D1562246

Joey W. Hill
Lacey Alexander
Elizabeth Lapthorne

ELLORA'S CAVE
ROMANTICA PUBLISHING

*W*hat the critics are saying...

෨

5 *Cups* "Lacey Alexander's characters in Mardi Gras are so compelling and lifelike, readers will care about them from the first page. The sex between the two is scorching and thrilling. " ~ *Coffeetime Romance*

5 *Cupids* "Sooo romantic and sexy! (Mardi Gras) gets you hooked straight from the start and you won't be able to put it down. This was my first Lacey Alexander romance but certainly not my last." ~ *Cupid's Library Reviews*

4 *Angels* "*Behind the Mask* is a wonderful collection of stories that capture the beauty and seductive powers of Mardi Gras." ~ *Fallen Angel Reviews*

5 *Unicorns* "This anthology is filled with exciting characters and wonderful scenes that leave the reader begging for more. Each author brought an amazing story to the mix." ~ *Enchanted in Romance*

"Ms. Alexander writes with a sensual style that will capture the reader with the first page. (All three stories)paint an erotic picture that will delight and at times make the reader so hot they will need a cold shower." ~ *Love Romances*

"*Behind The Mask* is a wonderful collection of stories that capture the beauty and seductive powers of Madri Gras. Each author deals with the eroticism of light bondage." ~ *Fallen Angels Reviews*

5 Cups "I was reading faster and faster to see how the couple moves forward. This is a wonderful, realistic and loving story, and I have already read it again. My suggestion would be to have a cool drink, or even better, a significant other available when you are done reading this outstanding book. Behind the Mask is an extraordinary read and definitely worth 5 Cups." ~ *Coffee Time Romance*

"In *Hidden Desires*, Ms. Lapthorne is back with a sensually decadent story set in Mardi Gras that is sure to make the reader sit up and take notice of how a mask can be a deeply sensual experience. Her characters are full of life, sensual promise and mystery as they come together exploring their desires. Her stories are always full of erotic passion but this one is sheer vividness in erotica." ~ *Love Romances*

An Ellora's Cave Romantica Publication

www.ellorascave.com

Behind the Mask

ISBN 1419952498, 9781419952494
ALL RIGHTS RESERVED.
Board Resolution Copyright © Joey W. Hill
Mardi Gras Copyright © 2005 Lacey Alexander
Hidden Desires Copyright © 2005 Elizabeth Lapthorne
Edited by: Briana St. James, Heather Osborn & Martha Punches
Cover art by Syneca

Electronic book Publication March, 2005
Trade paperback Publication September, 2005

Content Advisory:

S – ENSUOUS
E – ROTIC
X – TREME

Ellora's Cave Publishing offers three levels of Romantica™ reading entertainment: S (S-ensuous), E (E-rotic), and X (X-treme).

The following material contains graphic sexual content meant for mature readers. This story has been rated E–rotic.

S-*ensuous* love scenes are explicit and leave nothing to the imagination.

E-*rotic* love scenes are explicit, leave nothing to the imagination, and are high in volume per the overall word count. E-rated titles might contain material that some readers find objectionable—in other words, almost anything goes, sexually. E-rated titles are the most graphic titles we carry in terms of both sexual language and descriptiveness in these works of literature.

X-*treme* titles differ from E-rated titles only in plot premise and storyline execution. Stories designated with the letter X tend to contain difficult or controversial subject matter not for the faint of heart.

BEHIND THE MASK

ॐ

BOARD RESOLUTION
Joey W. Hill

~11~

MARDI GRAS
Lacey Alexander

~151~

HIDDEN DESIRES
Elizabeth Lapthorne

~263~

BOARD RESOLUTION

Joey W. Hill

ജ

Trademarks Acknowledgement

ഇ

The author acknowledges the trademarked status and trademark owners of the following wordmarks mentioned in this work of fiction:

Rolex: AEGLER S. A. COMPANY SWITZERLAND
REBBERG WORKS HOHEWEG 82 AND 82A

Grinch: Dr. Seuss Enterprises, L.P. Geisel-Seuss
Enterprises, Inc.

Coke: The Coca-Cola Company

Valium: HOFFMANN-LA ROCHE INC.

Monopoly: HASBRO, INC.

MENSA: American Mensa, Ltd.

X-Men: Marvel Characters, Inc.

Pierre Cardin: Cardin, Pierre

Chapter One

∾

Savannah put down her briefcase in the immaculate powder room of Kensington & Associates and straightened before the mirror. When meeting with piranhas, it was important to look appetizing but unattainable. She wanted the hunger to be there, but restrained, her opponents recognizing the attractive armor for what it was. A mask for a predator as scary as themselves.

A necessary step when the piranhas were Matthew Lord Kensington and his management team, and the subject of the meeting had yet to be disclosed. He'd simply issued an invitation to discuss a business opportunity over drinks at his office on Friday night. Knowing Matt, that meant glasses of water evenly spaced around the formal conference room table.

She checked her makeup, the arrangement of her streaked blonde hair, the smooth fit of her mid-thigh skirt and the blazer over it. While her father hadn't believed in using blatant sex to close a deal, he'd had no problem with strategically using the arsenal one had at hand, and that included one's looks or charm. She had been blessed with an abundance of the former and he'd encouraged her to use it, though always sparingly.

Geoffrey Tennyson's Rule Twelve: People keep class and elegance around them. Trash gets thrown away after it serves its purpose. The lace of her bra was faintly visible through her white silk blouse if one looked hard enough, and she'd enjoy seeing Matt strain his eyes.

Their negotiations had always been cordial and lucrative, but she'd seen the flare in his gaze when he thought he'd pressed an advantage on her, the tightening of his sensual lips when she proved him wrong. She knew he loved it, how they sparred at a table and never could came away claiming anything other than a mutual victory. He craved that, she suspected, hungered to take something from her she wasn't willing to give. It made things flutter inside her to play the game, to fence and win a draw. Often she went home aching for something nameless, something she was afraid was the desire for him to outsmart her just once, to make her surrender.

If she was totally honest, her interactions with Matt were as close to having sex as she ever got.

Savannah shook herself out of the odd direction of her thoughts, and was appalled to find the crotch of her panties damp. Appalled, but not surprised. He might be surprised though, if he knew how often she'd curled into a fetal ball between her expensive sheets, her thighs squeezed together as she thought of that hard body between her legs, pounding into her, his hands clamped on her wrists, mouth ravaging her neck.

Perhaps it was the time of night making her think this way. A meeting at eight in the evening on a Friday turned her mind to frivolous thoughts, though she didn't know why. It wasn't as if she'd be doing frivolous things. While she might have planned an outing with a carefully chosen escort to a gallery showing or movie premiere, that would have been to further the interests of Tennyson Industries. Otherwise, she'd have been home, reviewing the upcoming week's schedule and analyzing her recent decisions for flaws or holes.

Another of the twelve rules her father had drilled into her to guide every action and reaction. They'd been posted on her bedroom wall like the Ten Commandments, ever since she was old enough to read. *Tennyson Rule Eight: A good captain never stops going over every inch of the ship.* Every once in a long while she might give herself a Friday night off to watch a movie she'd rented. She'd view it from the couch in her father's study...her study, now that he was gone.

This might have been such a night. It had been a hard week and she was feeling a bit...well, the armor was a little thin.

Even her disciplined soul wasn't immune to the flood of anticipation that infused this Friday night with the sense of possibilities. The whole weekend stretched ahead like an adventure.

Mardi Gras had happened this week, and this corporate tower was still feeling the powerful vibrations from the celebration as much as the streets of New Orleans. Several strands of colorful beads and a feathered mask were placed as decoration on the vanity counter. It always bemused her why her father chose to keep their corporate headquarters here, versus New York or Chicago, but whenever she asked, he'd only said that New Orleans was a place where anything was possible. He'd met her mother here, and she suspected the truth was to be found in that. She had died shortly after Savannah was born, of a virulent cancer that had been discovered while she was pregnant. Refusing treatment to protect her unborn child, Portia Tennyson had died nearly six months after the birth of her daughter. She left Savannah a locket containing a curl of her hair and a tiny folded piece of paper, with the scent of lavender and a short message.

You were worth it.

Her father had never liked her wearing the necklace, so until his death she kept it in her bedside table.

She took a deep breath, closing her eyes. Yes, a wise captain would have chosen tonight to stay on the ship, fight the battle Monday when there were fewer titillating portents in the air. The wild desires and dreams that Mardi Gras madness stirred up like a fairy dust storm could impair her judgment seriously. Especially with this particular man.

Regardless, she'd accepted the invitation and chosen to come alone. She always negotiated with Matt and his Intimidation Team by herself, as if underscoring that she had no fear of any of them. Having spent most of her teen years apprenticing in Tennyson's corporate and manufacturing offices, she had no apprehensions about discussing any aspect of the business on her own. She'd been accepted a year early to a prestigious Ivy League school, finished the coursework and passed the bar a year before her classmates. Serving the four subsequent years as a trial lawyer with a ruthlessly aggressive Washington firm her father had chosen had seasoned her enough to serve as his CFO. She'd had five years at his side in that capacity before he'd died, leaving her a relatively young but extremely capable CEO of a Fortune 500 company whose wealth and power was based in the male-dominated world of steel manufacturing.

Plus, if the desolate truth was known, she'd become attached to working with Matt's team on their many mutual interests. She wanted to keep them to herself. As though she'd adopted them as her family. Or not so much like a family as something more, something even stranger.

She choked on a laugh. She was definitely off her game tonight. Maybe Matt knew that Friday night, when the empty weekend yawned before her, was her most vulnerable time. The bastard seemed to know everything else. Their buildings, corporate high-rises, were just across the street from one another, and she wouldn't put it past him to have planted spies in her ranks.

Well, it was her challenge to show him he wasn't as smart as he thought he was. Then she could fill her weekend with victorious gloating.

Savannah gave herself one last appraising look. The jacket of the pale tan suit followed the shallow curve of her back, nipping in at the waist to flare out in two layers, like a modest bustle of an old-fashioned Victorian dress. The snug linen skirt revealed a teasing picture of the back of her thigh with the slit in back. Modest and professional, even to the faint whiff of perfume, the outfit was perfectly appropriate for a woman to be wearing after five in the evening. She'd left her hair clipped up on her head, but had loosened a few tendrils, giving her a softer look. She wanted to tease.

"Boys, you're goners," she decided, but she knew there was only one man who mattered.

She clipped down the hall in her slender heels, the echo loud in the quiet building. Other evidence of the festivities that had occurred earlier in the week caught her attention as she passed open office doors. Sparkling beads hanging on doorknobs or left across a desktop. The inexpensive plastic masks.

The security guard had indicated they were waiting for her on the top floor. When she rounded the corner and saw the conference room door open, she had to suppress a smile. While there were no water glasses on the table, a crystal pitcher and a tray of tumblers were within easy reach on a side credenza.

Then her attention flickered to the man sitting at the head of the table, and her amusement was swept away by something entirely different.

Matt Kensington was a powerful man on Wall Street, even from the distance of New Orleans. But what made him even more potent was that he was a physically dominating man. Over six feet tall, he had dark eyes, raven hair and a swarthy Italian complexion provided by his mother. However, his father's Texas roots ensured he had none of the prettiness of Italian men that could suggest weakness. Just all of their sexual charisma.

Her blood hammered harder in her arteries when she saw he was alone, not flanked by his usual four-man management team. Though, regardless of who was in attendance, Matt always overwhelmed a room with his presence. Or maybe he just overwhelmed her.

Tennyson's Rule Two: Always be brutally honest with yourself. Otherwise, you won't know the difference between the truth and a lie from anyone else.

Every detail of Matt spoke of power and discipline. From his charcoal gray suit that fit his broad shoulders to perfection, to the white line of his cuffs and the gleam of his Yale class ring. Even his manicured nails in no way diminished the capable strength evident in those hands. His bent knee, visible over the edge of the table, hinted he had his foot braced on a leg of the table so he could lean his chair back. The pose was casual. Disarmingly so. She couldn't help it that her gaze strayed over the column of his thigh.

He rose as he always did, an act of Southern courtesy she'd teased him about with appropriate feminist acidity. He did it for all women, but somehow the way he did it for her, with his gaze locked on hers as he rose, always set butterflies in her stomach into a tailspin. He didn't smile, those firm lips and aristocratic nose an inspiration for a sculptor trying to depict a warrior king.

It was an apt comparison. The elegance of the board room was a façade. Strip it away, make it the walls of a tent, then prop armor, shields and swords against the wall, and its nature would not change. It was the domain of a conqueror, and every time she came here, she felt it. His desire to claim, control, invade. He'd managed the last, for he'd captivated her mind, but she could accept that.

Tennyson Rule Three: Accept your weaknesses and, if you can't fix them, compensate for them.

Cleopatra had been no different. She always knew she walked the knife edge between holding the reins and being the spoils of war. Savannah surmised that the Egyptian monarch had kept to the upper side of the knife by being queen first and woman second. If she'd ever forgotten that, had let her woman's desires completely take her over, her allure to a man of power like Marc Anthony and Caesar would have been fleeting, a piece of candy consumed and forgotten.

Savannah ignored the twist of pain and fatigue such a thought gave her. An emotional reaction, and one she wouldn't indulge. Men like Matt sought the powerful woman, but a woman wanted a man with whom she could be just a woman occasionally. The problem was that Savannah only wanted a man like Matt. The chicken and egg dilemma of human nature.

She gave a mental shrug, set her briefcase on the table. "Where are your child prodigies, Matthew?"

His wunderkind, they were called. Lucas. Jon. Ben. Peter. The young, hungry men who supported him in the world of manufacturing, now a very dynamic area since technology changed the production playing field almost on a daily basis. They were all attractive twenty- and thirty-somethings who worked hard in the office and played hard in the gym. She wondered if, like a wolf pack, they showered and slept together, and was instantly amused and aroused by the visuals conjured by the thought.

Yes, Savannah, you're definitely in a strange mood tonight.

Matt had yet to speak, and there was something in his eyes. Something similar to what she'd recognized there before. But tonight it was more direct. Unleashed. For a despicably weak moment, she was glad the length of the table was between them.

Okay, Savannah, enough daydreaming. Time to get a grip or he is going to eat you alive.

And that was entirely the wrong thought, because it summoned a flood of images so powerful they shuddered through her body. She closed her hands on the briefcase to cover the reaction, as if it were a shield she could use against his overpowering attraction.

"You call me Matthew just to irritate me."

"Would you prefer Mr. Kensington? Or perhaps *Lord* Kensington?" She added the last in a saccharine tone.

It was a standing joke in the corporate circles, the use of his middle name, bandied about equally as an admiring quip or a bitter insult.

He did not laugh. In fact, he seemed to consider the notion, then his gaze centered on her in a way it had never done before. Perusing her in detail, his attention moved from her face to her throat, pausing over the frantically beating pulse, before continuing down to her breasts, the indentation of her waist, the flare of her hip, just visible to the right of the briefcase. She suppressed the urge to shift out of view.

"If you like," he said at last. His grin was quick and unexpected. Feral. Pure sex. And it made her focus flounder in a wash of heat. "But I think I prefer Master, or *my* lord, if you're using it."

She blinked. "I'm sure you would."

"While we're on the subject, *your* name is an interesting one." He seated his hip on an edge of the table. The way he was looking at her across the dimly lit room made her feel the table was not that much of a barrier after all, and that the protection of her briefcase was laughable at best.

"It doesn't suggest a hard-edged business woman, someone able to shrivel a man's testicles with a glance, though I have seen you do that. Almost as often as I've seen you arouse my men with the simple scent of your perfume, or a glimpse of those killer legs. Particularly when you lean back and cross them so modestly, and you show just the hint of the lace top of your stocking before it's gone, like a mirage to a man dying of thirst."

Savannah stayed stock-still, her fingers gripping the handle of her case. "Are you making a point, Matthew, or have you lost your mind?"

"We're discussing names, I believe, and my point is that a name very much reflects who a person is, deep inside. Savannah suggests a soft, giving woman. When I look at you, Savannah…" He paused, lingering over the name, making a flush rise on her neck. "…I see you waking up in my bed, the cotton sheets caught between your calves, that soft, luscious body molded by a satin sheath with spaghetti straps. One of those straps is falling off the shoulder, so your breast is almost completely exposed, though just not quite. And when I come to you, touch you, make you smile, all that fine, beautiful hair is rumpled and framing your face…"

His gaze flickered over the loosened tendrils that she suddenly wished she had not drawn free of her usually impeccable twist.

She pulled the briefcase off the table, a jerk of motion so he wouldn't see that her hand was shaking. Men did not affect her that way. "I don't know what this is, Matthew, but it's not a business meeting. I'm leaving."

"Sit. Down."

The snap of his voice caused her to jump, which made her angry, frosted her voice. "I beg your pardon?"

He straightened off the table, one lithe, quick movement, but his steps toward her were measured, the intent but slow paces of a wolf stalking prey. Or in his case, a shark, those dark glittering eyes promising no mercy.

"You heard me. Sit your pretty ass down, now, or I'll wear it out so you can't sit for a week."

Shock gripped her, both at the words and at the serious look in his eyes, which told her he very likely meant the astounding thing he had just said. She should be giving him a disdainful look, turning and making her exit, but she couldn't make her feet move. As if his words were a lightning bolt that had immobilized her in a crackle of powerful current that charged her entire body, all the cells vibrated with apprehension and something else, something rising in her, responding to him and his ridiculous words.

He took another step toward her. Then another. "You drive a man to distraction. Not just the sneaky bit of leg, but that drape of neckline revealing a tiny cup of lace just barely holding your breast in when you lean forward to make a point. The way you touch your hair just behind your ear, lightly, or moisten your lips when you talk."

"Stop it," she whispered. "Stop."

But he didn't. Not his forward movement or his words. "That's the thing. You're teasing my men, but you're challenging me. From the first moment we met, you've known you were mine. Every negotiation has been a dare, a taunt. You want me to prove I've got what it takes to make you submit, claim what's been mine all along."

Why was her pulse pounding like she was hearing a terrible truth instead of the ravings of a lunatic?

"You're a tough nut to crack, aren't you, little girl?" He was almost around the table, and still she couldn't move. His footfalls were silent, hushed in the carpet.

"Don't call me that."

"Oh, that's right." He nodded, dark brows drawing down like the shadow of a hawk's wings. "You're not a little girl. You've never been a little girl. Groomed from birth to take the reins of your father's empire. Daddy's closer all your adult life, and then you stepped right into his shoes when he died. You've never allowed yourself to be vulnerable, never allowed yourself to be a woman, never daring to risk it. You've become so good at it you don't even know you have a warm, wet, soft pussy, aching for a cock. My cock.

"Tell me, little girl. What would you do right now if I turned you over my knee and gave you a spanking?"

She'd gone from shock to fury, and she didn't care what game he was playing or the fact her panties were soaked and her hands were damp with nervous perspiration.

Yes, she had a subliminal awareness of what the slit of a skirt or a glimpse of cleavage would do to powerful men, had even enjoyed fleeting thoughts of them struggling to focus, though she'd never gone so far as he had intimated. She'd never imagined the crude reality of erections distracting them under the table.

That subliminal awareness was part of the charge. Sex and negotiation. Power. Control.

Her eyes widened at the connection, the understanding of her own body's unexpected response. This was the same as a negotiation, only he'd taken it to a whole new level. A level on which she had almost zero experience, and he knew it.

Her eyes narrowed and her lips firmed. He'd changed the game level, but not the game itself.

She didn't know what Matt was up to, but she'd beaten him before. She could beat him at this as well, whatever it was. Make it to a draw, with both parties satisfied. Business played the way they normally played it was as much of a rush as sex, and the line could get thin between the two. She understood that, gripped the truth of it like a lifeline to steady herself.

"What would I do if you tried to spank me? I think I'd leave a nice set of scars down that handsome jaw of yours."

"You like to fight, don't you? Let's really fight, then." His voice dropped to a rumble that sounded suspiciously like a growl. "Tear at me, leave behind the civilized façade that we pretend to have at this table. Go for it. Fight me. Because come hell or high water, I'm going to have you tonight. Take you right here in this room, and have you call me Master."

"I think those giant balls you're rumored to have are going to be rolling around the floor first."

"Hmm." One black brow now arched and the dark eyes glittered like coal exposed to candlelight. "I've never heard you be crude, Savannah. But you probably don't realize that's not really your way, do you? You've been meeting someone else's expectations so long you've never developed an identity of your own. Geoffrey engineered the perfect chameleon, straight from his loins. If you'd submit to me, maybe you could find out who you really are."

"Using personal insults to get a woman to spread her legs for you. That's a unique come-on. I've got things to do, Matthew. Good night."

"You're not leaving."

As he loomed over her, oddly she chose that moment to notice how white his shirt was, fresh and pressed. She knew how that would smell, the clean starch of a well-laundered shirt. The smell of him beneath it. His hair was shaved perfectly at the nape and she wondered how that would feel beneath her fingertips, how those big, restless hands would feel on her body, what he could do to her with that unsmiling mouth. She could almost feel her skin prickle in anticipation of the rasp of the five o'clock shadow.

She *was* a chameleon. He was right about that. *Tennyson Rule Four: Never show fear.*

She couldn't go around him, and she had a momentary, dangerously appealing image of a desperate feint to scurry for the elevator. She quelled the ridiculous image and the apprehension that had fueled it, and set her briefcase deliberately back on the table. She faced him, her back straight, hands at her sides. "Fine, then. You're right, Matthew. We're two adults. We have a sexual attraction. It's obvious. Let's relieve it. We'll have sex, get it out of the way. I'm sure you've indulged the itch as often as I have on a boring Friday night."

Coal became fuel with fire. She was reminded of that by the expression that flared in his dark eyes, even though his voice remained mild. Dangerously so.

"That's good, Savannah. Very good. But I don't want to scratch an itch." He closed that last step and his arm went around her waist, his other to her hair. He yanked out her barrette in a rough motion that sent her hair tumbling down, around her face and over one eye. She would have shaken it back, but he immediately had a fistful of it and yanked it, letting her feel the brute strength that was his to command. "You won't make any more references to anyone you've ever fucked. You're mine, Savannah."

"Go to hell," she snapped, and gasped as his mouth came down on hers, hard, hot and hungry, his hands still tight on her hair and waist.

At the first touch, she knew she'd lost the edge. He was pure male beast, heat and superior strength. All the images she'd fantasized late at night in her lonely bed, with him as the center feature, now flooded her senses. Fantasy combined with reality to make her weak, out of control. His tongue caressed hers with a skill that let her know what he could do with it elsewhere, but he wasn't seducing her. He was taking over, demanding unconditional surrender.

But you only surrendered unconditionally if you had no weapons left, and she sure as hell wasn't there yet.

She bit down on his tongue, got her hands in between them and shoved at his face to break away. When she wrenched away, he tore her blouse open, revealing flesh barely confined in the shelf cups of the lacy bra, as he had described them. Savannah slapped him, used her nails with pleasure to draw blood. He caught her wrist before she could jerk back and, despite her struggles, he brought that hand back to his face, rubbed her fingertips in the welts. Taking three of the fingers into his mouth, he slowly sucked at his blood and her flesh, freezing her in place with the sheer ferocity of the gesture, the flame in his eyes as he did it.

She had known he was fit, toned. She hadn't realized he was so bloody strong. Catching her other wrist, he swung her around and pinned her against the wall, pressing his body against the full length of hers, lifting her. As he came up against her, he insinuated his knee between hers so her snug skirt rode up at pressure of his leg. With her toes stretched to hold onto the floor, her pussy was her center of gravity, pressed hard against the muscular length of his thigh. She automatically tightened her muscles to hold her balance, and the feel of that, the close relation it had to clamping her thighs around his hips, made her breath leave her. She yanked at her wrists, her legs thrashing, but he simply held her in place. She bent her fingers back into claws, prepared to strike if he gave her the chance.

With his gaze never leaving hers, he brought one set of those sharp fingertips back to his face.

She stopped struggling, realizing she was just wasting energy she might need when he shifted his grip and gave her another opening. It was senseless to fight him on ground where he had the advantage. She had to wait for the weak moment.

At least that's what she told herself, to explain why she suddenly went so still, like a frozen rabbit, as the hunter took her hand into his mouth again, stroking the crevices between her fingers with tender touches of his tongue, down to the palm. Down to the sensitive pulse point of her wrist. Her hand now curled over his eye and nose, her nails within a lash length of his vulnerable brown iris, and she could not make herself move. Her heart hammering against her ribs, she could only stare at him.

"This is rape," she managed.

"No, it's not. You're not trembling because of that. You're the type of woman who'd fight a mugger to the death to keep his filthy fingers off your Rolex, and just be pissed off if he pulled a gun."

He feathered the knuckles of his free hand down her cheek, startling her. "If there's one thing about you that scares me, Savannah, it's that."

"I'm not afraid of you."

"Yes, you are. You're afraid I'll make you do and feel things you don't let yourself feel. You're afraid if you expose your throat, I'll rip it out. You don't believe you can trust anyone, especially a lover."

"We aren't lovers, Matthew."

"You are such a liar." The offensive words were spoken softly, like a caress against her skin, putting her further off balance. Pressing her up against the wall, he rubbed his thigh, slow and strong, against her mound. Her feet left the floor, his grip on her wrists her only way of staying upright, a precarious position that made her thighs clamp harder around his, increasing the pressure of her clit against lean muscle. "We've been lovers since the moment we met, the first time we sparred at a conference table." His face and lips had somehow gotten closer, so his cheek was now almost against hers, his five o'clock shadow sliding along her jawline, his breath tickling her ear. "Every offer and counteroffer has been a thrust and withdrawal, a teasing foreplay that you felt as much as I did. You think I didn't notice when you'd lean back in your chair and cross your legs, like you were listening to me make a point, but I saw the slight tightening of your thighs. You were aroused and indulging the sensation, giving your pussy a sweet, secret squeeze."

Savannah drew in a shuddering breath as he pressed his lips just beneath her ear, his hair brushing the side of her face. Her hands balled into fists of need rather than anger.

"Or that time you stood at my shoulder, leaning over to point out something in a report. You had your hand on the back of my chair, and your blouse fell open just a bit, like the petals of a flower, showing me that ripe breast. I inhaled the smell of your perfume, imagined you touching yourself there with the wand of your perfume bottle first thing in the morning. When I let out that breath, the heat of it touched you. Your nipple got tight. When you straightened, I saw it pressing against your blouse, even through your bra."

"I don't know what you're talking about." She jerked her head away from his mouth and swung, knocking him smartly in the temple. Seizing his ear between her teeth, she bit.

He snarled and she twisted, thrashed, threw them both off balance. She managed to scramble off his thigh, but her heel twisted and she went to one knee. He was on her in a second. Amazingly, she thought she heard him chuckle, but that turned into an oath as she palmed her fist and elbowed him in the chest when he tried to pounce on her. She spun to her feet and had a flash of that clean white shirt she'd admired earlier as he caught her by the hips and lifted her, maneuvering her onto her back on the slick surface of the table. Keeping himself between her thighs, he locked her wrists down with his hands as he leaned over her, breathing hard.

The position rucked her skirt all the way to her hips and his eyes coursed over the lace thigh-highs, the swatch of white lace panties. "Class and elegance, wrapped in a fuck-me-if-you-got-the-balls package. So what about it, Savannah?" He moved against her, and his hard cock rubbed the damp crotch of her panties through his trousers. "Have I got the balls to fuck you, make you scream for me? Whether you want to or not?"

He was taunting her, and she wanted to hate him, be repulsed by him. "I'll scream if I want to scream. You won't have anything to do with it."

She bit back a gasp as he released her wrists and caught her by the back of the neck, one large palm supporting her skull as he lifted her up against his chest, bringing them eye to flashing eye.

"You'll scream for me, even though you don't want to. You'll beg, despite the fact every cell of your stubborn, rebellious mind will be telling you not to do so. Before this evening is over, you'll belong to me, heart, body and soul, and you'll be cursing me, even as you accept that you'll never be free of my claim on you again."

"Stop it, Matt."

"No." But his tone gentled, as if, by her use of the shortened version of his name, she had alerted him to her desperation, the sudden vulnerability that leaked through her armor and made her doubt herself.

"You know what I fantasize about sometimes, Savannah? I'm sitting at the head of that table, listening to my team give me a report on something... Hell, anything. Could be the weather in Shanghai, for all I care." A light smile touched his lips, simple, startling her with its ease in comparison to the intensity of the past few moments. "I have you sitting on my lap, and you're completely naked, your arms bound behind your back. That tight little ass of yours is squirming against my cock because I'm fondling your breasts, just idly stroking the curves, caressing the nipples, pinching them, watching you get more and more aroused."

He slid his arms around her back, anchoring her against his chest, banding her to him with those long arms. His mouth took hers again. She pushed against his shoulders with the heels of her hands, but he only deepened the kiss, widened her mouth with the pressure of his, delving deep into her, his tongue exploring every moist crevice. She could have pulled his hair, twisted, done several things to buck the embrace, but being in Matt Kensington's embrace did not suggest battle. It screamed for surrender.

Savannah ignored that path, but compromised with a momentary cessation of hostilities to experience the most potent mouth she'd ever tasted, or been tasted by. Not that she'd really tasted many, but this one had to be exceptional. She came to that conclusion from the simple realization that if there were men's mouths more potent, there would have been reports of women dying from experiencing them like this.

When he lifted his head and they stared into each other's eyes, his lips wet with her mouth, she could not say her body was her own. It seemed to have melted into soft pliancy against every hard curve of his, and her pussy throbbed against the hard reminder of his cock. A disturbing reminder, a return to the reality of what he wanted from her today. The impossible.

She was making more of this than there was. Her hormones hadn't been indulged often enough, and Matt had hit the right buttons. She repeated it to herself fiercely, though her mind screamed that she had just drop-kicked Rule Two, always be honest with yourself, right out of the ballpark. Or was it Rule One?

As if he were reading her thoughts, his voice dropped to a rough whisper. "You said a moment ago you're willing to have sex. Why are you fighting me?"

She managed a shrug, not an easy body language to pull off with her body shaking and her chest heaving with the exertion of their struggle. "If you want to fill tonight's dance card, then I had to make sure you worked for it."

His lips curved up in something that would have been a smile if it wasn't so cold and deliberate. "You deny there's anything special between us." It was a statement, not a question.

"That's your arrogance talking, Kensington. Nothing is between us but lust and about a hundred million in costs in three start-up ventures. You want me, and it's the hunt that's got you so worked up. Tomorrow, when we've sated it, you won't even remember. We'll get an equal thrill from seeing that steel prices went down."

"Then I suppose I'll have to show you that, even though your body can be pleased in other ways, your mind and heart have only one avenue to fulfillment. I'm going to straighten up now and lay your wrists on the table on either side of you." He unfolded her arms from her chest between them and did just that, stretching them out and placing her wrists against the smooth table surface. "I want to unfasten your bra and see your breasts. If you move your wrists, lift them from the table, I will spank you. I'll turn you over, pull those pretty panties to your knees and make your ass rosy with the palm of my hand. I'll enjoy it." His voice lowered, his eyes glittering with purpose. "So do me a favor and disobey."

She set her jaw, lifted her chin. "You're a pig. If you're going to do this, don't play your sick games. Just do it. You might be better than my…vibrator, but I doubt it."

"Just any guy will do, if his cock is hard enough?"

She managed to keep her voice from breaking, but she suspected only a lifetime of discipline made it possible. "I'm sure you can get me off easy enough. You've had the practice. I'm just another Friday night paper doll fuck to you, same as you are to me. Change the hair, clothes, shoes. Same person, forgettable after it's over."

"I see." With a warning glance to reinforce his earlier threat, he spread open her torn blouse. It was a back fastening bra, but he simply took hold of the piece connecting the cups in the front and tore it, holding the tension on the two separated cups so she was arched off the table. His cock, still pressed against her through his clothing, slid an inch along her panties at the change in position. When he looked at her exposed breasts, to her shame, the nipples were elongated and erect, as if begging for attention. As he lifted her, her wrists slid along the table, but did not leave it, as if they were chained to the table in reality. Her hips wanted to move, to writhe against him to relieve the painful build up of pleasure vibrating along the nerves between her pussy and abdomen.

She tried to keep an indifferent look on her face, though she was perilously close to losing control completely. What she wanted to do was scream, fight him with everything she had just to get away from him and what he was doing to her. He seemed determined to take her choice away from her. Her body and mind were getting lost beneath that intent gaze and sexy firm mouth, both of which gave her imagination a thousand ideas, just watching them as he studied her.

"I knew this would be difficult." His gaze never left the quivering slopes of her breasts, the upward tilt of her rib cage. "And I prepared for it. You say you'll fuck me because I've turned you on, but it could be me or any other guy to scratch your itch. Is that right?"

"Are you having a hearing problem?" she retorted. "That about sums it up."

"Then I guess I'll have to back you down and prove you wrong." He bent close to her. "You want me with a hunger so bad you'll tear my flesh off my bones to crawl inside me. I know it, have known it for months, and so have you."

"You—"

"Do you want me to hurt you, Savannah? Is that preferable to me being gentle, tender with you? Cherishing you? You won't make me rush this. And one other thing." She felt like a desperately cornered mouse staring into a hawk's eyes. "I won't let you out-negotiate me. There is no draw. Tonight you'll surrender to me completely and give me everything I ask for. And I'll make you glad you did."

"You wish," she said, more faintly than she'd intended. A light smile touched his mouth, but something else was in his eyes, more frightening than hard purpose. He cupped her face in both hands. "You can fight me, scratch at me with your nails or that biting sarcasm of yours, but I won't hurt you, Savannah. Except in ways that will bring you pleasure. And I'm not ever going to let anything else hurt you again. You've already had your quota of pain for one lifetime."

"No."

"Yes. And it's time for you to realize that." His hand reached under her, one hand coming around her back to hold her up as he smoothly unbuttoned the top button of the skirt, lowered the zipper, his fingers sliding down the satin-covered crease of her buttocks as if they had every right to be there.

She *did* want to have sex with him, so why not just help him along, get it over with? Why stay rigid under his touch now?

Because he wanted more than that, and he wasn't asking. He was taking, stripping off more than her clothes, and it frightened her in a way the physical discrepancies in their strengths did not. She understood everything about how this moment had come about, had enough of a history with him to know tonight wasn't about rape. He wouldn't force her if her body said no, but he had to realize, when his hand slid lower, smoothed over her pussy and found the crotch of her panties wet to the touch through the satin, that her body was screaming for him.

To hell with it. As he pulled her slightly forward to get the skirt down past her hips, her feet touched the floor. She reared up, stomped on his instep with the spike, managing to land a blow in between the side opening of the expensive shoe and the thin black dress sock, a poor protection.

He swore, flipped her and plastered his hand against the center of her back, used his weight to bear her back down onto the table. Holding her there that way while she thrashed uselessly, he bent, pulled off first one shoe and then the other, tossed them across the room. He stripped her skirt off, sliding it down over her kicking feet. Then, with a violence that dropped her stomach to her knees, he tore the remains of her blouse from her, leaving her in stockings and panties only. He stripped the bra down her arms, but instead of taking it off, he used the garment to tie her wrists behind her back.

"Kensington, what are you doing?"

"Something I've been planning to do for a while. A great while, so that I planned it out to the last minute piece. I've heard you admire my attention to detail." He paused, holding the pressure on her body to keep her still. "Actually, that's my interpretation. The rumor was that you called me first cousin to the Grinch, who didn't overlook even a last crumb for the Who mouses. Which shocked me only because I didn't think you'd ever been allowed to read Dr. Seuss.

"I intend to impress you with my level of detail tonight. Often, and well."

He yanked her to her feet, turned her to face him. "But first, I'm going to explain some things to you. Just consider this one of those corporate trust retreats where you stand on a stage and fall back into your co-workers' arms."

"I always hated those things."

"I'll bet." He produced that sexy, easy smile again, which kept tempering these moments between absurdity, terror and wonder. "We hate them because of the hypocrisy, because we know there's no peppy corporate organizer in the real world, inspiring fuzzy feelings in people so they'd want to catch strangers in their arms. But didn't you despise it even more because you wanted it to be true, a group of people willing to take care of you, to catch you when you fall?"

She wished he had left her shoes alone. Standing before him in her bare feet was discomfiting, and not just because it increased the difference in their heights. It increased her awareness of his gaze traveling over her bare breasts, thrust out because of the restraint of her arms behind her back. He traced a finger along the sensitive crease of her thighs, along the lace of her white panties. She was trembling, which she also hated, so she focused on being still, standing like a statue before him, determined not to give him anything other than the responses of her body, which she could not control under his touch, and the disdain of her expression, which she could.

"That's good." He reached her face at last. "You're the strongest woman I know. But you're going to learn you don't have to be tough with me.

"Here are the rules. You can give up at any time, admit I was right, that I do affect you. That you're absolutely crazy about me." That smile grew broader, even more arrogant and infuriating. "And then, if you want, we can call it an evening. You can walk away and I'll let you. For tonight." That smile shifted, became more of a threat with the devastating promise implied in it. "But both of us will know I won. So, just say the word. And you're free to go."

She smiled back, a quick, feral gesture, and rammed her knee into his groin.

It was a suicidal move, all in all. She was by herself, with her hands tied, with a man who physically outmatched her several times over. Her hands were tied, her clothes scattered in tatters on the floor.

But she didn't intend to run. She merely took one step back, threw out her chin and waited.

He'd made it a competition, and she didn't quit or surrender. She intended to walk away with every hair in place, figuratively if not literally. She'd call tonight an amusing diversion of sex games to his face, her sophisticated indifference intact.

It didn't matter that the pit of her stomach was quivering with nerves or that she was way beyond the deep end of the pool. She was in the middle of the ocean with no land in sight. A long time ago, she'd learned to mask fear, turn the energy that fueled it into her weapon. With this level of trepidation, she should be able to come up with a nuclear missile.

He'd bent over at the waist, no choice there for any man. When he straightened, he did it slow. Pure fury was in his gaze, and something else, that indefinable look again, the one that frightened her far worse than the threat of physical retribution.

"That's not going to be enough to drive me away, Savannah," he said softly.

He unbuckled his belt, his gaze remaining on hers. Savannah flicked her gaze over the action, came back to his face. "Well, it's about time you got to the fucking part, isn't it?" She tried to say it casually. "Most men aren't into this much foreplay and conversation."

"The cynical wisecracker. That's the face I saw through first, did you know that?" He slid the strap free, dangled it loosely in his hand, his other hand over the fastening of his trousers. Her action apparently hadn't dampened his enthusiasm. She could see his erection pressing against the placket of his zipper, and she had to force herself not to wet her lips. She couldn't fight the dampening of her pussy, which responded to the sight, oblivious to her admonitions.

"But I didn't get the whole picture until a few weeks ago. Do you know what happened then?"

"Why should I care?"

He shook his head at her. "It was two in the morning. I was coming home from a client's fundraiser, and I stopped at a traffic light. A diner on the corner was still open, and I looked over, thinking about getting a cup of coffee.

"I saw a girl sitting on a barstool at the counter. Wearing jeans and a sweatshirt that was too big for her. Sipping a fountain coke, laughing at something the late-shift waitress was saying to her."

Savannah's throat constricted, but it didn't matter. She wasn't going to say anything. She wasn't going down this path with him. This was just sex. Rough, kinky sex, the kind she'd heard about. She could take it, as long as she stayed away from danger signs. Like the one that was going up right now, with every word he spoke.

"Something about her caught my eye, and then it hit me. The light changed and I didn't even notice. I was looking at Savannah Tennyson, the indomitable *femme fatale* of Tennyson Industries, as some of my staff call you. Fondly, I might add. When the waitress left you, you went back to playing with your straw in the Coke. You looked out the window, but you didn't see me. There was something in your face. A softness, a wistfulness, and I realized just how lonely you really are. An incredibly independent, dynamic woman sitting alone at two in the morning in a diner, so she doesn't have to be home during the loneliest time of night."

"Stop it, Matt." Her fingers clenched against the soft fabric of the undergarment binding her wrists. "This isn't funny. You want to fuck, we'll fuck. Don't pretend you give two damns about me, just to get into my pants." She shifted her expression to pointedly look at her mostly naked body. "You're already there, and I've told you I'm agreeable. So quit the dramatics, before you piss me off and I get out of the mood."

"You talk like you have a choice." She yelped as he grasped her arm. In one effortless motion he had taken a seat in a chair and pulled her down on his lap. Face down, her hips crooked over his thigh, her ass in the air, her head hanging down so she saw the bottom of the chair, the backs of his legs.

"Kensington, you son of a —"

Crack!

Total shock was her first thought, followed by the pain as he slapped her buttocks, hard. He hadn't held back, or if he had, she sure as hell didn't want to know what he had in reserve.

"I told you, I won't tolerate that type of language from you. You're not that kind of person. You won't pretend to be something you're not around me."

"No, I'm the kind of person who's going to personally shoot your fucking balls off if you don't —"

Whack!

She was right, he did have some in reserve.

"I'll use the belt if you keep it up, Savannah. You want to go for round three?"

"You like abusing women, Matthew?" She made her voice go cold, though she was perilously close to tears. Not from the pain. That would have been bad enough. This was something else, something the pain was breaking loose in her chest, something terrible dislodging its claws from its secure place in her vitals where. As long as its claws didn't move, she could bear its weight. If it started moving around, stirred by whatever it was he was doing to her, she'd start screaming and wouldn't be able to stop. What was wrong with her?

"No. No, I don't." His touch turned even more dangerous, for instead of punishing, it became a caress. Stroking her abused buttocks, he traced his fingers down the crease through the panties so the fabric rippled over her tender skin. His other hand remained flat on her back, keeping her in place. "There are things I could do to bring you more pleasure than you've ever known, if you'd just let me. I'd make love to you for hours, let you sleep in my arms without worry. Put fresh flowers in your room every morning before you wake so they're the first thing you see. Take care of you."

"I don't need anyone to take care of me."

"I know. Which makes it all the more important that someone does."

"Stop fu…messing with my head!"

He chuckled, and she despised her cowardice, but her nerve endings were still screaming from his last smack, and she wasn't eager for a repeat performance. She pitied the backsides of his progeny, if he ever had any.

He continued that gentle, maddening stroking, at odds with his inexorable hold on her. "Would you like to see a recent modification we made to this room?"

"Would it matter if I didn't?"

His arms shifted, turned her so he held her cradled in one arm. She felt small there, tucked in against him, unsettled because it was not an unpleasant place to be at all. His thumb slid under the lace edge at her hip as his hand moved up her thigh, and her breath caught in her throat at the potency of that touch. How could something so light cause such heat to spread through her blood, like an oil fire?

He removed his touch for a moment, reached under the table.

"Sit still."

She twisted her head, startled as he slipped a Mardi Gras mask over her forehead. She had a momentary impression of its face, painted with exotic slashes of color and trimmed with feathers, before he had it seated over her eyes. Lifting her hair, he secured the band under it, so the elastic tie followed the back line of her ears across the nape of her neck. Tassels sewn along the cheek edge of the mask fell to her jawline, caressing her face.

"What's that for?"

"Sshhh. Spirit of the holiday. Watch this." He reached for the table control panel this time.

She heard a whirring of gears, and the sound reminded her this room had five video conferencing monitors mounted in the ceiling that could be lowered to the eye level of the meeting attendees. As she lifted her gaze to follow the noise, she saw those were gone. What was coming down from the ceiling was a contraption of soft black straps and nylon mesh, connected to something that looked like an upholstered bench without legs, only far more narrow than a bench.

"Notice that it's connected with wires to the ball bearings that slide along the circular track, the same system as we used for the video conferencing units," Matt confirmed. "It gives more options for movement. And access."

He was lifting her, and with her arms bound behind her back she couldn't stop him. He made her feel weightless, as if it were nothing for him to carry her. He put her on her feet beside the table. Then his hands were on her face, making an adjustment to the mask. Suddenly she was blind, darkness covering the eye holes.

"Matt, what are you —"

"I think it's best for this to be a surprise," he said gently.

"No. I don't like this."

"You're just afraid. You don't have to be afraid."

"I'm not," she snapped. She felt desperate, like a cat squalling and clawing inside a burlap bag, knowing that she was about to be thrown into the river with nothing but a brick for company. The fear wasn't rational. She could tell him to stop, he'd told her she could quit at any time. But she couldn't quit. Not in this type of game. Not with him. She swallowed, biting down on her tongue ferociously to calm herself.

"Matthew, save your sex games for whatever bimbo you're screwing right now and just get this over with. I can be a lot more fun with my hands free. I've…got plenty of lovers who will vouch that I'm worth the time in the sack."

She heard him sigh, and then his hand was against her back, pressing her down to the table, making her lie there on her stomach. His thighs brushed the back of hers, and she choked on feminine fear. *My God, he's going to... No, not like this.*

One of the nylon straps was under her upper arm, telling her the contraption was just to her left. There was a sliding sound, a click of metal, and for a moment she thought he was adjusting the device. Then she realized he had picked up something to her right. Something he had laid on the table earlier, before he pulled her over his lap. She swore.

"Goddamn it, Matt—"

"Two things," he said in a hard voice. "The cursing, and referring to lovers you've never had, and never will have."

Snap!

The belt was like a lick of flame, striking her across both buttocks. She cried out, startled, her mind not able to keep up.

"Matt, don't. I'm sorry."

"No, you're not. You'd gouge my eyes out if you could right now."

Snap.

Her body quivered with the pain, but she clenched her teeth, even as she felt the first tear spill out.

"Why are you doing this?" She lost her resolve, her voice breaking. "Why can't you just...not do this? Why does it have to be like this?"

"Sshhh...it's okay."

His body covered hers, completely blanketing her, his legs against hers, his pelvis against her hips, the pressure of his cock firmly against her aching ass, his waist against the small of her back, his chest against her shoulder blades, his neck and jaw against her temple. For some reason, instead of wanting to bite him in retribution, she wanted to press her face into the curve of that warm male neck, feel the rough scratch of his

38

afternoon shadow, his breath moving the soft hair along her face. She needed oxygen, or her entire body was going to decompress from the pressure. *Tennyson Rule Four: Show no fear*, was about to fly out the window.

"How did you imagine it would be with us? You and me?" His voice was a husky whisper.

Like you described. Forever, making love to me forever, with fresh flowers in the room… The thought was almost as shocking as her next thought. She'd also imagined it somewhat like this. The heat, the wildfire and sexual violence mixed with exhilaration. Not this tearing emotional pain. But one couldn't come without the price of the other. She was a negotiator, a closer. She knew the cost of the biggest deals. And tonight was a very big deal, though she kept trying to minimize it. Matt was ruthless at the negotiation table when he wanted to be, and he wasn't holding anything back.

All the wildness of the past few moments faded back as a stillness settled over them, the sacred, unassailable intimacy of two bodies that wanted to be together, no matter what her mind denied. The press of his weight against her perversely soothed the vibrating pain of her bottom. His hand reached up, stroked back her hair, freed a piece caught in an uncomfortable position in the mask.

"Trust me, Savannah. Tell me you want me, what I've always known. Then we don't have to do this. Just surrender."

She shook her head. "I can't. Please, Matt. Just…don't."

"No." He nuzzled her ear, and she couldn't help moving her cheek against the touch. "This is a deal I'm going to win, that we're both going to win. You've got a lot of starved passion in your body, and I'm going to devote tonight to appeasing its hunger. And when your lust is sated, there will be only one truth, one you won't have any excuse to deny. There's only one man that can give you what's pounding for release in that heart of yours." His hand slid down, his fingers probing beneath the crotch of her panties, making her shudder. "Your pussy knows the touch of its Master. It wants my cock buried up to the hilt in it. Before the night's over, you'll beg me to fuck you."

"So you can say bad words, but I can't," she said petulantly.

"I said it in a way that makes your nipples hard and your mouth go soft." His dry chuckle reverberated in her ear. "The way you said it made me doubt you had love in your heart."

She bit down on a retort. The cool smoothness of the table pressed against her bare upper body as he rose, keeping a palm on her back to hold her in place. He began to remove her jewelry. Her earrings, her bracelet, the ring she wore on her left index finger. He was stripping her of everything, and the quaking in her stomach acknowledged the power of it, the meaning, even as her mind refused to embrace it.

"Cleopatra at least had an asp," she said.

"I don't intend to drag you in chains through the streets of Rome."

"No…" She jerked as his hands settled on her neck, on the locket. She cursed herself for the emotional reaction, but his hands gentled. He still removed it, but his knuckles stroked her neck soothingly.

"It will be right over here. I won't let anything happen to it. I promise."

And everyone, friend and foe alike, knew that he kept his promises. She relaxed slightly, on that point at least.

He loosened the bra from around her wrists, but before she could take advantage of that, he was replacing it, strangely enough, with a pair of gloves. He worked them over her cold fingers and she discovered from the touch of the air they had open finger holes. Lacings on the back of the right and the palm of the left allowed him to lace her two hands together so they were flat, sandwiched together at the small of her back, the knuckles of her left hand against the dip there. Then he put a set of cuffs on her wrists, as if her inability to move her fingers apart was not enough.

He shifted her quivering body onto the upholstered narrow bench piece of the device he'd lowered from the ceiling. It ran from the base of her throat to just above her pubic bone. It wasn't as wide as she'd thought it was, perhaps about five inches. Supporting her sternum, it separated her breasts, pushing them out so they were on either side of it. She tensed as Matt's hands moved over her breasts, but his intention was to extend four bars, two on each side, that were apparently joined to the bench at its base to swivel out as needed. She felt a moment of trepidation when he positioned the bars at the top and bottom curve of her breast on either side, and then he began doing things with the straps in that area. Things that compressed those bars together, holding her breasts snugly, so her nipples pressed harder against the table surface, immediately increasing their sensitivity to any friction.

"That feels good, I know, but I won't make them any tighter. You need to have good circulation, because I'm going to have you in this for a while."

Two extensions came out near her hips to give them a wider area of support on the bar, and then one more set at her shoulders for the same purpose.

As he made all the adjustments, she found her breath was getting more shallow, not from constriction, but from a dizziness swamping her, her arousal compounding exponentially with every action he took to make her more confined, less able to control anything. With constant gentle touches and quiet reassurances, he balanced the panic that caused, and the power of the arousal took care of the rest. It seemed perversely okay for her body to be reacting the way it wished, now that he was transferring all power and control to himself.

He increased that helpless sensation tenfold when he went behind her and produced another set of bars from beneath the back end of the bench. She felt them extend and press against the line of her thighs. Swallowing against a rising tide of panic and arousal, she couldn't suppress a shiver as his

41

fingers hooked into the delicate swatch of panties and removed them, sliding them down her legs and off her feet before he gently adjusted her knees outward. These bars had a cuff at the end of each one, into which he guided her knees. He locked the top part of the cuff at her thigh just over the knees and then slid a bar into a lock hold between the two cuffs. Her legs were now spread and held open.

"I'm going to lift your feet off the floor now," he warned her. "Ah, sweetheart. Your pussy's absolutely gushing. You're loving this, aren't you?"

She couldn't reply without her voice shaking, and she couldn't risk that. Her fingers clutched one another, tangled in the lacings. Another set of cuffs went on her ankles, and then he gently bent her legs to a ninety degree angle and connected the ankle cuffs with another straight bar to the cuffs just above her knees, like the hypotenuse of the two sides of the triangle formed by her calf and thigh.

Why was she so violently aroused by being restrained? Why on earth would she, a master of controlling her life, be so completely seduced by the lack of it? She could not ask, imagining that smug look he'd have in his eyes if she admitted the confusion. Of course something this unsettling had to be a weakness.

She was sure she could play sex games with the best of them. This was no more frightening or dangerous than any hostile corporate takeover. He'd think her stupid and naïve if she said she'd never had any restraints during sex, not even some innocuous silk scarves. But why couldn't she stop her shaking?

She started out of her thoughts as another motor engaged and suddenly the straps were tightening across her body, the bench pressing firmly against her, taking her weight as the contraption began to retract, lifting her.

"Matt—"

"Don't worry. I'm just moving you all the way onto the table."

As good as his word, he stopped the motor after just a moment. Another lever engaged and she was moved forward, over the table she assumed. An assumption confirmed when there was another adjustment downward, and he had her settled completely on the rich mahogany.

In the position which the harness system held her, she was on her bent knees, her upper body sloped downward so her cheek rested on the table, her backside exposed in the air, a disturbing and ignominious position she began to protest, but then he was touching her face, telling her he had moved to the opposite side of the table, directly in front of her.

"Open up, baby," he murmured, and with his thumb at her jaw and the corner of her mouth she had no choice. The moment she parted her lips he slid a ball of soft rubber into her mouth, preventing further speech. He strapped it securely around her head, and now she could not speak or see.

Her breath rasped around the ball in shock and panic. His hands smoothly stroked her head, her quivering back.

"Sshhh...sshh...you're fine. You're beautiful. Don't be afraid. Not of this. Not of me."

She couldn't think of any moment she had been more afraid, but it wasn't the sick fear she'd experienced when her father had made her ride amusement park rides that terrified her, teaching her not to indulge weakness. This fear tangled with a desire so strong she wasn't sure she'd be capable of speech if her mouth was unobstructed.

His hands continued to caress, reassure even as he put a strap across her forehead and under her jawline, testing their fit. His touch moved to her shoulders, and he attached those facial straps to the horizontal restraint there, so her head and neck had a support to hold them up comfortably, in a physical sense at least. The inability to duck her head or shield her face in any way was somehow much less comfortable. Her backside and spread pussy were still the highest part of her body, which enhanced the feeling of total exposure and vulnerability to him. The motor engaged, suggesting he had a remote control, and her upper body was lifted up about an inch so her chin was not pressed uncomfortably on the table.

"I can adjust any part of your body up and down, to just the right height for what I want to see or do to it. Tilt the bar like a seesaw, put your hips even higher in the air, so I can see your pussy and ass better. Straighten you up to your knees, so I can see your beautiful breasts in that parallel restraint. If you start getting a tingling or a numbness anywhere, you let me know."

How? How on earth did he expect her to do that with her ability to speak denied?

He was behind her again, and his finger trailed down the sole of her right foot, tickling her through the sheer stocking. She wiggled the foot in reaction, curling her toes, and his low chuckle was more sensual reaction than humor.

"That's the signal, Savannah, if you're in any type of physical discomfort. Wiggle your right foot. I'd say curl your toes, but I intend to give you the type of pleasure tonight that makes them curl, and I don't want to misread you."

His voice continued, stroking her even when his hands were not. "I had this suspension system made for you specifically. Knowing where you get your clothes custom-tailored, I obtained your exact measurements. The length of your body overall, then from just beneath the breasts to the hips." He caressed these parts of her. "They made the steel bench and support extensions strong, so you'd be completely supported while you were suspended, and I talked to a master suspension artist about pressure points to be sure you'd be fully supported, safe. We made this on our own shop floor." His hand passed over her still smarting flank. "We had the covering on the bench made of the softest material available, because you have such delicate skin. I didn't want you to feel any discomfort, except for the discomfort I want you to feel.

The straps are a new synthetic we're working on for restraining people in hospitals when certain surgical procedures require it for their protection. They're lined, made so they won't chafe you even when you're straining against them."

He bent down, touched his lips to her ear. "I've taken away your sight, your ability to wield that vicious tongue of yours, your freedom of movement. Not to punish you. Not to frighten you. I'd rather cause you pleasure than pain any day, though one certainly can be the avenue to the other. But I want you to *feel*. Feel it all. Get past your mind, back to your heart. Because I'm there, waiting for you. I'm going to leave you no place to retreat except there, until you have to admit it's me that you've wanted for months now, same as I've wanted you. And you'll know why and how I knew your body would respond like this to sexual domination, to my mastery over you."

She wanted to tell him '"Fuck you", but she had neither voice nor eye contact to convey it, nor the freedom of her arms to make a suitably rude gesture. And she wasn't sure she had the strength to force the words past her lips, even if she wasn't gagged. Not with her body reacting as if it was gripped by some type of overwhelming palsy, where she was no longer in control of the most basic movements or speech. Even now she had an inexplicable desire for him to stay bent close to her, where she could smell the nuances of musky male heat that her flared nostrils recognized so distinctly as Matt.

Then, unbelievably, she heard a door open.

Chapter Two

ൟ

"Good evening, gentlemen." Matt's voice was abruptly smooth and professional, and above her, telling her he had straightened, taking that reassuring scent further from her face. "Come in. Feel free to sample the refreshments offered on the table, remembering the rules we discussed."

There was a whirring of gears, and Savannah felt the straps along her sides tighten, begin to lift her from the table. The upper body lifted a few more inches, the lower body much more significantly. When the gears stopped, she realized, to her horror, that Matt had lifted her up just enough so the tips of her breasts brushed the table surface. Her hips were still higher than her head, only now her knees barely brushed the table, taking away a sense of grounding. With her legs held open by the steel bar, the bench separating and displaying her breasts, she was baldly displayed to… How many pairs of feet did she hear? She realized abruptly it had to be his team, all four of them.

"Any cock will do, right?" Matt had bent down, was whispering in her ear again. "At any point, this can be over." A cloth pressed into her open right palm and she automatically gripped it, making both sets of fingers curl over it, due to the lacings holding the two hands together. "That's my handkerchief, your white flag of surrender. If you've had enough, if you're ready to admit that I've had you pegged right from the beginning, you drop it. As long as you hold it, I'm not granting you a moment of mercy.

"Whenever we do a hostile takeover, we itemize the obstacles, group them until we know how many gates we need to take to get to the prize. We're fairly sure there are about five gates we'll have to crash through to get you to surrender.

You're going to come often and hard tonight. Not when you want to, but when I want you to, when each of these men wants you to, because that's our will."

His palm slid along the side of her face, his thumb flicking the tassels of the mask along her cheek, causing the sensation of watered silk flowing across her skin's surface. "They all know who you are, of course. But psychologically, I think the mask and the blind provide you a sense of anonymity that will give you the space to let yourself truly go. At a certain point, I'll want you to see us, see how you affect us. But for now, I want you to forget that you think this is a battle, and just imagine what you would do if this was all, not against you, but for you. To give you pleasure, to bring you where your deepest desires, the ones you don't even admit you have, want to take you."

She heard his words, understood them, but all she could think about at the moment was there were four ambitious young men in the room. Men who had put in a full day, probably starting at the crack of dawn. Now in the early evening, ties discarded and sleeves rolled up, they wanted something to help them unwind for the weekend. And she didn't think they were thinking of an old movie in the study and a healthy dose of ice cream like she had been planning.

"She's beautiful, isn't she?" Matt slid his hand up the slope of her back to her raised ass, stroked down her hip. "There are only a few rules, if you'll recall, and I'm going to restate them here, where Savannah can hear them."

Rules? They had discussed this like...some takeover strategy?

"Rule number one, I won't repeat. You heard it clearly enough before and she's not ready to hear it right now."

She suspected it was not the same Rule One she knew.

Tennyson Rule One, the most important one of all, the one her father had spent her entire life teaching her. *There is no such thing as failure. Only quitters.*

His tone altered, his words more pronounced, deliberate. She picked up the tension and could envision that shift in vocal cadence had drawn their attention from the display of her bare body in the same way wolves of the pack took their attention from a kill when the leader laid back his ears, lifted his lips in a snarl.

"You can play with her in as many and varied ways as you wish that will give her pleasure, but you can't fuck her pussy. Understood? And if you touch her, you have to make her come. For each time you make her come, you get an extra percent share in this company, of my own stock. The man who makes her come the fastest tonight, from the time of the initial touch, will get a five percent share."

His hand shifted back to her head, slid down the side of her face, touching her lips, their stretched state around the ball making them even more sensitive to the stroke. She would have bitten off his thumb if her mouth wasn't obstructed by the gag. They were making her into a game? It was one thing to play with Matt, but if she were free now, and had known what the plan was, she *would* have screamed rape, torn his eyes out, done whatever was necessary to get out of this room.

Big talk, Savannah. And every word he's just spoken has made you even wetter between your legs. Had she lost her mind? What was the matter with her? And why did it bother her so much that he was offering a stock incentive? Was she seriously entertaining an ego in this outlandish situation?

Tennyson Rule Six: The body and heart do what they please, but it is the mind's choice to follow. So basically, it didn't matter if her body was responding or not, her outrage could still be intact. Of course, she was aware that her attempt to use the rules of a lifetime to keep her head on straight was faltering miserably.

"She's very special." His voice softened to a purr. "Don't frighten her. Show her what it is to be desired and loved by more than one man, gentlemen. Take her beyond her wildest notions of desire. She's waited a long time, and she deserves to have it done right."

Something within her trembled hard at the words, especially when his hand tightened on her hair, reminding her that he was convinced she belonged to him, then the grip loosened and he stroked his knuckles down the inside of her shoulder blade, a sensation she hadn't thought could be so incredibly intimate. "She's never felt a man's all-consuming passion, so strong he'd kill just to be inside of her. This is the deal of a lifetime, gentlemen." He paused for a significant moment. "Don't let me down."

Then his touch left her and he walked away. She heard him, strained her ears to figure out where he was going, suddenly panicked at the idea that he was leaving the room altogether. Instead, she heard him move to the head of the table, take out his chair. A moment later, another man's hands touched her.

It made sense it would be Lucas, his CFO. Every breath in this room was like taking in the primal odor of a wolf's den, and in a pack, dinner was served in pecking order.

Savannah could barely breathe around the gag in her mouth. She had gone from active trembling to a vibration that kept her shivering as if from a flu, and it grew even more intense as Lucas touched her.

It wasn't that any of these men were strangers. It was just that Matt had always dominated her fantasies. In this situation, Lucas was an unknown quantity, the equivalent to a stranger emotionally.

She knew it was Lucas, for several reasons. One was that scent. Lucas wore a light cologne fragrance that reminded her fantastically enough of Egyptian pharaohs. The heat of the desert, the power of kings. The kohl used to outline piercing eyes, aristocratic brows. Bodies inviting touch in their light robes, cuffs of beaten gold emphasizing powerful wrists and muscular biceps.

She could visual him in reality well enough, but the image that came to mind was not of him in this conference room, in office clothing. Lucas was as tall as Matt, with a lean, athletic build developed from his primary extracurricular activity, cross-country bicycling. The pale gold of his hair spoke of the many hours out in the sun. He biked to work, a ten-mile trek, and one hot summer day she'd pulled into the parking deck for an early morning meeting at Kensington in time to see him parking the bike. He'd removed the helmet, and the hair that was a little long, just past his ears, had been casually pushed back, blond mixed with dark streaks from perspiration. He stripped off the short-sleeved skin-tight cycling shirt and started toweling off. She knew from casual inferences that he kept his change of office clothes in the building, but she had not known he performed this drying ritual first.

She'd sat in the front seat of her car, two rows away in the shadows, ready to duck her head as if searching through her briefcase if he looked up and caught her watching, because she could not keep herself from her inexcusable ogling. Something about watching all the sculpted muscles of that body move in the simple act of removing sweat held her motionless, her body pulsing with a rhythm that she wanted to ignore. The rhythm of wanting.

Two ladies from his office had passed by, one whistling and both engaging in some flirtatious banter with him. He'd grinned, held his shirt in front of him in mock horror as if protecting his modesty. She'd heard the other wunderkind ribbing him about the fact he shaved all his body hair. She liked the dark hair that curled at the base of Matt's throat, intimating a nice pelt beneath his ironed shirts. However, watching Lucas towel off that smooth golden skin made her realize that women didn't have to have just one preference. Just like chocolate, there were many favorites to appreciate.

Savannah had wished she'd been settled enough to get out of her car, walk past him, make some friendly remark as they did, but all she'd thought of was how warm that skin would feel under her touch, what it would be like to be touched by those hands…

Well, she was about to find out.

Those strong, gentle hands were stroking her ass, lingering touches that told her he was examining her in detail from that angle. The pulse that had been jerking in her throat from trepidation settled uneasily back into the rapid cadence of arousal, the conflicting emotions keeping her body vacillating between need and nerves.

"She smells exquisite," Lucas observed. His finger traced up the back of her thigh, to the inside, and her muscles clenched, straining against the cuffs that made closing her legs impossible. "You've already made her pussy wet, Matt." Male amusement entered his voice, teasing his boss. "Or maybe *we're* responsible for that. I think I'd like a taste."

She felt his body shift, his warm breath slide down her spine. It filtered between the clench of her buttocks, the moist heat of his mouth coming closer, closer. A moment later, his warm, firm lips closed over her clit, his hair tickling the inside of her thighs. Her head jerked against the restraint, her eyes widening at the sensation. A moan came around the ball gag, and she'd not told her vocal cords to make any such noise.

"Lick her slow and easy, Lucas. She's never had a man do this to her. Let her find out how hard she'll come under a lover's slow touch." Matt's voice.

"Screw the five percent," Lucas murmured against her skin, making her shudder. "I'd rather eat this pussy as long as I want. She's sweet, like honey."

His mouth lifted away and she could almost sense how his nostrils flared as he took a deeper breath, for she felt the shift of the rhythm of breath inside her thighs. She made a quiet whimper, a plea. Though she didn't know for what.

"Do you know how much my men care for you, Savannah?" Matt asked, his voice a calming stroke of reassurance. "After the negotiations we've had, the long hours we've spent here, sometimes until the morning sun struck the office windows? We know you've felt the synergy among all of us."

"It was something you did one night that made us start thinking of this." Lucas picked up the thread from Matt. "At about two in the morning, long after we'd all shed our coats, loosened our ties, you got up, unbuttoned the one button of the pale green jacket you were wearing, and slipped out of it. Laid it with perfect precision over the chair. Every movement elegant, ladylike. But then, you put your hand to the small of your back, kneaded it, stretched it. You raised your other hand and let down your hair. Not a calculated move at all. You just pulled the clip free, ran your fingers through it to ease the pull on your scalp, kept up that kneading on your back. You rolled your shoulders, turned and came back to the table. You had no clue how riveted we all were, as aroused as if you'd just stripped. The human woman inside the inhuman armor revealed. An armor you've created solely from the core of strength inside yourself."

Stop it, she wanted to say, though she knew he wouldn't listen, would never obey her commands the way her body was obeying the stimulation of his words.

"On our playing field, you're a knight who obeys the same code of honor we do." Matt spoke now. "We've worked together five years, our two companies, and in the past two years, since your father died, we've worked even more closely together. Every man has grown to care for you, desires to protect you. Desires you, period. When we were talking about it early that morning, Lucas made the comment that, somewhere along the way, we'd decided you were ours."

"Like a sister, but definitely not." Now there was a smile in Lucas's voice, and she heard a chuckle from the others, those who'd yet to approach her, but if Matt's words were heeded, would be doing so soon.

"This is hard to explain, complicated," Matt said. "But we suspect you don't really have to hear the words, because your body already knows the truth, and your heart is close behind."

It was as if they knew she had a desperate need for a rational explanation of what was happening to her, but the explanation they were giving her was not the one she needed to keep her insides from breaking up into pieces.

"You always come alone to us." Matt observed softly. "You don't want to share us. We think you consider us yours as well."

Lucas's breath hovered just above her hips, making her lower belly clench with need. "That may be true, but there's only one of us she'll let all the way into her soul. There's only one of us she's in love with. And we all know it."

His thumb followed the valley of her spine, and he wouldn't stop telling her things her mind couldn't digest, a combination of disorienting sensations. "I wanted to lay you down on the sofa that night," Lucas said, his voice a rumbling purr. "Rub your back, your shoulders, until the tension went out of them, until my touch put you to sleep. I imagined you'd look like a princess lying there, your fist tucked up under your chin, your golden curls falling around your face. When you finally slept, your legs would draw up, and you'd turn on your side. There would be a gleam of dim light on your stockings, and I'd reach up under the skirt..." His hand slid down her flank, over her buttock, to the top of the thigh-high. "...and ease them off, for your comfort."

His hands did just that, his fingers insinuating themselves under the lace top of the left stocking, taking it down the contours of her thigh, the back of her knee, working it gently past the hold of the cuffs at thigh and ankle. The nylon whispered over the sole of her foot. He removed the other the same way, with painstaking, breathtaking slowness. Then, barrier gone, Lucas set his lips to her calf.

She had brashly told Matt she'd have sex with him. But this wasn't sex. This was seduction. Matt had locked her into some strange dream. She was beyond wondering whether he really would release her if she asked him to do so. All she knew was the slow rub and heat of Lucas's mouth on her calf. Oh God, the back of her knee. Nibbling kisses, each one like a tiny massage, arousing sensual response and emotional pain that held her in a strangling grip. Tears were moving down her face, and she didn't know why, couldn't stop them, and she hoped the mask would absorb them so the men wouldn't see them roll beyond it, down her chin.

Lucas's large, fine-boned hand was on her other thigh. He slid his hands into the cuffs holding her spread open and made an adjustment that spread her even further apart, so she choked around the gag at the sensation of increased vulnerability. His hair brushed her leg, that soft, straight hair.

"What do you put here?" He tilted his head, just the tip of his nose brushing that sensitive pocket of bone formed between the juncture of her thigh and her pussy. The heat of his breath tickled the fine hairs of her mound, and arousal made her feel as if there were a shimmer of electrons on her skin. The room became warmer, it seemed. "It smells like baby powder, Matt," he said quietly. "Like she trims her pussy with a razor and soothes her skin with baby powder. And some lavender here. Maybe lotion. I love the way women put different fragrances on themselves." He rubbed his nose against her clit deliberately, shooting sparks of sensation straight into her womb. His mouth was so close, so close to her. She'd never had a man...do that to her, but she'd watched the movie *The Big Easy* on one of her "off" nights. Savannah remembered Ellen Barkin's sensuous expressions in the scene that implied Dennis Quaid's Cajun character was doing what Lucas's proximity suggested. She'd sat, still and motionless in the study, her pillow hugged up to her body, wondering if the scene accurately reflected what a man's skillful mouth could do between a woman's thighs.

"Like a flower garden," he said dreamily. "Something different every time you inhale."

Without warning or hesitation, he put his mouth fully over her, his tongue delving deep within her. She surged forward, shocked by the heat of his lips and tongue, but of course with the bindings, she could go nowhere.

She could see nothing, and she found she wanted the anchor of Matt's eyes, something to focus her, his reaction to Lucas's servicing her with his mouth. Something that would help her keep resistance and basic lust to the forefront, but with her ability to speak removed, her eyes blinded by the mask, she could only face the reality of Lucas's miraculous mouth and what it was unleashing within her.

He sucked on her clit, made appreciative, wet noises against her, and her hips responded, lifting and rising the infinitesimal amount permitted by the restraints, creating glorious friction, and she strengthened her efforts, following instinct to drive it to a pinnacle.

"None of that now." It was Matt's voice, Matt's hand now on her back. A more erotic stimulation she couldn't have anticipated, to have one man's mouth between her legs and another's hands upon her. He did something with the waist strap and suddenly Lucas adjusted his position. Motors hummed, and her knees left the table fully, perhaps a couple inches, so she couldn't move in a rhythm, only sit, helplessly squirming and gasping against the gag as Lucas's mouth returned, his tongue delving deep within her pussy again, thrusting, rolling her clit, licking.

"I can smell her, now," Jon spoke from the end of the table.

"Same here." Peter responded directly in front of her. "She's got a sweet pussy, just as you said, Lucas."

"I want her to come, Matt," Lucas said, lifting his mouth from her just a fraction.

She shook her head. No. No… But hadn't she just wanted that? But no, not like this, not when everything was up to them.

"I think she's refusing you, Lucas." Matt's cool voice came from the end of the table again. "Make her come in the next two minutes. Despite her best attempts to resist. Mouth only."

"Done," Lucas said softly, and moved in to close the deal.

She expected him to redouble his physical effort, had tensed and braced herself against it, and so was surprised when there was a pause, the noise of wheels. He'd taken a seat in a chair, pulled it up between her legs. The fine hair over his temples brushed the inside of her thighs as he moved in close again.

"You know…" He administered a tiny lick on her clit that made her shudder. "Eating pussy is my very favorite thing to do with a woman. I love the smell, the taste, the feel of her thighs as she sits on my face. I love squeezing her ass in my hands as I shove her hard against me, taking away her choice, pushing her into that pleasurable abyss. I love to listen to her scream as she falls. I love knowing when she falls to the bottom, it will be my arms there to catch her. We'll be here to catch you," he whispered huskily. "All of us. Stop being so afraid. Don't you know how much you mean to Matt, to all of us?"

She made a noise of forceful and furious protest against the gag.

"Didn't sound flattering, Lucas." Ben spoke this time.

"One minute," Jon warned.

"More than I need, though nowhere close to how much I want."

Lucas put his mouth over her clit, sucking her back into the heat and wet. He began to lick her, strong, sure strokes, not too fast, pushing up against the volatile area, starting at the bottom, pushing up on it again, scoring her lightly with his teeth. That bite and push again, as if pressuring that tight bud of flesh was like nudging a switch.

Things were happening inside her, things that defied description. A spiral of reaction that had strings drawing taut everywhere, her whole body starting to hold itself tight as if in some form of self-imposed paralysis. Her breath darted in and out through her nose, her teeth sinking into the ball. Something gathered, gathered, just out of reach. No, she couldn't reach for it...couldn't stop herself from lunging for it...

"Come for him, Savannah." Matt snapped out the order. "Now. At my command."

The orgasm exploded from somewhere between Lucas's mouth and her pussy and erupted through her. Going over that pinnacle, her brain reversed its will. Instead of freezing her in place, now she was wriggling gracelessly, helplessly. In her suspended restraints, screaming against the gag, she made words that could only be heard in her own mind, shocking her.

Touch me...touch me... Never stop.

She wanted Matt. But he could not hear her wish with the gag, and what little mind she continued to control told her to be glad.

It wasn't just about the battle of wills. If she threw open the door to her heart, he could deny her. Leave her with her wishes echoing against the walls, empty and desolate, like a house where everything was gone, leaving only the harsh regret of memory. Like a child being told that little girls who ran to their Daddy to get hugs wouldn't amount to anything except a takeover acquisition for some man.

She felt suddenly like the men in the room were all weapons turned against her, the sword of Eden, turning in every direction, shining upon her weakness, her every shortcoming.

With so little sexual experience, she didn't know if this was normal, this flood of overpowering emotions that made her feel completely adrift on an unfamiliar ocean. Flailing, she tried to pull herself out of that darkness, onto the far more rational thought that this was similar to eating too much chocolate, or taking one too many Valium to help her sleep. Those things made her body no longer in her control, subject to macabre dreams or frenetic nervous energy she could not rein in. It was a physical, chemical reaction. It said nothing about herself, who she was or what she truly wanted.

Lucas kept his nose and mouth pressed hard against her pussy, continuing to eat her out. Running his tongue over her clit, he dipped into the well between her legs, making a noise of pleasure at the taste of her come on those sensuous lips. His hair brushed her thighs, the planes of his face touching her as he continued the soft nibbles through the hard aftershocks. She bleated at each touch like a lost sheep, a sheep who in this moment had no doubt who the shepherd was who held her fate. She wanted to see Matt with the fervor of a dying wish, and her hand clutched into fists to keep from dropping that kerchief, from begging with her body what her mouth was thankfully prevented from saying.

No. She wasn't that far gone. This was a whole new situation, like the first time she handled opening a plant on her own. There would be some weak moments, some stumbling as she figured out her approach to get the upper hand with the players who didn't think she had the right to the upper hand.

There is no situation in life that cannot be explained by the same principles we use in business. Geoffrey's voice resounded in her mind, hammering the point home. "If a person is making you feel something you don't want to feel, take the reins away from them. If you can control yourself, you can control the situation, bring the tiller back to your hand. Keep your wits about you and wait for the opportunity."

Sound advice, though she was certain even her dispassionate father could not have predicted this situation. And somehow, hearing his voice in her head now, thinking of applying his logic to this situation, swept her with a desolation that made her wish to be free of them all, her father and these men and Matt, in her bed with the covers over her head. And then the most unnerving thought of all intruded on the image.

What if Matt were there, putting his knee on her bed, lying down on top of her covers, curving that powerful body around her? Scooping up the covers and her into the heat and warmth of him, providing a shelter that was simply that, a place to draw strength and sanctuary, demanding nothing she was not willing to give? Or take it a step further…accepting something she'd always wanted to give but had been afraid to offer, mainly because no one had ever come right out and asked for her heart.

Get a grip, Savannah. He's won the round, that's it. He wasn't proving anything except that she could enjoy oral sex, like any independent, healthy woman. What woman in her right mind wouldn't enjoy this, even if she had been dragged kicking and screaming to it?

It meant nothing. *Nothing.*

Abruptly the gag was removed and a mouth was on hers, hard, hungry, as Lucas kept up with his soothing and stirring kisses along the insides of her quaking thighs. All her arguments shattered, because it was Matt's mouth on hers, Matt's scent filling her nose, Matt's warm skin so close, that rough, handsome jaw that she ached to touch.

Sheer fulfillment flooded into an emptiness yawning open in her chest like a wound. His lips were the healing touch, reassuring her, yet spinning her off her axis once again so that something within her screamed in fury and desperation. Giving in to it, her lips pulled back from her teeth in a snarl and she bit, latching down on his bottom lip.

Instead of him jerking away, allowing her to rip and tear at him as he was ripping and tearing at her insides, his hands cupped the back of her head, holding her still. Despite her painful vise on his bottom lip, he kept his mouth crushed over hers, his tongue plunging along her clenched teeth, his own lips persuasive, gentle. Responding not with matching ferocity, but with devastating tenderness. When his touch slipped forward to caress the sides of her throat, her cheek, she realized she had let go. The acrid taste of his blood lingered on her tongue.

"You're doing beautifully," he said in a whisper against her, his breath touching her cheek just below her mask. "They all love you, don't you know that? You can't do anything to drive us away. We're your family. Your lovers, your friends, the adversaries that challenge and stimulate you. Your real social life, not the theater and charity events, the occasional dinner with a man just for show."

She shook her head. No. She would not let this outrageous situation become that personal. She wanted an end to it, to go home.

Which meant she had to admit they had broken her, that she was as soft and vulnerable as Matt claimed she was. Capable of being hurt, manipulated. That he affected her so strongly that she couldn't see this through to the end he had planned.

She went rigid, refused to let her body respond. After a moment, she heard a sigh, felt him draw away.

"Do you know it's often the women who are strongest in public that most desire a man's Mastery behind closed doors, Savannah?"

She shook her head, in protest or denial she couldn't say, but she had no words with her body throbbing with the aftermath of the climax and the sense of loss his withdrawal caused. Lucas had pulled back as well, and now stimulation came in audible form only. Matt's voice, hearing the shifts of their bodies around her, the rustle of clothing, the sound of their breathing.

"You have this overwhelming desire to surrender, to submit to a man strong enough to Master you. It's like an aphrodisiac to the man who senses it. I know the exact moment I recognized it in you. It was like a punch in the gut. Or a light bulb going on."

She heard the smile in his voice, and cold fingers gripped her vitals. Just by speaking the word, he had evoked the memory. A memory she had replayed over and over in her mind, not understanding why it was so fascinating to her. But he had known, and now so did she, despite her strongest desire to deny it.

"I know you remember it." His voice took her back with him to the uncomfortable recollection. "I know I do. I've relived it every day since it happened. It led us to this moment. Didn't it?"

* * * * *

He'd come back from the dinner break early, ostensibly to make a couple of phone calls, but there was always the possibility that he would see Savannah and could spar with her for a few enjoyable moments.

It made him frown, though, knowing he would find her in her office. She went on business luncheons, attended banquets and gala events with the right escorts, but never did he see her sitting on the edge of one of the downtown fountains, eating a sandwich and taking in the pigeons' play, engaging in idle people-watching. Or, even more shocking, out with a girlfriend, laughing, having some female conversation. Doing some playful male-bashing.

"She's not a woman, she's a fucking robot," he'd heard one competitor say. "Geoffrey Tennyson didn't spawn her, he had her built in one of his plants."

It had made Matt angry, and he'd made sure to scuttle the man's plans for overseas expansion with him. Lucas had pointed out it was an emotional, rather than a fiscally intelligent act, and he had not disagreed with that assessment. Nor had it erased his satisfaction in doing it. He wondered often if Savannah realized she had a circle of devoted knights trying to protect her from harm when she wouldn't even let them into the inner circle of her life. Geoffrey was gone, and what protection the man had provided, as well as the damage he had done, was gone. She was as alone in the world as a person could get. He wanted her in his world, and she wouldn't even give him an opening to make a move in that direction.

He rounded the corner, his peripheral vision sharpened so he could see if she was in her office. The door was open, her desk light on. And she was standing on top of her desk.

She hadn't taken off her shoes, and he assumed it was to give her extra height to reach her objective, though he shuddered to think about her stepping on her unstable wheeled office chair in those skinny heels.

He detoured. Determining in a few strides what she was doing, he quickened his pace.

Apparently a bulb had burned out in the incandescent ceiling lighting she preferred to fluorescent. Anal-retentive plague that she was, she was changing it herself, rather than waiting to have a maintenance person with solid shoes and a ladder do it tomorrow. She was on the ball of one foot, the other off the ground, straining, her right breast clearly outlined against the fabric of her turquoise turtleneck. The ceiling was too high for her to use one hand to steady her upper body, and as she worked to free the panel over the light fixture, she was precariously balanced. When it came free with a jerk, she overbalanced.

Matt got there in time to clamp his hands on her hips, his palms curled over the hipbones, his fingers on the soft curves.

"What are you doing? Get down from there."

She was flustered, and he didn't often get to see that. She backed out of his hold, and he nipped the panel from her fingers, taking it to the floor.

"I'm trying to change a light bulb."

"I can see that. Get down."

"I just need to—"

"Get. Down. Now."

Instead of coming back with another sharp retort, he saw something incredible happen. A moment of confusion. Nervous tension. Something came over him, too, an instinct, and the remarkable feeling that a door had just swung wide open. And he wanted to test it.

"You heard me, Savannah," Matt said softly. "Come here. Now."

It was a long moment. Then she shifted her gaze away from his, *down*, and moved toward his reaching hands, her neck and cheeks flushed.

Still reeling from the revelation, he almost missed his cue, but he recovered in time to take her elbow as she reached down for him. He gripped her waist and she put her hands after a brief hesitation on his shoulders, curiously docile as he lifted her clear of the chair, pushing it out of his way, and lowered her to the floor.

It was a moment before he found his voice, and he managed to make it gentle, since she was blinking at him with the startled look of a deer, not anything like the Savannah he knew.

"Don't you attend the corporate safety seminars you torture your employees with?"

He saw the snap as the spell was broken. She even took a defensive step back, looked around herself, and that familiar disdain and faint irritation took over her features.

"We fulfill all OSHA requirements, Kensington."

"Oh, yeah. That was definitely an OSHA-approved maneuver." He flicked a hand out, caught a loose lock of her hair, enjoyed her look of shocked anger at the casual familiarity.

"I know you think you have to live up to your Savannah Cyborg image, but you don't have to be and do everything yourself, you know."

He actually saw a split second of hurt at the nickname that was used too often for her not to have overheard it countless times before. It made him angry with his clumsiness. And with her, for being so worthy of the name, but only in how she closed herself off to any advances of affection or friendship.

"You delegate administrative tasks to your assistants. Why can't you let other people help you with things?" He let his concern for her show, hoping to amend that inadvertent barb. "Damn it, if you'd fallen, there'd have been no one to see you fall."

"That's the plan," she said dryly. "Better to bust your backside when no one's looking." Some of the spunk was returning, but in the shift of her eyes, he saw she knew something significant had happened. He wondered if she understood what she had revealed, if she even knew it about herself.

The thought brought out a fierce possessiveness in him, a desire to crush anyone who'd taken advantage of such a sweet gift. He enjoyed the many faces and forms of sex, and having an excess of alpha in his personality, he'd often let the natural Dominant in him take over with his casual lovers who liked BDSM. The idea of exercising it in a less casual mode with the woman who'd become his obsession was so intoxicating he had a hard time keeping his cock settled in his trousers. Fortunately, she chose that moment to distract him.

"Fine." She tossed her head, presented him with a bulb from her desktop. "You want to do maintenance, here's your chance. And don't worry. I'll stand right here and catch you if you fall."

Typical Savannah. In the time he'd had two thoughts, she'd marshaled her defenses and reorganized her strategy. He thought if Napoleon had had her, the world would have undone the Tower of Babel and everyone would speak French now. The Russian winter couldn't have defeated nerve that cool. But he'd seen the heat just for a moment in her eyes, in that soft expulsion of breath as he set her down. He'd also felt the warmth of her skin beneath her clothes. Maybe she would have melted the ice in Russia, if she couldn't match it.

He grinned at her, fast and reckless, enjoying her, and her look of startled surprise at his reaction. He became less amused and more absorbed as her gaze lingered on his mouth, changing the look in her eyes. Testing, he took the bulb from her fingers and had to grasp it quickly to keep from losing it as she did her best to let go before he touched her fingers.

"Careful, don't drop it," she admonished, a snap to her voice.

He gave her an even look, toed off his shoes and slid onto the desk. His height helped him reach the bulb with a few inches to spare, and he unscrewed it and put in the new one, blinking as it came to life in his eyes.

"Jesus, Savannah, you could have turned off the light first." He took the panel from her and replaced it.

"Then how would I know the bulb worked while I was up there?"

He looked down and found her staring at his feet.

"What?"

"You..." Her lips pressed together, and then he saw a corner curl up in a tiny, shy, totally out-of-character smile. "You have a hole in your sock."

He sat back down on the desk, brought one leg to the floor and put his ankle on his knee, blinking around the flash image still popping within the spectrum of where he focused his vision. There was in fact a small hole worn just over his big toe. Not big enough to push through, or notice when he got dressed this morning.

"So I do." He looked up at her, at the unusual expression on her face. "What is it?"

"I just never think of you as someone with holes in his socks."

"Come here." Before she could evade him, he caught her hand, tugged her over. As he did, he put both feet on the floor so she was eased between his thighs. He took his fingers and carefully raised the hem of her skirt on the right side a few inches, so she could see what he had seen when she stood on her desk. A pencil-thin run in her stocking, starting just above the knee.

"And I don't think of you as someone with a run in your stocking."

She looked up at him, but the rest of her body didn't move. She was suddenly as still as a wild animal again, and he was even more aware of the feel of skin and silky nylon beneath the pads of his fingers.

His hand shifted, slipped up several more inches and encountered a lace top, the short skirt hem forming a folded crescent around his wrist. Her scent filled his senses.

She jerked back as though he'd slapped her when his fingers touched bare skin. Moved back so quickly she bent her heel and would have stumbled if he hadn't straightened just as fast and caught her by the waist, a touch she threw off as soon as she regained her balance.

"The office isn't a dating pool, Matthew. Go get yourself a one-night stand from a club like a regular guy."

He seized her by the elbow and whipped her around so fast that the shock was still in her face when he put her up against the wall and his body against hers. His fully aroused body. She felt perfect, her little pussy rubbing against him as she squirmed. It fulfilled his intention to let her know how she affected him, though it was more direct than he'd planned. Nevertheless, he pressed his cock harder against the juncture of her thighs.

"If you're going to flirt," he snapped. "Expect to get a response."

"I wasn't flirting." She shoved at him. Panic flickered across her face as she realized what he already knew, that she was ineffective against his strength. Though she tried to mask it, he felt her shiver down through her legs and arms. "Let go of me."

It registered like another fist in the gut. The trembling of her body, the emotion in her face, the wonder and desire followed by the panic and confusion. It was the shock of the truth, more than her demand, that had him easing his touch, gentling it.

For he *was* a very sexually experienced man. Enough to recognize a woman with none.

She'd never known a man, never handled his lust or accepted it into her body. Savannah Tennyson, the cold-blooded CEO of Tennyson Industries, was a virgin at the age of thirty-five.

* * * * *

"I can see from the way you're holding your mouth, the tense line of that classic jaw, that you remember that night as vividly as I do. I knew a couple things after that." Matt's fingers sent tingling jolts of pleasure down her neck as he drew short lines on the soft skin just beneath the straps holding her head up. "That you craved a man's Mastery, and you were untouched. And to a man like me, *already in love with you,* there was no way I was going to settle for less than total possession. Then came Lucas's summation of the situation, and we know the best way to take a fortress is to trick our way in, or use a battering ram. The only way to keep it is to win over the inhabitant, make her admit she can't do without you. So here we are."

...already in love with you...

He said it with such simple assurance, with no guile in his voice... What did she know about love? There had never been any such ship on her radar. She had no idea what it looked like, felt like. Her feelings for Matt were sexual, a strong sexual obsession. Professional admiration warring with animosity, most of the time. And he was using his knowledge of that to take advantage of her, to make her another conquest.

She couldn't explain why the simple telling of a story about a light bulb had made her body, so recently roused to climax, aroused again, the dampness between her legs heating with new moisture. Her nipples were so taut their light contact with the table was almost painful. But that was a physical reaction, not an emotional one. Wasn't it?

"You want me to believe that Matt Kensington would let himself fall prey to a weak illusion like love?" She scoffed, though she didn't like the harsh sound of her voice. "The idea of love is only used as a weapon."

"We'll see," he said after a long moment. There was a forced lightness to his voice. "Jon is going to give you pleasure next."

His hands lingered on her face, and she felt his reluctance to leave her side. It infuriated her. The whole situation, his ridiculous, patronizing assumptions, his gall in saying... *God, why did he say that?* Already in a tailspin, now she was diving out of control, all her thought processes lost, and all she could fall back on was frightened fury.

He returned to his chair, but from the creak of its frame, she suspected he'd turned away, was looking out over the panoramic view of the city. She'd gotten so familiar with his habits that, even blinded, she knew what he was doing.

It was something he did when he was contemplating something that disturbed him, and the fact that mattered to her made her even angrier.

"If you're ballsy enough to do this to me," she grated. "You should be ballsy enough to watch your men grope me."

The frozen stillness that settled over the room told her the arrow had hit its mark. There was the sound of the chair again as he turned, and she imagined him laying his hands on the table. One palm flat, fingers straight, the other laid casually upon it, like a lion lying at the edge of a meadow, watching a deer with every appearance of casual regard, all the while mulling whether he was hungry enough.

She'd seen the pose, knew it elicited tremendous discomfort in his prey. She wasn't sure she could be more disturbed than she was at this moment, but she wasn't going to give him the satisfaction of thinking he'd unsettled her further, not after his declaration and his peeved withdrawal when she hadn't fallen fawning at his feet in gratitude. Then he spoke.

"Jon. Proceed."

Chapter Three

ഇ

"Can I have the lighting aimed at the center of the table, please?" Jon voice revealed that he was behind her. Directly behind her.

If Matt was known as the fearsome Lord Kensington, Jon's nickname was Kensington's Archangel. Savannah remembered the first time she'd heard him speak and she, like everyone else, had done a mental double take. Words came from his mouth in such fluid, resolute tones that it was nearly impossible to imagine arguing with him over anything, even if he calmly indicated the sky had orange polka dots and grass sprang out of the ground purple. With the inexorable strength of water, he could break down financials into their most elemental pieces as quickly as he could an engine's components, revealing every flaw, and not use any visuals to get complicated points across. In the most turbulent conditions, Jon could bring absolute silence and attentiveness to a room the moment he began to speak.

But it was not just his voice that gave him that power. It was his expressions, his body language. He always brought to mind the words of Han Suyin: "There is nothing stronger than gentleness". It was an honor just to agree with Jon, because he seemed to take so much joy in a person's accord.

The others teased him, because his passion was reading enlightenment texts. Not the new age and self-help works with their generalizations and crunchy granola messages carried over from the sixties. The ancient works of Eastern gurus or Greek philosophers. He would bring up excerpts during their meetings, amusing them all, but the observations were never trite. Savannah had noted that often those quotes served a purpose. With them, Jon gently reminded all of them that their negotiations to win more stock shares or acquire companies could never be treated as a Monopoly game. That jobs, livelihoods and local economies were involved. He provided perspective and, according to him, helped them all keep their karma slate clean. No one disputed it.

There was a different kind of beauty to him. Slender, not tall, with luminous blue eyes and a black mane of silk that fell like feathers over his forehead and past his shoulders. Pale, for his interests kept him in offices and laboratories most of the time. Holding a dual Master's in accounting and mechanical engineering, he could slip from one topic to another as smoothly as he now began to touch her with the cool firmness of his hands. Down the crease between her buttocks and lower, where she was still wet and dripping from her climax, something she'd chosen to ignore until he reminded her of it. The embarrassed flush on her cheeks was something she could not stop or hide, particularly when Jon's request was met and the spotlight warmed her skin.

Typically it was used to highlight marker boards set up on easels on the table. Now it highlighted every bit of data concerning her.

She heard his footfalls as he came around the table, the roll of the chair a moment before she felt the touch of his hands on her face. He removed the mask's blinder section so she could see. She blinked a moment, despite the dim light of the conference room.

"Savannah, I'm so glad we decided to do this." In his magical way, he almost made her feel like she'd had a hand in planning the evening. "I'd like to do something to give you pleasure, something I've invented. You'll be the first woman I've tested it on, and I'd like your permission." His long, clever fingers stroked her forearm, making her shiver.

She was wrong. She *had* fantasized about these five men, in one way or another, for months. Matt had always been central, but they'd been steamy appetizers. They'd been her sex life, all in the realm of her mind.

What does it do? Her eyes asked the question she couldn't bring herself to ask. Of course Jon read it easily. Every man in the room was an expert at reading body language. Even with the gag, they'd likely understood her every wish. Though Matt alone seemed to have a clear window to her darkest fears, with no curtains to keep out his shrewd gaze.

"It brings a woman to climax almost immediately, and keeps her there, through programmed adjustments of the angle, for a prolonged period of time, to satisfy her fully. It stimulates her between the legs and the buttocks both."

"I'm not sure. I'm… I've never…done that." She'd actually never done any of this, but she'd never contemplated anything in that back area, even in her fantasies. She didn't know if that was naïveté or revulsion, but she didn't feel revolted about the idea now. Just nervous.

"It will be very gentle," he promised. "Not invasive at all. And I'll stop if you want me to stop."

It was strange, feeling as if she were alone with him, but at the same time being aware of the others that were listening. Of Matt in the shadows, watching over it all, his presence a pulsing awareness in her body.

He'd known Jon would be perfect at this juncture, after that first hard climax. To slow her panic, after having lost her infamous control. The handkerchief was in a ball in her sweaty palm, her fingers clutched tightly on it, as if her subconscious was afraid she'd drop it by accident and be misunderstood.

She'd seen Matt choose a moment of conflict to have lunch brought in by a pretty, cheerful office assistant, diffusing tension. Or he'd suggest a break, and they'd adjourn to the roof garden to enjoy the spectacular view of the city. It changed the moment, made his opponent feel cozened, good about giving Matt and his team nearly everything he wanted. He did it so strategically that the calculation was obscured. Even recognizing it, she felt its effect stealing over her own senses, as if that emotional part of her could care less about what her rational mind knew.

She could set him back on his ass by denying Jon now, but she *was* curious, extraordinarily so, about what Jon had devised.

It was as if her body, so long suppressing its enjoyment and exploration of physical desires, now could not get enough. A lever had been flipped, suggesting she could safely do and explore everything tonight. Had Matt known that? Provided her a unique way of losing her virginity?

And when that moment came, would it be him, in front of all of them? Or would it be all of them? Somehow, despite the titillation that such a thought should cause, based on how aroused she was, the idea did not please her. She could not block the vision that rose within her of more private desires. Just her and Matt, the ruthless hands becoming gentle, the weight of his body bearing her down, taking her into its shelter…

She reined back that thought. It didn't matter if it was him, or the whole group. In fact, there was no reason to get emotional about this situation at all. *Tennyson Rule Eleven: Unpleasant experiences at the hands of your enemy become lessons to turn against him later.* While she wasn't certain she'd call this an unpleasant experience, and Matt was an unpredictable business partner versus an outright enemy, she'd known her physical innocence combined with her looks was a handicap in an industrial world dominated by men. She'd put on a good façade, and managed to do well enough without full understanding, but by losing her innocence here tonight, in these many ways, Matt was really doing her a favor, giving her a leg up.

"I really want you to be the first woman to try it," Jon repeated the appeal.

"But I just…climaxed."

"It won't matter," he said. While she'd been subconsciously aware for some time of the sexual undercurrent between herself and all of them, seeing the desire unmasked in his direct gaze slammed it home so that she could not draw a deep breath under the intensity of it. "That's its magic. By the time I give you the full setting, your body will be more than ready, and when you come…" That light smile touched his lips. "Let's just say we could go through the entire first quarter financial report and you wouldn't hear a word of it."

It was an intensely erotic image. Her body, writhing and straining through climax after climax in the center of the table, while business was conducted as usual. Only she could vividly imagine the way that the words would drift off to silence, into a sexually charged stillness as the attention of every male was absorbed by her display. Their bodies, so marvelously different from a woman's softness, becoming even more hard, aroused, waiting to be unleashed.

The way this team interacted during meetings to go over market trends, cost analyses and production reports often reminded her of a dinner scene from *Seven Brides for Seven Brothers*. Ben gesturing with a carrot stick off the vegetable tray, making a side riposte, Lucas coming back with a quelling retort and then continuing his point with barely a break in stride. Peter pacing, working the latest MENSA-level brainteaser in his hands as he considered the issues of contention and fired thoughts from different sections of the room. Matt interjecting a vital piece of information, seemingly out of left field, but which tied everything together. Jon smiling at them all and working the numbers.

As their latest cooperative ventures had required more and more frequent meetings with her, they'd included her in the banter, in such a natural way that it had taken her awhile to recognize the tone of her inclusion was somewhat different, low-level flirting dynamics. Something she found she liked, even if she parried it with appropriate cynical retorts.

She'd enjoyed being surrounded by them so often, being the one-woman beneficiary of their mingled scents, voices, the feel of their heat and strength around her as palpable as physical touch. Once, she'd even caught herself letting out a breath when she sat down among them, as though she'd arrived somewhere she could relax. Be at home.

"That might be a bit distracting, to all of you." Her voice shook with nerves. "You could miss a crucial piece of information, lose your advantage."

"We could at that." His lips curved. "Maybe we'd make you participate, get you to go through your numbers with us, answer our questions. See if we couldn't catch you in a mistake, make you lose that infamous cool of yours."

"I'd hardly call it infamous."

"Honey, you don't know the half of it. Don Blatovsky said you were ice from inside out, though he put it in less than flattering terms." Jon's eyes took on a gleam. "Which is why Peter utterly destroyed him in racquetball."

There were a series of chuckles around the table, male sounds of satisfaction that made her feel…protected. Championed.

"Plus, he didn't have this crucial bit of information." Jon leaned forward, bringing his face close to hers as his hand slid across the table, under her suspended body, and found her pussy. He dipped into her heat and wetness, making her gasp. "There's no ice here. In fact, there's heat enough to burn." He smiled at her from inches away, those glowing eyes dominating her vision. "I'm waiting for your answer to my original question."

She had to struggle to remember. "I'd like to try it." Then, because it made her feel raw to see the warmth in his eyes, and sense the pleasurable approval of all men at the table, she added, "Maybe I'll buy the first one off the line. The Who-Needs-A-Man vibrator."

Jon withdrew his hand, brushed his knuckles over her cheek so she smelled herself on his skin. "Honey, I've never seen a woman who needed a man more than you do. You've needed one your whole life."

Before she could fashion a reply to that appalling and confusing statement, he had removed the device from his suit pocket. After all that talk, she would have expected a complicated design. Instead, it was innocuous and sleek, and appeared to have three main pieces. An oblong disk of a soft material, a curved shaft, and a circular piece about the size of a silver dollar. The circle looked like a tiny wagon wheel, with a short, thick piece of rubber as the hub and a pinwheel of silver spokes. A network of slim straps tied the whole thing together.

He laid it on the table before her and rose. Placing his hands together before his chest in an attitude of prayer, he bowed, nearly touching his forehead to hers, then straightened. "I see the divine in you, the face of love, and I honor it."

At her curious look, he gave her his angelic look. Not quite a smile, but then the expression didn't need it to convey the same delicious feeling inside of her. "That's the namaste. It's from Hindu culture, used in various ways, but in Tantra it's a way to begin lovemaking, a reminder that coming together with a lover in true sexual intimacy is a way to spiritual development."

The knowledge he gave her of its meaning caused that delicious feeling to spread out through her torso into her limbs. It should have seemed incongruous to be restrained the way she was and yet to feel so suddenly...cherished, but she couldn't deny the reaction. Lucas's mouth on her body, Jon's quiet approach, even Matt's watchful regard abruptly became something else.

This night, for all its volatile moments, had the quality of a ritual. And suddenly she felt like the center, like she was being worshipped, an incredible thought that she nevertheless could not deny.

"I was trying to resolve how to stimulate and please a woman in all her most erogenous areas at the same time, without overloading her nerve endings." The inventor part of his personality took over and she was almost amused to see it in his body language. "I want to incorporate some stimulation to the nipples eventually, but right now I wanted to keep it to the areas below the waist. Matt, if you could come and help me?"

An involuntary ripple of need surged through her as she heard Matt leave his chair, move behind her. Jon gave her cheek a reassuring caress and then joined Matt, where she could not see them.

"Touch her here," Jon's voice said softly. She quivered harder as Matt laid his palms on the curves of her ass, his thumbs inserting between them and then spreading her open, causing her breath to catch and hold in the back of her throat while a hard spasm of sensation rocked through her, like an aftershock of climax.

"She likes it very much when you touch her, much more than when we do. Hold her open like this."

Such a simple, truthful statement from Jon, no slyness. Almost as if he were trying to reassure Matt. Did Matt need such reassurance?

"I don't want her hurt." Matt's voice was rough, odd. "Is that lubricated enough?"

"It is. She'll feel nothing but pleasure, I swear it. Savannah, what you're feeling now is my finger. I'm very gently placing some lubrication in your anal passage. I'm only going to be putting some pressure on your sphincter, not going all the way in, but I want you to be comfortable."

There was a gentle, rubbing sensation around the rim that made her buttocks tremble under Matt's grip. Instinctively, she lifted toward Jon's touch. God, it felt…good.

"Now, let that breath you're holding out slowly, for a count of five. One, two…"

She followed his direction, and felt something rounded, smooth and slick ease into the opening of her rectum. Not deep, as he had said. It just stretched the opening, made her want to squirm with the stimulating sensation. He'd seated the short rubber hub in her passage, she realized. The "wheel" was placing the firm pressure against the rim of the opening.

"While many women enjoy getting fucked in the ass, the sensation is ninety percent psychological and ten percent stimulating the opening," he confirmed her reaction. "With a device like this, therefore, I've focused on the sensitive nerves there. Plus, we agreed your ass would be Ben's specialty. Just like your breasts are Peter's area of expertise."

Savannah froze at that remarkable statement. "Don't worry." Jon's hand stroked her back. "You'll love having him there, and this, as well as Peter, will help you prepare for him. Now, Matt, with your permission, I'd like to take it from here. Savannah, this next piece will stimulate your clit. "

Jon's long fingers slid up her thighs. With her legs spread apart, she felt the trepidation again, but no one had hurt her yet, physically, and she decided to rely on the empirical data she had and tried to relax.

"Good girl," Jon murmured. His fingers moved under her, past the pussy. The material of the oblong piece felt like good quality linen, now viscous with some type of adhesive. He completely hooded her clit, pressing firmly, making her breath rasp as the two sensations twined together and pulled pleasurable tension down even lower in her stomach. "The adhesive is a warming oil, so it won't feel much different from your own fluids after a moment, and it's fragrant, a vanilla smell to make it pleasant to your nose, though I personally prefer the smell of a woman's aroused cunt to any other scent on earth."

He withdrew and shifted, placing the flat of one palm against her lower back, just at the rise of her buttocks. Something touched the opening of her pussy, the shaft piece, she realized. "Now, the phallus. It's up to you how deep I'll go. I don't want to break anything that's not mine to break."

It took her a moment to understand, then she gave a nervous half laugh. "The gynecologist took care of that years ago." She felt shy about saying it, but she did it, forcing herself to try and be as sophisticated as they were being about all these things she'd never done, things she'd never even realized *could* be done. "Just…don't go any deeper than you know…you know."

"All right, then. You tell me if I cause you a moment of discomfort." There was the glide of something within her opening, and then pressure. She tensed. Jon immediately stopped, his palm obviously on her back to register such a reaction. "I think an additional distraction might be good. This is low setting."

Savannah sucked in a breath as current ran through the hood over her clit and through the pinwheel. The oblong clit piece hummed against her in a wave rhythm, like experiencing a tongue and a vibration at once. And the anal piece…there were tiny electrons of sensation leaping all over there. She couldn't track them all, but it robbed her of the ability to retain any control over her voice. She was making soft moans of pleasure, unable to stop herself, and she wished for the gag, so the embarrassing noises would be muffled.

Jon eased the phallus in on one of the tiny undulations she could not help making, and seated it against a dense spot that reacted immediately, almost spasmodically, to the touch.

"Perfect. God, you're perfect. That's it, honey. The current goes through the spokes of the wheel and all around the rim, and there's a different rhythm pulsing through the hub, the part that's inside you. It's key to the whole thing, because the flow and speed of the vibration alters constantly in all three pieces, so they keep stroking you, over and over, but in different ways. When you finally go, that lack of consistency will prolong the orgasm, much like when a man changes the angle of his cock during lovemaking between the clit and G-spot."

She knew nothing of those things, only that his words were goading her further.

"Jon," she gasped.

"Hang with me."

Being an engineer, and therefore very detail-oriented, he was making some more adjustments. His hands moved quickly over her now, and she felt the satin ribbons of the straps tighten over her thighs, between her legs, so the components were held firmly against her anus and in her pussy. The clit piece was left alone, and its greater freedom to vibrate against her made all three sensations even more excruciating.

"Oh, God…" She was so close. It was going to be hard and intense, more than she could handle, but she wanted it, craved it like the relief of an excruciating pain being taken away.

Jon wasn't in the mood to let her go so quickly. Abruptly, the vibration stopped.

"No," she blurted out. "*No.*"

Matt stepped into her field of vision, his hand cupping her face, his expression dangerous with brutal male desire, telling her he was not there to soothe, but to see her agony. With no outlet for her passion, she bit him anew, this time his palm, too wound up to exercise restraint. She tasted his blood again and reveled in it, the taste of life.

He growled in response and buried the fingers of his other hand in her hair, but not to yank her away. In the same instinctive way she knew how to breathe, she knew he wanted to grip her with such force at this moment, make her feel his dominance over her. She snarled against his flesh. It eased the grip of her jaw and he drew the hand back, showing her that she had marked him. She wanted to mark him everywhere. That gorgeous chest, flat abdomen, hard thighs, his feet, his…

"Start taking her up, Jon," he muttered.

"Five minutes at low setting," Jon responded behind her, his voice thick with his own reaction. His hand slid over her buttock, squeezed hard, and she whimpered at the bolt of electric reaction. Matt's spanking had made her hypersensitive there, in a way that made pain irrelevant. Pain or no pain, it was all pleasurable. "That will build her reaction, make it even more intense."

The three pieces activated again. They weren't just vibrating. The dildo began a slow, measured stroking, like a man's cock must, only still not deep enough, making her want to struggle, pull it in, even as the terror of what that desire meant swept through her.

Matt stepped back, though his attention never left her face, and then he was outside the range of her vision. She could feel him to the left of her, and Jon was before her again.

With his beautiful face, the long sensitive fingers, the curve of his mouth, Jon would never need a device such as this to get a girl to go to bed with him. But with it, women would elevate him to the stature of a god, bow down and worship him. At the moment, she'd cheerfully volunteer to be High Priestess of the cult of Jon.

"Now," he continued. "Before I raise the setting, I'm going to put the gag back in your mouth. I want something seated on your tongue to keep you from biting through it, though I'd love to hear you scream for us. I'm going to draw up your head a little higher, because we all want to see your face. That will enhance the sensation of your bondage, your slavery to us, to Matt." At that amazing statement, one she would not have expected from Jon, he put his fingers along her cheek again, pushing the ball gently against her teeth. "A most cherished slave. One we couldn't do without. Open up, honey."

She didn't have much choice with her head held rigid and his thumb cleverly inserting into the hinge of her jaw, making her obey.

"Put her on display in the center of the table," Matt commanded.

The gears whirred at the far end of the table. The mechanism began to lift her even higher into the air and move her forward, toward the center. With her knees and ankles connected by the straight bars, and the cuffs holding open her thighs, her legs remained bent and spread, as if she were on her hands and knees, only she had her hands bound behind her back, her head slightly lower than her raised hips. She felt the table recede, and when she came to a stop, the heat of the spotlight told her she was about three feet above the table, allowing the men in the room to examine her from every angle, including the parts of her stretched by Jon's wondrous torture device. It was demanding even now that she twitch her hips in futile attempt to establish a rhythm with the three alternating pumping, stroking and vibrating currents, all individually tailored to maximize response from the three erogenous zones. She couldn't move much, but the little amount she could her body was using, making her feel the weight of her breasts quivering with her shameless, involuntary movements.

"Matt, I'm ready for my turn." Peter's voice came at her from the table level, suggesting he was sitting just to her right, just below her breasts. "I want to suckle those pretty tits and make her come just from that alone. Jesus, she's built. "

There was a hoarseness to his voice, the savagery of desire, and she felt it pushing on her from all sides, every man's need in the room swamping her, mixing with her own arousal until she could think of nothing so exciting as being buried beneath them all, helpless beneath their hands, mouths...cocks. What would it be like to taste each of them, feel one or more of their cocks stretching her mouth, while the others shoved into her wherever they could find an opening?

Did she really have that thought?

"All in good time. Lucas." Matt's voice filled her like the warmth of a promise. "Give her some visual stimulation."

"With pleasure."

She was turned on the track, rotating like displayed artwork. She was stopped when she faced Peter and Ben. Peter's gaze devoured her breasts in a way that made them tremble and ache. Just beyond the two men the panels of the wall slid back as Lucas operated a switch, revealing a grid of twelve screens, which Matt and his team used to monitor different stock markets and news channels at once, as well as manage video conferences.

The dozen different images that flickered to life now were montages of her recent experiences in this room. She saw not only herself, but the men when she had not been able to see them. Lucas's expression as he had run his palm down her back. Peter, watching her strangled cries with rapture on his face. Jon, placing the devices within her most private areas with quiet capability, his lips firm with concentration.

Matt. His eyes intent, flamed with raw passion, presumably while Lucas went down on her. His quick, predatory strength as he tied her, then stood over her while she lay flat on the table. There was an expression on his face at that moment that she did not dare give a name, because it had no place in this room, she was sure. Definitely not lodged in her heart like an arrow.

She wished she had the blindfold back, or that the straps holding her head were not so relentless, as she saw images of herself. From the back, her buttocks clenching as Lucas's blond head worked his magic between her thighs, the pale line of them on either side of his face, the pink soles of her feet outside his shoulders. Then a shot after she had been fully restrained in the harness and was listening to the entry of the men. The press of her lips not just suggesting trepidation, but sensual excitement.

Jon doing his namaste to her, the easing of her jaw revealing her change in feelings at that moment. Embarrassing close-ups when he placed the items against her pussy and anus.

But the worst was a clip from the beginning, when she was still mostly clothed. Matt's first kiss, her body visibly softening into his as his hands wandered possessively down her.

"Waiting five minutes like this, doing the low setting, is also a Tantric practice," Jon said seriously, behind her again. Heat rose in her face, because now she knew exactly what he was looking at. Her attention was caught by Ben's gaze, his eyes the color of green sea glass, multifaceted, jewel-like, a rich compliment to the sculptured jaw and firm, unsmiling lips.

Out of all of them, she knew the least about him, Matt's legal pit bull. Remembering what part of her body Jon had said was reserved for him, she flicked her gaze nervously back to the screens, not able to handle any greater level of anxiety at this moment. She focused on the comparatively soothing quality of Jon's voice instead.

"Prolonged pleasure makes not only the climax but the spirituality of the moment even more intense." His voice was as compelling as a priest's. "When I turn it on full, Savannah, I suggest you fight it. Fight it with everything you've got. The best things in life are those you hold off from enjoying as long as possible.

"You'll understand that best at the end of the night, when you finally stop fighting Matt. You'll discover an intensity ten times greater than anything we do to you, because it's something he has that none of us can offer you, no matter what pleasure we bring you tonight. Something that you won't see until you accept that you're more than worthy of it. And when you do, Matt will be the luckiest man in the room. Here we go."

She was turning now, the suspension straps moving along the circular track, taking her around the table. It was a disorienting experience that managed to sway her body and increase the effect of Jon's device within her. When she stopped, she faced the head of the table, her gaze locked with Matt's. She knew he could see every expression of her countenance, tense with desire, her lips pressed hard around the ball gag, throat working against the forces that were going to overwhelm her in no time, take her back to that place where Lucas had taken her. Only, if Jon's device worked, it was going to keep her there, in screaming, mindless pleasure, where everything was beyond her control. And Matt was going to see it all, every vulnerable moment.

She would fight, but not for the reason Jon suggested. Her body didn't rule over her mind and, her father's tenet be damned, she wouldn't learn a lesson from failure because she wouldn't fail. She wasn't going to be made to do something just because someone wanted her to do it.

She realized she sounded a little desperate, even in her own head, and another rule came to mind. *Never lose emotional control, even in your thoughts. Discipline is bone-deep, not just skin-deep.* She had no idea what number it was, though she remembered thinking once it was somewhat redundant with Five, which she couldn't remember at the moment, either.

The clit hood started pulsing harder, rippling strokes like the tide rolling up over a shore after a large vessel had passed, the tongue sensation electrical. The slight roughness of the linen and the fact there were no straps holding it firmly against the clit, the adhesive doing that work, meant it created even more friction as her hips rocked the very tiny amount her bonds allowed her. She tried to stop the movement, but then the other two areas were turned on at the higher setting Jon desired, and she was lost.

Oh God, oh God, oh God. It was everywhere, inside and outside, radiating from the top of her head to the end of her toes. In that moment, if she could have spoken, she would have said things that would have embarrassed her far more than having Matt see her face, which was unthinkably embarrassing in itself. The electric current ran along the spokes of the wheel firmly pressed against the opening of her rectum, and that short rubber stem rotated very gently, sliding against the opening of the sphincter muscle, rocking the wheel like a spinning top, so it was stroking the rim of her in a way that made her strain against those straps. And the phallus... Jon had it perform several seconds of simple vibration, his fingertips briefly touching her, verifying how wet she was before he set it in motion again. Slow short glides in and out of her, stroking her pussy lips, with a rotation movement that kissed that dense spot within again and again and again, the mere brush of an electrical tongue.

She fought. She gave it all she had, in total panic, shutting her eyes, unable to look at Matt, her breath rasping around the gag so harshly the saliva escaped, making the ball slick. She bit it hard, desperate to hold back.

She lasted seven seconds, and then the storm crashed down on her.

Against the gag, the scream that ripped from her throat reverberated back in her chest, choking her, accelerating the rate of her heart. Her body was shuddering, vibrating, convulsing, bucking impossibly against straps too snug to allow her room to buck. Whereas the climax Lucas had given her had given her the sense of falling backwards into the embrace of a bed piled high with pillows and quilted covers, this was like catapulting from an airplane, that terrifying feeling of falling, spinning out of control toward bone-breaking impact. She wanted to undulate against something, something solid, something that would rock back against her, ease this tearing need in her.

And it went on and on. There was no pinnacle. She kept thinking she had hit it, and then she'd launch straight across to another peak, the tiny wheel at her anus, the busily stroking dildo and enthusiastically vibrating clit piece alternating their rhythm and patterns as Jon had said they would, giving her no relief, only merciless pleasure for the enjoyment of the men watching, all at the command of one man.

Look at me, Savannah.

Did he say it? Whisper it in her mind? She opened her eyes and met Matt's dark gaze, raging with the fires of heaven and hell, with everything she could want from both and in between. Jon was right. At this moment, she had no rational thought. She utterly and totally wanted Matt's Mastery. She wanted to be his. And if she could speak, she would have begged for it.

Tears slid down her face, her nose running from the excruciating pleasure of the multiple climaxes. When they finally began to lessen in intensity, she thought her stomach and buttocks would forever be in a state of clenched response, all muscles tight as stretched rubber bands from the onslaught of the orgasms. However, as the sensations drifted away, leaving her shuddering and sniffing helplessly, everything went limp with exhaustion. The place between her legs still pulsed, almost quivering with exertion.

"Her pussy is as full and juicy as the prettiest peach you've ever seen. Lucas?" Jon's soft voice, not quite steady itself.

Oh...no...yes. Lucas's mouth ever so gently closed over the distended area, and she let out a guttural, animal sound of near pain, exhausted pleasure. He licked her tenderly as Jon worked around him, eased out the dildo, which felt slick enough to be dripping. It was Lucas who held open her buttocks as the anal piece was removed. Through it all, she stared at Matt, her body heaving with gasping breaths.

When he rose, leaned toward her, her mind dragged her gaze where it wanted to go, to see the enormous erection straining against his slacks.

"Do you want my cock?" It was a throaty demand that she respond, his voice beyond civility, commanding her. Prying open her fingers, he took away the handkerchief, using it to wipe her nose and around the corners of her mouth. That tender cozening perversely seemed to underscore his right to impose his will upon her, rather than lessening the force of his demand. When he didn't give back the handkerchief, she knew she was being told her choice to call an end to it all had been rescinded. "Answer me, Savannah. Do you want my cock?"

She nodded as much as she could. *Not just that. All of you. Everything.* But she couldn't say it, even if the gag weren't there. He caught the strap holding the gag, ripped it away, pulled the ball from her mouth in a rough move. She didn't expect it, the way his hand gripped her jaw, her throat, in a hold just a step below bruising. No more than she expected to delight in the pleasure of the pain.

"Say it. Say it now."

"Yes." She was hoarse, her lips and throat dry.

"Lower her," he ordered. "Leave her ass in the air so Jon can get her ready for Ben. Just her head, to the level of my cock. And spin her, so she can take me deep."

Her eyes widened as Peter and Ben moved to either side of the table. Their arms went under her body and they tightened the straps that held her to the bench. Jon slipped the S-hooks of the suspending chains and they turned her and replaced the chains so she was facing the ceiling. The long narrow bench supporting her front simply held her torso straight as the chains were adjusted. Her head was lowered, lowered, lowered, Matt's fiery gaze staying pinned on her even as the back of her skull touched the edge of the table, while her lower body went to approximately a forty-five degree angle above her, her legs still spread for Jon to do…whatever Matt had just told him to do. She couldn't remember, not with Matt's crotch this close to her face.

"I took her lower body down a little bit." Lucas this time. "We don't want all the blood to rush to her head and make her faint. She's still pretty spun up."

"Remember to move your foot if you feel faint. Mouth me. Let me know you want my cock in your mouth."

She didn't think, didn't review any rules for this situation. Her mouth opened and closed over the fabric of his slacks, her lips pressing hard against the thick width of him, her tongue reaching out to lick and wet the straining cloth, as she made noises of animal hunger in her throat.

"Jesus Christ." Matt unfastened his pants and shoved them and a pair of black jersey boxers down to his hard thighs. The organ was so close to her that she couldn't see it clearly, but her nose brushed the heat, smelled the animal musk of him. He seized the chains holding her, pulled so her head tilted over the edge of the table and she was essentially upside down. He reached past her, took something Jon was offering, a lubricant of some kind, and rubbed it over the broad head.

"Open up, Savannah."

She barely had her lips parted before he shoved into her mouth, stretching her lips as she'd imagined, as she'd craved. He seated himself deep, and then stopped, holding his cock against the back of her throat, moving it slightly, as if he were rubbing it against her. She gagged, and his fingers stroked her throat, soothing her, and then the gagging desire was gone, though he pushed in deeper, against her tonsils.

"Another of Jon's many tools," he growled. "Benzocaine to coat the back of the throat, so you can take me deep. You want to take me deep, don't you? In your throat, in your ass, in your pussy. You want me everywhere."

The tears were starting again, for the pleasure and truth were coming together, tearing her apart. She couldn't see through them, in the literal or figurative sense, so she simply tilted her head more, giving herself up to this moment.

Matt withdrew slightly, then moved back in. She stroked him with her lips, just wanting to taste him, feel him. With no experience at all, she simply licked him with her tongue, sucked on him to get that taste, that scent in her mouth, her throat, her nose, where she could keep it. She imagined the earth of a humid jungle would smell like this, exotic and mysterious, brutal and honest. She even scored him with her teeth, tasting the meat of him.

She was vaguely aware of Jon, applying something soothing onto her clit, just inside her pussy lips and around her anus, something she supposed would keep her from getting raw before the next assault. But then another sensation invaded, something less pleasant. She fought against it, and the fighting made it worse. Dizziness, black spots on her vision. She kept on, furiously, desperately sucking on Matt, not wanting to lose the odd sense of comfort in the act of servicing him, but it was overtaking her, sweeping her body, turning her shudders into a sick trembling…

She wouldn't wiggle her foot. That would be failure. And she needed this, didn't want it to stop…

"Matt." Peter's sharp voice seemed to come from far away and she made a noise of wailing protest as Matt withdrew from her. Suddenly his arms were under her, lifting her, making the chains holding her upper body go slack, lay cool against her skin as he brought her head even and then slightly above the rest of her body. She opened her eyes, saw his face close above hers, the concern in his strong face.

"I should have known you wouldn't ask for help when you should," he muttered, his hands impossibly tender against her temples.

She wanted to say she was sorry for making him angry, but his lips were soft on hers, making it all right. Making nothing necessary but to simply be.

Just like she had felt at her father's funeral, if only for one moment.

It wasn't an entirely unexpected thought to have right now. Matt had given her that one moment, just as he had made this night something far different than she anticipated.

Overwhelmed, she let herself spin comfortably down a gray tunnel, into that memory.

Chapter Four

80

Among all the offers of sympathies, the unwelcome press of strange hands and bodies near her — acquaintances, hangers-on, a few genuine friends of her father's who had little to offer to her beyond their formal support as she stepped into her father's corporate shoes — Matt had been close. She remembered the heat of his body near her throughout those long several days. The supporting touch of his hand, the only contact she had welcomed, at the small of her back.

After the funeral and memorial service, deep into the third or fourth hour of the never-ending wake at her father's sprawling estate, she had escaped to her room for a few minutes. Burying her face into her pillow, she'd screamed, beating the mattress, wishing for tears that never came. Though she stayed in there a good thirty minutes, trying to compose herself, she'd been undisturbed. It was only when she took a deep steadying breath, checked her hair and makeup and stepped back out in the hallway, that she'd found out why.

Matt sat on the top stair, with a brandy loose in his hand and a plate of untouched funeral food. Keeping watch. Keeping them at bay, the barbarians away from the gate.

"I don't need a watchdog, Kensington," she said uncharitably, frightened of how relieved she was to see him there.

He lifted a shoulder, took in everything about her at one glance. "Humor me. It gives me an excuse to stay away from them." He picked up a carrot from the plate, took a bite. "God, I hate these things."

"The vegetables?"

"No. When I die, I'm going to have a fast cremation and leave instructions for Lucas to throw a street party in my honor for a few thousand drunken revelers who have no idea who I am and couldn't care less. They'll toast my memory because I bought the drinks, and the people who love me won't be put through a dog and pony show."

"Nobody loves you, Kensington."

He smiled. "You do." He patted the step beside him. "At least the food's good. Come have a taste."

She found herself quite willingly moving toward him. "Is Morris Johnson still downstairs?"

"Of course. He and his executive staff. Trying to schmooze up to the CEO of Bank of America and eating as much free food as he can get his hands on."

"If we slip a laxative into his crab dip, I'll bet we get a great interest rate on our next six-month cash loan from BoA."

"How diabolical, Miss Tennyson. Remind me not to eat anything you've provided next time we're having an important meeting."

"I thought that's why you employ Ben. To be your official royal taster."

"Cute."

She lowered herself beside him, in the small space his large frame and splayed knees allowed, but it felt good, not crowded. She absorbed his warmth with a welcome shiver.

"Cold?"

"A little. It was overcast at the graveside."

"I'm sure Geoffrey arranged it. He did like the appropriate setting for all occasions. Here."

"I can go get a sweater." Her words died as he shrugged out of his coat, bringing a whiff of his cologne to her delicate nostrils, and laid it around her shoulders.

"There."

Suddenly, she was struggling not to weep. Why did she want to weep now, when she felt nothing in her room except rage? She made a snort that sounded suspiciously to her own ears like a sniffle. "I guess if we were in high school, you'd ask me to go steady now. Give me a broken coin and we'd each wear half."

A corner of his mouth lifted in a smile, and he reached over, tugged free a tendril of her hair trapped under the collar. "I was on the wrestling team. You're the football quarterback type. You'd have turned up your nose at the likes of me."

"Wrestling?"

"Absolutely. You know how punishing football is on the adolescent bone structure? At least, that's what my mother told me, over and over again, *ad nauseum*, when I whined to sign up. We compromised with wrestling."

"Matt Kensington, whining?" She leaned back against the opposite wall, which made her knee brush his. The contact felt right, so she didn't take it away and he didn't seem to notice.

"Like the proverbial girl. But something tells me you never whined."

She gave a half laugh and some of the coldness returned. She crossed her arms over her breasts, gripped the edges of the jacket closer to her, letting go of the ball of tissue in her hand so it fell into her lap. The coat smelled of him. She pictured a closet of such suits, all smelling like this, and her falling into them, holding on in the quiet, tranquil darkness of his closet.

"Geoffrey didn't believe in it. He taught me that if you want something, you strategize how to get it. You never beg. And if you fail, you accept the failure, analyze it, go back and win what you lost."

He nudged her knee with his own. "What's that in your lap?"

"Just a tissue..." She looked down at his puzzled expression and instead of the tissue, she saw a tiny rag doll, little bigger than the length of her hand. She'd left it on her bed earlier, hadn't realized until this moment that was what she had clutched in her hand as she screamed into her pillow. She'd apparently had held onto when she left the room. "Oh." She lifted a shoulder, tried for a casual look, even as her hand settled protectively over it under his shrewd gaze. "At my father's corporate Christmas party, one of his business associates brought a little gift for me as the 'lady of the house'. When I was six," she added, at the twinkle in Matt's eyes. Her eyes could not linger on his face, so she looked back down, fingered the doll. "He knew nothing about me of course, was just trying to win favor with my father."

He had no clue that fawning on Geoffrey's child meant nothing to Geoffrey.

"But I liked it." Extraordinarily liked it. Kept it with her that night, slept with it hidden under her covers where her father couldn't see. But Geoffrey had known. "One night, I was tired over something, and I whined, I guess as children can do, and he punished me by taking it away. I found it in his closet when I was looking for a suit for him...for this."

"He never gave it back?" Matt raised an eyebrow.

She shrugged. "Of course not. As I said, he'd told me whining didn't get you anywhere. It meant the things that mattered got taken away from you, and when you lose things from your own actions, you must learn from them." Savannah shook her head. "Don't look at me like that, Matt. I know it sounds dysfunctional, and maybe it is, but you know, kids from good income brackets get about everything they want these days, and for the most part, they *are* whiny, self-indulgent, spoiled brats whose parents don't know how to say no to them. Geoffrey may not have been a loving, affectionate father, but he taught me everything I know about how to be successful. How to be hungry only by choice."

Reaching out, Matt put a hand to her face, startling her. She was immobilized by how good it felt, that human contact freely offered, pressed against her skin. "You were the best thing that ever happened to him," he said quietly. "He had all

94

the money in the world, and he got his most valuable acquisition the day you were born. And not just because you could run his company better than he could run it himself."

Savannah didn't know what to say to that. She looked toward the bottom of the stairs. "It's odd no one's walked by here to disturb us."

"I told them there was free food in the main courtyard. It drew them off. Here." He offered her his plate. "As I said, the food's quite good."

"Of course." She shook her head at it. "Geoffrey already had his menu planned out. It wouldn't be less than perfect. Hungry by choice, remember?"

"The best kind of hunger there is," he said. Suddenly, she knew exactly where his knee pressed against hers, and what hunger he was talking about, because it had her lower extremities in a perilous grip.

"I want to give you something for later." He broke the charged silence between them. Withdrawing the handkerchief from the breast pocket of his jacket, he folded it into her hand, his own remaining over it.

"What, is my makeup running?"

"No. It's for when everything about this day hits you, and you finally cry, even if it's for no other reason than you don't feel like crying and *that* breaks you down." He rose. "Keep the coat until you're warm. I'll get it back later." Then he leaned down and kissed her forehead, just a gentle brush of lips, his hands holding the lapels so she was in a light embrace within the jacket. "I'm here if you need me, Savannah. I'm always here. Come down when you're ready. Lucas and Jon are in the foyer hallway, keeping people from coming this way. You don't have to come down at all if you don't want to."

"Of course I do." The dangerous temptation of such an image broke the spell. She rose to her feet, slid the jacket off her shoulders and handed it back to him. "I don't need this." But she kept the kerchief. It was a gift, after all.

She was on the step above him, so their positions put them at eye level. His expression had hardened with an emotion she couldn't read as he studied her face. In a surprising move, he suddenly slid an arm around her back and legs, swung her up in his arms and turned, carrying her down the steps.

"Matt," she hissed. "What are you doing?"

At the bottom, he let her feet touch the floor, but he held her elbow another moment. "That was to remind you that someday, you might need someone else to carry the load for a while. And you can trust me to get you where you need to go, no matter how steep the hill is. Up or down."

He left her there, amazed, speechless. Oddly happy and hurting at once. And that was when she used the handkerchief for the very first time.

*　*　*　*　*

She'd kept it folded under her pillow ever since.

The fuzziness receded and she became aware of her surroundings again. They'd adjusted the chains so she was level and turned her over so she was once again on her stomach. She was lying on the table, still bound, but the straps had been loosened back to their prior snugness, rather than the snugness that had been necessary when she didn't have the back support. They'd also let her head down so her cheek was on the table.

Matt was sitting in the chair, leaned forward, his face no more than a foot from her.

"I guess we got a little carried away. You carried us all away. You were something else."

She coughed, her voice raw from her screaming. "But I'm still tied up. So you're not done with me yet."

"I'll never be done with you." He drew even closer, so the depths of his brown eyes were all she could see. "You've scared yourself, and you're retreating again. I can see it. I'm not going to let you. I'm going to feed you."

A weak chuckle, somewhere close to a sob, broke from her abused throat. A throat that remembered vividly what it was like to have him slamming against the back of it. "You can't bribe me with food, Kensington, at least not unless you plan to keep me like this for several days without food and water."

"An intriguing possibility." He cocked his head. As sensation returned to all her limbs, she realized he was stroking her forehead, playing with her loose hair. "Actually, while manufacturing this invention and renovating the room for it, I've thought about it a great deal. Imagining what it would be like to have my woman suspended in it every day, accessible to me whenever I wanted to play with her nipples, slip my fingers or cock into her wet cunt. Put her on display for business associates who come in here for meetings, a mesmerizing centerpiece for my conference table. I think my competitors would give me anything for the privilege. But just to look at you. No man other than those in this room tonight will ever touch you again. You're mine."

That harshness came to his eyes again, and just as naturally as command came to him, resistance to capitulation flooded her. But this time she had no sarcasm to offer, just simple denial. "No," she whispered.

"Yes," he responded, just as quietly. He supported her skull in his hands as he readjusted the straps so her head was lifted, her facial expressions exposed to them all again. The chains tightened and she was raised from the table, only this time she was only lifted about two feet, and it was her upper body that was raised higher than her lower, so her breasts thrust out at Matt at eye level, in a blatant display that roused an embarrassing heat along her throat and face. His eyes followed the track of it, and when his gaze got to her face, his own fire was a match for it.

"Here." Lucas slid a small plate to Matt's elbow and Peter placed a gold-edged wineglass next to it. Savannah smelled the rich scent of red Merlot.

"You need to eat and drink," Matt said. "We don't have a good strategy for getting rid of your body if you die from too much pleasure."

His eyes glinted with humor, and she bared her teeth at him. He brought the tumbler to her lips, cradling her cheek with his hand, touching the corner of her mouth, compelling her lips to part. The angle was awkward with her position, and before she could take more than a sip, he took it away.

"A better idea." There was a pause while he took a swallow. She wondered and imagined and then hoped, and then his mouth was there, sealing over hers, opening, letting the wine on his tongue spill onto hers, his hand still along her face, the grip of his hand moving along her throat as if to help her swallow the liquid.

She didn't drink much, having a low tolerance for alcohol, and just this swallow was made more potent by the method of delivery, by his care for her, by the stroke of that tongue on hers. He pulled away reluctantly, and then she smelled one of the snacks they often brought in for meetings from the gourmet deli down the street. Goat cheese flavored with thyme, wrapped in a finger-sized, seasoned flatbread.

"Your favorite, I believe," he said, those eyes watching every inflection on her face, his own expression still a little intimidating, reminding her that he was not going to brook resistance. Savannah decided she was going to let him win this minor point to fortify herself and regroup. She wanted to try a different strategy. An experiment, really.

She ate the entirety of it from his hand, even obeying the sensual urge to clean the soft cheese off his fingertips, taking the taste of his skin with it, those strong fingers resting in her mouth.

The tension and lust poured off him as she did it, and she knew her experiment was successful. It wouldn't be easy, but with the power of that knowledge, she knew she could turn this to her advantage, make him *her* slave if she wanted to.

But something else came with the thought. Anguish. She didn't want to make Matt a slave. She wanted his harshness, his power, his command. She wanted the tender protectiveness and chivalry as well, and wondered if there were even more gentle sides to him than he'd yet revealed to her, aspects of his personality that might exist in a softer world, one outside these corporate walls.

"God, you make me insane, Savannah," he muttered.

Join the club, she thought. "How did you know these were my favorites?"

It was Lucas who spoke. "You don't eat much that we have brought in. Or at least you didn't at first. But then we started noticing the things you would eat, more than once."

"We wouldn't touch any of those," Peter put in. "And made sure that portion of the tray was closest to you. Then we figured out if we ordered more of that type of snack, you'd eat more."

Southern etiquette. Never eat the last one. She remembered a gradual increase in the food she'd eaten at their sessions, an ample variety of her preferences present.

"We made it a competition, coming up with foods we thought would become your new favorite." Peter laughed, caressed her bare calf from somewhere out of the range of her vision, reminding her forcibly of the view he had of her spread legs. "I knew you'd love those chocolate cream finger cakes."

"I lost a five hundred dollar bet on it," Lucas grumbled good-naturedly. "I was sure you'd pick the caramel creams."

"When Ben baked the cakes himself and slid them on the tray like they came from *Dean and Deluca's*? Not a chance."

Savannah choked. "Ben baked…"

"It isn't the sleazy lawyer routine that gets him women. It's his culinary skills," Jon added.

"Yeah, like you don't use the lost angel thing to seduce women." Ben snorted outside of her vision.

"Five hundred dollars on whether or not I'd eat a sweet?"

Matt dabbed at the corner of her mouth with one finger, put a missed bit of goat cheese on her tongue. "We always have a betting pool running on something. At the end of the month, the winnings go to the preferred charity of the final winner."

"What's your chosen charity?" she asked.

"A man's charities are a private thing. Not manly to discuss," Lucas interjected.

"And I think our guest has recovered enough," Matt said, his eyes studying her face.

Anticipation sprang up in her, thick as heated blood.

She wasn't sure she could take anything else. Emotionally, she felt as delicate as an eggshell, just Matt's words creating a shiver through her body. But wetness touched her thighs, her pussy leaking a tiny drop, her body's betrayal of her interest. It was as if Matt's multiple-layered strategy had already trained her body to such a level of sensual awareness that the mere suggestion of sexual activity could get her revved up again.

He rose, his fingers whispering across her cheekbone, and leaned over where she could see him touch the table controls. The motor engaged and she was moving along the track, down the table. As she turned in that direction she saw she was going to the very end, where Peter had moved and now waited, just to the right of the rounded table end.

Peter would have looked more at home at a monster truck rally. With a corner lift to his mouth at almost all times, as if he were sharing a private joke, he had a soft Southern drawl and a way of wearing his clothes that suggested he'd be most at home in jeans and a T-shirt from a seventies' rock band. His fingers would tap restlessly as they conducted their meetings and at times she'd hear him humming a heavy metal tune under his breath. He wore his hair cropped in a short military cut that emphasized the strong lines and corded neck of a bodybuilder. He wasn't a bodybuilder, but an Army reservist. He spent a great deal of time staying in shape to serve his country if called. He'd taken a leave from Kensington to volunteer for a year tour in Afghanistan. During that time Matt had casually mentioned many were sending shoebox care packages to the soldiers. He'd left her a copy of the instructions that were circling the corporate offices, encouraging participation. In the margin, he'd noted how to get one specifically to Peter, if she wanted to have her staff make up one for him.

Before she knew it, she was collecting items, especially as she had watched the news reports and thought of Peter's face, the laughter so often in his gray eyes, the strength in those broad shoulders, a strength that the media footage made clear could be erased in an instant by the fragile reality of mortality.

Moist towelettes, sample-size toiletries, a pack of playing cards she'd found that had images of New Orleans integrated into the depictions of numbers and royal personages. She remembered he had a weakness for ice cream and put in a bag of hard candy that boasted fifty-one flavors similar to ice cream. The latest Dean Koontz novel and a Nightcrawler X-Men comic book. The others called him Nightcrawler, because they claimed he preferred trawling the New Orleans nightlife over sleeping.

And then she put in something she hadn't expected to buy. On one of her layovers, when she was browsing in an expensive airport jewelry shop, she'd seen a gold St. Christopher medal. She'd purchased it with not a thought for the three-figure price, because it didn't matter. Getting him back safely did.

She'd never done something so…nurturing before. Filling the list in the privacy of her home, she didn't involve her staff. She even mailed it herself.

She'd never prayed. She suspected there was a God out there, but had always imagined Him like her father. Not Someone from whom she could seek support or comfort, just Someone who expected the best, or dire consequences would result. But in that moment, when she took the medal home and tucked it in the box, finishing the care package, she offered something that she supposed was like a prayer to that saintly figure. *Please keep him safe. Bring him home.*

When Peter did get home, at the first meeting where she'd seen him again, he'd been wearing it. He'd ruffled her by putting his arms around her and hugging her, a close hold that he prolonged five still seconds before he let her go, looked in her eyes and nodded. Then he asked her one question.

"Have you tried the God-awful chai tea Jon's trying to make us drink today?"

He always wore the necklace.

"I love your breasts," Peter said simply, bringing her back to the present. He had sat down, and had his elbows on the table, his chin resting on his fists, as if they were two children, facing each other on their stomachs on the limb of a tree. The whole world fallen away below, so that the only things around them were things that could fly or flutter, crawl to great heights to see the world from a higher perspective. "I try not to stare, because I know women think men are creeps when they stare at their breasts during conversation, but since you and I don't have to talk directly that often in meetings, it's seemed okay to stare at them."

It startled a smile out of her, and he returned the favor, showing her white teeth so symmetrical she knew an orthodontist had been part of his youth.

"Of course, sometimes it ticked Matt off." He grinned more broadly. "You like lace, just a bit on the edges. You've never worn a bra for us that didn't have it." His finger reached out, traced one bare curve, the line such lace would follow if it had been there. In her raised position, her breasts were right before his face, at the level of his mouth, and she could not block the images that thought evoked. This position also put her where she could still see the wall screen. New images had been picked up. Her writhing, screaming response to Jon's stimulus, all muted, but no less potent, particularly when Peter's large callused hands reached forward now and began to fondle her. She was getting very, very attached to the magic of men's hands. At least the different textures and types of touch these men had.

He traced the crease under the left breast, started up the opposite curve, making her feel his appreciation of her shape, her fullness. Her nipples ached, but he did not touch them, just the soft flesh around them.

"You're too thin," he observed in a warm voice that implied no judgment, no criticism. "You don't eat enough, though you're in good shape. You use your corporate gym daily, I know. When I've crossed the city overwalk between our two buildings, I've seen you running the track on the tenth floor. Covered in a light sheen of sweat, wearing a black sports bra that holds you so tight and immobile, no give. Much like your life, don't you think?"

"And all of your lives are so perfect," she said, but with much less acidity than she would have had a few hours ago.

"Well, I can't think of a moment much better than this one." He gave her a charming look and then continued on, unperturbed.

"I can't stand it when women diet themselves down to zero cellulite thighs and a tiny ass. They lose their breasts, the curves of hip and bosom that make them a woman. I wish we could go back to the fifties, and see women who were firm and healthy, with generous breasts, soft asses, whose thighs were like soft pillows for a man's hands. I'd be in heaven."

"Sounds like I'm a disappointment to you, then."

He chuckled and weighed one breast in each hand, pressing her nipples to the heated cup of his palm, eliciting a soft whisper of pleasure from her. "Not in the least. You're a beautiful woman." The Southern accent got deeper, richer. "While you and Matt spar, or Jon drones off one of his never-ending financial reports—" there was a snort from the end of the table, "—I've imagined them a lot of different ways.

"Bare, like this, nothing clothing them but the touch of my hands. Anticipating the feel of your nipples in my mouth when I close my lips around them and suckle them." He gave them a gentle pinch, a mere pressure, and she arched, moaning. "Or in a beautiful satin bra, with sheer cups so I can see the suggestion of your nipples and the color of your skin behind the cloth. The kind with underwiring that pushes you together, makes that deep cleft that I want to run my tongue down, like the cleft of a woman's cunt lips.

"Or a shelf bra that your breasts are just barely tucked into, the plump tops rising high like the smooth tops of freshly baked cinnamon rolls. You've worn that style before, and the images it conjured have made me nearly insane. I want to sprinkle powdered sugar over the top of them, lick it all off."

She was shuddering, and his touch had turned into a gentle kneading, slow, torturous, a manipulation of the sensitive globes even as his thumbs idly, all too infrequently, passed over the distended nipples.

"And then there's the bra with cutouts for the nipple, so you can have all the support and shapeliness a bra provides, but your nipples are as prominent under a shirt as if you're not wearing one at all. No man can resist looking, hoping for a rain shower to soak the cotton, make them even more noticeable.

"Nipple jewelry is also something I'd love to see on you. D-rings and barbells for piercing, dangles, chains to attach them to one another and adorn the neck. Weights with uncut gemstones. All of which stimulate the nipples and keep them distended, aching for touch." His hands kept up their complex composition on her, and she thought he would make her come, just from the combination of words and skillful fondling.

"There are hundreds of ways to appreciate a woman's breasts, and every day I think of a new way. If I had you to myself for an entire afternoon, I'd lay you out on my bed, apply a henna paste to your tits, decorating them with a Celtic design. And then when I was done, and it was dry so I could touch you, when your body was screaming for fulfillment, I'd place your breasts in a parallel bar restraint like this and tease you with my teeth and tongue until you screamed for release. But not release from that bar. Release from the passion you would be feeling."

His voice dropped to a rough whisper, a sensual friction against her senses. Her entire breast tingled as if she could feel the weights he spoke of, the touch of the henna paste, the squeeze of those bars distending her, making her more aware of touch, of the need to be tasted.

"Would you like me to suckle your breasts, Savannah?" Peter asked. "I want to, very much. Tell me you want that."

"Yes," she managed. "I want that."

"Good." His mouth curled up at the corners. "Because I was going to do it whether you agreed or not." He leaned forward, his face even with her breasts, and looked up at her. "While I'm doing this, Ben is going to be preparing you for a very different sensation. Together we're going to rouse you to the pinnacle of climax, but hold you there longer than you think is possible, until we reduce you to mindless sense again, the pure being that you are, nothing else."

"I'm not sure I can take much more..." The weak words were out of her mouth before she could stop them, appalling her, but the totally male smile from Peter ran fire through her, obliterating the cold frisson of fear.

"You can take it. You'll have to, because it's not a choice."

He lowered his head, covered her with the heat of his mouth, and swamped her with the sweet satisfaction that her nipple had been craving, so sharp that she cried out as he drew it in, teased it in the wetness, pressing on it with his lips. He brought his hands up, framed the rack of her breasts and squeezed just in front of the grip of the bar restraints, causing a moan, an outright whimper.

She'd never had each part of her so focused upon, so worshipped and cozened as it had been in the past several hours. Her entire body, every expanse of skin and the restless nerves beneath, desired something, a level of fulfillment Peter had just indicated they would not deliver. But it didn't matter, because the spiraling need felt so good that she shamelessly angled her hips in wanton display. Peter deepened his suckling, making appreciative wet noises as he drew succor from her. Her fingers ached from clenching into one overlapped fist, the desire to touch, to hold his head closer, denied to her.

She shifted her gaze and saw Matt standing in front of the screens, a silhouette against the many images of her time in this room. Someone had dimmed the lights so she was in spotlight again. Feeling his claim on her as if he had uttered it like a war cry, she understood then the appealing fantasy of a slave girl being prepared for the warlord's pleasure. For she knew in looking at him, she was not being shared equally among friends, but pampered, her body made malleable for claiming by the man who had fully intended to have her from the first. And that time was drawing very close.

Peter's teeth scraped her left nipple and the shudder of reaction went all the way to her womb.

Then Ben touched her. The man who turned the legal screws when Kensington's rights were challenged in any situation. It made sense Matt would pull him into this last phase, to ensure there was no challenge left in her. Though Matt underestimated her if he thought that was possible. She would go down fighting. She had to. Didn't she?

Ben's hands were slick as they touched her backside. She smelled an oil, heated musk like opium, and he was sliding it down her buttocks, oiling them, somewhat as Jon did, but then suddenly, he was working his fingers and the oil into her anus, and slid past the resistance before she could react.

"My apologies, Savannah." His voice was a sexy baritone with the faintest hint of Cajun accent because of his parentage. He'd spent most of his formative years in New England, including the acquisition of his law degree at Yale, where he and Matt had met. "I didn't want to warn you because you would tense up, and I don't want to cause you pain."

She highly respected Ben, because while he was in fact as aggressive as the proverbial pit bull, like all of Matt's team, he played as fair as he played hard. When she'd been privy to meetings where they'd been on the same side of the fence, she'd noted that Ben did not hesitate to tell Matt whether or not Kensington could do something. Matt followed his direction most of the time, never undermining Ben's expertise with CEO ego.

It was more difficult to relax with Ben touching her, however. She'd had to acknowledge she had a more affectionate and intimate bond with each of the other four than she would have admitted prior to tonight. But Ben had been more distant throughout her relationship with Matt. The man she knew least was obviously preparing to invade the area she'd explored or fantasized about the least, mentally or physically. Jon had barely entered her there, and with Ben's firm though gentle hands, she understood implicitly that he was planning a full invasion, as the last step in Matt's plan to completely break her down.

Her resulting anxiety created a strange dichotomy of sensation, trepidation shooting like a distracting arrow through her reaction to Peter's mouth, teeth, tongue and hands.

"Stop," she rasped. "Don't."

Peter's mouth slowed, but did not still. Instead of nips and eager sucking, now he laved her softly, tugging her in slow, lazy sucklings in his mouth so her pussy, already wet, flooded with new heat, moisture Ben picked up on his fingers to rub over the outside of her pussy, stimulating her there, and then raised his touch to use the rest to lubricate her back opening.

"Matt." She reacted, didn't think of appearances. "This is scaring me."

Her voice quavered slightly, but for once in her life, it did not embarrass or appall her. There was no room anymore for the cold pit viper she was described as being. She was just Savannah, a woman aroused and captivated by the five men in the room, captured by the demands and desires which had roused her own. It was the first time she'd been afraid of the physical portion of the evening. She had been afraid of what they would do to her, afraid of where they would and wouldn't stop, where that would leave her when it was over. Afraid of Matt. Of his relentless determination, so much greater than she had ever suspected, to have what he wanted. Afraid that she, in the end, did not have the strength to resist him or hold him at arm's length, stay safely behind a shield so he couldn't get to who she was. She also was afraid the night's events revealed all too clearly that he had figured that out a long time ago.

Ben's strokes became even more gentle, his palms turning so she felt the caress of his knuckles on her buttocks.

"There's nothing to fear." Matt spoke quietly. Firmly, which told her he wouldn't alter the plan for her fear, but with a note of tenderness in his voice that she recognized as similar to a parent reassuring a child. "It will be all right. Trust me. Trust us. You're trembling with pleasure even now."

"Is he going to…" She licked dry lips, and was surprised when Peter's covered her mouth, moistening them, just a light touch, there and then gone, before she could savor it. Not a kiss, just a very functional action, meeting her needs. Only Matt had *kissed* her on the mouth. The significance of that struck her.

"Yes. But not his cock. You've never been stretched there before and that would be painful. But his fingers will bring you pleasure, as well as the gift he's brought for you."

And before she could think of another word, Ben's oiled hands were spreading open her cheeks assertively, so he would see her anus in embarrassing detail.

"Very pretty." Amazingly, she felt his lips brush over the opening, then he licked her there, probed, his roughened jaw tickling her buttocks, the tops of her thighs. Peter blew heated breath on her left nipple, closed his mouth over it again, his right hand continuing its tortuous kneading and gentle pinching of the other breast.

She was aroused, but at the dual sensation, something turned over inside of her stomach, some tightly wound spring, and something was catapulted into her chest, choking her with need and desire at once, flooding her body, an exquisite sense of pre-climax. It was so close she could see it, but she wasn't there, she was just at that perfect viewpoint to see how amazing and steep the cliff edge was that awaited her, as Ben and Peter bore her toward it like a cherished sacrifice. Her gaze fastened on Matt's, and she was invaded by a wild thought. He was the god of this volcano, the volcano of molten response ready to erupt within her, held back only by their skill and his command, the knowledge of it in that sensual gaze. She needed his power around her, over her, spreading her wide, filling her, taking her sacrifice.

He was watching her shifts in emotions, the reactions of her body, and somehow she knew part of that attentiveness was because he was ready to move and act as needed if the line was crossed and fear or pain entered the picture in a way not intended. Matt would never hurt her, or allow someone else to do so.

That had to be insane thinking, brought on by the physical and emotional duress of her climax. Even her father had made that clear to her. *Rule Nine: The people who claim to love you can hurt you worse than those who don't. Don't let anyone past your guard, and you'll know what to expect from friends, lovers or children, as well as enemies. It won't matter which mask they wear.*

Underneath, every person operated on self-interest, and that would obliterate any sentimental attachment when challenged by stress.

She'd seen him proven right, again and again. People were what they were. He hadn't meant it as a qualitative judgment. Geoffrey hadn't gotten sentimental or emotional. He'd been protecting her in his way, or rather protecting Tennyson Industries, but at times she had wondered if certain returns were worth the pain. She expected her father would have said, "It depends on how much you're willing to pay".

"You're tensing, Savannah," Ben observed. "I want you to do something for me."

"Wh— What?"

"I want you to tell me a fantasy you have when you're afraid. How do you make yourself feel safe?"

Safe? Had she ever felt safe? Certainly from the common things of the world like thieves and muggers, but she'd never felt safe from emotional attack, not in a world with Geoffrey Tennyson, though she'd loved him. She'd had different fantasies to comfort herself when the stress of always having to be on her toes got to her. But over the past couple of years, one fantasy had dominated and erased all the others. She couldn't tell them that one.

"I won't pull down the blinder, but close your eyes," Ben insisted. "Then say it as you'd say it if we weren't here. We don't have any secrets here."

Of course they knew she was afraid to say it. Maybe they even suspected what it was, which made it absurd for her to pretend otherwise.

"My fantasies are always shadows," she murmured. "Just impressions, just for a moment, then gone, as if I'm afraid someone will come into my mind, turn on the lights and catch me doing something I shouldn't be doing. Worse, the lights will be harsh, and make something I want to be beautiful become something ugly."

"What's the fantasy?" His hand gently probed her, making her suddenly wish to weep. He shifted his thigh against the back of hers.

"You may get emotional when I do this." Again, he seemed to read the confusion of her mind as if she had expressed it. "That's normal, because a lot of issues are held in this region. Tell me the dream. Your fantasy."

"To be held," she whispered. "…Someone…comes to me, to my bed, and holds me." She couldn't be specific. A lifetime of protecting herself couldn't be undone in one night, though if anyone could do it, she suspected they were in this room.

The "Someone" was Matt. She didn't know why it was him in the fantasy, but it always was, ever since she'd met him.

Peter was brushing his cheek against her breasts now, a comforting gesture. She felt an almost maternal, fierce need to have her hands free so she could touch his head, his hair, hold him to her, perhaps rub her mouth, her cheek against his hair, smelling his varying scents. Nurture as well as be nurtured.

"I'm in my bed, and…that someone comes to me. He's there, sliding in behind me, but not just to hold me from behind. He turns me, so I'm in the shelter of his body, facing him, my face tucked beneath his chin, his arms around my back, and all I have to do is just…be. He sees me. He doesn't say anything, or want anything I'm not willing to give. He fills me in my heart, my mind and body. He's there, with me, for me."

"And you're comforted."

For that short period of time. Until the alarm goes off. "Yes."

One of Ben's fingers slid within her, the oil taking it easily deep into her rectum. His other hand squeezed her right cheek, a sexual gesture as well as one of comfort. "Breathe deep, Savannah," he said.

As she drew in a breath, he kept speaking in that deep, musical voice. "I love women with tight asses. I have thick fingers, and I love the feel of them clenching around me. And I think you'll enjoy this even more."

He leaned forward, his soft Pierre Cardin dress shirt brushing her back, and in the oiled hand he held before her, just to the right of Peter's head, he clasped a strand of gleaming freshwater pearls.

Her father had given her jewelry to appropriately decorate her for the functions they attended. Not once in her life had she been given jewelry as a true gift, something offered for her pleasure. She certainly could afford to buy herself something like that, but this...

"Ben...they're beautiful. I...can't..."

"They're yours," he said simply, and then he was bending over her, laying a kiss, tender and lingering, on the nape of her neck. He trailed the pearls down her spine, left them in a coil in the small of her back. "I'll use them for your pleasure, then I'll take them with me tonight, get them cleaned and return them to you, so you can always remember how they were used when you wear them."

"And how is that?"

"I'm going to double them over, and insert them into your rectum. As Peter rouses you to even greater pleasure with his mouth and *his gift*, I'll slowly draw them out. It'll make you crazy."

Before she could think of a response to that, Peter was turning, taking a velvet box from Lucas.

"We've all brought you gifts tonight." Lucas leaned his hip against the table next to Peter. "Jon is giving you his device, the prototype, to keep for your private enjoyment. Ben has brought you the pearls. Peter and I picked these out together."

"One from each of us." There was laughter in Peter's voice. "I think you'll like them." He withdrew what looked to be a pair of genuine diamond chandelier earrings, and then she realized they were not earrings.

He leaned forward, covered her with his mouth and wet her again, then his fingers were there, placing the jewelry on her distended nipple. "Tell me when it's uncomfortable. It's an adjustable clamp."

She only had a moment to be fearful of that particular word in association with her nipples before he was tightening the screw on the jewel. The pressure was exquisite, wringing a whimper from her throat, and he looked at her face, registered that the noise was pleasure, and he took another turn. "I'm going to stop there, darlin'. You're aroused enough to like the feel of it, but it will be painful if it's at too tight a setting for long. Now the other one."

"I'm taking the pearls into you, Savannah. Take in another deep breath for me."

Ben again. Good luck in that, when she could barely draw an even breath, let alone a deep one. Peter slid his tongue over and around her curves as if washing them, nudging the jewels, tugging on them, his fingers twisting the slick nipples, causing wrenching bolts of pleasure to rocket from her nipples to anus and back again. The diamonds brushed the lower curves of her breasts like feathers of sensation.

She drew in the breath, tried to hold it, though her pussy was so wet she could feel that the soft curls were drenched, cool against her skin.

"Now let it out. Slow. Count of five. Just like with Jon. One, two, three…"

She obeyed, and she felt Ben's fingers gently push round, smooth pearls into her. They were lubricated with the oil of his fingers, and she began to move against the straps, she couldn't help it. It was equal reaction to both stimuli, so aroused she couldn't find a rhythm, only this desperate movement. Ben began to play with the beads, pulling on them slightly, not taking them out, just turning them around, wiggling them a bit, and then his finger amazingly joined them, a thumb she thought, for she felt impossibly filled, her pussy contracting as he began to move the digit incrementally inside of her, tiny back and forth pressures as his thumb stretched her opening.

Savannah cried out, her hips jerking, shuddering, her cunt weeping for a release being held just out of reach. Neither man touched her clit, and in the air, she had nothing she could grind against, the damn bench on which she rested stopping just above her pubic bone. She still could have forced herself down against it, pushing against the loose skin just above the pussy to somehow massage the clit, but as if Peter knew that, his hand slid under her belly, between the board and her body, and held her away from it.

She didn't know when she had lost an anchor on her senses, control of her bodily or mental functions. She only knew that she was completely adrift, rolling in a heated, searing cloud of sensation and emotion, immersed, just a blink before the panic of climaxing. The men's furor had increased, as if picking up on her desperation. Their own animal instincts responded, pressing the advantage, the sensual parallel to closing in on a kill, feeling the bloodlust take over, without the blood.

She saw their faces and her own reaction grew more primal. She wanted to see them below the waist. She was disappointed that Lucas sat with his hip on the table, that portion of his anatomy turned away from her. Jon and Ben were behind her, and Peter was pulled up to the table so he could more easily tug at her breasts. Matt had moved outside her range of sight.

Then she remembered the screens.

When her eager gaze shot to it, she saw some of what she wanted. Lucas's body was highly aroused, his profile intent upon her. Jon likewise tipped back in his chair, watching Ben's work, his cock straining against his khaki slacks, unembarrassed in his blatant arousal. And Ben...well, if the size of his erection against his summer wool trousers was any indication of his true size, she was glad it was pearls and not him inside of her. All of the men were as much or more aroused than she, and suddenly she again had that amazing desire to satisfy all of them, to be as open to their raging needs as to her own.

There was a current close-up of Peter suckling her nipple, nothing of her visible but her breasts. Straining the curve of her throat, she arched more in response to the visual stimulation as his hands framed and squeezed her, giving him more to suckle.

"Please," she gasped, emitting a short scream as Peter's tongue went from a swirling rhythm with the sucking pressure of his mouth to a hard flick, bouncing the weight of the jewelry against the nipple. Ben replaced the thumb caressing her opening with his tongue, tickling the tender inside flesh of her buttock with alternating pressure of teeth and tongue. Then the pearls started to come out.

Pop, pop, pop... At each expulsion, she made a guttural noise of reaction, her nostrils flaring, seeking air.

Clit stimulation or not, her pussy had reached its capacity. It contracted, squeezing around nothing, preparing to let her go, pushed passed endurance. Her mouth opened on a long, desperate cry, through which Matt's voice cut like the smooth power of a shark's passage.

"Stop."

Chapter Five

෮

She'd never brought herself to climax with knowledge. Once, when she'd watched a romantic movie with a mysterious hero, she'd found herself rocking on the couch, her hand somehow finding itself between her legs, just a tentative pressure, and all of a sudden there was a snap of sensation that shuddered through her, hard and fast, somewhat unsatisfying but intriguing and shaming all at once.

She willed the two men not to listen, knowing from earlier experience tonight that what had been coming was that pop a million times over, like a sparkler compared to a full Fourth of July fireworks show.

Unfortunately, Ben's mouth and the last pearl withdrew, as did Peter. He gave her breasts a lingering caress as he pulled away, a gentle tug on one of the diamond jewels. She had a brief glimpse of his aroused countenance, his wet lips, before he slid the blinder of her mask back in place as if on signal from Matt. She fought him, thrashing her head, snapping at his fingers, but Peter had the advantage of mobility, if not of calm. Hearing the ragged edge of his breath, feeling the tremor in his fingers, she wished she could see his reaction like she had the others. It had been hidden by the table's height, but she knew it would be there, as enormous as her own need.

Ben's lips brushed a fleeting caress on her left ass cheek, a tiny nip of teeth that made her jump a little, before he stroked the small of her back with a slick finger and withdrew.

Like a creation of flame, she vibrated with energy, all her exposed secrets throbbing with the need for more fuel, more friction. She felt like weeping or screaming or both, a wanton creature with no desire for control, only possession.

She shouldn't have recognized herself, this strange, mad creature who had been brought to this pinnacle so easily these three times now, but she did. She knew the face, she'd seen it inside the mirror of her mind, a reflection she never let out. A Savannah that had crept out of hiding, willing now to roar out every desire, every secret, every shameful need, to a roomful of men who had coaxed that alter ego out. It was dangerous, frightening thinking. Some rational part of her said this whole evening was a terrible mistake, from which she'd never be able to reclaim her life, but at the moment all she cared about was the aching want between her thighs, and within her heart.

Fill me with what I never believed existed. And if she was wrong and it didn't exist, she knew whatever sense of Savannah she had outside of her father's mold would die. She would die, in all the ways that mattered. But that was perhaps better than living with the emptiness, the lonely pain.

"Savannah, are you listening to me? Can you hear me?"

Matt's voice penetrated the roar of arousal within her, and she jerked her head, whether in a nod or negative, she didn't know.

"I knew we could offer you passion tonight, make you understand what could be yours if you were willing to trust and be vulnerable. You've given every man in this room an incredible gift. No matter what happens in the next few moments, what choice you make, I want you to know that." He hesitated, and the raw quality of his voice, the rough desire and emotion mixed, caught more of her attention. She wondered where he was going with this, but hoped it was somewhere that would ease this craving need. And soon.

"You'll walk out of here as cherished and respected as you were when you walked in. Every man enjoys teaching a woman the ways of pleasure, especially a woman he loves, and every man in this room loves you. I wanted you to experience a wide range of sensual possibilities and fortunately, each man here has very individual specialties."

What was the phrase she often heard her secretary use to describe something blatantly obvious? *Boy, howdy.* She was close to being hysterical, she realized, and tried to take some deep breaths, get a grip on her raging body.

"I wanted you blindfolded now, because I want you to search only your heart for the answer to this next question. You can go back to the reality of your life as it was before you walked in here tonight. There will be no recriminations, no sense of favoritism. It will all end here. Everything will be the same tomorrow. You've won the right to choose."

"Choose?" The word felt awkward, somehow unwelcome on her tongue. She didn't want to have choices. When she lost control, she'd been given mind-altering pleasure, made even more intense by the fact she no longer had to worry about whether Savannah Tennyson was making the right decisions. She realized in a heartbeat the significance of Rule Five.

Discipline is a 24/7 exercise. Lose a grip on it even for a moment and you could lose everything you've worked for.

Get out of my fucking head.

The reaction froze every system in her body, even shut out Matt's voice and her surroundings for a blink of time. Everything tonight had been a surprise, something unexpected. But that vicious thought, targeted at her father's memory and coming out of her subconscious like a snarl from behind the gates of Hell, was the biggest shock of all.

She *did* have choices. For the first time in her life choices existed for *her*, Savannah, and she was free to make them. Peter, Lucas, Jon and Ben had helped her see that. And Matt. *Matt.*

"I want to see," she said sharply.

"I want you to think," he responded. "I need you to think very carefully about something, and I want you to have no distractions."

When he was delivering a deal breaker, his voice would change, modulate, and just like a regular poker opponent, she recognized it. This was dead serious, no bullshit, no games.

"Here are your choices. Choice number one. You're obviously in need of physical release. Jon has brought a larger invention, something that will fill you as fully as a man's cock. Every man here would enjoy watching it give you the level of orgasm your body is ready for.

"Choice number two. You can choose to call it over. We'll clear the room. I'll untie you, help you dress, and tonight will never be referred to again, by any of us. Or..." There was a slight pause, and she waited, not sure how she felt about either option and hoping there was another, one that this straining need in her would recognize as the right one and eagerly embrace.

"Choice number three. Your final choice. You can choose one of us to do what Jon's invention will do."

It took a minute to sink in. "You mean..."

"Any one of us." His voice was firm, resolute now. "The rest of us will go. The man you've chosen will stay with you, meet your desires, whether they be physical or emotional. He'll make sure you get home safely afterward. No demands after that."

"No demands," she said hollowly.

"None."

Unexpected pain landed like a load of bricks on the shuddering waves of pleasure still gripping her, which made her feel like a dog that had been kicked by a beloved master, uncomprehending of why, making the pain that much worse. But the analogy cleared up the source question, and she struggled to channel the pain into fury and lash out.

It built in her, so suddenly that she felt lightheaded, all the blood rushing to her face, but at the same time she was swept by a desolation so exponentially fierce that she couldn't draw breath from anger, or control the direction of her thoughts or words.

"So you don't want me," she said.

"What?"

It was a very rare moment to catch Matt Kensington by surprise, to the extent it could be heard in his voice.

"This was all…a nice game. Fun…amongst colleagues." She managed to create a sharp laugh, like a razor blade along her own skin. "I can't thank you all enough for devoting your evening to fulfilling every woman's erotic fantasy."

She was at an atavistic level of need, to the point where action could be the only communication, but Matt had restrained her so there was nothing she could do to influence events. Roused to a painful, raw state by Ben's pearls and clever fingers, Peter's mouth, by everything they'd done and shown her tonight, her insides were like the slopes of a California hillside under pummeling rain. Mudslides were roaring to life, revealing the primal underside of her earth, smothering her civilized façade. The images still flickering on the wall stimulated her body still, even without the benefit of her sight.

Anguish squeezing her lungs, she choked against the hard, relentless force of strangulation. There was nothing left but a burning ache, desire and loss come together in a head-on collision at fatal speed. She tasted tears on her lips, and knew she should be horrified by her weakness, but they had forcibly dissolved that concern an orgasm or two ago.

"Savannah." Gentle hands removed the blinders, and Lucas was there, his eyes thoughtful, a little sad, but with a light that suggested he had hope for them all. "You've rendered him speechless. I think he's one step from apoplectic."

She looked at Matt through her tears and suddenly wished she was untied. Out of a sense of self-preservation. Matt looked more angry than she'd ever seen him. Not a cold controlled anger, either—the enraged passion of a man pushed past some boundary of restraint.

"This is your own fault," Lucas said, unperturbed.

She glanced back at him, startled, realized he wasn't talking to her.

"Just tell her straight out, for Chrissakes."

"Leave us, then," Matt said.

Savannah felt a sudden surge of fear, but Lucas laid a hand on the tender area between her shoulder and neck. He lowered the harness so she was on the table. Ben helped him free her legs. Hands straightened her, caressing her thighs, bringing her feet back to the floor. The suspension device and all its components were removed from around and beneath her. With gentle pressure, Lucas kept her upper body on the silken mahogany. He slid off her mask, though, laid it aside and smoothed her hair back, his thumb brushing over the path of a tear. He leaned down, kissed her temple. "You'll be safe with him."

"Lucas."

"Going." He straightened, made a quick gesture with his head and they all left, melting into the shadows and stepping out the door, four men who had profoundly altered her reality in the space of an evening. Now she faced what her destiny would be tomorrow.

Despite Lucas's not-so-subtle hint, she pushed her body up. Naked though she was, she felt less vulnerable facing Matt with her back straight. And her clothes were folded over the chair not more than a yard from her.

She discovered two things immediately. One was that Lucas had had a practical reason for encouraging her to stay down. The body she had walked in with several hours before had suddenly become heavy and unbalanced, her knees trembling, her vision blurring and tilting as blood rushed back into her torso.

The second thing was that Matt moved a lot faster and more silently than she anticipated. With her head spinning, she wasn't even aware of his approach, but suddenly he was there, the heat of his hands on her hips, the faint scratch of his slacks pressing against the back of her bare legs, his white shirt against her shoulder blades, the silk of his tie a caress against her spine.

It got very quiet between them, and Savannah could only hear the sound of her own harsh breathing, the echo of her words, obviously laden with hurt, lingering in the room. She had no choice but to lean, but in truth, it was a relief to feel him there. That he was still angry she'd no doubt, but he obviously wasn't intending to take it out on her in some frightening way. She hoped.

"I don't know you enough to trust you like this," she mumbled, but still she didn't move. If anything, she settled back against him as he took a more secure, possessive grip on her waist, his hold sliding forward so his arm was over her abdomen, his palm over the opposite hip as he raised his other hand, applied gentle pressure until her head was on his shoulder, the upper slope of his chest.

"Yes, you do," he said quietly.

He'd gotten her to admit she wanted him, not as a moment of passing lust, not to act on a curious attraction. All the desires he had roused through his men had culminated in one raging truth—that it was him she wanted, him whom she now leaned against, the only one she trusted enough to reveal such a need. From the very beginning, she had denied it in every way, that he was the culmination and solution. He'd exposed the lie by not offering what she had expected him to offer to close the evening's deal. She'd been outmaneuvered, and now there was just the frightening truth between them. He held all the poker chips, and he could tear her to shreds. But she still had his desire for her to bargain with, shift some of the balance to her side of the table.

"So what does Lucas want you to tell me?" She leaned her head into his touch, nuzzled him with her lips deliberately. He pulled loose, lowered his grip, closed it over her throat. Feeling her fragile pulse beating against that powerful hand made it beat harder.

She looked up into those dark eyes, sensual lips, imagined them moving over her. *That's it, Savannah.* Focus on what he could give her on the surface, two bodies satisfying each other. What was beneath didn't matter. Couldn't matter.

"I'm sorry I was catty," she said abruptly. "You set this up and we all enjoyed ourselves. I just went all female on you for a moment."

"Did you?" He cupped her chin and held it so she was locked into looking up at him, into his unfathomable gaze.

"You know I did. It was a slip, that was all. It won't happen again. There's no reason we can't enjoy each other—"

"And keep all our commitments tomorrow, meet every appointment. Savannah, I am not your bloody fucking father."

Her body went rigid. The anger was still there, blasting her with its heat, but his eyes held something else, something close to pain, that she'd never seen in his eyes before. A part of himself he was deliberately revealing to her. He turned her, his hands closing over her shoulders.

"Well, I certainly hope you aren't him," she managed. "Otherwise, what just happened in this room—"

His grip tightened further, nearly dragging her to her toes.

"Matt—"

"Just shut up, before I decide to strangle you." He placed his finger on her lips. "Listen to what I'm saying. Look into my eyes and stop being afraid of what this is. It wouldn't have hurt you so much, my proposal to let you choose anyone, if it weren't real, what you're thinking."

"Let go of me," she said.

"Never again." He shook his head. Shook her. "We wouldn't want you to go all female on us, would we? Hell, don't stop there. Let's not be human while you're at it. Why should you have needs, desires and, God forbid, express anger or pain where someone else can see it? I *want* a human woman with a healthy mixture of weaknesses and strengths, who sometimes laughs inappropriately, or gets in real fights with me. Someone from whom I beg for forgiveness, even if I know I was right, because I know making her happy is more important to me than being right. Someone who doesn't want to be alone."

"I've been alone all my life."

"Lonely all your life."

"Yes, goddamn you." She shot it back savagely, and there was a rough, tearing quality to her voice, somewhere before a shout and a snarl. She startled him enough she managed to pull away, back up several steps, and snatch up her blouse. "Yes, I have been, Matt. Boohoo for me. The princess in the tower, given everything she wants except her daddy's love. So what? You're going to make it all better? Is that what the hell this is all about?"

"Yes."

"Well, tough, because it doesn't work that way."

"Yes, it does. It can. It should." He took a step toward her, like a man approaching a wild and dangerous animal, not with fear, but respect and caution, not wanting to harm the creature. "I love you. It's as simple as that. And if you're willing to give that a try, even give it just a moment of belief in your heart, I promise I won't let you down. You won't feel lonely anymore."

"You're out of your fuck...idiotic minds, all of you." She nearly screamed at the amusement that came into his eyes at her avoidance of cursing. "Don't you dare laugh at me, Matt Kensington." She snatched the belt off the table, flung it at his chest. He caught it, the amusement turning into annoyance. *Good.*

"You've stripped me down, great. You blithely tell me you love me, without taking off one piece of clothing, metaphorical or otherwise. For all I know, it's just a good con, the whole thing, because as far as I can tell, you haven't even broken a sweat tonight. So, tell me what Lucas wanted you to say. Get off of your high horse and tell me what this is all really about. "

"It's about asking you out on a goddamned date."

He shouted it so fiercely it echoed through the room. She even imagined she heard the windows of the high-rise rattle.

"What?" It was such an unexpected statement, she had to grope for something to say, particularly when he continued to glare at her without further explanation. "Matthew, this is *not* your average first date."

He chuckled at that, but it was a harsh sound. "You've got that right. 'Didn't break a sweat.' Jesus Christ. I ought to wring your neck." He rubbed a hand over his face, through his dark hair until it stood on end in a very appealing tousle. "This entire night, the idea of it, started because I wanted to get involved with you, and I didn't think anything short of something this dramatic would work.

"If you'd accepted my invitation to go out on a date, and treated me in that clinical, detached way you do those other losers I've seen you attend political functions and movie premieres with, I think I'd have had to kill you."

She stared at him a very long moment, and there was no motion in the room except for the flickering light of those many different screens, showing the story of her life for the past few hours.

She lowered her gaze to the blouse she was holding. It was an odd contrast to her pale naked body, and the soft glitter of the lovely chandelier nipple jewels. She liked the way those looked, and how Matt's eyes kept straying to them. Savannah struggled past those thoughts, to what was going on in her own head. To what she knew she had to be brave enough to say, if she truly wanted to believe Matt's words.

It was five minutes before she found the courage, and to his credit, he waited, motionless, through the extraordinarily long pause.

"You know," she said, her voice thick, not her own. "One day I was in the elevator with this young girl doing summer work in the mailroom. She had on the prettiest pair of sandals. I kept staring at those shoes, and I thought… 'I bet she really enjoyed buying those. I bet she likes looking at the way they look on her feet.' And it made me feel so sad…"

"Savannah." He took a step toward her, but she closed her eyes, shook her head. "And I knew then, though I didn't admit it to myself. I've never bought clothes, shopped for fun, done anything out of a sense of spontaneous whimsy." She took a deep breath, raised her head and met his eyes squarely. "You're right. You're all right. I was Geoffrey Tennyson's cyborg, from the day my mother died. So you are all absolutely right. As much as I've fantasized about you, and wanted you, I would have treated you exactly that way. I wanted to be cruel to you tonight, finish up with all this and walk away, but I can't. I want you, Matt. And admitting that terrifies me."

"And love?"

She lifted an uneasy shoulder. "I don't know what that is. I do know…" Her voice lowered and he came to her, so when she raised her head, she was looking directly up into his face, her bare body erotically almost pressed against his fully clothed one. "I know you're the 'someone' in the fantasy to comfort myself. Every time. You always have been, since the day I met you."

Reaching down, she picked up his hand. After only a brief hesitation, she brought it to her lips, pressing her face into his palm. Something seemed unusual and she raised her face enough to look at a wound on his palm. A deep wound, like a puncture. His blood had coagulated, but the wound was hot to the touch, sticky. "What—"

His other hand touched her face, tracing the light impressions she could feel where the mask had pressed against her face.

"I kept digging my hand into the screw set under the table to keep myself from breaking down and releasing you. I almost broke, every time one of them touched you, every time you came, every time I heard the fear in your voice. I wanted this to be the right thing. And I told myself I was sure. But every time you got upset…" A tremor ran through his hand, amazing her. "Don't ever make me go through that again."

"Make you—" She saw the trace of a smile in his eyes, a moment before her knees gave out on her.

"Whoa." He caught her at the waist as she gripped his coat lapels for balance, and before she knew what he was about, he'd lifted her off her feet and was headed to the couch.

"I didn't feed you enough, I think," he observed.

Not to mention what three or four mind-blowing orgasms in one night can do to someone.

He laid her down on the couch and then straightened, retaining one of her hands in his, studying her.

"Matt," she whispered. "Matt," she repeated softly, seeing what was in his dark, intent eyes. She was afraid to put her arms around him, afraid to stroke her fingers through his hair, afraid to do anything. Struggling against all her natural instincts to curl into a protective fetal ball and deny what she was so scared and hopeful was the truth.

Never lose control. Her father had told her, from her very first tantrum. *You give the enemy the advantage when you lose control.* And it took her very little time to understand he meant that to apply to everything, because to him there wasn't any time that wasn't about business, the business of life, the ultimate corporation. You ruled your life and everyone around you with iron control, or you opened yourself to defeat, to takeover. To failure.

To the disappointment in her father's face.

Oh, God. To think that her whole life, the compass she followed each day, had always pointed to that. One tyrannical man's expectations, a man who was dead.

Nobody could possibly understand how hard it would be to let that go, when her whole life had been structured on it. The idea of turning to something different was the same as detonating a bomb that would blow up her foundation, her world. She'd been called a Daddy's girl, but that implied something soft, with golden curls, like Lucas had described. She'd been his weapon, his tool.

But tonight had been about who she was, Savannah. And by making it about that, Matt had told her clearly, through action, that it was *her* he wanted. Not the weapon of Geoffrey. *Her.* And though she might not have much of an idea of who Savannah Tennyson was, when she looked into Matt's eyes, she saw *he* knew. As if his eyes were the mirror she'd never been able to find to show her what her true face was. And there she finally had the truth of why he was always the center of her comfort fantasy. Of every fantasy.

"You really do love me."

His hand reached out, smoothed her hair from her temple, tilted her chin so she had to look up at him, into his unsmiling, devastatingly handsome countenance.

"And you love me, sweetheart. I'll wait for you to know it, the way I do."

It was such a reflection of her own thoughts, she had to stifle tears. "We don't…we haven't even gone out on a date. I'm *not* counting tonight, Matthew."

"I beg to differ." He caressed her hand, playing idle finger games with her, a wonderfully intimate pastime that fascinated her. "Over the past two years, we have had over thirty-eight dates. We've played the same fencing games that dating couples play. We've even spent the entire night together, several times. We've ordered food."

Her mouth turned up into a shy smile. "Matt, you're as dysfunctional as I am. Those are meetings, not dates. Next thing you'll say is that the video we saw on the new line of hydraulic nailers was the same as going to a movie."

"I laid an arm over the back of your chair. I would have tried to cop a feel, but figured you'd chew my arm off at the shoulder."

She laughed then, and it wasn't as hopeless a sound as she expected it to be.

He removed his hand from hers, began to loosen his tie.

"What…what are you doing?" Her throat had gone dry, knowing exactly what he was doing. The trembling in her thighs increased, and all the passion stroked to life but unfulfilled by Peter and Ben flared as if there had never been a lull. Every cell of her body begged.

"You know what I'm doing. You're mine. And notions of twentieth-century promiscuity be damned, we both know the way I intend to stake my claim on you, make you mine forever."

Chapter Six

ଗ

"Have you thought of just asking?" she asked softly, stilling him in the act of unbuttoning the third button of his shirt, exposing the fine dark hair of his chest that her fingers longed to stroke, tangle in, clutch when his body slid into hers.

"You know the rules of negotiation. Never give them a chance to say no."

A full smile curved her lips this time, and she watched his eyes settle on her mouth with erotic intent. "Be brave, Matthew."

Matt seemed to weigh her words, every aspect of the moment, down to the ticking of the clock and the hum of the lighting.

"Don't calculate the risk, Matt," she said, the silence driving away her tentative assurance, making her eyes prick with the threat of tears. "This is so hard for me. Please, just...believe..."

In something larger than us both.

His eyes softened, and the crucial moment of connection was made, a moment of such impact she almost heard the click. "You're right." He dropped to one knee beside her. "I am very much in love with you, Savannah. I've wanted you from the very first moment I saw you. Since the moment we met, you've stirred me up, made me think thoughts so fantastic you'd laugh at them."

"Like what?" She touched his face, grateful that he stayed still, letting her fill with wonder at the simple pleasure of feeling his jaw beneath her fingers, knowing from his expression he wanted her hand there. It was a miracle to be wanted. She wondered if he could possibly understand that.

"You're crying," he said softly, and she nodded.

"You haven't told me an example of fantastic thoughts."

"Forever thoughts. A house. A dog. A shared portfolio."

She laughed then, a quick hitch into a sob. His gaze on hers, he stayed on one knee beside her, but finished unbuttoning his shirt, drawing her attention down to his hands. Her body's urgent hum increased, disrupting her emotional focus. She had never felt so many different things at once. Her fingers trailed down his neck, followed the opening in his shirt to feel a man's chest, again for the first time. A shudder ran through his body. A new miracle. She lifted amazed eyes to him.

"You've brought me to a place I've never been tonight, Matt," she admitted. "And I've no idea where to go at this point but to lead with my feelings, even knowing that I'm giving you every opportunity to cut me to ribbons. I want you. Please. Just don't..." It took every ounce of courage to say the words, and she was proud they came out, not as a trembling plea, but a quiet, steady request. "Please don't hurt me."

She wasn't talking about the act. She knew he understood that. She'd never asked anyone for protection or defense. Instead, she'd become a master at preventing people from hurting her. She'd crafted herself into a knight forever trapped in her mail, the metal becoming her true skin while everything inside withered away from lack of sunlight, stimulation...touch. He'd broken her out of the mail, and she was shivering, naked, completely vulnerable. Completely alive.

"Never." His voice was rough with emotion, and he came close, held her face cradled in his hands as he pressed his forehead to hers, touched her lips with his mouth. She cupped her hands over his strong, warm ones. "I've wanted you to say that to me for so long," he murmured against her. "To hear that you trust me enough to ask it. Never, sweet Savannah. I'll destroy anyone who causes you a moment of pain."

The totally male, totally unrealistic promise nevertheless squeezed her heart into her throat, stopping her breath as much as when he straightened and slid out of the shirt, his tanned skin a golden gleam beneath the room's dim light. He had beautiful musculature under the fine layer of male fur, and she could not help following the sleek lines of him down to the waistband of his slacks.

"Do you want more?" he asked quietly, his hand at the fastener.

A tiny smile curved her lips. "My specialty is production. What do you think?"

He chuckled, but she did raise one hand, holding them just a moment. "Just…go slow. You're kind of overwhelming. Actually, this whole night's been a bit overwhelming."

"I know," he said, a trace of regret in his voice. "If I were any kind of gentleman, I'd wait, but Savannah… God, it's like a vampire thing. I have to make you mine by dawn or I'm afraid I'll lose you, that I'll see you tomorrow and you'll be back behind your armor, convincing yourself it didn't mean what it meant, any of it." His heated gaze traveled up her bare body, spreading fire. "But if you feel the soreness, the stickiness of my come drying between your legs, the smell of me on your skin, see a red blush on your jaw in the mirror tomorrow from the rasp of my beard, you won't."

"It's a signed deal, then," she whispered. She lifted her arms. "Will you come and just…lie on me a few minutes, before you take everything off?"

He had bought a man's couch for his boardroom, so it was a good seven feet long and nearly three and a half feet wide. He tossed the small cushions scattered on it, except for one, which he adjusted under her head and shoulders, making her comfortable, before he stretched out upon her as she had requested. His finger trailed along her thigh with gentle pressure so she widened their span to accommodate his hips and long legs between them. She liked how he adjusted the pillow beneath her, scooping his arm under her shoulders, holding her face close to his chest, his chin brushing the top of her head as he saw to her comfort. What would it be to get used to that, someone caring how she felt, not because she was responsible for thousands of people's livelihoods, not because she was a legacy, but because he cared? And what would it be to care for him the same way, hold his hand at a movie, stroke his brow after a trying day, see him laugh at something on television, see that toe poke out of the end of its sock?

"How's that?" he asked in that sensual, bedroom-hushed voice. "Am I too heavy?"

The pressure of him on her was like the pressure of too much happiness on her heart, something so unfamiliar it was almost painful. It was a feeling close to heaven. His arms curled on either side of her head, her vision totally dominated by his handsome face, the dark eyes, that incredible mouth. Daring, she lifted her chin, reaching, and like a miraculous telepathy, he came down to meet her, with a soft, gentle kiss that was perfect. She parted her lips, shyly tasted him with her tongue, touching his lips, then his tongue, and felt the new sensation of his body tightening in response to the provocation. The friction of him against the juncture of her thighs, separated only by the trousers, pressed insistently, male power and strength held back only by his caring toward her. She closed her eyes as the kiss deepened, and a hundred things flashed through that darkness, things that had always been there, that she had refused to see. A hundred ways he had supported her, contributed to her reputation, respected her. She had focused on the battles, never allowing herself to see what else was there.

A million kindnesses. She remembered now, in stark detail, tiny things. Him reaching toward the center of the table, filling her water glass when it was almost empty, though his was full, underscoring that he was doing it as a courtesy to her. Silly, but now it seemed full of meaning. The many times he'd called her during the week, to discuss this or that detail on their mutual business interests, but in some subtle way he'd lifted her spirits by making a dry joke or witticism about something they both understood. The fact that he'd sent her flowers every Friday since her father's death.

She loved roses. She supposed he'd found that out from her office assistant. He'd sent her the first bouquet right after her father's death. She'd thanked him for it, assuming it was the usual condolence gesture. Then they'd kept coming, every Friday for the past two years. She hadn't acknowledged those bouquets at first, figuring if she ignored them he would stop sending them. He didn't. In all those two years, he'd never sent her the same shade, and never a dyed flower. Always beautiful palettes of hybrids from gardens all over the country. One bouquet had even been shipped from England. At some point she'd started saving one bloom from each delivery, getting them pressed and preserved, and added them to a dried bouquet she kept in her bedroom. Often, it was what she studied as she lay down at night, somehow not feeling so alone by the simple act of gazing at them.

"You've always been there for me, since we first met." She accepted it. Said it out loud.

"Not as often as I should have been. I should have done something like this a long time ago." He bent his head, put his lips beneath her ear and cruised down her neck. She arched, pulling on her bottom lip with her teeth as the movement rubbed her body against his, the soft skin of her inner thighs sliding against the outside of his, instinctively pushing her aching center against his hardness. She was amazed at her own wantonness, unleashing itself now that she...

He raised his head as if he felt her reaction to her own thoughts. "Savannah?"

"I trust you, Matt. I've never trusted anyone, not in my entire life. I think that's why tonight was...possible. I kept asking myself why I wasn't screaming and fighting you, why I wasn't dialing 911 when I got free, and this was it. You knew, didn't you? Since that day on the desk, like you said."

He nodded, his heart and his desire for her in his gaze. "I knew."

"And that I would…" She suspected "enjoy" wasn't the proper word. "…respond to this type of thing?" She wasn't worldly about sex. She just knew it felt good, that she craved more.

"Yes." He kissed her nose, lingering so she closed her eyes, savored. "I knew you were mine the first time I saw you, and I knew you'd be willing to be submissive to the right man, the man you could trust to take care of you when you have to be in control of everything else.

"You're a strong, strong woman. The most basic way to prove that to you, the way the predator in you would understand, was to take you down the way another predator would. Make you expose your throat and concede my dominance over you." He tilted her head back with a thumb to her chin, and set his teeth lightly to her jugular, flicking it with his tongue. "As your mate. The one who cares for you and needs you the most. Who would never hurt you."

The words were offensive, but the truth behind them was so primal, so intuitive and beyond the realm of political correctness, her pulse leaped, not in anger, but in response, and her thighs relaxed, accommodating him further, sending exactly the message he had said he would pull from her. Total submission.

"I…I don't want to be free to choose any longer, Matt." She got out the words, and she meant them so deeply, it was hard to form them. "I want to belong to you."

With an almost feral growl of need, he lifted up from her, just enough for there to be a space. "Open my slacks."

With trembling fingers, she found the hook fastener, slipped it, took down the zipper, her wrists brushing the hard heat beneath. He reached back, pushed them off his hips.

"Matt," she said softly, not daring to look him in the eye. "Will you…can I feel all of you at once? Will you be…"

135

"Naked?" His eyes smiled at her, though his jaw was tight with his desire for her. "Anything for you. Anything you ask, I'll give you."

He lifted off her, meliorating her immediate sense of loss by taking her hand as he rose, kissing her knuckles in a gallant gesture that ran electricity down her arm, tightening her breasts and the wet folds of her sex.

Then he took off his shoes, one by one, pulled off the black dress socks, making her smile when he put his hand in one to show her the hole in the toe. His slacks were open during the process and her eyes were drawn to the play of his well-defined stomach muscles just above the band of his underwear, the black soft jersey boxers. He slid the slacks off, tossed them over one of the conference room chairs, then removed the boxers as well. He saved his watch for last, and she was able to watch the play of muscles in his arms and chest as he bent his elbows to perform the removal task, and look her fill at his bare body. He made no move to adjust his stance, keeping his blatant arousal, his whole body, open to a thorough appraisal.

She was shy about him watching, and he must have noticed. "Look all you want," he said gently. "There's no shame in wanting to look, and the way you're looking at me just makes me want you more. This is as much your body to look at as yours is mine. I'm all yours, sweetheart."

The heavy sac of his testicles rested against his thighs, the long, stiff cock jutting from a nest of soft, dark curls, midnight like those on his head. The outline of his hip suggested he had as fine an ass as she'd always suspected from surreptitious study of it when he was clothed.

"Did you know that I looked, sometimes?" She couldn't take her gaze away, and in a spontaneous gesture, she wet her lips.

He groaned, gave her a half laugh. "Yeah, I did. A lot of times I caught you eyeing my ass. Once I caught you studying my crotch." Her gaze shot up, sparking, and he laughed outright. "Well, you did. It was the airline contract."

"Well, those were very tedious negotiations," she defended herself. She was getting cold. She wanted him here, on her again, to feel that comfortable, solid weight pressing her into the couch. "You don't have to remove the watch."

"Yes, I do. It can catch a nipple or a hair unexpectedly, and I don't want to cause you a moment more of discomfort than I have to. Savannah, have you ever used anything inside of yourself? A vibrator?"

At her confused look, he explained, in a husky voice. "I need to know how tight you'll be, honey. So I don't hurt you."

She shook her head, flushing. "Of course not. Good grief, Matt, I have a houseful of domestic staff. What would they think if they heard it or…found it?"

He smiled, propped an arm on the couch and came back down on her with an animal-like deftness that took her breath. He used his knee to nudge her a little further apart, and then put the other hand between them, stroking through her labia, finding her slick and warm. Savannah gasped on a moan, and his eyes darkened.

"What will they think the first time I take you to bed there, make you scream and tear the wallpaper because I have your wrists cuffed between the slats of the headboard? Ah, sweet Christ, your pussy just rippled against my touch. Feel me, baby." And he slid his fingers into her, slow, pressing upward so she felt the flesh of his palm against her clit as he explored her pussy.

"Matt." She gripped his biceps, holding on, her neck straining, her head against his shoulder as her body struggled beneath him.

"Beg your Master to take you, Savannah. Tell me you belong to me again."

A lifetime of distrust somehow had no ability to withstand the flood of emotion that his words evoked, the

137

overwhelming lust gripping her body, a different intensity than even what she had experienced with his men. That had been physical, she realized. This was more, a longing for fulfillment on all levels.

Now she understood what Jon had meant, the pleasure that would be ten times greater than anything else that had occurred tonight, if she recognized and accepted it. Surrender. Love. Full submission to the man she loved, an intense emotional and physical pleasure like she'd never known swamping her at the simple verbal declaration.

But she had one last holdout, one last need to be met, and she would ask it, because she knew now she could trust his answer.

She managed to get her hands from his arms up to his neck, caressing his jaw, so their eyes were locked in a moment that was simple, mutual absorption.

"If I tell you that, will you keep me, forever and ever? Never leave me? Never leave me in any way, never stop loving me?"

Please don't be my father. Don't live in the same house and let your heart not be there.

He took his fingers from her, making her shudder, and closed his hand on one of hers, laying it to his heart. "I will never leave you, not in any way, Savannah," he said, his voice laden with emotion. "From today forward, for all eternity. You're marrying me this weekend. I'm never going to let you know loneliness again. There's a diamond ring in the pocket of my slacks, and it's going on your finger before you leave this office tonight. That was my gift."

The tears welled up then and as he bent to kiss one off her cheek, he shifted, his eyes still locked on hers, and his cock seated itself in her channel, just the head. Her muscles closed around him in a fist of reaction, tightening his features. "Don't tense up, honey."

"Who's tense?" she gasped. "Please, Matt. Just do it. I need you inside me now."

He slid his arm under her waist, tilting her up to him, and nodded. "Hold onto my shoulders, then."

She did, spurred by the hoarseness of his tone, the obvious desire for her expressed by every part of him, even parts she could not see, but could feel, surrounding her, empowering her.

Her passageway was ready for him, but he eased in, using small strokes. She felt in wonder the sensations of his flesh brushing her inner thighs, the hard flesh of his abdomen, his soft hair rubbing against her belly and chest. She slid one hand down, following the plane of his back, and curved her fingers over his buttock, digging her nails into him in reaction as he stroked her again.

He growled, his body tensing under her touch, and he came all the way into her in one inexorable deep stroke, a claiming she gladly welcomed, binding her to him.

She could hear her father's voice in her head. *It's what all men want, Savannah. A woman's capitulation to their desires. It's a hunt, a game to us, a deadly game. Once they win, they may indulge you or even themselves that their emotions are involved, but that passes.*

He'd never allowed for the reality of love, and so, being a good daughter, she'd never allowed herself to believe in it. But she knew now her woman's heart must have protected some tiny spark of belief, like a fairy captured inside her ironclad soul, and kept alive all these years by the things she'd noted subconsciously. The old couple walking hand in hand in the park, not part of a slick diamond commercial, but real. The always painful sight of a young father in the office, holding his wife protectively and proudly in the circle of his arm as he introduced the new baby daughter to his co-workers. Or in the hospital, when her father was dying, she remembered a room where two men sat, one dying of AIDS, the other holding his hand, rubbing ice on his dry lips.

She'd only touched her father when he was in the final coma, beyond consciousness. She'd briefly held his hand, wondering if she'd feel a tightening of his grip. If she had, she knew it would have been a physical reflex only, but she could have pretended it was a response to her.

The flowers, the times Matt had called, the time at the funeral, those had been gentle insinuations into her life. A taming more than a hunt, teaching her patiently to trust him, so when he chose to claim her, she walked willingly into his arms, into his thrall.

"Say it again," she said softly. "Say it so my heart will hear it."

He had stilled within her to give her time to adjust, and he pressed his cheek to hers, his breath in her ear. "You're mine, Savannah. Now and always."

He withdrew slightly, then moved back in, and pleasure rippled through her abdomen. She raised her legs higher, tightening them over his hips, drawing him deeper. He filled her everywhere with this act of joining, and it was so easy, so clean. She wrapped her arms more tightly around his shoulders, feeling all his power, now all hers, as much as she was his, as he raised his hips, lowered, raised, lowered. Controlling her, sliding along her passage, building up a fire that had the power of a detonation. He was deliberately teasing it to the surface, making her cling tighter, her breath growing harsher against his neck. Her nails dug in again and her teeth as well, tasting his heated flesh, the cord of muscle along the line of his broad shoulder.

"That's it," he muttered. "Let it go."

What had occurred earlier was earth-shattering, on the field of matter. This was a feeling beyond anything she had ever known or imagined, this incredible emotional and physical coupling. She had no experience to know if casual sex felt like this, but if so, she was sure sex done in love would kill the participant. This had to be love. Had to be. In their entire relationship, she'd never known Matt to lie to her about anything.

If he said he loved her, he did.

"Let go, honey," he urged again. "Trust me. Let go. You're mine, all mine, and I'll never let you go."

Her arms held him tighter.

"You're so strong and fragile both," he said. "So delicate. Such soft curves, your hair against my face, your perfume. I've never been so aware of a woman."

"Never?" She thought of the many she'd seen him with, though she knew she'd been out with a similar number of men and they'd meant nothing to her.

He raised his head. "Never, Savannah. This is the way it is for a man in love. You're in control of my destiny now. You're a goddess to me, but you're also terrifyingly mortal. I couldn't stand losing you."

"But what if…" She bit her lip as he moved, and his eyes gleamed with amusement and lust, as she struggled to get the words out, to meet his playful challenge. "What about in five years? When you know everything about me?"

He groaned, half chuckled as she tightened muscles on him, testing her own power. "How could any woman think that revealing herself to a man would destroy her mystery, her allure?" He bent, caught her lips, touched them with his tongue, spoke against her mouth. "Love has a million rooms to discover, sweetheart, and I'll spend the next ten lifetimes and not know everything about you. I'll only crave more."

Her body trembled on the precipice. In her mind, she saw the old couple again, the young parents, the gay couple soon to be parted by death. People bound together willingly, to share all the moments good and bad. Because that was what life was about. Not strategies and concessions, deals and coups. She saw her father's face, saw its coldness and lack of understanding. Saw it at the end, crumpled in pain, the shields that had kept him from the knowledge of love the only thing left intact.

What Matt offered might be Purgatory or Heaven, but she was willing to risk either to escape her cold, emotionless room in Hell.

"Enough talk," Matt whispered, and he began to move in her again. Long, slow strokes, one arm beneath her body, holding her to him so she felt him pressed all along the length of her, his thighs rubbing the inside of hers. She pressed her face into his neck, heard the rasp of his breath against her ear as he lifted and lowered his hips, and her hands crept down, felt his buttocks clench, release, clench, release with each slow pump into her. Her body trembled, swept by heat, and her breath began to match his rapid rhythm.

"Your pussy knows its Master, doesn't it, Savannah?"

"Yes...yes..." She couldn't hold her head up, dropped it back, and his mouth took her throat as she felt her hair brush her shoulder blades. God, he was so powerful, so all-consuming. *Ah, God...*

"Take me, Matt. Please make me yours, all yours."

His strokes grew stronger, his gaze more intent, never leaving the clasp of hers, and as the pleasure swept up through her, inhibitions left and she said the words he'd said she'd say, words she wanted to say, just as the climax began to break over her.

"I am yours, Master. You're my...Master..."

It was a swirling tornado of images and emotions and physical completion, all spinning her up into the relentless fist of the orgasm. His powerful body stroked her without breaking rhythm, nothing to stop the flow of a tidal wave up through her pussy and lower abdomen, spearing out through her limbs, making her clutch him even more tightly, cry out against his skin, seeing their bodies bathed in the flickering light of the muted television sets. The screens had picked up this moment, so she saw the two of them on the couch, the muscles rippling along his back, buttocks and thighs as her slender legs clamped around him, her fingers digging into his shoulders.

"Yes, baby. Let me hear you."

Her voice was a long, smooth utterance, like a wolf howling in low, urgent demand, her need for her mate calling him to her. Everything she longed for was in that one, prolonged note of desire. And as her hands tightened on him, Matt's body stiffened and then slammed forward into her urgently, over and over. His grip shifted to the couch arm so he did not shove her head into the arm with the force of his movements, his rapid pistoning into her, the hot spill of his seed inside her womb.

He had chosen not to use any protection, she realized, and that too was another statement of his claim on her. A very significant one.

He came to a gradual slow halt, keeping up slow strokes that made her mewl with pleasure, until at last he stilled, laid his forehead against hers. She reached up, cupped the back of his head in her hands, felt the damp line of perspiration on his nape.

Her heart was so full, she wanted to give him something, something he'd know she was giving to him, sealing her belief in his words, his desire for her.

"I read it last year."

Matt raised his head, looked down at her. He curled her in the crook of his arm, turned them so he was lying on his back and she was in the shelter of his arm on the wide couch. He touched her faintly smiling lips and she saw it coaxed a smile from his own. "What?"

"The Grinch. That's how I knew about the Who Mouses. I was Christmas shopping and there was a storytelling hour going on in the corner of the bookstore. I lingered in the shelves nearby and listened to it. So I guess I didn't technically read it. I heard it read."

She reached up, surrounded him with her arms and squeezed. A hug. A basic, wonderful hug he reacted to by closing his own arms around her and hugging her back.

With a groan, he hauled them both to a sitting position, moved her so she was cradled against his lap, her bottom against his wet cock, which stirred against her as he snugged her down on it.

"You're…" A faint blush rose in her cheeks.

"Getting hard for you again." He tipped her chin, held it so she looked directly into his piercing eyes. "I have so much need stored up for you, I'm probably going to have to close down the whole damn fortieth floor for a week to preserve your reputation while I keep you here, ravishing you over and over again."

She didn't know how to respond to that, but her body did. She saw by the intentness of his gaze that he registered the shudder that ran through her.

"So," he said lightly. "You'll marry me, then?"

"You're giving me choices, now?" She narrowed her eyes. "If I changed my mind, would you invite your team back in for a renegotiation?"

He laughed then, a male sound of appreciation that coated her with heat, and she pressed against him instinctively, making his eyes darken with renewed desire.

"From now on, I think we'll keep our negotiations strictly a two-person executive session. Kiss me. And for once, don't be afraid of anything."

She reached up, brought her lips to his and lost herself, and it was the easiest thing she'd ever done, to obey his command, now that she'd surrendered herself to him. She deepened it, played with his tongue, enjoyed the feel of his canines pricking. Shuddering at his growl, she whimpered in delight when he shifted his grip and put her under him once more, parting her legs and putting himself against the opening of her pussy, making it obvious that his cock was close to being able to take her again.

"Tell me what you want, Savannah." His voice was harsh with lust, but his eyes were asking for more. For everything.

Cleopatra couldn't ever give up being perceived as a woman of power. Be just a woman, and no man like Marc Antony or Matthew Kensington would want her.

That's what you think, Daddy.

Tennyson Rule Seven: Never be afraid to face your destiny.

"I want..." God, she suddenly wanted everything. "I want to live somewhere else. I want to have a yard, and...learn to garden. I want to have mismatching pictures."

His eyes told her he understood, which brought forth the thing she suddenly wanted the most. She pressed her face into his neck, her lips against his thudding pulse.

"I want to be your wife."

His arms tightened around her. "Those rules, the ones Geoffrey posted on the wall of his office that you haven't taken down? They come down tomorrow. From here on out, your life is governed only by one rule, the one I wouldn't tell you at the beginning, but that I've told you several times now. Do you know what it is?"

His lips were very close to hers, sending spirals of pleasure through her lower extremities, making everything tighten with need for him again. She opened herself to him further, felt his cock slide into her tender opening.

"That I'm yours," she whispered throatily. "Yours, forever and ever."

And you're mine as well.

"Close." He looked at her, his sensuous mouth serious and firm, and she wanted it on her again. "Rule One, the first and last rule you'll ever need, Savannah, to get through anything. Are you paying attention?"

"Yes," she said. But instead of letting him say the words, she spoke them first against his lips.

"I love you."

Also by Joey W. Hill

෨

Enchained (*Anthology*)
Forgotten Wishes (*Anthology*)
Holding The Cards
If Wishes Were Horses
Make Her Dreams Come True
Natural Law
Snow Angel
Virtual Reality

About the Author

❧

Joey W. Hill is published in mainstream, paranormal and erotic romance, as well as epic fantasy. Most of her erotic romance falls into the BDSM genre. She has won the Dream Realms Award for Fantasy and the EPPIE award for Erotic Romance. Nominated for the CAPA award and the PEARL, she also has received many gold star reviews from Just Erotic Romance Reviews, multiple Blue Ribbon reviews from Romance Junkies, and a Reviewer's Choice award from Road to Romance. She regularly garners five star reviews from erotic romance review sites. In 1999, she won the Grand Prize in the annual short story contest sponsored by Romance & Beyond magazine.

Following the dictates of a very capricious muse, she often brings in unexpected elements to a storyline – spirituality into erotic romance, paranormal aspects to a contemporary storyline, an alpha male who may believably perform as a submissive… all with intriguing and absorbing results for the reader. As one reviewer put it: "I should know by now that Ms. Hill doesn't write like anyone else." All of her erotic works emphasize strong, emotional characterization and the healing power of love through sexual expression.

Joey welcomes comments from readers. You can find her website and email address on her author bio page at www.ellorascave.com.

Tell Us What You Think
We appreciate hearing reader opinions about our books. You can email us at Comments@EllorasCave.com.

MARDI GRAS

Lacey Alexander

ଖ

Chapter One

స్రు

"Morning, sweet thing."

As the plate glass door fell shut behind her boss, Mia Sanderson looked up in time to see him whisk past her desk, into his office. She smiled too late, he was already gone. "Morning, Ty," she called after him anyway.

Oh well, it didn't matter. None of the other smiles she'd flashed his way over the past few years had suddenly seduced him, so she was reasonably certain today's wouldn't have held the magic ingredient, either.

If you only knew, she thought, peering lustily toward his office door. *If you only knew how badly I want you.* From his handsome face, his dimpled chin covered with just a bit of brown stubble, to the sandy blond hair that usually needed a trim but still looked perfect on him, to the well-built, slightly muscular body that looked as if it had been made to pleasure a woman—Ty Brewer was everything Mia desired in a man.

As for his daily endearment, sadly, he'd been calling her "sweet thing" since she was thirteen. He'd been a freshman at Tulane at the time, and he sometimes came home with her older brother, Tim, in the evening or on weekends. It didn't mean any more now than it had then—and hell, it had probably meant more *then*, now that she thought about it. At least then he'd seen something in her—something cute maybe, something worthy, something that had earned her a little playful flirtation despite the difference in their ages.

Now the nickname and the wink that sometimes came with it were both habits, she supposed. She was sure he had no idea how she gobbled up the silly, playful words every morning, or how his wink turned her lace panties wet. Ty was a friendly guy, teasing and flirtatious, especially with women he knew well. And given that he'd known Mia for—God!—eighteen years now, it only stood to reason he'd flirt a little.

Although the realization of just how long they'd been acquainted was sobering, making her slump in her desk chair. It wasn't as if they'd been in constant contact all that time, of course, but she *had* been working for Ty for five years now, which pretty much indicated that "sweet thing" meant...nothing. Because if she knew anything about Ty at all, it was that he didn't hesitate to go after what he wanted—in business or in pleasure. And he'd never gone after *her*.

Letting out a sigh, she peeked toward his door once more and began to imagine a different scenario. Her breasts felt heavy and her pussy slightly swollen as she envisioned herself being a much bolder sort of woman...

"Morning, sweet thing."

She flashed him a sexy smile, then reached out, curling one finger toward her in a motion that summoned him closer. "Come here. I have something to show you." In the fantasy, the words left her in a silky, sassy tone she'd never really used and didn't know if she even possessed.

Rounding the front counter and the desk situated behind it, Ty gave his head a playful tilt that said he was intrigued.

She stood up, revealing a short skirt and a black see-through blouse with a lacy bra underneath. Not that she would ever wear anything like that to work—if she even owned it—but this was a fantasy, so she pressed on.

"Nice," he said of the outfit, raking his gaze from her shoulders to her knees.

"Thanks, but that's not what I need to show you."

He raised his sandy-colored eyebrows in anticipation. "I'm all eyes, sweet thing. What have you got for me?"

She gave a teasing pout and glanced downward. "I hope you won't be upset."

"Well, let's find out."

Reaching down, she hooked one finger into the slit on the skirt and drew it slowly upward until her pussy was on display. "I forgot to put on my panties this morning. Very unprofessional of me. I hope you aren't angry."

When she lifted her gaze back to his, fresh heat burned in his eyes. Her nipples turned to tiny bullets against her bra.

"Not angry," Ty said, a slow, sexy grin growing on his face. "But there are consequences for girls who forget their undies when going to work."

She lifted one fingernail to her lip in faux worry. "What are they?"

"Well," he said, his voice going lower as he stepped up to slide his hands smoothly over her hips, "it's a known fact that if you forget your panties, your boss is going to fuck you."

Mia bit her lip, her body flushing with warmth. Glancing down, she could even see the reaction to her hot fantasy—her nipples had hardened not only in her imagination, but also in reality, now jutting through her bra and fitted yellow blouse.

She glanced again toward Ty's office. *Do you ever notice them? Do you know they're like that for you?* Then she sighed. *Or does it only make you think I'm chilled, despite that we live in one of the hottest cities in the country?*

She shook her head, then decided there was no reason not to sink back into her fantasy, especially since she'd just gotten to the good part.

"Kiss me," she said.

No. That was too tame. It was fine for the more romantic daydreams she sometimes indulged in, but today's imaginings were all about heat, so she changed it to *"Fuck me."*

Then she eased her ass onto her desk, parting her legs for him to step in between. As he worked to undo the buttons on her thin blouse, she reached for the snap on his jeans.

God, she *loved* it when Ty wore jeans. He ran a totally casual workplace, and most days found him in long, baggy shorts, but colder winter weather often brought out his blue jeans, and fortunately, the air outside was brisk today. She'd noticed the worn denim even in just the short glimpse of him she'd caught. She adored the way they molded lightly to his butt, and in front, to his sexy bulge. And speaking of sexy bulges...

Bending to kiss her, he pushed her blouse open, then lowered her bra straps from her shoulders so that the lace cups drooped enough for her breasts to tumble free. As he closed his hands over them, she finally got his jeans unzipped and spread wide, reaching in to pull out his big, hard cock.

"Oh, fuck me, Ty," she said again, more urgently this time. Then she shared the truth with him. *"I've wanted this for so long."*

His smile was warm, happily surprised. "Well, why didn't you say so, baby?"

Grabbing onto her ass, he curled his hands around her flesh, firm and sure, and drove his stiff shaft into her – wonderfully deep.

"Mmm," she purred without quite meaning to.

"You say something, Mia?" Ty's voice sounded from within his office.

She flinched. "Um, no. Just...talking to myself."

Ty chuckled softly at her—that was the easy sort of relationship they had—then the office fell quiet again...

And he was in her again. Thrusting in smooth strokes, each one packed with pleasure. Mia closed her eyes. *She was unbuttoning his shirt, running her hands over his chest, then pressing her bared, sensitive breasts warm against him.*

"You feel so good, baby," he was murmuring in her ear, low and sweet. "Why haven't we been doing this all along?"

"I don't know," she whispered up to him, *"but it was definitely worth the wait."*

"I want to make you come," he said, sliding his hands further around her ass and lifting her up off the desk. *"I want to make you scream for me, sweet thing."*

And, of course, he knew exactly the right angle at which to hold her and exactly when to slow his thrusts as she writhed against him, approaching climax. "Soon, lover," *she cooed.* "Very soon."

"Now," *he demanded so harshly it stunned her — and set her skin to tingling in a whole new way as he stared into her eyes, insisting on her orgasm.*

Oh yes, she could feel it gathering, getting closer and closer, climbing higher, higher, escalated by his rough command, and by his eyes, his sexy, sexy eyes, until — "Oh!" *she cried out as it overcame her — the hot, almost violent spasms of release rushed through her like a river of fire, and she bucked against him, riding it out, as he murmured,* "That's right, baby, that's right. Keep coming. You're coming so good for me, sweet thing, so fucking good."

The trill of the phone sent her leaping from her seat as if someone had just stuck a tack in her butt. "Jeez!" she squealed, then pulled herself together and snatched up the receiver. "Bourbon Street Messengers."

"Hey Mia, it's Brad. Is Ty in yet?"

Their tax guy. It was that time of year. "Sure. Hang on." She pushed the hold button, then called, "Ty — Brad on one."

She could feel Ty's grin as he said, "Uh, you okay out there?"

"Fine, thanks," she lied, cheerful but short. She was sweating profusely from the fantasy, and from the shock of being jarred back to reality.

Then came his familiar chuckle. "After five years of answering the phones here, I wouldn't think it would scare you so much."

And after five years of me mooning at you constantly, I'd think you'd notice by now.

But then again, maybe he *had* noticed, and just wasn't interested. She was Tim's little sister, after all, and she was pretty sure Ty wouldn't ever think of her in any other way. Which meant all her sweating was for naught.

Even now, she couldn't help recalling instances of his brotherly affection. Although he had no qualms about dating every wild woman in their wild city, he was always quick to give his opinion if he thought *she* was dating someone who wasn't good enough for her, or who "seems a little rough for you, sweet thing", or "has one too many tattoos, if you ask me".

It always made her laugh, precisely because everyone knew Ty was no angel, yet he assumed *she* was, and he seemed to like her that way.

But those rough guys with tattoos, it turned out, were more her type than she'd even known, and they'd taught her quite a bit about fun, and sex. She might not own a see-through blouse, and she might not have ever left her apartment without panties, but on the inside, she definitely hovered on the edge of being a bad girl.

Ty would never believe it, of course. He'd probably have a heart attack if he found out. The truth was, she supposed, that they'd just known each other too long. He had certain ideas about who she was, what she was about—ideas that had been true for a very long time—but what he didn't realize was that she'd grown up. For God's sake, she was thirty-one years old.

Yet Ty, she knew, still saw the silly, playful teenager she'd once been, the girl who was good for some laughs and a little harmless flirtation. And she guessed he also now saw her as a competent receptionist and accountant—she was pretty much his Girl Friday at the bicycle messenger service situated in the heart of the French Quarter, where bike traffic often moved a lot quicker than vehicles. But when it came to sex, she was certain he thought she was a much nicer girl than she actually was, not to mention a much nicer girl than she wanted to be. And that was definitely her loss.

Just then, the front door opened again, admitting Ty's best friend, Jack Wade. Jack ran a P.I. business just a couple of blocks away. "Hey there, Mia."

"Hey," she returned with a smile. She'd known Jack nearly as long as Ty, since they'd both hung out with Tim back in college. Jack's dark good looks complemented Ty's sandy beach boy image perfectly. She'd even heard rumors among common friends that Jack's recent bride, Liz, had let the two guys share her one night early in their relationship. The very thought made Mia's pussy hum with desire.

"He in?" Jack pointed toward Ty's office.

"On the phone," she said, "but he shouldn't be long."

Jack lifted his elbows to the counter and leaned over. "Well, while I'm waitin', I can tell *you* what I came to tell *him*. Liz and I are ringin' in Mardi Gras with a big party Saturday night, and you're invited. You bring the mask and the beads, we'll provide the jambalaya and the alcohol. Think you can make it?"

A party at Jack's place? Where Ty would almost certainly be in attendance? It wasn't the first such occasion—Jack liked to throw parties from time to time—but even knowing nothing new would transpire between her and her sexy boss, it was still an invitation Mia couldn't resist.

She smiled up at Jack. "Sure. Sounds fun. What time?"

"Starts at eight." He grinned down at her. "Liz'll be glad you're comin'—she thinks you're sweet."

Mia resisted the urge to roll her eyes. Even Jack's wife—who by all accounts had been a prim and proper lady before meeting him—thought she was sweet? She was doomed. But she forced a smile. "It'll be nice to get to know her a little better."

Just then, they both heard Ty hang up the phone, so Jack made his way into the office.

"Well, if it isn't the old married man come to pay me a visit," Ty greeted him with a laugh, and Mia decided it was time she do something constructive—for the first time so far today.

Rising from her desk, she tried to ignore the slight swell of her cunt as she leaned in the office door. "Ty—Dan and Annie are out on early runs, but Bobby's not here yet and there's a delivery due at Jackson Square by ten. Since it's quiet, I'm going to walk it down there before it's late."

Her boss nodded. "Thanks for taking up the slack for him, sweet thing. You're the best," he concluded with a wink, and as usual, her pussy surged.

* * * * *

"*You* ever think about settlin' down, gettin' married?" Jack asked in response to Ty's greeting.

Ty drew back with a slight laugh. Up until a year or so ago, that question wouldn't even have appeared on Jack's radar screen. But marriage had changed his best friend—at least in some ways. "Me?" he asked. "No way, compadre."

"Come on now, *ami*, it's not like I got the plague or somethin'. In fact, you well *know* what I got—a beautiful, sensual woman who loves to fuck as much as I do. Not exactly a life sentence or anything."

Oh yeah, Ty knew what Jack had in Liz, all right. And if *he* could find a girl like Liz—well, who knew, maybe the "M" word wouldn't sound so terrible. But as it was, he just didn't think it was in the cards for him.

"Besides, you're gettin' just as old—just as fast—as me," Jack added.

True enough. He'd just turned thirty-six. Hard to believe, given that his libido felt like it belonged to a kid of nineteen, but he knew his mother and sisters back home in Michigan had just about given up on getting him married off. Which was just as well, the way he saw it. "You know how it is with me and women," Ty replied.

Jack leaned back slightly, quirking a grin. "No, *ami*—how exactly is it?"

Ty put his feet up on his desk, stretching out as well. "I know a lot of women who like to fuck and who do it damn well. But I've yet to meet one who…" How to explain? "…has anything more to offer."

Jack blinked. "Not sure what you mean."

"Just that I never have any trouble connecting with chicks *sexually*, but in my experience, girls who like to party aren't girls who make me feel…well, anything more than a stiff dick."

Jack tilted his head. "I thought that once, too, but then Liz walked through my door and changed everything. Just takes findin' the right one is all."

Ty gave his head a shake. "You got lucky, but that doesn't mean there's a Liz for every guy. The girls I meet are either a hundred percent cute and sweet, or a hundred percent down and dirty. I can't live without the down and dirty, so I *have* to live without the cute and sweet."

"Quite a sacrifice," Jack quipped.

Ty flashed a light smirk. "Believe it or not, the lack of substance gets a little old."

This time, Jack let out a hearty laugh. "You're so full of shit. You forget, I was exactly where you are until a year ago. Findin' the right woman is the greatest thing on earth, but either way, you can't tell me hot sex gets old."

"Maybe I'm just reaching a point you never reached," Ty suggested. He shook his head, half laughing at himself along with Jack, but still trying to figure out what he was attempting to convey. "I'm just…kinda bored lately, I guess. I mean, it's same old, same old after a while. Different girl, same experience."

"What exactly is it you're not gettin' that you want so bad?"

Ty lowered his feet back to the old hardwood floors beneath him and cocked a slight smile toward his friend. Given the direction the conversation had taken, he was glad

Mia had stepped out for a few minutes so he could speak freely. "Have you ever been...tied up by a woman?"

Another chuckle echoed toward the ceiling, an easy grin gracing Jack's face. "Sure. Liz and I play around with that sorta thing sometimes. We play around with *everything*."

"Does it get you off?"

Jack flashed an *are-you-serious?* look. "It's *Liz*. Everything Liz does gets me off."

"What if it were somebody else?"

"Who knows. Can't say."

Ty leaned back in his chair once more. "I guess I've just been thinking about that kind of stuff. Believe it or not, I've never been with a woman who was into the bondage thing, and I suppose I'm looking for something new to keep sex interesting."

Jack sat up a little straighter in his chair. "Well, you know, there *are* bars you can go to, places to meet women who are into that."

He nodded uncertainly. "I know. But I'm not sure I'm into the whole gagging, nipple-clamping thing. Nothing hardcore. I just wanna...you know...experiment a little."

"Sounds like you need a wife, *ami*," Jack said on a chuckle.

"What?"

"Get yourself a wife and you can experiment with anything you want."

But Ty shook his head. "No, get myself a wife like *Liz* and I could do that. But I don't think *all* wives are that accommodating."

And the truth was, Ty had been dating strictly naughty, sexy girls for so long—he didn't even know what he would look for if he were able to switch his attentions to sweet girls. That perfect combination Jack had found in Liz...well, he figured that was once in a lifetime, that she was one of a kind.

And besides, sweet girls and him? It just didn't add up.

Take Mia, for instance. She was about as sweet as they came, and he loved hanging out with her, working with her, bumping into her at a bar or a party, but when it came time for intimacy, well...he was just too accustomed to hot, wild sex to want to give it up, and any good girl worth her salt would probably faint if he said he wanted her to tie him up and fuck his brains out.

"Speaking of Liz," Jack said, "that sort of leads to why I stopped by."

His voice drew Ty back to the conversation. "Oh?"

"My lovely wife and I are throwin' a party Saturday night to kick off Mardi Gras. Eight o'clock. The usual suspects, plus some people from Liz's office."

"Did you invite Mia?"

Jack nodded. "Of course. Why?"

He shrugged. "She's fun to hang out with."

Jack gave his head a speculative tilt, and Ty could almost read his thoughts before he spoke them aloud. "Now that's who you oughta ask out. Mia's a sweetheart."

Ty simply laughed. "Are you deaf, Jack? I just told you, sweet girls and me are like oil and water. It would never work. And besides, she's Tim's little sister. I've known her since she was a little girl. It wouldn't feel right if we got anywhere even *close* to sex. Not to mention that she's a great employee and I wouldn't want to risk fucking up our working relationship."

Jack sighed. "Well then, maybe you'll get lucky and hook up with somebody else at our little *fete*."

"Does Liz have any hot girlfriends who like to play with whips and chains?"

Jack grinned. "That you'll have to find that out for yourself, my *bon ami*."

* * * * *

Mia stood frozen in place at her desk. When she'd returned to the office for her purse, Ty and Jack had been laughing about something and hadn't heard her come in.

They very *clearly* hadn't heard her.

Because they were talking about *fucking*, and being *tied up*. Her entire body had sizzled with shock…and arousal.

The conversation she'd overheard had certainly confirmed *one* thing. Ty had no interest in her whatsoever as a lover. As she'd suspected, he just didn't think of her that way—apparently *couldn't* think of her that way.

The part that really caught her attention, though, was when he'd told Jack he wanted to be tied up. Her blood ran hot just envisioning Ty, naked and bound, at her mercy. Until this moment, she hadn't been aware that she wanted to experiment with bondage, either, but the heavy pulsing of her pussy said she did.

As she stood there, quiet, purse in hand, not quite sure what to do next—or how to sneak back out without them hearing the door—an idea flashed in her mind. A really *naughty* idea.

Could she, the infamously sweet Mia, ever pull off such a thing?

If she wanted to try, it would take some work.

First, she'd have to hit her favorite craft store down on Royal—they stocked tons of great glitter and feathers this time of year. And as luck would have it, her latest craft project was making Mardi Gras masks. It had started as a way to help her fifth-grade niece with an art assignment for school, but now she suddenly realized the craft could have a much more personal—and satisfying—benefit. She'd have to do some other shopping, too, of course, but if she was seriously considering this, maybe she should start by making a special mask and letting that be her guide.

To her shock, the longer she stood there, the more concrete the idea became. Turning into something she would definitely do, something she *had* to do, in fact.

Because Ty had confirmed her suspicions. He thought women were either nice girls or naughty ones, with no in between. It was a shame, but not a surprise. She was crazy about Ty, but he was sometimes a very typical guy's guy. Clearly Jack had been enlightened by Liz, yet Ty remained in the dark.

She knew now that Ty would never see her as anything but a good girl. And the truth was—given how long they'd known each other, and that he still kept in touch with her brother in New York, and that he seemed to like and even *value* her sweetness—she just didn't think she could ever bear to disillusion him and risk his high opinion of her.

But now that she understood all that—and knew that, sadly, nothing romantic would ever take place between her and the object of her affection—she was going to give herself a really big gift this Mardi Gras season.

She was going to have Ty, once and for all.

He just wouldn't quite realize it.

She felt a wicked little grin unfurl across her face, anticipating her plan.

"Well, I'd better get back to work. My cases aren't gonna solve themselves," Jack said, giving Mia just enough time to duck down behind her desk as he exited Ty's office.

"Hey, you making your world-famous jambalaya Saturday?" Ty called behind him.

"Wouldn't be a party without it, *ami*," Jack said. "See ya then."

"Okay, dude. Later."

Trying her best to think fast as Jack pushed through the door, admitting a *whoosh* of chilly air and the vague sounds of traffic and a honking horn somewhere in the distance, Mia popped up from behind the desk, let out a sigh, then slammed a desk drawer.

A few seconds later, Ty leaned through the doorway. "Mia? When did you get back?"

"Just now. Passed Jack on the way in—he held the door for me." *Which is why you only heard it open once.* "Forgot my purse," she added, holding it up. "See?"

He looked puzzled. "I...didn't hear you say anything to Jack."

She blinked. "We...exchanged nods."

"Exchanged nods?" He was looking at her as if she might belong in a mental ward.

"Yeah," she said, dropping her gaze to her purse and the two small packages in her arms. "Gotta go. Don't want these to be late," she said, then rushed past him and out the door onto Bourbon, where she finally breathed a sigh of relief. Sheesh, that had been close.

But she couldn't be sorry it had happened.

Because of what she'd just overheard, she was going to make her dreams come true. Well, not *all* of her dreams—there wouldn't be a wedding, or a honeymoon, or two-point-five children and a dog with Ty. But she was going to make her *sexual* dreams come true, and in the process, she was going to give Ty a night he'd never forget.

Chapter Two

§๑

Mia's skin prickled as she stood before the floor-length mirror in her bedroom.

Her plan had worked even better than she'd hoped or imagined. If she didn't know she was looking at her own reflection, she'd never have recognized herself.

She'd hidden her pale brown hair beneath an auburn wig of long curling locks, and she'd disguised her blue eyes behind contact lenses of forest green. She'd applied her makeup much heavier than usual, highlighting her eyes with lots of liner and mascara, and accentuating her lips with a warm shade of red.

She didn't think Ty would recognize her from the neck down, either. She might not have owned any sexy, see-through clothing before, but one daring shopping trip had changed that. As in her fantasy the other day, she donned a lacy black bra under a transparent black blouse. Below, her black mini possessed every element from the fantasy except the sexy slit. And under *that*... She felt positively sinful in the black lace thong and matching garter belt that attached to black, lace-edged stockings.

Reaching to the dresser beside her, she snatched up two long strands of onyx beads and slipped them over her head. She doubled them, pulling down until one loop chokered her neck and the other draped her breasts.

To top things off, she added the *pièce de résistance* — sliding a lush, sexy mask of black and silver on, so that only the vibrant green of her eyes shone through. Two thick, downy feathers jutted provocatively from one side of the glittery black mask, its edges lined in sparkling silver cord. Three silver sequins highlighted the outer point of each eye.

"You are a sex kitten, baby," she said to her reflection in the slightly lower voice she'd been practicing, making sure to enunciate her words more than usual. "And Ty will never know it's you."

* * * * *

As Mia strolled up the old sidewalk at what was usually the quiet end of Bourbon Street, music and voices drowned out the click of her high heels. Clearly, Jack and Liz weren't the only people throwing a party tonight, as the scents of spicy food and hot grills filled the air. Rock, jazz, and Zydeco vied for sound supremacy, along with the notes of a lone saxophone being played somewhere in the distance.

She passed two young boys with taps attached to the bottoms of their tennis shoes, dancing for tips, and a court jester on stilts walked along as if he were any other person headed out for a night of debauchery on Bourbon. Her gaze was drawn to the opposite sidewalk, where two girls were lifting their tank tops, flashing their breasts for beads. The group of guys surrounding them whistled, adding comments like, "Nice, baby," as they surrendered the shiny necklaces. Judging from how heavily laden the girls' necks were, they'd already been very busy tonight.

Mia's pussy swelled a little more with each step she took. Not only due to the sensual sights around her, but because beneath her sexy clothes, her lace lingerie hugged her tight, and her garters rubbed against her thighs and ass with every move. And despite all the color and people and breasts to behold on the street, more than one set of male eyes had perused *her*, as well, adding to how sexy she felt.

"Want some beads, darlin'?" a man in a cowboy hat asked as she approached him on the sidewalk. He stared hungrily at her chest, but she didn't mind—he was handsome, in his mid-thirties, and she was so on fire that the suggestion only added fuel to her flames.

"No, but thank you," she said with a smile in her new lower, more sophisticated voice.

Every balcony along the historic street was strung with streamers or beads of purple, gold, and green, and most were filled with partiers. Every balcony she noticed, looking up, except one. The sight brought a sinful smile to her face.

The quiet, dark, wrought iron balcony she spied was less than a block from Jack's place, and the apartment attached to it belonged to her Aunt Sophie. Her aunt—the sort of chic, refined woman she hoped to be by the time she reached her fifties—was a jewelry collector and the proprietor of a pricey store on St. Peter, which she made a habit of closing during the few weeks preceding Mardi Gras. It was too loud and crazy for her taste, both at work and at home, she always said, so she used the time to head to the Caribbean with her longtime lover, Morris, every year.

And she always invited Mia to use the apartment while she was gone, given its prime location on Bourbon, but since Mia's own apartment was only a couple of blocks away on St. Phillip, she'd never taken her up on the offer—until now.

Get ready, Ty, because here I come.

Straightening her shoulders and pushing out her chest, she walked tall and proud up the street and through the archway that led to Jack's apartment. Disguised as she was, she thought she should have been nervous, but instead, she felt more confident—and more sexy—than ever before. It was as if the mask and the wig gave her some sort of permission to do all the things she wanted with Ty, without any worries. No worries about it changing his opinion of her. No worries of it messing up their relationship or her job. The only thing worrying her at the moment was wondering how she'd stand the wait until she could get his clothes off and have her way with him.

She'd waited until after ten to arrive, and as she'd hoped, the party appeared to be in full swing. As she climbed the outdoor stairs to Jack and Liz's place, she found partiers—

some masked, some not—who had stepped outside to smoke. Jaunty Cajun music came from inside the door that stood wide open. Leave it to the Cajuns, she thought, to make the accordion sound sexy.

She couldn't have been more pleased to step casually through the door to find a large crowd in a low-lit room. Some people were decked out in Mardi Gras regalia of the obligatory purple, gold, and green, while others chose regular everyday clothing. She blended in perfectly, without even trying.

Much of the crowd stood back around the edges of the room, forming a circle around Jack and Liz, who performed a sexy version of the two-step. Mia had never seen Jack look at any woman the way he always looked at Liz—like she lit up his life.

Some of the guests moved to the music themselves, but it was clear this dance belonged to the host and hostess. Liz smiled into her husband's eyes, and Mia could see the sparkle in her gaze, even through the red mask she wore. She wasn't sure she'd ever seen two people more into each other.

God, I want that with Ty.

She flinched when she realized what she'd just allowed herself to think.

Because she couldn't *have* that with Ty. What she *could* have with Ty was hot sex. And friendship. Independent of one another. And that was all.

When the sizzling Cajun song came to an end, the crowd gave a smattering of applause, and Ty suddenly appeared, stepping up to slap Jack lightly on the back. "You almost make him look like a good dancer," he said to Liz with a laugh.

"Whoa there, *ami*, I'm the one who's been doin' the teachin' here."

When Ty raised his eyebrows, Liz replied, "It's true. Jack's been taking me out to a place on the bayou for barbeque and two-stepping every Friday night for the past couple of months."

"Gotta get some Cajun in her soul," Jack added with a grin.

"I'll just take some Cajun in my arms instead," his wife said, pulling him into a steamy embrace Mia envied.

But stop envying Liz and Jack. In fact, stop thinking. And start getting into your game.

Fortunately, watching Ty from across the room made that easy. Since spotting him, everything inside her had tightened with excitement, and with the knowledge that tonight she would finally have him. Her cunt went wet remembering what she'd come here to do.

It was high time she slake her lust with this man, once and for all.

* * * * *

Ty checked his watch for the fifth time in the last hour. Where was Mia?

Not that it really mattered, but she'd said she'd be here, and she was usually punctual, and it worried him if she didn't show up someplace she was supposed to. He'd known her for so long, he just kind of liked to look out for her when he could. As a favor to Tim, and because she was a friend, he told himself. That was all.

As Liz passed by, a few empty plates in her grasp, he lowered a hand to her arm. "Have you seen Mia?"

She shook her head. "Now that you mention it, no. But Jack said she was coming."

He gave a slight nod, then let Liz go on her way.

Yet he couldn't stop a wayward pang of envy for his best friend. Liz had it all. In fact, he'd gotten the opportunity to get a taste of Liz in bed back when she and Jack had first met—they'd wanted to experiment with a threesome, and who was he to stand in the way? Fortunately, things had never been awkward after that. He'd understood it was a one-time experience and from that point on, he'd been happy to get to know Liz as a friend and Jack's future wife. But as he'd implied to Jack earlier in the week, he often found himself wondering how Jack had gotten so lucky to have his soulmate walk right into his life when he wasn't even *looking* for anything like that.

Hell, maybe he did want to settle down. If not, then why was he so jealous of Jack's happiness lately?

He was having stupid thoughts, that was all. And if he was smart, he'd quit dwelling on those stupid thoughts and do what he'd planned to do at this party—find some lovely, wild woman who wanted to cut loose and have some Mardi Gras fun.

It was at that precise moment he saw the lady across the room. Even behind her mask, he felt her watching him.

A redhead with a smokin' body. They made eye contact and she slowly licked her upper lip. Sexy as hell.

As he felt the first hint of a reaction in his cock, he decided that maybe his wish was coming true—the redhead must be a friend of Liz's and she looked *exactly* like a woman who wanted to get together and get naked.

If his experience held, they'd have a good night or two— or five, or ten—of sex, and then it would be over, but that was okay. Despite his brief moments of wife-envy, he'd pretty much accepted that having sex without romance was just part of how his life worked. And if he'd needed a sign to prove it, the sexy lady in black and silver was it.

Even now, with her gaze intent upon him from behind that alluring mask, she dipped her finger into her glass of wine, then sensually slid it into her mouth, sucking it dry. His chest went warm and his groin tightened further. *Very nice, baby*, he thought, and hoped like hell she could read the response in his eyes.

Just then, someone bumped into her—a guy, someone else Ty didn't know. The dark-haired corporate type began talking to her, making her smile, and an unbelievable, and unreasonable, ire rose inside him at having their silent flirtation interrupted. It made his cock go even harder, made him want her even more, feeling as if Mr. Clean Cut over there had just invaded his territory.

Just as he was contemplating walking over and finding some way to stake his claim without seeming like a madman, the guy moved on. Looking after him, the lady in the mask switched her glass from one hand to the other, and in the process dropped her cocktail napkin. It fluttered to the floor at her feet.

To Ty's surprise, she cast a quick glance in his direction. To make sure he was still watching her?

Then she turned away from him and bent over at the waist, going down, down, making her skirt rise so far in the back—past the sexy, lacy tops of her stockings and well up onto black garters stretched tight—that he stood waiting to catch a glimpse of the mound between her thighs. The skirt didn't quite go *that* far, but by the time she retrieved the napkin and stood back up, he was so stiff it almost hurt.

Just then, a piece of silverware tapped against a wineglass, and the buzz of voices filling the room went quiet, leaving only a slow Cajun waltz in its place. "There's plenty more jambalaya in the kitchen for anyone who wants it," Liz announced.

Standing beside her, Jack added, "And if you're ready for dessert, we've got fresh beignets and, even though it's a little late in the season, a great big king cake."

"Never too late for king cake!" someone yelled in a heavy Louisiana drawl.

Traditionally, the king cake was supposed to be served on January sixth, the *epiphane* and official start of the Mardi Gras season. A plastic baby, to symbolize the new year, was baked into the cake, and whoever got the piece with the baby had to host the next *soiree*. But, tradition aside, king cake was a pretty common treat right up through Fat Tuesday—it wouldn't be a Mardi Gras party without one.

Turning his attention back to the hot redhead, Ty found she'd left her spot to move toward the dessert table. He decided to hang back and avoid the crowd for the moment—he'd approach her when there weren't so many people around her.

Looked like she'd volunteered to help hand out the cake as Liz cut it—he watched as she picked up two purple paper plates topped with cake and took a few steps into the room until two partygoers relieved her of them. The same scenario repeated three times until it hit him that he was totally caught up in staring at her. But he couldn't help it. He was getting intoxicated by her lush cleavage and that sexy see-through blouse, and her black strappy heels were so hot he thought he might like to feel one of them digging slightly into his back. *Oh yeah.*

Just then she grabbed up another slice of cake and started weaving through the crowd until she reached…him. She held up the plate with a come-hither smile. "Hungry?" she asked in a low, drop-dead sexy voice.

He felt the question in his cock. "Very," he replied, peering down into warm green eyes.

"Enjoy," she said as he accepted the cake, then she turned and sauntered away, the sway of her hips entrancing.

As Ty bit into the sugary-sweet confection, he found himself thinking, *Hell, who needs a meaningful relationship when you've got this—a super-hot woman ready for what promises to be a fun night ahead.*

That was when he realized he was chewing…paper.

Reaching into his mouth, he drew out a tiny slip of crumpled yellow paper. It said in sharp black letters, *Want to fuck?*

His cock threatened to burst from behind his zipper at any second. He lifted his gaze to find the redhead back across the room, still handing out cake. Lowering his plate to the nearest table, he made a beeline for her.

As she bent to scoop up two more plates from the dessert table, he leaned in close behind her, letting his body graze hers from the waist down.

She flinched lightly, but didn't move away—only straightened and turned to look over her shoulder.

"Yes," he breathed low in her ear. "And I want to do it hard."

Maybe he shouldn't have been a hundred percent certain *she'd* sent the note, but he was. He just knew—without a shred of doubt. He moved half an inch closer, so she'd feel his hard-on pressing into the crack of her ass.

Setting the plates back down, she turned, handily extricating herself from between him and the table, and grabbed his hand. "Follow me."

Just the touch of her fingers added to his heat as she led him across the floor, around a corner, and into the bathroom, currently candlelit. He shut the wooden door firmly behind him and spun to look at her.

Her eyes blazed with the same fire that burned hot in his veins, and her ample chest heaved slightly, begging for his touch. A pouty mouth painted with dark lipstick made her look all the more like a mysterious piece of forbidden fruit. And he was ready to take a bite.

They stepped toward each other at the same time, moving into each other's arms. His settled around her waist and hers circled his neck. "What's your name?" he asked, his mouth hovering an inch above hers.

She hesitated slightly, then licked her upper lip. "Mina."

"Nice to meet you, Mina. I'm Ty," he said, then lowered a kiss onto that dark, sexy mouth.

She responded with eager pressure, hungry and willing, just the way he wanted her. She tasted sweet, like the cake he'd just eaten, as he eased his tongue between her lips. Her breasts pressed firm against his chest and his cock molded perfectly with the indented slit he could feel beneath her skirt.

Her skin was warm to the touch, and her movements against him filled him with longing. Damn, he couldn't remember a time when he'd gotten this hot this fast. He'd wanted her badly enough before, back out in the crowded room, but his desire had skyrocketed since stepping behind a closed door with her.

Her tongue circled his in kisses that grew slower, but more heated. He could hear them both breathing heavily as his hands roamed her back and she ran her fingers through his hair. When he drew one hand around to her breast, it was like heaven and sin colliding in the palm of his hand. The feel of her lush flesh, even through her blouse and bra, made him thrust at the soft spot between her thighs, the move almost involuntary.

She moaned when he raked his thumb across the hardened nipple he could feel through the thin blouse and the lace underneath.

"Want your breast in my mouth," he breathed as her lips left his, venturing downward. He leaned his head back as she rained kisses across his neck and onto the top of his chest through the "v" in his shirt.

"Mmm, I want my *pussy* in your mouth," she purred between kisses.

He groaned. What a dirty girl. He was wild about her already.

When she raised her gaze, drawing her splayed fingers down his chest, he reached to take off her mask. He wasn't sure why—he hadn't even planned it. He guessed he just wanted to see her better—this hot, sexy woman who was kissing him senseless. He wanted to see who he was about to fuck.

Biting her lip, she stopped him, holding the mask in place. "No."

He didn't argue. Instead he went for the next best thing, the button between her breasts. Flicking it open and reaching inside, he curved his fingers around the lace cup of her dangerously low-cut bra.

She let out a sexy sigh at his light, sensual kneading, but quickly pulled his hand away, grabbing both of his wrists to keep him from going further. "No," she said, firmer this time.

He didn't know what to think. Even as she held his wrists at his sides, he leaned down to rake a hot kiss across her lush mouth. "I thought you wanted me to fuck you," he said, his voice coming out raspy. "Did I do something wrong?"

She shook her head, her eyes just as passion-filled as before. "But I don't want to hurry, baby. I want to make the pleasure *last.*"

Something about the way she said it heightened his lust, straining his zipper even more than it already was. He leaned his forehead against hers, delivering one, two more small kisses designed to entice. "What did you have in mind?"

She let go of his wrists and flashed a hint of a sexy smile. "Follow me."

She was already reaching around him for the doorknob when he grinned and said, "Didn't we already do this part?"

"This was just warm-up, lover," she said in that husky voice that made him lust harder. Opening the door, she glanced over her shoulder at him, that sexy, concealing mask still framing her eyes with dark glitter. "For what I want to do to you, you'll have to take your chances and see where I lead you. Are you coming?"

Placing his hands on her shoulders, he leaned down to whisper in her ear as a guy moved past them into the newly vacated bathroom. "You haven't made me come just yet, but I have a feeling you will."

He felt the words travel through her in the sexy stretch of her shoulders, the forward thrust of her breasts.

"I'll go wherever you want me to, honey," he added. "Just lead the way."

* * * * *

Mia's skin tingled with heat by the time she led Ty up Bourbon Street toward her aunt's apartment. The mood outside only added to her excitement. People milled about, girls were still flashing for beads, and a party atmosphere permeated the warmer-than-average February night.

She was still quaking over the name she'd told him— Mina. She'd feared she'd given herself away even as it left her lips, but he'd seemed to accept it without thought. Thank God she'd never told him Mia was short for Mina, which was short for Wilhelmina—a great-grandmother on her father's side. Apparently, Tim had never had occasion to mention that little bit of trivia to Ty, either, for which she was now eternally grateful.

She'd also nearly fainted when he'd tried to take off her mask. Thank goodness he hadn't persisted. Everything depended on keeping her sexy mask *on*, and her face hidden.

She didn't look back at him as she walked—she didn't dare. She was too amazed that this was really happening, really working. She'd been confident, but maybe she hadn't been truly *prepared* for how it would feel to have his hands on her, his mouth on hers. To finally kiss the much-lusted-after Ty had been at once magical and the most natural thing on earth. He kissed exactly like she'd imagined, with a soft, insistent heat and a slow urgency that could drive a woman insane. She'd almost thought she could come just from kissing him. And when his perfect and delightfully large hard-on had pressed into her—mmm, her cunt had nearly melted from the flames he'd ignited there.

Now her anxious pussy hummed with desire. But she had a long way to go before she'd actually have him, his cock, inside her. She had plans for her man. Plans for an evening he'd always remember.

Chapter Three

❧

She drew him across the street and through a group of twenty-something guys, aware they were staring, aware that her blouse remained unbuttoned past her bra. She decided she must be an even naughtier girl than she realized, since she didn't mind being displayed for them, didn't mind that it was probably very clear she was about to seduce the man following behind her.

Leading Ty through a wrought iron gate, she climbed the stairs to Aunt Sophie's second-floor apartment. She couldn't help wondering if her ass was in his face with each step she took, and if perhaps he was tempted to reach out and push up her skirt, and go after her right here and now. If he did, she wasn't sure she'd have the will to stop him.

But you have to stick to your plan, she reminded herself. *If you want to give him a night to remember, you have to take it slow and do it right – get him where you want him. Get him where he wants to be, too.*

When they arrived on the landing, she reached into her bra, sliding her fingers across the soft lower curve of her left breast, and pulled out the key.

Raising her gaze, she found he'd been watching.

"That's damn sexy," he said in a low, pointed tone.

She replied in her super-sophisticated voice. "I like to travel light."

He grinned, his eyes all fire and anticipation.

When she unlocked the door and pushed it open, she didn't reach for the light switch, instead letting the glow shining through the front windows guide them through the apartment.

Only when she stepped into what Aunt Sophie referred to as her front parlor, just off the balcony, did she turn on a lamp—one operated by a dimmer switch. She kept it low, both to protect her true identity and create a seductive mood.

Next, she walked to the French doors that led onto the balcony. As much as she wanted to be alone with Ty, she also regretted having to leave the infectious decadence of Mardi Gras behind. On impulse, she opened the doors wide, admitting the sounds of music—snippets of Dixieland, jazz, and Zydeco all emanating up from the street below. With it came the vague static of voices, laughter, and the wafting aromas of sweet pralines and any number of spicy Cajun delicacies. It all drifted inside, seeming to inhabit the room with them.

She'd dropped by the apartment on the way home from work yesterday to situate everything just the way she wanted it. Turning to see the kitchen chair she'd placed in the middle of the parlor floor reminded her that—with her passion already at a fever pitch—she'd best put her strategy into play before he grabbed her and started kissing her and the whole plan was forgotten.

"Sit down," she said. Not too harsh or bossy. Just a request.

He moved toward the sofa that rested against one wall.

"No. There." She pointed to the wooden chair.

He lifted his gaze. Grinned slightly, uncertainly. "Uh, why?"

She returned a small, pointed smile. "Just do it, lover."

He tilted his head in speculation, as if maybe he was tuning in to the idea that she was about to fulfill his private desires—then he moved toward the chair and took a seat.

Of course, the way he was looking at her now made her simply want to leap on him and decide *Screw the plan*, so she had to work to stay calm in order to go on. Still, her thighs ached and her cunt pulsed with need. Even her arms and hands felt heavy, hungry. Pure want soaked her entire body in a way she'd never quite experienced before.

"What now, baby?" he asked in the sexiest, raspiest voice she'd ever heard leave his mouth.

This is what it's like to be his lover, she thought.

But, no—that hot anticipation leaking from his eyes was only the *beginning* of being his lover, the before part.

She felt herself taking steps toward him, her shoes clicking across the polished hardwood without her consciously deciding to go. Suddenly, he was like a magnet to her. Reaching him, she boldly lifted one leg across his lap, her skirt rising nearly to her hips as she straddled him.

His hands came to rest low on her outer thighs, skimming quickly upward, past the lace tops of her stockings, under her skirt, onto the thin elastic strap of her panties. A low growl left him and her entire body pulsed, heavy as the beat of a drum. Her pussy pressed against the delectable length of his cock through his jeans, setting off waves of pleasure that felt like tendrils stretching out through her cunt. *No, this is what it's like to be his lover*. Or it was getting damn close, anyway.

"Kiss me," she said feverishly.

Their tongues met at the precise second their lips did, in a warm, sensuous connection that felt natural and right, the sensation melting through her like ice cream left out in the hot Louisiana sun.

She never made the conscious decision to begin unbuttoning his shirt, but the buttons slipped free beneath her fingers, one by one. His hands left her hips, then grazed her sensitive breasts as he worked at her buttons, too. Each kiss grew more intoxicating until she was finally pushing his shirt from his shoulders, running her hands over the muscles there, splaying her fingers across the broad, sexy expanse of his chest.

He shrugged out of the shirt before finally undoing the last button on her blouse and urging it off her shoulders as well. She didn't bother taking it off completely, letting the sheer gauzy fabric fall about her upper arms in a way that felt lightly — deliciously — binding when she moved. Besides, it was too much trouble to pull her hands away from his finely sculpted body, half of it now bared for her.

His kisses trailed from her mouth over her jaw, onto her neck. She arched against him, pressing her hungry cunt harder into his erection, leaning her head back to welcome his barrage of kisses. His mouth soon sank to her chest, the upper swell of her breast. Her pussy tingled and her pulse raced.

His hands found the two sensitive mounds of flesh just below, lightly cupping the outer curves as he brushed his thumbs across her lace-covered nipples. A slight whimper escaped her as his kisses spanned the valley between, then traveled up onto the other rise. Her breasts had never felt so sensitive, like a gift she wanted to give her man.

He dropped his touch back to her hips, her ass, helping her, because without quite realizing it, at some point she'd begun to move against him, grinding against the irresistible column of stone beneath his jeans. Oh God, at this rate, she would come soon, before the action even really got underway, which she didn't want — but how could she resist?

Her body was in charge now, writhing against him of its own volition.

He nipped at the hard peak of her breast through the lace that barely covered it, and she cried out. The delectable sensation shot straight to her pussy and nearly pushed her over the edge. She moved harder against him, wanting more, more.

His palms roamed her body oh-so lightly, his touch at once a tease and the most wonderful stimulation. She heard herself panting — him, too — and looked into his eyes to find the same fire as before, only burning hotter now. "You're so sexy, baby," he murmured. "So fucking sexy."

He framed her face with his hands and drew her in for a deep kiss that reached all the way to her soul, just as he slipped his fingers beneath her mask and began to remove it over her head.

She pulled it back into place, yanking his fingers away. "No," she snapped.

It killed her mounting pleasure, and the orgasm that had felt so near... But that was actually *good*, despite the frustration roaring through her body. Because she'd clearly forgotten her plan, gotten off track.

Time to get back on.

"Why?" he asked. "I want to see you. I want to see your face, Mina."

She shook her head, and then—as painful as it was—extracted herself from his lap.

The move racked her body with loss, but that, too, was worth it, since his attempt to remove her mask was a wake-up call. No more letting her own desire get the best of her. Time to take control. Completely.

"What's wrong?" he asked, rising to his feet.

She pressed her palm to the center of his chest and pushed him back down. "Sit."

"What?" he murmured, looking confused.

"You've been a bad boy," she said, moving to the shopping bag she'd placed just a few feet away on her previous visit to the apartment. She pulled out one length of the heavy white rope she'd purchased and walked behind his chair. "Give me your wrists."

He cast a brief glance over his shoulder, clearly surprised, but then his expression softened as he shifted his arms behind him, through the lowest opening on the ladder-back chair.

Mia drew in a deep breath as she placed his wrists one over the other, then began to tie him up. She purposely avoided tying him to the chair, wanting him bound but still able to move around at her will. A dart of dark pleasure pierced her chest as she wrapped the rope, tightly, over and under, wondering if it was biting into his skin, wondering if he was enjoying that.

Even after her initial delight at hearing Ty and Jack's conversation in the office earlier in the week, she'd never truly expected to derive any deep thrill from taking on the role of dominatrix, but already, she could tell she'd been wrong. She liked tying him with the rope far too much, each twist of it around his wrists filling her with a sense of forbidden heat.

When she'd knotted the rope and walked back around in front of him, his expression hovered somewhere between aroused and amused. "You know I can't touch you like this?"

Yes, she knew. A sacrifice, but one worth making. "That's all right." Then an idea hit her, a slight amendment to the plan. "Maybe I...should do it for you."

With that, she walked to the stereo system and pushed the play button to start a CD she'd brought over the day before. The speakers boomed with a super-sexy song that always got her hot. Above a slow, throbbing rock beat, the singer urged a woman to be his lover, promising to show her his dark secret.

Mia had never stripped before, and even with the plethora of men's clubs to be found just a couple of blocks away, had never seen a stripper perform live. But she was going to try to be one now, for Ty, and she was already so excited that her arousal squelched any fear.

Turning away from him, she began to sway her hips sensually back and forth with the driving rhythm. Then she arched, leaning her shoulders back to let her transparent blouse slide from her arms and drop silently to the floor.

Revolving, she rested against the wall, one knee bent, her arms stretched up over her head. Slowly, she drew her hands down, letting them skim sensuously over the round globes of her breasts, the flat plane of her bare stomach, then she splayed her fingers as both hands pushed down her thighs.

"Damn, that's hot, baby," he said, sounding totally spellbound.

Curling her fingers around the hem of her skirt, she met his gaze as she playfully lifted the fabric inch by teasing inch.

"Oh yeah. That's nice. Keep going."

When the skirt rose past her lace stockings, she eased her fingers onto the flesh of her thighs, beneath the tight black garters. Gliding her fingertips upward, she lifted the skirt to her hips. She heard Ty sigh at the sight of her mound, which had gone swollen and achy now. It was a pleasure for both of them when she slipped her middle finger between her legs for one slow upward stroke over her panties. She felt it deep inside, especially when Ty purred, "Mmm, yeah."

Reaching behind her as she resumed her slow sway to the sexy song, she unzipped the black mini and used both hands to push it down, down, until it loosened at mid-thigh and dropped to the floor. She stepped carefully free of it, very aware of how she looked now, wearing only sexy black lingerie, ultra-high-heeled shoes, and her feathered, glittery mask.

"Stand up," she said.

He rose to his feet, looking all-too-good in nothing but those pleasantly snug jeans, his hands tied behind his back. But he was about to look even better.

Stepping up to him, Mia ran her hands down his hard, muscular flesh, from shoulder to waist, where she folded the fingertips of both hands into his jeans. Sliding them to the center, she met an astonishingly hard obstacle that made her go weak. "Mmm," she said, unbuttoning the jeans, then slowly easing down the zipper. "You're so big for me."

Reaching into the open fly, she ran her palm up his erection.

He leaned his head back with a long, sexy sigh. "Aw, you're killing me here, honey."

She grinned up at him. "Good. Nothing like a little torture to set the mood."

They exchanged feral looks and he bent down to sweep a hungry kiss across her mouth as she squeezed and caressed his cock through his briefs. She was awed by how large he felt and it only added to her excitement.

Moving around behind him, she hooked her thumbs into his jeans and underwear and dragged them down to his knees. She nearly shuddered at the sight of his tight, round ass, his wrists roped just above it.

As he kicked off his shoes and began maneuvering out of the denim, she ran her hands around him from behind, caressing his hard chest, his hips, the tops of his thighs — everything but the cock itself.

He leaned his head back in frustration. "Please, baby."

"That's right, lover. I want to hear you beg. Beg me."

He hesitated a moment, letting out a small growl, then said, "Please — touch me," adding, "Come on, honey. Do it."

She withdrew her hands.

"What?" he asked, clearly disturbed.

"That sounded more like a demand than begging." She purposely sounded miffed.

By the time he spun to face her, she'd returned from another trip to her shopping bag, from which she'd retrieved a black leather riding crop. She stood sternly slapping it into the palm of her free hand as she gave him a look meant to quell any arguments.

He raised his eyebrows. "You intend to use that thing on me?"

"You've been a bad boy. Clearly, you need to be disciplined."

He stood looking uncertain, as if perhaps he was having second thoughts about wanting to be dominated. But given all the trouble she'd gone to, arranging all this, she'd be damned if he was going to back out now. Lifting the fringed end of riding crop to her shoulder as he watched, she slid the length of the tool along the swell of one breast, the leather braiding that circled it creating a pleasant sensation as it passed over her skin.

As she'd hoped, the fire returned to his eyes. "Does using it turn you on?"

She nodded. "Very much."

"What do you want me to do?" he asked, seeming ready to acquiesce.

"Do what I say and only that. Don't question me or argue with me. Take what you're given and like it."

She sensed the exacting command sinking into his arousal, making him want to obey.

And for the first time in the midst of her attempted discipline, she noticed his cock. It was even bigger than she'd imagined. Certainly the largest specimen she'd ever had. The sight of it made her bite her lip with hunger as she reached out with her new leather toy. Sliding it behind his erection, she pulled it forward a bit, then removed the crop, letting the shaft slap softly against his abs. He let out a soft, quick moan.

But she couldn't let herself be sidetracked by his hard-on, no matter how colossal and beautiful it looked, so it was back to business. "Turn around and lean over the chair."

She watched Ty take a deep breath, then pivot, bending slightly at the waist, his wrists still bound behind him. "Like this?"

"Yes, that will do. Now tell me you've been a bad boy."

He hesitated, so she took the opportunity to snap the crop lightly against his lovely, masculine ass, surprised at the pleasure the strike delivered...to her. "Say it," she commanded.

He sighed, still looking reluctant. "I've been a bad boy."

She smacked his ass with the crop again, slightly harder this time.

"Oh *God*, I've been a bad boy."

Mmm, yes, that time it sounded like her little spanking was starting to feel good to him.

Her cunt throbbed when she slapped the crop harder across his flesh, this time leaving a pink mark. He moaned.

Each successive strike of the riding crop elicited another groan from Ty, each sounding deeper, deeper, until she asked him, "Do you like your whipping from Mistress Mina?"

He nodded vigorously, even if he looked a bit spent with desire. "Yes."

"Mmm, that's a good boy," she purred, her pussy humming with delight at his submission. "Now, sit back down."

He obeyed, and when she next saw his eyes, she knew she had him utterly excited, and ready for whatever came next.

"Do you want to see more of me?" She drew the riding crop sensually through her legs and up her pussy in case he needed some inspiration.

He answered deeply. "Oh yes."

"Beg me."

He didn't hesitate this time. "Please let me see you, Mistress Mina. Let me see your breasts, let me see your pretty pussy."

Oooh, she liked him this way—so much so that it increased the pulse in her cunt and she could barely wait to *let* him see more of her.

Abandoning her riding crop on the couch behind her, she reached up to curl her fingers into the cups of her bra, slowly pulling them down to reveal taut pink nipples, standing thick and erect. The beads she wore fell between her breasts. He let out a low groan and she ran her hands over them, tweaking the rosy tips.

"So pretty," he murmured.

"Beg to see my pussy some more," she instructed him.

The request brought fresh heat to his expression. "Please, Mistress Mina, show me your pussy. Show me your hot, pink cunt. I want to see how wet and open you are."

Mmm, just what the dominatrix ordered. Like before, his begging upped her excitement, getting her even more turned on than she already was.

She turned, putting her back to him, then slipped her fingers beneath the elastic at her hips. She drew her panties down over her garters and stockings, bending at the waist to give him a hot view from behind. When the panties were at her ankles, she stepped free and turned to stand before him, exposed.

"Oh God," he breathed, his gaze glued between her thighs.

"You like it, lover?" she asked, reaching down to run her fingers through her damp slit. She glanced down at it herself, aroused at the sight, because she'd shaved away all of her pubic hair except for a narrow swath above her cunt.

"Fuck yes," he growled, sounding as excited as she was.

Following her instincts and highly aware that he loved watching her auto erotic touches, she sat down on the couch and parted her thighs wide.

"Unh…" he breathed.

Biting her lip, she reached for the riding crop, then began to run the leather-fringed tip over her clit and inner lips.

"Oh God, honey, that's so damn hot. Let me fuck you now."

Mia couldn't quite believe how wonderful it felt to rub the leather crop through her slit while Ty's eyes drank it all in. She'd never touched herself for a guy before, and like everything else that was a first for her tonight, the rawness of the act thrilled her almost more than she could understand. "You like watching me play with my pussy?" she purred.

"God yes, baby." His voice was a low, hot rumble. "But I need to fuck you now."

She lowered the crop to the cushion beside her and squared her gaze on his. "Are you being a bad boy again? Trying to take control when you know it belongs to *me*?"

Ty looked like he was ready to come bounding off the chair at any second, but at this, he collected himself. She saw him take a deep breath. "No. Whatever you want, Mistress Mina. Whatever you say."

"Good." She smiled. "Now, get down on your knees and come over here."

Their eyes met. His seemed to say he wasn't sure he liked this part of the game. She kept her gaze steady, though. Commanding.

Finally, he left the chair and dropped to his knees, his hands still firmly tied behind him. He began to move toward her, placing one knee in front of the other.

Ty looked amazingly sexy coming closer to her, his hard cock jiggling with each move, his eyes hungry, his hands still trussed. Knowing he was willingly following her demands only made it better. She parted her legs farther—as far apart as possible—as he neared her, pleased that his burning gaze had fallen back to her cunt.

"Now, eat me," she said, when he was kneeling between her thighs.

Without a second's hesitation, he lowered his face to her pussy, closing his mouth over her engorged clit. She cried out at the instant pleasure. Hissing as he began to suckle, she realized her joy ran deeper, much deeper, because the man who mouthed her was Ty. *Her* Ty, the guy she'd had a crush on for most of her life. And now they were suddenly playing naughty sex games and he was licking vigorously at her slit, getting her wetter and wetter, making her think *yes, yes,* and making her *know* that disguising herself to be his secret lover was the best thing she'd ever done.

"Oooh, yes, lick my pussy," she cooed over him, watching as he dragged his tongue all the way from her opening up over her clit. "Oh God, yes, baby, that's good."

She lifted one high heel to the couch, her knee bent, to give him even better access, beginning to raise herself toward his ministrations. All the while, she caressed her breasts, gently massaging, lightly twirling the nipples, her black beads clicking together lightly as she thrust at him.

When he looked up, his eyes going glassy at her self-caress, she upped the heat by pushing one breast as high as she could with her hand, then bending toward it—just barely able to rake her tongue across her own nipple. She felt a shudder run through him and cast a sexy smile. "Don't stop," she told him. "Lick your Mistress Mina's pretty pussy."

Mia's body was on fire. She wanted to raise the temperature in the room even more, though, so when she caught sight of the riding crop next to her shoe, she took it up and began to swat Ty's ass in time with her light lunges against his oh-so skilled mouth. In one way, she hated to think of all the other women she knew he'd been with over the years, but in another, she couldn't have been more pleased to have a man of such experience between her thighs. She moaned as the pleasure grew and grew—glad she hadn't climaxed before when he'd been in the chair, glad she'd saved it up for now, because she suddenly wanted, more than anything, to come in his hot, sexy mouth.

She whimpered as she drove at him, her Mardi Gras beads snapping together harder. She soon stopped hitting him with the crop, instead reaching past his bound hands to slide the tool up and down the valley of his ass. The new sensation made him moan deeply, so she kept it up, thinking of the leather braiding passing back and forth across his asshole as she got closer and closer to orgasm.

She lowered her free hand to his thick, sandy hair, thrilled by the simple sensation of running her fingers through it, but soon enough she was using it to guide him, to force him, to make him press himself deeper against her as she fucked his mouth. "A little more, baby, just a little more," she murmured, pulling him to her pussy while she stimulated his ass with the crop.

Both of their moans filled the sultry air, drowning out the CD of sexy songs she'd made, as well as the noises from outside. She wondered briefly if anyone beyond the balcony could hear them, and she hoped so. She hoped all of the French Quarter could hear them making each other so hot.

And then his lips clamped tight around the swollen bud of her clit, and she thrust at him harder, and—oh God—it broke over her like a tidal wave, more consuming and overpowering than anything she'd ever experienced. She heard her own screams without being fully conscious of making a sound. The pleasure pulses were wild, drenching, filling her ears, her whole body—every limb seemed to vibrate with the intense waves.

She lifted, attempting to pull her pussy away from his mouth because it was too much, she couldn't take it, needed to let it pass and then recover—but Ty wouldn't release her, following after her cunt until he was pressing her into the back of the couch to keep sucking at her clit. His insistence should have been something to be punished, but it dragged her orgasm out, longer, harder...*better*. Mmm, yes.

So when the flood inside her finally calmed and he drew back to kneel before her, she didn't say anything about discipline. In fact, she could barely move. She felt limp and heavy, thoroughly fucked without having been fucked yet. Amazing.

Even more amazing was that Ty sat patiently waiting between her knees for his next instructions, suddenly her obedient little sex slave.

"Was it good?" he asked, looking as if he very sincerely hoped he'd pleased her. His face glistened with her wetness.

She nodded, still trying to come back to herself. "Are you ready for more?" she asked, maintaining her sultry voice.

"Oh *yeah*, baby. I'm ready for whatever you want, Mistress Mina."

She couldn't keep a wicked little smile from spreading across her face. "My, my, aren't you just a good little boy now? Maybe I should reward you."

His eyes sparkled with fresh anticipation. "How?"

"Go back to your chair, and maybe I'll suck your cock."

Chapter Four

ဢ

Ty could barely breathe by the time he sat back down. His entire body felt on edge. God, even his ass, from the way she'd rubbed him with the riding crop. He'd never felt anything like that. Had never even thought he'd want to. But Mistress Mina was teaching him a thing or two—just when he thought he knew everything there was to know about sex.

She slowly got to her feet, her fuck-me-now shoes accentuating those long, silky legs, leading up to her sweet little pussy, shaved so smooth. He didn't think he'd ever been with a woman so incredible.

As for the bondage stuff—he'd been right, he liked being tied up. But he hadn't even thought about issues like *discipline* coming with that, and that part...well, it wasn't easy, but he'd decided to give himself over to it as much as possible, just for this one night. After all, he'd wanted this, hadn't he? And like an answer to a wish, here was the mysterious Mina, bringing his fantasies to life and adding to the mix with her hot little commands and that sexy riding crop she used so well.

She walked toward him, her lush lips gleaming with the hint of a smile, and it was only then that he realized she must have reached into her bag of goodies when he wasn't looking, because she held more rope in her hand. His stomach tightened with strange arousal to wonder what she was going to do with it, and to know he was pretty much at her mercy. At her mercy by choice, yes, but there wasn't much a guy could do with his hands tied behind his back if he decided he wanted the game to end.

She kneeled between his thighs, looking delectable. He could still taste the sweet tang of her cunt—she'd been so wet, he felt like he was wearing her juices all over his face, and the sensation hardened his anxious cock all the more.

Pressing one of his ankles back against the front leg of the chair, she began to tie him to it. Like before, when she'd bound his wrists, the harsh rope bit into his skin, pleasurable only because she was the one making it that way.

As she began her work on his other ankle, he couldn't help asking, "I thought I was being good now. Why are you tying me up more?"

She flashed a naughty grin from beneath that sexy mask. "Just because you're being good *now* doesn't mean you won't try to take over in five minutes." She looked down at her work, circling the bottom of his left leg with more rope, pulling it snug with a motion he felt in his dick, and then raised her gaze to his again. "Besides, I like the way you look tied up."

He didn't answer, only felt his cock swell more.

As he watched her work, he thought about that mask of hers, wishing like hell she'd take it off, wondering why she was so adamant about not letting him see her. Must be part of what turned her on about this hot little game, he decided.

He wasn't sure why seeing her face mattered so much, but when she kissed him... He couldn't explain it to himself, but something about her felt so familiar, almost as if he knew her. Yet he didn't think he'd forget having met Mistress Mina, so he dismissed the idea.

"Beg me to suck your cock," she commanded.

At first, he'd felt weird about that—begging. But he'd grown more used to the discipline now, and even though he didn't think he'd want to do this all the time, begging her to lower those lovely lips onto his erection wasn't a challenge. "Please, Mistress Mina, suck my cock with your pretty, pretty mouth. Please suck me."

Kneeling low between his thighs, she surprised him by licking his balls, then dragging her moist tongue up his length. When she reached the tip, she hungrily licked off the heavy accumulation of fluid at the end. "Mmm," she said. "Delicious."

He could have come right then, given all he'd endured so far, but no way was he ready to let himself go just yet. He had a feeling that sexy and mysterious Mina was just getting started on him.

"Tell me again," she said.

"Please, baby, suck me. I want to be in your mouth so bad. I want to feel your sexy lips on me."

Rising up slightly, she rested her elbows on his knees and slid her splayed hands upward on his thighs until her bared breasts came to rest around his hard-on. "Oh God," he said on a moan.

"How about these?" she asked. "Would you like to feel these on your cock, too?"

They were delectable, round and lush with the prettiest mauve nipples, which he couldn't believe he hadn't managed to get in his mouth yet. On his cock, though… That was even better. "Mmm," he said, barely able to talk as he looked down at the titillating vision of the two soft mounds curving around his hard shaft. The stiff lace of her bra abraded his balls. "Yes, please."

She lifted her hands to the round, white globes of flesh, pressing them more fully around his erection, her beads caught up and intertwining with her long, tapered fingers. As she began to softly slide her breasts up and down his cock, he shuddered and groaned—again so close to coming that he wondered how he was managing not to. He was generally in firm control over that, but being with Mistress Mina changed things.

"Does that feel good, baby?" she purred, peering up at him.

"God, yeah."

"Mistress Mina likes to please you when you're a good boy."

"Can I thrust?" he asked, fearing that if he did it without asking, it might suddenly put him in bad-boy land again, which he didn't want at the moment. He was enjoying her attention too much.

"Lightly," she said, her voice a mere lilt, and he immediately began helping her, pushing his hungry cock up through her gorgeous breasts. Damn, what he wouldn't give to have use of his hands right now, so *he* could be the one holding her mounds around him. But he wasn't complaining. Her pretty, tapered fingers, their nails painted a sexy blood red, looked hot as hell curving around her breasts. And this whole game had turned out to be even more arousing than he could have imagined.

"Now," she said in that sexy voice of hers, "how bad do you want me to suck this big, hard cock?"

He looked down at the vision before him. His aching erection being pleasured between her beautiful breasts, her hot eyes glimmering through that sexy black mask, her pouty red lips teasing him with the possibilities. He let out everything he was thinking. "I want it *so* bad, Mistress Mina. So bad I can hardly breathe. I want to watch you suck me. I want to see how much of my cock you can take. I want to fuck your mouth the same way you fucked mine on the couch. Please suck me, Mina. Please."

Her eyes never left his as she rewarded him with a wicked little grin and poised her lips at the head of his erection. She licked a hot little circle around the tip, again taking the bead of moisture from the end and making him utter, "Oh yeah, baby."

Then she lowered her lovely lips over him, smooth, swift, taking an astounding portion of his length. He was well over eight sturdy inches and she'd just swallowed most of them. He could feel the tip of his hard-on touching the back of her throat, wet and warm as she held him there, as if showing him exactly what she could do with his cock.

Finally, after a breathtaking moment, she pulled back and began to move her mouth up and down on him, taking him almost as deep each time.

"That's so good, baby."

He let himself lift slightly, fucking her mouth just as he'd told her he wanted to. She didn't object, or even flinch, and he loved her boldness, loved how much she enjoyed what she was doing.

She continued delivering the luscious ministrations for what seemed a long and generous while, and he relished each and every second. More than once he tried to reach for her, to run his fingers through her hair, or to draw her down on him harder—only to remember his hands were bound behind his back. He strained helplessly at the ropes, both frustrated and pleased by the harsh rub of them against his skin. But all the while she kept working over him, sucking him so thoroughly he thought he'd die of pleasure as he pumped up into her wet, lush little mouth, and by the time she released his shaft from the moist passage, he felt more enamored of the sensuous masked woman than he could easily understand. He wanted to tell her what a bad girl she was, and how much he loved that, but as her submissive slave tonight, he knew it wasn't the time, so he held his tongue.

Finally pushing to her feet, she said, "Now it's time for you to pleasure *me* some more."

He gave her his most wicked grin. "Want me to lick that pretty pink pussy again, Mistress Mina?"

She shook her head. "No. I'm going to ride you instead."

With that, she lifted one leg over the chair, giving him an incredible view of her cunt, then circled his shaft with her fist, and lowered herself onto it with shocking ease.

They both moaned at the smooth, deep entry.

"You have a marvelous cock, Ty." She leaned in to brush a sensuous kiss across his lips.

"You have a warm, wet, sweet little pussy," he returned.

She bit her lip at the dirty compliment, sinking onto him a little farther, and he groaned.

"A very *deep* little pussy," he added.

"Fortunate for you, yes? So that I can accommodate this very lengthy erection."

"Does it feel good inside you?"

She gave a languid nod. "So big and hard. You're filling me."

"Are you gonna fuck me now, Mistress Mina? I mean, *really* fuck me? *Really* ride me? Hard?"

He could have sworn the question turned her beaded nipples a little firmer before his eyes. "Is that what you want, Ty? To be tied up and fucked hard?"

He simply nodded. That's what he'd wanted before tonight, but now he wanted it more than he'd ever known possible. And he wanted it with her. His dominatrix, Mistress Mina of the Glittery Mask.

"Then I'm going to give you what you want, baby. I'm going to give it to you so good, going to make you come better than you ever have before."

"I believe you," he said. And he did.

Mia felt nearly undone. Still in control of the situation, yes, but on the inside, she was drowning in a passion so thick that it was all she could see, all she could feel. Taking his cock into her mouth had been more fulfilling than with any other guy, ever, and although it had never been an activity she minded, with Ty, she could have kept going all night, just pleasuring him that way, just feeling the stretch of her mouth around his hardness and the way he slid himself in and out, so deep.

As for how far she'd managed to go down on him, it wasn't that she was unusually skilled, only that she was so hot for him. And it was also because he was Ty—*her* Ty—and she'd simply wanted to take every ounce of his perfect cock inside her in some way. Then…and now, too.

Lowering herself onto him just now had been more than incredible, an experience she'd literally awaited her whole life. Now, as she thrust downward, her arms around his neck, her clit meeting the flesh just above his erection, it felt...like coming home. Possibly the corniest thought she'd had since high school, but there it was. It seemed at once new, yet familiar, like a thing that was supposed to happen, a place she was meant to be.

She looked into his eyes and got even hotter, rubbing her clit against him as she rode him in tight, heated little circles, his cock doing just what she'd told him—filling her, so very well.

"I wish I could touch your breasts," he said, and they both peered down at her pearled nipples. The globes of flesh felt heavy, achy, and she wished he could touch them, too.

"Suck them for me," she whispered, their foreheads softly meeting.

He moved in for a hot kiss on her mouth, and then she arched for him, her Mardi Gras beads falling around the breast he sought as he bent to capture the pink nipple between his lips.

She let out a whimper at the added pleasure. As she moved on him, bucked against him, offering her breasts up to him, she felt wild, dirty, alive, free. Her beads bounced lightly on her skin. The tight lace of the bra that still framed her moved against her with each rhythmic stroke. The garters, too, stretching taut down her thighs and across her ass, provided more sweet, hot friction as she moved against Ty.

"Fuck me," she whispered. She didn't plan it, wasn't being demanding Mistress Mina anymore. It just came out spontaneously, was simply what she wanted, needed.

His thrusts came harder in response, his mouth's grip on her breast more intense.

"Yes," she murmured, "*yes.*"

Everything inside her was rubbing together just the right way, and though she wasn't normally a multiple orgasm sort of girl, she knew that tonight she *was*, and she also knew the second would be even better than the first, by the mere fact that he was inside her, the way she'd always fantasized. Of course, the mask and the ropes were *new* parts of the fantasy, but the lovely hard cock and the sucking of her breast, and the blond hair she ran her hands through—all that was the same. Only better. So much better.

"Yes, fuck me," she whispered urgently. "Fuck me more. Don't stop. Don't stop."

This time the orgasm rose slow and steady, until she reached a point when she knew it was upon her, and she said, "Yes, now. Now, baby." And it rocked her against him, filling her body with electricity at every hot lunge, vibrating through her like live wires whipping about. She cried out—loud, screaming cries—until finally the climax began to wane, leaving her to look into his eyes as he lifted his head from her breast.

Just as she'd anticipated, coming was even better that time. With him inside her. *Because you waited for it so long*, she told herself. *Because you've had a crush on him most of your life.* That's the only reason it had felt so...fulfilling, so profound. She had to believe that.

He continued to pump up into her and she could see, sense, that he was on the edge, too, and she wanted to feel Ty come in her, wanted to make him climax just as hard as she'd promised.

Of course, she'd already said lots of very dirty things to him, she'd already tied him up and made him obey her, she'd stripped for him, she'd gone down on him, she'd played with herself for him—what could she do to make it better for him, too, better than ever?

Following her instincts, she simply brushed against him, grazing her firm nipples across his chest as they moved together, before lowering her hands to stroke *his* nipples with her thumbs. Then she bent to kiss his neck—soft little kisses, like raindrops on his skin.

His moans had begun low, but now grew louder, more intense with each tiny kiss and touch she delivered, and she heard herself murmuring against the tender skin of his neck, "Come. Come for me."

"Oh God," he breathed above her. "God, yes, I'm going to. I'm going to. I'm…ahhhhhhhh," he yelled as he thrust up into her hard and deep, lifting them both from the chair. Once, twice, three times, then four—he raised her entire body with his cock, pumping, pumping, and she loved knowing he was emptying inside her, that she'd made it happen. She'd brought his fantasy to life, but for her, being with Ty was more than mere fantasy—it was a dream coming true.

As they slumped together, recovering, she instantly felt weird. She'd not thought about the after part, still having to keep her mask on after they finished, but certainly she had to. No other choice.

Still, she didn't want the moment to end. She sat pressed against him, their chests molded together, her arms around his neck, her head on his shoulder. She thought she could stay like that forever.

Finally, though, his mouth quirked into a wan smile.

"What?" she asked.

"Are you going to untie me now, Mistress Mina? Or am I stuck this way?"

Biting her lip, she dismounted from him, sorry for the loss when his cock left her, but wanting to free him from his bindings. The truth was, she'd sort of forgotten about him being tied, but now that she remembered, she felt bad, suspecting his arms were probably sore.

Behind him, she stooped to undo the knot, and when the rope fell away, his shoulder blades spread apart and he groaned, stretching.

As he bent to work at one ankle, she returned to the front of the chair to untie the other.

Finally free, he sat up, looking down to where she kneeled before him. "So, Mina, what now?"

Come to bed with me. Stay the night. Let's make love. Without the whips and ties. They were fun, but I want you the normal, easy way, too. I want your hands on me.

She longed to say that, all of it, in the afterglow of sex. But of course, she couldn't. In fact, she could only think of one thing it made any sense to say at all. "You get dressed, and we say goodnight."

He gave a short nod, but as he bent down, reaching for his jeans, she couldn't help wondering if he'd been hoping for something else.

Just then, he muttered, "Awww...damn it," and bent his forehead into his hand.

"What?" she asked without moving from her place near his knee.

He gave her a look drenched in regret. "There's a condom in my jeans, but I never even thought...and even if I had, my hands were..." He sighed. "I fucked up."

The same regret rushed through her now, as well, leaving her unable to believe she'd forgotten, too. Somehow with Ty, someone she knew so well, it just hadn't been at the forefront of her mind like with other guys.

"Well," he said, "I'm sorry I can't tell you I'm a chaste guy who doesn't usually fool around on the first date, but I *am* always pretty careful. Up to now, I mean."

She nodded, encouraged. "Me, too. And I'm on the pill."

After cleaning up with a tissue from a nearby table, he stepped into his jeans. She pushed to her feet, as well, wondering if she should find her panties, adjust her bra, but she settled for not doing either, since as far as he knew, she didn't have to leave the apartment in order to be home. It would seem silly to cover herself for any other reason after the things they'd just done.

As he pulled on his shirt and slid his feet into his shoes, he tilted his head, peering down at her. "Let me see your face." Then he added a playful grin and a teasing voice. "*Please,* Mistress Mina."

Bizarrely, she was almost tempted. Crazy. "No," she said.

"Why?"

Good question. "This way I'll always be your mysterious Mistress Mina."

"Why do you have to be mysterious?"

"Because…that's the way I am, the way I like it."

"Can I see you again?"

Oh God. He wanted more of her? It was a dream come true. And also a nightmare. "No."

He looked undaunted. "Why?"

"Well, maybe," she amended, fumbling but trying not to let it show, wholly unsure how to proceed.

"Maybe?"

She nodded, thinking, *Please leave, Ty. Just go. I can't take this much longer.*

"When?" he asked. "Give me your number."

"No," she replied quickly, "*I'll* call *you.*"

Looking around, he grabbed up a notepad from Aunt Sophie's desk, along with a pen, then scribbled down both his home and work numbers before ripping off the top sheet and shoving it into her hand. She looked at them, particularly the one he'd labeled "wk", thinking, *Little does he know, I'm the person who* answers *this phone for him.*

After that, he turned and walked to the door, so she followed, beginning to feel a little sheepish in her revealing lingerie and high heels now that the hot sex was over.

"Let me see you," he said once more, sounding a bit more insistent this time.

She simply shook her head.

He gave her a long look, letting his gaze drop all the way to her feet before rising back to her eyes. "Well, honey, even if you won't let me see your face, I can tell you this—the rest of the package is beautiful." Then he pulled her to him in a firm embrace to lower a long, thorough kiss to her swollen lips. It traveled all through her, leaving her nearly as weak as her orgasms had.

"Thank you, Mistress Mina. It was a hell of a night."

"A memorable one, I hope."

He nodded. "Like no other."

Then he pushed through the door, leaving her there with nothing but what she'd left him with—memories.

* * * * *

By the time Mia reached work on Monday morning, she couldn't believe she was actually considering seeing Ty again. Sexually. Bringing out Mistress Mina for one more spin before retirement.

But sex like that—God, she'd never *had* sex like that.

Before Saturday night, she'd thought she'd had some good lovers. She'd thought she was an energetic bed partner herself and had never gotten any complaints. But her domination game with Ty had been different. She'd been making it up as she went, knowing little more about true domination than what she'd been able to read on the Internet over the few days prior, yet whatever she'd done had clearly worked—at least for her. Her whole body had been left practically humming from the two spectacular orgasms Ty had delivered to her at Aunt Sophie's place. Even now, her pussy tingled at the mere thought of them.

"Hey, sweet thing, what's shakin'?"

She looked up to see Ty walk in with a big smile on his face. At the sight of her unsuspecting lover, her stomach contracted and her breath trembled. *Get it under control.*

"You're awfully chipper for a Monday morning," she managed to say.

"Had a great weekend," he replied easily. Rather than making a beeline for his office, as usual, he stopped and rested his arms on the counter, looking almost giddy.

"Oh?" she asked, trying to hold her voice steady. "What was so great about it?"

"Jack's party. Met a woman. She rocked my world."

It wasn't unusual for Ty to give her little snippets of his sex life this way, but this was the first time she could remember hearing about it without the news making her insanely jealous.

He tilted his head. "Hey, wait a minute. Speaking of Jack's party, where *were* you?"

Excellent question. For which she—stupidly—had not prepared an answer. She reached for the simplest reply at hand. "Met a guy," she said with a smile. "*He* rocked *my* world."

Ty blinked, looking understandably surprised. While he generally knew who she dated and had even met some of the guys on occasion, she *didn't* usually allude to her sexual encounters, even in simple terms like this.

He raised his eyebrows. "Please tell me he's someone I would approve of."

She couldn't help smiling. "Well," she began, leaning her head to one side, "I can't be certain you'd *approve*, but I think you'd get along with him."

His eyes narrowed. "Any tattoos?"

She shook her head. "Unfortunately not. That's his one flaw."

"What is it with you and tattoos anyway?"

She shrugged. "Turns me on, I guess." Then she squared her gaze on him. "We all have our little turn-ons, don't we?"

As she'd hoped, she could almost see his thoughts traveling back to Saturday night, to rope and riding crops. Finally, he gave a short, almost-sheepish laugh. "Yeah, I guess we do." Just as quickly, though, his eyes turned serious and protective again. "But listen, Mia, just be careful. Okay?"

"Of?"

"Guys who…well, just guys you don't know very well. This is a crazy city with a lot of unusual people. I just…wouldn't want you to get hurt in any way."

"You forget, Ty, *you're* the transplant. *I* grew up thirty minutes from here. I'm well aware of where we live."

He sighed. "I know. And I don't mean to treat you like a little kid or something. I just…you know."

"No, I *don't* know. What?"

"I care. That's all."

Her heart constricted lightly, and one of her most frequent thoughts came back to her. *If you only knew, Ty.*

If you only knew how deeply it touches me that you care, but how badly I wish you cared in a different way.

She added a new thought, *If you only knew how much of a little girl I'm not. If you only knew I was the woman who tied you up and fucked you senseless Saturday night, just like you wanted.*

"Any calls?" he asked, getting back to normal.

"Yeah, Bobby called in. He's going to be late again."

Ty responded under his breath, rolling his eyes, "Bobby might not have a job for much longer."

"And Rich from Sure-Pak called. Wants to set an appointment to show you their new line of baskets and carriers."

He nodded. "Anyone else? Like a woman with a sexy voice?"

She almost smiled, but held it in. "No, that's it."

He responded with a sigh. "Okay. I'll be in my office."

Mia watched him walk away, and again, had the burning urge to don her wig and mask one last time. In a way, it seemed crazy—she'd managed to pull it off and had given them both the night of their lives, so why risk messing it up now? Yet on the other hand, how was she supposed to resist that hungry, happy look in his eyes? Or the letdown expression that had replaced it when he'd learned she hadn't called? She was suddenly the object of Ty Brewer's affection. He *wanted* her. *Madly*. How could she refuse that?

Glancing up at his open office door, she let out a sigh of her own and answered herself.

Simple. She couldn't.

* * * * *

Ty sat in Jack's rundown old office on Royal Street, waiting for him to get off the phone. He was used to this, but…well, not this *exactly*.

He was used to waiting for Jack to get off the phone with *clients*. But lately—the last year or so—he'd been waiting for Jack to get off the phone with Liz.

You guys can't get enough of each other at home? he always wanted to ask. Apparently they couldn't. And today, for some stupid reason, it made him feel sort of…lonely.

He ignored the emotion the best he could, though, because it was likely just one more effect of riding an emotional roller coaster. The memories of Saturday night, still so fresh in his mind, filled him with a deep, glowing sort of satisfaction he couldn't ever remember feeling—or at least not since he'd been very young, getting first kisses from girls he really liked and thought would be in his life for much longer than they actually had. His masked Mina had really done a number on him.

But the dips in the ride came when he recalled how thoroughly underwhelmed she'd seemed by his request to see her again. Had he done something wrong? Had he not been good enough for her? He'd always felt pretty accomplished at fucking, but...well, this had been new. Maybe he hadn't been submissive enough? After all, that part sure hadn't come naturally. For her, he'd done it—and he'd enjoyed the results—but giving up total control had been difficult. Hell, for all he knew, maybe she'd wanted him to fight back more. He just didn't know how these games worked well enough to accurately analyze it.

And since when did he feel he had to analyze his sexual performance, anyway?

Since Mistress Mina had whisked into his life with her sexy leather riding crop, he supposed.

Finally, Jack hung up, leaned back in his chair, and crossed his ankles on his desk. "What has you lookin' so jumbled up this mornin'? And where did you disappear to so early on Saturday night?"

"Same answer to both questions. A woman."

Jack raised his eyebrows. "A woman has you jumbled up?"

Ty was less than thrilled to hear he looked "jumbled up", but decided to move past it. "Yeah, and I need to find out who she was. A redhead with a killer body in a black see-through blouse and a black Mardi Gras mask with feathers. She was handing out the king cake."

Jack blinked and lowered his feet to the floor. "I remember who you're talkin' about. But I never spoke to her, so I don't know who she is. Hang on a minute," he said, holding up one finger.

He picked up the phone again, dialing Liz back, Ty figured. Two minutes later, he hung up once more and gave Ty a perplexed look.

"Well?"

"Liz doesn't know, either. She saw her, too—helped her with the cake, she said—but she thought it was somebody *I* knew, a client or something."

Ty leaned back in his chair. "Unbelievable. The best fuck of my life, and I can't find her."

Jack sat up a little straighter. "The best fuck of your life?"

Ty nodded. "Ropes and everything."

An amused expression grew on Jack's face. "Really? And *everything*?"

Ty was beginning to feel sheepish, but given some of the stuff he'd been through with Jack over the years, he didn't know why. "Everything as in—there was a, uh...riding crop."

Jack nodded, grinned. "Weapons, now, too. Interesting."

"And she wouldn't let me take her mask off, so I never saw her face."

"Mysterious."

"Yep."

"So, was bein' tied up everything you hoped for?"

"And more, unfortunately."

"Unfortunately?"

"I want her again. Like I've never wanted a woman before. And I have no idea how to find her."

Twenty minutes later, he walked back into the messenger service, no closer to locating Mistress Mina. He found one of his messengers, a college girl named Cara, sitting behind Mia's desk. "Mia went to lunch," she said. "I told her I'd cover the phones until you got back."

He nodded. "Thanks. Any messages?"

"I think Mia put a couple on your desk before she left."

Making his way into his office, he scooped up the two small pink slips of paper. One was from an architectural firm—they wanted to negotiate terms for a new account. He

208

lowered the message next to the phone, then moved on to the other one.

His heart nearly dropped to his stomach as he read it. In Mia's neat handwriting, it said, *Someone named Mina called. She'll meet you Friday night at 8:00, outside the Café du Monde.*

Chapter Five

Ty nearly felt faint when he set eyes on Mina Friday night. She was a vision. She'd been alluring enough before he'd known what she could do to him, but with that added knowledge, she made him hard as a rock on sight.

Tonight she wore a tight, slinky dress of purple that showed lots of cleavage and lots of thigh. Same hot black heels, and he only hoped those stockings led to garters again—he had a serious thing for garters.

Of course, to his frustration but not his surprise, she was wearing another mask. Tonight's was covered with tiny glistening purple sequins, and three dark purple feathers fanned up from the left eye. Two strands of shimmery purple beads hung from either side of the mask, draping below her chin.

Her vibrant green gaze seemed to pin him in place.

"Mistress Mina, I presume," he said with a smile.

"You presume?" God, her sexy voice sifted down through him like warm brown sugar.

"The mask," he said, pointing. "I wasn't sure what to expect, but I suppose this means we're still playing domination games tonight."

She pursed her lips. "Does that disappoint you?"

He shook his head shortly. "No." Although that was a bit of a fib. The truth was, he'd hoped to take a little more control this time, get back into his usual comfort zone. The fantasy had been fun, if a little unnerving, but he wanted something else tonight. And now that he knew what it felt like to be tied up, he kind of had the urge to tie *her* up. He wouldn't have minded dispensing with the mask, either. Sexy as hell? Yes. But despite that, he still wanted to see her face.

She took his hand. "Ready?"

So she intended to lead him straight to her apartment and get right to the action. He wasn't complaining, but... "I'd hoped to take you out to dinner first."

"I already ate," she said, then stepped up close to him — so close that, despite all the partiers and revelers around them, no one noticed when she pressed her palm against his cock through his khaki pants. "And I want to fuck you, lover. Now."

Warmth encased his body as the hot pressure from her hand turned him even harder. He loved that they stood in the middle of a crowd, but no one knew she was touching him so intimately. "Don't suppose I can argue with that," he murmured, peering heatedly down into her eyes.

Turning, she grabbed his hand and began to guide him across the street to Jackson Square. "One thing, though," he said behind her.

When they reached the sidewalk, she stopped to look up at him. "What's that?"

"Don't tie me up this time. I want to touch you."

"You didn't like how things were last time?"

"I loved it, baby. It was...as if you read my mind." And that was the truth. "But this time I need to have my hands on you." He decided to keep it as simple as that. The last thing he wanted to do was piss off Mistress Mina by refusing to play her little game.

She gazed up into his eyes, the expression in hers pointed, almost feral, giving him the impression that she might want the same thing. "Will you do what I say if I don't tie you up? *Exactly* what I say?"

In actuality, he wasn't sure he could resist taking control if he wasn't bound. He wanted to turn the tables on this exciting, delectable woman. But he wasn't about to tell her that. "Yes," he lied. "Anything."

He sounded so earnest, so needful, it tore at Mia's heart. Part of her was tempted to rip off her mask and wig and say, *It's me, Mia*. Pure insanity, of course. But a big part of her wished he knew she was the woman making wild love to him, the woman he was begging, wanting to touch.

Still, she couldn't. She'd gone too far into this crazy game now. She had to keep playing or she'd lose everything. Her friendship with Ty. Maybe even her job. Definitely this second night of passion. She wasn't willing to give up *any* of those things.

Taking his hand again, she led him up to Bourbon, the crowd and the excitement growing with each step toward the famed street of debauchery. Music played everywhere around them. Guys threw handfuls of beads from balconies to girls who were lifting their shirts below, baring their breasts to the cheers of passersby. Hurricanes and daiquiris and enormous glasses of beer were being drunk, or splashed, or spilled. A glance to her right found a college-aged girl purposely oozing a slushy daiquiri onto her exposed breasts while two guys licked and slurped the drink away.

Mia had never been into that sort of random revelry, even during Mardi Gras. She loved sex, but before Ty, she'd never fucked someone on the first date, and public displays of decadence on the street generally didn't affect her much one way or the other. But tonight, with a river of heat already flowing through her veins and flooding her pussy—everything around her added to her arousal, with or without her permission.

When finally they reached Aunt Sophie's place she reached into her bra and drew out the key, letting them inside. And just like Saturday night, she wanted him so badly that it was all she could do not to just leap on him. She needed to catch her breath, get control of the situation, if she wanted to play his Mistress Mina again.

Whisking into the front parlor, she opened the French doors wide and stepped out on the balcony for a breath of fresh, calming air. The weather was cooler tonight than last week. But the crowd was wilder—Fat Tuesday, the culmination of Mardi Gras, was only three days away, and you could feel the Quarter's tension building with each successive night. This weekend would be the pinnacle of the heavy partying, all the stops pulled out. Maybe this wasn't such a good place for attempting to calm herself.

She stood there unable to think clearly, her desire rising to a fever pitch, when Ty stepped up behind her. His arms slid around her waist as he pressed his hard-on into the center of her ass. She let out a sensual sigh, and rubbed lightly against him, unable to resist.

Reaching up to pull back her red locks, he lowered a tender kiss to the ultrasensitive skin on her neck, letting the sensation flutter down through her. Then he whispered in her ear, "I don't mean to be a bad boy, but if you don't come inside and have your way with me, I'm gonna push up your dress and fuck you on this balcony right now."

She turned into his arms, her soft body raking against his hard one. Invisible sparks flew.

He drew her close against him with one hand, using the other to eagerly massage her breast. "Ooooh," she purred, thinking—*Oh God, yes*, his hands were a welcome addition to this evening already.

Without a hint of hesitation, he tugged on her bodice until one taut nipple appeared above the fabric's scalloped edge. Molding his hand beneath it, he bent to lick. She moaned in response, never giving a thought to whether anyone below could see what they were doing as she reached out and found his erection through his twill pants.

By the time he came up for air, they were both panting, hungering for more.

It was almost enough to make her abandon her plans — to just let him fuck her however came naturally, to just have normal, wild, writhing sex. There was even a part of her that wanted to *submit* to Ty, to find out what he would do to her if she let him.

But she'd liked the sense of control she'd felt last Saturday. She liked it and…well, she also thought maybe she *needed* it — to help her keep her false identity at the forefront, to ensure keeping her secret safe.

So she pushed him away. "You *are* a bad boy," she said pointedly, no humor in her voice. She motioned toward the open doors. "Go inside and prepare to take your punishment."

She couldn't read his look. Disappointment or excitement?

Either way, though, he withdrew from her and went inside as he was told, and recapturing that sense of power gave her the security she needed to maintain her ruse and press forward into another evening of hot sex with Ty.

Following him inside, her heels clicking across the floor, she reached behind her, unzipping her dress. She found Ty standing in the middle of the room, exactly where his wooden chair had been located last time, waiting and watching. Hooking her thumbs through her shoulder straps, she drew the dress off, shrugging free until it fell around her ankles. Her purple lace shelf bra was cut to expose her nipples, so they were both bared now. Her matching garter belt started at her hips, extending nearly to her thighs, cut to resemble a sinfully short miniskirt that barely revealed the crotch of the tiny thong she wore underneath.

She absorbed his long perusal of her body until he finally said, "You take my breath away."

As before, she longed to go to him, just kiss him, just fuck him, but she held her ground — and her identity. "Do you think that makes up for your misbehavior? You promised you'd do exactly as I said, yet I did *not* tell you to come out on the balcony and rub your cock against me. I did *not* tell you to kiss my breast. You've been a very bad boy again, Ty."

Her pussy swelled at the harsh reprimand, even if the dark sparkle in his eyes left her wondering if he was going to acquiesce this time. As much as she relished controlling him right now, the idea that he might not allow it made her cunt spasm further.

"Strip," she demanded.

She took a seat on the sofa and met his gaze, which seemed to silently challenge her. *He's going to fight me on this,* she thought. *He's going to fight me, and what then? Who would win?*

She had to. Because if she didn't, if she turned weak and submissive, she might do something stupid—she might act like herself, she might *sound* like herself. She might even somehow *look* like herself. He might see something in her eyes or hear something in her voice that said Mia to him more than Mistress Mina.

So she glared at him, as if just daring him to argue with her. "Strip, I said."

His eyes narrowed and he looked almost angry, but finally, Ty slowly began to undress. He pulled his polo shirt over his head, dropping it on the floor, then discarded his pants, leaving him in only a pair of gray boxer briefs. His tremendous hard-on made a big tent in front, practically causing her mouth to water.

"All the way," she said when he stopped there, then enjoyed the view as he pushed down his underwear and stepped free of them.

God, he was gorgeous naked. Maybe the other night she'd been too busy with her plans, or too nervous, making sure everything went just right, to really take her time looking at him like this, to just study him and savor it. But now she was doing both. "You have a fabulous body, lover."

"Thank you, Mistress."

His eyes still shot fire as he stared at her, and she suddenly knew she needed to put this man in his place—quickly—before he decided to put her in hers. "Get on your hands and knees," she instructed.

This time, he obediently followed the order, pleasing her. Reaching up, she absently cupped one breast, lightly twirling her nipple as she watched him. He kept his eyes on her, too.

"Now, crawl toward me."

As he did, she observed the muscles in his arms and shoulders working, gliding—he moved toward her like a sexy jungle cat.

When he neared her, she lifted one shoe to stop his progress, pressing the inch-high platform beneath her toes lightly to his forehead. He halted, letting her hold him there like that.

"Lick the heel of my shoe," she told him, a little surprised at the skittery reaction in her cunt. She had planned this part of it—wanting to experiment a little deeper with the notion of submission—never having a clue such an act would excite her, too.

She watched as he dragged his tongue up the smooth patent leather heel, her pussy weeping in response, and added, "Keep going. Onto my ankle, up my leg."

A slow trail of fire climbed her inner calf, past her knee, up her thigh, past the top of her stocking, until he was tonguing her clit through lace. "Ooooh," she moaned hotly, now fondling both her breasts, aware his gaze was glued to them.

"Now reach under my garter belt, and when you find a ribbon, pull it."

He did, his fingers barely whispering across her skin, and when he tugged on the ribbon, her thong loosened.

"Now the other side," she whispered. "Then pull my panties away so you can look at my pussy."

Her legs were spread wide, so once the scrap of lace was gone, her cunt was put on proud display, looking pink and slick and lush.

"Do you want to lick it?"

He dragged his heated gaze to her face, nodding.

"Too bad." She laughed. "Tonight that's a treat reserved for only *good* boys. Instead, you'll stay where you are and watch *me* pleasure it."

Ty couldn't believe her beautifully wet pussy was mere inches from his face and she wasn't going to let him feast on it. Her clit protruded, swollen and needy-looking, as if begging for his tongue, and he yearned to taste her, longed to feel those soft pink inner lips surrounding his mouth as he licked up through them and across the glistening nub of flesh. Just how long, he wondered, was she expecting him to put up with being denied like this? And just how long *would* he? Last time, she'd helped him live out a fantasy. This time, he was *trying* to indulge her dominance, but he simply wanted what he wanted, and he didn't like being told no.

He felt near to collapse when he watched her reach between the couch cushions and draw out a shiny gold vibrator. Even more so when she said, "Get it wet for me, lover," and inserted it into his mouth before he could even think of protesting.

She pushed it in slow and deep in a way that made his stomach contract, since he was unwittingly finding out what it must be like to take a cock in your mouth. She began thrusting the cylinder slowly between his lips, and he wondered how he looked doing this and if she liked it.

Finally, she withdrew the vibrator from his mouth and inserted it smoothly into her pussy in one swift action. "Mmm," she said, then turned the end with long purple fingernails, making the toy buzz to life as she began to slide it easily in and out.

Being that close made him fucking crazy. In one sense, it excited the hell out of him, but in another, he felt excluded, like he desperately needed to be involved.

And, damn it, he was *going* to be involved. Right now.

"Let me lick your clit, Mistress Mina," he said, a little more forcefully than he meant to. And he didn't wait for her to give him permission. Instead, he simply leaned in to lap at her hot, open pussy. *Oh God, she tasted good.* Her clit was like a thick, soft bead on his tongue. He drank in her pungent scent, letting it surround him, drown him.

Above, she bit her lip and whimpered with pleasure, thrilling him. Mmm, yes. His naughty Mistress Mina clearly didn't mind—or at least couldn't resist—letting him take a little control. And he was more than happy to suddenly find himself back in the driver's seat, where he liked to be.

He continued licking, matching the rhythm of her thrusting gold toy, which still vibrated just below his mouth, occasionally bumping his chin. It at once excited and irritated him that she was pushing the hot little rod in and out of herself while he licked her—he wanted *all* her pleasure to come from him.

Reaching up, he covered her fingertips with his at the base of the vibrator. "Let me do it," he murmured against her pink flesh.

She released the toy into his grasp without argument and he instantly pushed it in farther and deeper, harder than her own strokes, loving it when she cried out. *Yes.* He wanted her to feel it coming directly from *him*.

He fastened his mouth tight around the bud of her clit and sucked as he continued fucking her with the vibrator, delivering insistent thrusts. He didn't want her to have any sort of soft, gentle orgasm—no way. He wanted it to hit her hard. He'd taken back control and he was going to use it for his own satisfaction.

She responded to his mouth and the vibrator, meeting the intense drives of the toy, and letting out a hot little cry at each. He drew hard on her clit and made her sob. And he was just beginning to wonder if maybe he'd gone too far, sucked too hard and actually hurt her, when he felt something at the back of his head, bracing him against her.

He looked up from his task, over his shoulder, to see she had locked him in place with their old friend, the black riding crop, placing it behind his head like a bar, holding tight to it with both fists.

"Lick me!" she demanded, pressing on the crop so that he had no other choice. He sank his face back into her wet pink folds and got lost in the work of licking and sucking at her hot nub, still pummeling her with the vibrator, only wishing it were wider and longer so he could give her more.

"Mmm, mmm, mmm," she began to sob in a hot, rising rhythm, and he knew she was about to come. He licked and sucked her simultaneously, effectively French-kissing her clit, and she pulled the crop tighter, pressing him deeper into her. He fucked her as thoroughly as possible with the vibrator, nearly inserting his fingers up inside her along with it.

"Oh God, yes!" she yelled then. "Yes, yes, yes, baby — God, oh God, yeah!" She fucked both his mouth and the vibrator hard, pumping, pumping, filling him with so much satisfaction as she came that he rose up, shoved her to her back on the couch, and buried his cock in her in one brutal thrust.

They both let out ferocious moans and Ty didn't move, just kept her pinned there beneath him, around him, enjoying the simple, feral pleasure of having taken back full control.

When she finally came down from the high, she looked pleasantly spent, filling him with masculine pride. "How was your orgasm, Mistress Mina?"

She gave him a scolding, angry sort of smile. "Excellent, naughty boy. But you're going to be severely punished for your insistence on licking me."

He lowered a soft, tiny kiss to her nipple, then gazed up at her, delivering a wicked grin. "Maybe I've decided I'm through being a good boy. Maybe I've decided to change the rules of our little game."

He had no idea how she would react, but he could tell from her sharp intake of breath that his switch to dominance fueled her excitement.

Even so, she pushed him away and got to her feet before him, so that he was looking up into her smooth-shaven cunt. He watched her cross the room, loving the way she walked around with her breasts and pussy exposed, all the while leaving on her super-sexy lingerie and those fuck-me heels, which he thought he might be officially developing a fetish for, now that he'd actually licked one of them.

"What if I say the game is over then? Meaning the sex is over?" she snapped, turning to face him.

Ah, so she was excited, but resisting it. He knew he was playing with fire, but gave her a truthful answer, still flashing his most devilish look. "I don't think that's going to happen. I don't think you can say no."

She looked defiant. "What makes you so sure?"

"Your pussy's too wet. Your nipples are too pointed. And you might be able to hide your face from me, but you can't hide the excitement in your eyes."

"Lie down on the couch. On your stomach," she said, her voice all business.

"No."

She looked stalwart, angry, and he suddenly understood—if he took *all* her power away, *all* her control, it changed everything she was—or at least everything she'd chosen to be for him. When her expression turned into something new, giving him the idea that she felt a little lost, maybe didn't know what to do, it tore at his heart a little. He realized he needed to meet her halfway, so he spoke gently. "Tell me something, Mina."

He saw her swallow, but her answer still came strong. "What?"

"Have *you* ever been tied up?"

She hesitated, then shook her head.

"Would you like to be?"

She didn't answer.

"After you tied me up the other night, can you tell me, in all honesty, that you didn't wonder how it felt to be on the other side?"

Still no response, but her pink nipples stayed tautly erect, and her eyes glittered with passion.

He dropped his voice even lower. "Let me show you. Give me the power, just this once. Trust me."

She spent a long moment considering the request, then finally took a few steps back toward him, her sexy heels clicking across the floor. "Promise me that in the end, you'll let me...have my way."

"Define that for me, Mina."

"If I let you do what you want to me, you have to return the favor afterward."

He blinked, mulling over the bargain. If she was willing to bend for him like this, couldn't he give her a little something back in return? "Sure," he finally said. "Okay."

She gave a short nod, unsmiling, then strolled back across the room with her pretty ass partially on display beneath that lovely garter belt. She returned a moment later carrying some familiar lengths of rope in her hand, only more of it than last time. "You'll need this," she said softly.

"Indeed I will," he replied, a whole new sort of desire humming through him. He was about to tie her up, about to take her someplace as new as the places she'd been taking him.

"Lie down on the couch," he said, rising from it. "On your stomach." Just like *she'd* wanted *him*.

Mia obeyed, then watched over her shoulder as Ty placed one knee between her legs on the couch and reached for her arms, pulling them gently behind her. She waited as he proceeded to tie her wrists tightly together, unable to deny the excitement that coursed through her at the gnawing of the rope against her skin, at the sense of being truly confined by her lover, her Ty. She couldn't quite believe she'd agreed to this, but even as helpless as she'd felt having to give up her power, she'd wanted *this*, too—wanted to just give herself over to him, in every way.

Next he kneeled beside the couch to bind her ankles together, just as firmly. A part of her began to wonder just exactly what he planned to do to her, how helpless he wanted to make her. But at the same time, she couldn't deny the bizarrely pleasurable tingle in her cunt at knowing she was totally and completely at his mercy.

"What now?" she asked, her heart beating harder than she wanted it to.

He leaned near her ear and whispered, "Now I'm going to whip your firm little ass, just like you whipped mine the other night."

Her pussy seized slightly beneath her at the threat which, at the moment, sounded more like a promise, something she *wanted*.

The first strike of the riding crop was insignificant, just a pleasant little tap on her sensitized skin. The second and third were much the same—just enough to rouse her, to make her a little wetter than she already was.

"Naughty little girl," he murmured above her, that hot, sexy voice shooting another dart of lust to her cunt just as he brought the riding crop down on her ass once more—harder this time. She flinched at the sting.

"Did that hurt?" he asked.

She nodded against the throw pillow supporting her head. "A little. In a...good way."

"Good." Then he swatted her again, hard, the burn traveling all through her and settling firmly in her pussy.

She let out a small moan.

"Mmm, do you like that, naughty girl?"

"Yes," she said, breathless.

"Well, here's some more."

He hit her again, and again, the hot sting flashing through her like lightning, like something illuminating her from the inside out.

Then his rhythm changed—he struck her faster, but with a steady beat, like a drum…like sex. She cried out lightly now at each hot blow of the crop, stunned at the incredible pleasure, even more stunned at how good it felt to relinquish her power to him. She lay there, content to soak it up, enjoying each intense sting of her own mini-whip.

"Mmm, I wish you could see how nice and red your ass is," he cooed, sounding utterly turned-on.

"Me, too," she heard herself breathe without planning.

"I should kiss it and make it feel better," he announced, just before his mouth rained kisses across her bottom.

"Ohhhh," she purred. "That's so good."

"How's this?" he asked, his breath wafting over her skin as one finger eased into her anal passage.

She clenched her teeth and sobbed with fresh delight. She had no experience in that area, but dear God, his touches felt incredible—wildly consuming, more than she could have known. Her voice came out shaky. "So good."

He kissed her ass again, whispering, "Then you'll probably like this even better."

"What?" she asked a split second before she felt something bigger, more solid, nudging at the same hole.

She looked over her shoulder to see Ty easing her vibrator slowly into the tight opening. "Oh God."

Their eyes met and he flashed a dirty smile. "Have you ever been fucked here before?"

She managed a slight shake of her head. "And I never thought I wanted to, but…"

"But what?" he prodded.

"But, God, I do. Oh, I do!"

Just then, the vibrator slipped in, deep in her ass, and the pleasure seared her. She cried out, and Ty said, "Turn back around, baby, and relax. Just feel it."

Having little choice, she did as he instructed, not quite able to believe she'd ended up bound and being fucked in the ass with her own toy. But it was so good, in a way she couldn't have fathomed before this moment. She lay moaning beneath him, her whole body on fire with heat and deep sensation.

She found herself pumping against it, amazed that something there could feel so overwhelmingly hot. "Oh God, I think I could come from this," she admitted on a heated sigh, and he helped her, easing his free hand up between her legs, his fingers sinking into her moist folds.

"Mmm, yes, yes," she said as the heady delight took her to a place of swallowing intoxication. And within a few amazing seconds she was screaming her ecstasy as she drank in the pleasure delivered by both of his hands. The vibrations rocked her, rocked her…until finally they faded and she went still.

Ty eased the vibrator from her ass and bent to lower a kiss to her shoulder. "How was that, baby?"

Spent, she could only sigh her satiation, and they stayed that way for a moment, him bending over her, close enough that she could smell the musky scent of his skin as she listened to the Mardi Gras revelers outside.

Somehow, that sound reminded her—this had gone terribly awry. Or *wonderfully* awry, depending upon how she looked at it. But if she didn't get back some control here—dear God, for the first time it occurred to her that Ty could take her mask off if he wanted to and there wouldn't be a thing she could do to stop him with her hands bound!

"My turn," she said, soft but sure.

He hesitated before reaching to untie her. "Are you sure?" he said, amusement in his voice. "Because from where I sit, you handled the submissive role beautifully, honey."

She flashed a smile over her shoulder. "Okay, so I'm a flexible girl. It's your turn to be flexible again."

"About that," he said, working the rope at her ankles once her wrists were free, "I love the things you do to me, baby, but you might as well know, submitting doesn't come easy to me."

Freed, she sat up next to him. "Then I guess I should be flattered that you've given me as much power as you have."

"Yes, you should."

"And you're saying that's over now?"

His slight nod sent a stark disappointment barreling down through her. Because she wanted to do one more thing to Ty, just one more thing. He'd just inspired her, deeply, and she wanted to bend him to her will one last time.

Reaching out, she began to stroke his long, smooth cock, still standing at attention between his thighs. He pulled in his breath.

"Five minutes," she whispered. "Five more minutes of surrender and I'll take you to heaven, lover. I promise."

The combined heat and tension in the room were palpable as their eyes met in the dim lighting. "I don't think I can—" he began, but she cut him off.

"You can do *this*."

He let out a sigh.

"Pleeease." She flashed persuasive eyes through her mask.

He let out a soft chuckle. "I thought that was supposed to be *my* line."

She returned a small grin. "Unlike you, I'm perfectly willing to beg from time to time in order to get what I want."

His eyes narrowed in grim amusement. "What do you want me to do?"

"Simple. Lay down on the couch like I was, on your stomach."

He lifted a finger in the air. "I don't want to be tied up again."

She rolled her eyes playfully. "Fine."

And even despite his reluctance, Mia's soul filled with excitement as Ty rolled to lay prone on the sofa. She wasted no time, climbing onto the couch, straddling his legs, wondering if he could feel her pussy rubbing wet and open against them as she began to do what she'd done the last time they'd been together here—she slid the length of the riding crop along the crack of his ass.

"Oh God," he groaned.

"Mmm, yes," she purred in reply. Women weren't the only ones to find pleasure in ass play and she was going to give her man as much joy as he'd just given her.

She bit her lip, aroused by rubbing the leather braidwork over his asshole. Slowly to and fro she scraped the crop, sinking it deeper and deeper against him, playing him like a violin. Beneath her, his breath came hot and heavy, drenching her cunt with still more desire.

Before she knew it, their mutual excitement drove her to do something entirely new. She pulled the crop away from his ass, laying it across his lower back as she used both hands to spread him there, study him. She'd never really had much occasion to examine a guy's asshole so intimately, but given that this was Ty, her lifelong dream man, she couldn't have been more deeply thrilled. She stroked the fissure with the pad of her thumb and he moaned, something that she sensed grew from deep in his gut. A second caress produced the same effect, arousing her to her inner core, her very soul.

Drawing in her breath, glad he couldn't see the little experiment she was about to indulge in, she stroked her fingers between her thighs, getting them wet. Then she rubbed her juices in a gentle circle over his anus, watching it open slightly. He uttered a soft, light gasp that pleased her immensely.

Her heart beat faster as she repeated the motion, this time massaging the wetness in, applying more and more pressure to the hot little circles her fingers made.

"Uhhh…" he growled deeply and she knew he liked it.

Would he like what came next?

Taking up the crop again, she studied the handle — nicely rounded and covered in smooth black leather, no seams.

She drew in her breath, her chest tightening in anticipation, as she began to rub the tip of the riding crop's handle in a small circle over Ty's anus.

His groan stretched enormously, seeming to fill the room and drown out the partying and music still wafting up from Bourbon Street below.

She rubbed harder, harder, working it, pressing it gently, until the handle began to slip inside.

"Ah, God!" he yelled.

From shock or pain?

She stopped in mid-insertion, going still. Then she bent down to gently kiss his ass next to where the riding crop now entered. A purring sound left him and he lifted his ass toward her — toward the crop.

She smiled as a sense of fulfillment whirred down through her, settling deep in her pussy. She slid the riding crop's handle in a little farther, and he began to move up and down, fucking it.

Her every sense was on alert now, every pore of her skin extra-sensitized from watching his lovely ass take the riding crop inside, from knowing he wanted it and that she was delivering it.

He moaned softly at every stroke, and she pushed the handle deeper, deeper, making him cry out louder. Soon she was fucking him harder and whispering, "Yes, baby, yes," thrilled at her achievement.

But then she wanted more of him—*had* to have more.

So she carefully climbed down off the couch—still holding the crop in place, still gently fucking his ass and drinking in every hot moan and groan that left him—to kneel beside the sofa.

"Turn onto your side, facing me," she said, a soft command.

He hesitated, and she could understand why, given that she was fucking him with something so long and gangly and that shifting his body might be tricky at the moment, but she said, "Do it," anyway.

He turned slowly, and she carefully moved her tool along with him.

When she saw his face, she was filled with...God, with what? Some emotion that almost buried her, strangled her. He looked so pleasured, and it was all because of her—she was giving this to him.

"This is...the most intense sex I've ever had, Mina."

Her voice came out in a mere whisper. "For me, too." Then, still holding the riding crop in place, she bent to take his lovely cock in her mouth.

A ferocious groan erupted from him, pleasuring her profoundly as she took as much of him as she could, passionately sucking, working him over without reserve, rewarding him for his obedience this one last time.

She slid her lips up and down until her mouth felt stretched and achy and her hand cramped from the awkward angle of holding the crop at his ass, but his sounds of deep enjoyment spurred her on, making her want to suck his big, beautiful shaft dry.

"God, if you don't stop, I might come," he said suddenly.

She released him and met his gaze. "Do you want that? Do you want to come in my mouth?"

He looked surprised at her soft tone. But the last few minutes with Ty had drawn something from deep within her, something that demanded she be tender.

"I want to come inside you," he told her. "In your pussy."

She felt the words in her chest. Mmm, she wanted that, too.

"I want to be able to...fuck you hard, Mina. I have a feeling you like it that way, and I haven't gotten to do it to you like that yet."

Oh yes, she *loved* it hard. And she wanted it that way from him as much as he did.

"One more thing I want," he said softly.

She didn't look at him this time, because she already knew what he was going to say.

"I want to see your face, Mina."

When she didn't answer, he said, "Why are you hiding from me?"

She didn't reply, instead gently withdrew the riding crop, leaving him to sigh at the loss.

"If there's...if there's anything under your mask you're afraid to show me...don't be."

God, he thought maybe she had some sort of scarring or deformity or something. The part that pinched at her gut was the implication that he didn't mind.

She glanced up at him. "Your chivalry is impressive, but it's nothing like that."

"Then why?"

She swallowed, at a loss. No good answer existed. "Listen," she finally said, "I don't want to talk about the mask anymore. What I want is for you to fuck me. Just as hard and long as you promised. No more questions or arguments. Agreed?"

He sighed, but gave a short nod as she knelt next to him on the couch, one shoe curled beneath her stocking-clad leg. "How do you want me?" she asked.

"How do you like it?"

She thought a moment, then turned over, onto her hands and knees, facing the other end of the couch. "Like this."

He let out a groan. "That's so hot, baby."

"If you want control so bad," she said in a slinky voice as she peered over her shoulder at him, "take me."

Placing his hands on her hips, he entered her hard and swift, nearly stealing her breath. He was so awesomely big inside her, the very sensation of him there nearly consumed her. When he began to thrust hard, hitting her G-spot with each hot stroke, it made her feel as if she were going to explode, over and over again. She cried out with each fierce drive into her pussy, overwhelmed by the power of his cock.

Thank God he'd wanted to do it like this—she'd not realized what she'd been missing. Now she was filled with pleasure, filled with Ty...simply filled.

Between his groans of delight, he murmured that he wanted to make her come again, and the next thing she knew, one of his hands had snaked around her hip, between her legs, his fingers sinking into her wetness. "God, yes!" she shrieked.

Oh, it wouldn't take long, she knew without doubt. She was too excited. And his cock was so big. Part of her wanted to let him fuck her this way all night, but she realized it was impossible—her body was too racked with pleasure already, and he'd admitted to being on the edge, too.

"Yes, rub my pussy," she prodded him, still trying to hold onto a little of her authority as she approached climax—when, without warning, it shattered over her like her body was a piece of crystal breaking into stunning shards of heat and light, and all of them were shimmering down through her as she came against his hand.

And then he was yelling, "God, me too, honey!" and his thrusts nearly skewered her to the couch, they were so deep and penetrating. Again, again, again, he pounded into her, pummeling her, burying her in sensation.

The moment he withdrew, she turned in his arms, needing to see him, hold him, needing for *him* to hold *her*. Without quite meaning to, she clung to him, bitten by that same overwhelming emotion again. She'd meant simply to kiss him, share the afterglow in an easy embrace—but instead she was clutching him tight and never wanted the moment to end, never wanted to let him go.

Chapter Six

Ty rained kisses across her lips, her jaw, her neck and chest, soon nibbling at her perfect pink nipple, still jutting beautifully erect above her sexy, revealing bra.

"Tell me something, Mistress Mina," he said, basking in the lazy serenity that followed great sex. "Are you always this wild?" He flashed a grin.

He watched her blink beneath that damn mask she still wouldn't shed for him. Then she lifted her green gaze to his. "Could be I'm normally a shy, prim little schoolteacher who wears high-collared blouses and her hair in a bun. Or...could be that you can see me nightly, stripping at Club Venus up the street, and that my specialty is hot lap dances on guys just like you."

He tilted his head, sorry she seemed to be slipping back into game mode, after the intense moments they'd shared. He'd thought maybe he'd been starting to peel back the layers of his mysterious Mistress Mina, thought maybe he'd been getting a little closer to the real her. "Which is it?" he asked anyway.

"It's whichever you want it to be," she purred, pulling him down for a soft tongue kiss. "Now, *you* tell *me* something."

"Anything," he said, attempting to prove a point. "Unlike you, I'm an open book."

She ignored the sarcasm and asked, "Ever been fucked in the ass before, naughty boy?"

He grinned. Now that it was over, he couldn't quite believe that had happened or that he'd enjoyed it so much. "Um, no."

"So I took your virginity," she said on a light, sophisticated laugh.

He chuckled along with her. "I wasn't aware I had any virginity left to take, but…uh, yeah, maybe you did. Just like I took yours in the same place."

They shared a deliciously mischievous smile.

"What's next for us, Miss Mina?"

"Next?"

He nodded. "Next tonight? Next, the next time I see you?"

Her smile faded. "I'm afraid we'll have to stick to the '*I'll* call *you*' plan, like before."

A horrible thought struck him. "Are you married or something?"

She shook her head. "No, of course not."

"Then why so secretive? You obviously enjoy my company enough to come back for more. Why won't you give me your number, give this thing a chance?"

"This thing?"

He motioned back and forth between them. "Me and you."

She bit her lip, looking pensive, and it forced him to recognize the leap in thought he'd made—a leap for which he was usually on the receiving end. He'd never been on *this* side before—the side that wanted it to be more than just an affair.

"Wait, you don't have to say it," he told her, pulling back slightly.

"Say what?"

"That this is just sex. We're not *dating*, not *seeing each other*, this is fucking and that's all."

She turned away from him then, which he thought odd— since he couldn't see her face anyway.

"What's wrong?"

"I'm sorry," she said. "It *can't* be any more than that. I can't explain why, but it simply can't."

Ty sat up. His heart physically hurt in his chest, but he told himself he was still just recovering from so much kinky sex. He had *not* gotten emotionally involved with his masked dominatrix. He refused to even consider that as a possibility. Even as much as he wished she hadn't closed back up on him emotionally just now, even as much as he'd liked finding out she had a soft side when she'd agreed to submit to him a little. Taking a deep breath, he rose from the couch and went to retrieve his clothes across the room.

"You're leaving?"

He glanced over his shoulder to see her sitting up, as well. "Yeah. I mean, if it can only be sex, well…the sex is over for tonight, right?"

She nodded. And he got dressed, realizing he *wanted* to leave now. Even if he sort of hated leaving, too. But the damnable truth was—if it couldn't be anymore than just this, just the fucking part, he didn't want it.

He couldn't *believe* he didn't want it, could barely fathom that the great sex she'd shared with him wasn't enough for him, but he also couldn't fight whatever was going on inside him—and the fact was, it *wasn't* enough. He wasn't sure how it had happened, but he *had* gotten emotionally involved.

He walked to the door without looking back, feeling angry, even if a part of him knew that was stupid. God knew they'd never made each other any promises, and they'd never even had any reason to—it had been two nights of hot sex, plain and simple. Maybe he was angry at himself—for wanting more. Wanting to see her face so damn badly. His chest felt tight, achy.

Her clicking heels approached hurriedly behind him, but he didn't look back until she grabbed onto his wrist.

"Not even a goodbye?" she asked.

Their gazes met, held. Then he placed his hand on the back of her head amid all those wild red curls and kissed her lush lips, one last time. "Goodbye, Mina."

He walked out the door, hailed the first taxi he saw, and headed for home, feeling empty inside for reasons he couldn't quite understand.

* * * * *

Mia sat alone in her apartment the next day, flipping through channels, watching nothing, hating everything about Mardi Gras and wishing it would end. Wishing lots of things. Like that she'd never concocted the insane idea to put on a mask and seduce Ty.

Although tears rose behind her eyes at the thought, because how could she regret the wild intimacy they'd shared, at once so new and yet so comfortable? She didn't think she could have done those things with anyone else.

God, she'd thought she could do this—take this for what it was, hot sex. She'd thought it would fill a physical need, bring the fantasy to life, and maybe then she could move on, get Ty out of her mind.

Instead, though, just the opposite had happened.

She had no choice but to recognize the devastating truth—she was in love with him.

* * * * *

"Morning, sweet thing," Ty said on Monday as he walked into the messenger service, the plate glass door falling shut behind him.

"Morning, Ty," she said without looking up, pretending she was immersed in paperwork.

"Any messages?" he called from his office.

"Bobby's going to be—"

235

"Fired," he said before she could finish. "When he gets here, send him in to see me. And start looking through applications for a replacement."

Wow, he sounded like he was in a *bad* mood. Was it because of Mistress Mina? Was it possible he'd taken their time together that seriously?

Against her better judgment, she got up and walked to his doorway. "Listen," she said softly, "I know it's none of my business who you fire, but...Bobby's actually sick today. Really sick. He threw up while we were on the phone and I'm ninety-nine percent sure he couldn't fake that."

Ty shrugged. "A hangover during Mardi Gras isn't a good excuse."

Oh. Stupidly, perhaps, she hadn't thought of that—given that she was trying to forget Mardi Gras existed.

"Besides, even if he had the Russian flu, it's one time too many. I've got a business to run and I need dependable employees—like you."

She swallowed nervously, thinking her usual—*If you only knew*.

"Um, how was your weekend?" she dared ask.

"Shitty, thanks."

"Why? I...I thought you had a date with your hot chick from last week."

"I did. It didn't end well. End of story."

She nodded, still a little amazed that the things he'd indulged in with Mistress Mina had mattered to him so much.

"How was *your* weekend? Better than mine, I hope. Did you see your new tattoo-free guy?"

She nodded.

"And?"

"And...that didn't go so well, either. I...don't think I'll be seeing him again." She hurried to add, "I mean, at least not...romantically."

236

He tilted his head, his expression softening. "Sorry it didn't work out, sweet thing."

Her heart wilted a little in her chest. "Yeah, I'm sorry yours didn't go better, too."

* * * * *

Fat Tuesday. The last day of Mardi Gras. The night of the biggest blowouts, the most wild debauchery, the most hedonistic revelry. Ty sat in his apartment, the first floor of a grand old house on Esplanade, at the edge of the Quarter, watching the daily Mardi Gras report on the evening news. Picking up his fork, he dug into the reheated red beans and rice Liz had sent home with him after he'd had dinner at their place over the weekend.

I should go out and take part in that, he told himself, watching a bunch of beaded and masked people screaming for the TV camera.

I should go down to Club Venus and get a lap dance or five and see if Mina turns up straddling my crotch at any point. But he doubted she would.

No, I should just get drunk, hang out on the street, and give beads to girls all-too-willing to jiggle their bare breasts for me, then maybe get laid by one of them.

Or maybe I should walk into a store, buy a mask of my own, and pick up girls that *way.*

Only problem was—none of it sounded any fun. Not the least bit titillating or desirable. Shit, this Mistress Mina thing had hit him hard, harder than he could easily understand. He barely knew her. Why had he cared so much? Why had he wanted so much more of her?

Finishing his dinner, he stuffed his wallet in his pocket, grabbed his keys, and headed for the door, without even knowing where he intended to go.

He set out walking, glad the night was clear and warm— sorry each time he happened upon a group of early revelers getting amped up for the last big party of this year's festivities. He wanted…he wanted…

Something that felt…safe. Normal. Good.

He wanted to go someplace where he knew there were no worries, where things were easy, comfortable. He could only think of two places that really qualified — Jack and Liz's place, or Mia's. He chose Mia, thinking maybe she was lonely, too, given her romantic failure of the weekend just past.

And the closer he got to her apartment, the more *right* it seemed to hang out with her tonight. Maybe they could just talk, pour their hearts out to each other over a bottle of wine or something. Maybe he'd been foolish all this time — thinking sex was more important than a woman's personality. Maybe he should try thinking of Mia as more than a friend and see what came of it.

He stopped into a liquor store on the way, grabbing a chilled bottle of Chablis, remembering it was Mia's wine of choice.

Reaching her building, he let himself through the gate that led to the courtyard, walked past the pleasant little fountain that gurgled there, then headed up the neatly whitewashed stairs and down the veranda until he knocked on her door.

She opened it wearing denim shorts, a cute fitted pullover of pale yellow, and a surprised look. "Ty — what's up?"

Only then did it occur to him to feel slightly sheepish. But he decided to be frank. "It's Fat Tuesday and for the first time in my life, I don't want to spend it partying. I just want to hang out with a friend, drink some wine or something." He held up the bottle. "You up for it?"

She blinked. Looked confused. He started to regret coming. Maybe she was busy. Or maybe *he* seemed desperate.

But then she smiled. "Sure. Yeah. Come in." She stood back to offer him entry.

He hesitated slightly. "You didn't have any big plans for the evening, did you?"

"Me? No. I'm not...you know...much of a partier."

"Except with tattooed guys," he said with a grin.

She laughed. "Yeah, except for them." Before closing the door, she glanced down toward the courtyard, which was quiet and empty, other than some Zydeco music coming from someone's window, loud enough at the moment to override the sounds of Mardi Gras on the streets beyond. "Hey, do you want to sit outside and drink? It's nice out—warm."

"Yeah," he said. "Sounds good."

"Let me grab some glasses and a corkscrew from the kitchen. And I have a couple of folding lawn chairs in my bedroom, in the closet, if you want to go get them."

He said, "Sure," set his wine bottle on a table next to the door, and headed off in search of chairs as Mia went in the other direction.

Entering her bedroom, he made a beeline for the closet— but was stopped dead in his tracks by what lay on her dresser. Two Mardi Gras masks. One in black with silver cording. The other of purple sequins with dangling beads.

He actually blinked, hard, then opened his eyes again, somehow thinking he'd see them differently.

But no—they were the same. The same very familiar masks. He picked up both in one hand, his stomach wrenching painfully as he tried to make sense of it. Which is when it hit him. *Mina. Mia. Mina. Mia.*

All along, he'd had the bizarre feeling of knowing her, although maybe at the time he'd perceived it more as *wanting* to know her. But now, as it all slowly became clear to him...damn, how could it be?

How could his sweet Mia have been Mistress Mina?

My God, the intimate acts they'd indulged in together! The things he'd let her do to him!

Along with the general shock of finding out his seductress had been Mia came the surprise of discovering that apparently she wasn't the sweet, docile girl he'd always thought. Tim's little sister, the girl Ty had always wanted to protect, look out for. Apparently, it was the other way around—*he* needed protection from *her*.

Feelings of humiliation, stupidity, and anger warred within him. His hands curled into fists as his body tensed. Why the fuck would she do this to him? Why would she lie, pretend?

"Ty, did you find the chairs okay?" Her voice grew closer as she spoke, until she walked into the room. "They're behind..."

Her eyes fell on the masks he held. She went pale, still, and they stared at each other for a long, strange moment.

"Why?" he boomed at her. "Why the hell did you do it?"

Her eyes went wide and her mouth dropped open, but nothing came out.

"Why, Mia? Or is that *Mina*? Why did you lie to me? Answer me, damn it."

"I...I can explain." She looked panicky, shaky. He thought she sure as hell should.

"Well, start talking."

Shudders ran the entire length of Mia's body. How had she been so stupid, letting him come in here? He'd shown up at her door unexpected, and she hadn't even thought... Oh God. She'd just said she could explain, but could she? "I...I... God, Ty, I just...wanted to be with you."

He looked incredulous, and she couldn't blame him. "So you thought it would be clever to put on a mask and a wig and make me think you were somebody else?"

She nodded. Then shook her head. She was so confused. "I...I never thought you'd want *me*. So I just thought, with it being Mardi Gras and all, that maybe, just once, I could be someone else. Just for some fun. One sexy night. Something different and…memorable."

"So you thought it would be amusing to put one over on me, use me for some kinky sex, then cut me loose and never fill me in that it was you."

She'd never seen him look more disgusted, and behind that, in his eyes, just plain sad. She didn't know what to say, how she could possibly salvage this. The worst had happened — everything good they'd ever shared was ruined now.

Which made her realize she had nothing to lose. So she told him the unthinkable truth. "Ty, I've had a huge crush on you since I was thirteen years old. All these years, I've wanted you. But I knew you only saw me as a friend, or as Tim's little sister. I knew nothing would ever happen between us if I didn't *make* it happen. I'm thirty-one years old. I wanted to have wild, crazy sex with you. Just once. Just to get it out of my system."

"We fucked twice," he snapped, lips set in a grim, straight line.

"You wanted to see me again. You wouldn't let it go." Her voice quivered now that she'd told him the whole embarrassing truth. "So I…couldn't resist doing it again." When still nothing changed in his enraged eyes, she babbled on further. "I never meant any harm. I just wanted to have a good time, without any repercussions. I wanted to give you a good time, too. That's all."

"That's all, huh?" he repeated, sounding cynical. Then he dropped the masks back to the dresser. "I'll leave these for the next time you want to make some unsuspecting guy feel like a fool. I'm outta here."

With that, he stormed from the room, out of the apartment, slamming the door behind him before she could even catch her breath.

She plopped down on the bed, burying her head in her hands. How the hell had this happened? And just when she'd been ready to put it behind her and move on.

Well, she amended, not *move on*. Now that she knew she was in love with Ty, moving on sounded next to impossible — but she'd been ready to try resuming their old relationship, ready to attempt surviving the brutal emotion of love and maybe someday get past it. Now, everything was a colossal mess. And she couldn't imagine any possible way to fix it.

* * * * *

Ty stalked away from her building, heading for Bourbon Street, his entire body tense. She'd used him. Lied to him and used him.

Tied him up, for God's sake. Made him lick her goddamn shoe! *Fucked him with a riding crop!*

He shook his head in disbelief. It had been crazy enough back when he'd thought they were two strangers. But to find out his masked seductress was someone he knew, someone he knew *very well*, and that she was lying to him and using him because she wanted to experiment with some kinky sex was…mortifying. To think of how he'd pined over her. Tried to track her down. Longed to take that mask off and see her face.

Well, at least now he knew why she'd been so damned adamant about leaving the mask on.

Then new thoughts hit him. He'd seen, felt, *tasted* Mia's breasts now. *Mia's!* He'd seen, felt, tasted — *deeply* — her pussy. She *shaved* it. Never in a million years would he have imagined Mia was a sensual, sexual enough creature to do that. Or to own that kind of lingerie. To *want* that sort of wild, hedonistic sex.

He shook his head, extremely confused and sorry to acknowledge that his cock was getting stiff with the memories, with the realization that his wild, riotous sex partner was sweet Mia, who he'd thought didn't have a kinky, dirty bone in her body.

Turning a corner onto Bourbon was literally walking into an enormous, wild party. Everywhere he looked, people were drinking, laughing, making out. A jazz band played in the street. People in costumes—wizards, tigers, court jesters—passed by. Girls were lifting their shirts and collecting mountains of beads to weigh down their necks. Strippers stood in doorways, scantily clad, beckoning men inside.

Yet the only thing that really grabbed Ty's attention was one of the French Quarter's many sex shops—lit up and wide open for business.

He wandered inside, drawn instantly—for the first time ever—to the bondage section.

Anger at Mia still burned inside him—it hadn't even begun to slack off. But his cock burned, too, in a different way. Hungrily. Urgently.

Maybe, he thought as he picked up a package of leather ties, he should teach Mistress *Mia* a little lesson. Maybe he'd show her exactly how it felt to be used for kinky sex. Maybe Fat Tuesday would turn out to be a wild night yet—when he introduced little miss Mia to *real* dominance.

Chapter Seven

೫

Mia flinched when someone pounded on the door. Who on earth…?

Yet, as she ran to answer it, she knew who she'd find on the other side.

What she *didn't* expect was to find Ty standing there wearing a simple but sexy little black mask. Despite herself, her pussy went wet. "Ty…" she said uncertainly.

He barreled in without being invited and shut the door, turning the lock behind him. He still wore the same grim expression as before, but his eyes looked different now — they looked furious and…intensely passionate.

She noticed the shopping bag he carried only when he set it down with a thump.

Impatiently, he reached for the hem of her shirt. "Take this off," he demanded.

"What?" Had she heard him correctly?

"Lift your arms up over your head, damn it," he bit off, and she did as he said. He stripped off her top in less than two seconds, tossing it across the room. Next, he reached for the button on her shorts, briskly lowering the zipper and shoving them down, so that she stood before him in a lacy coral-colored bra and matching panties.

"Ty, what are you doing?" she asked, breathless.

He stepped up close enough that she could feel his erection pressing into the front of her undies, and spoke low and firm. "I'm giving you a taste of your own medicine, Mistress Mina. I'm gonna find out how *you* like being used for kinky sex."

She drew in her breath, both frightened and thrilled. She had no idea what Ty might do to her, and she'd definitely never seen him this angry or determined-looking, but she also couldn't imagine anything he could do to her that wouldn't excite her right now.

They stood looking at each other, the air filled with hot tension until he closed both hands hard on her ass and pulled her to him for a rough kiss that left her breathless. She twined her arms around his neck as he moved one hand to her breast for a brutal caress that filled her with more wet pleasure than she could have anticipated.

Still crushing her to him, he yanked one bra strap off her shoulder, baring her nipple, then possessively lifted it to his mouth. He sucked hard, making her whimper at the pleasure-pain of it. Even while it hurt, she'd never felt anything so powerful or intense, and it swept her away in a rush of hot desire. "Mmm, God," she murmured.

Then his hands were at the back of her bra, deftly unhooking it. "Take it off, all the way. I haven't seen your breasts without anything on them or around them," he said in that same commanding voice.

She shrugged free of the bra, then stood beneath his scrutiny, her breasts achy and tingling under his gaze. He cupped them both in his large hands, as if testing the weight, then began to knead them, hot and vigorous. Heated, thready sighs left her until he urgently lowered his mouth to the other breast, suckling hard again. The sensation shot through her like licks of flame. She cried out, grabbing onto him for balance, and he gripped her ass once more, this time lifting her up into his arms and carrying her into the bedroom.

He tossed her on the bed and she lay there, aroused and unsure, waiting until he returned with the bag he'd brought.

The first thing he drew out was a long, black strip of leather. Straddling her in the bed, he pushed her arms up over her head and tied her wrists with it, pulling the leather into a tight knot. Then he attached it to the wrought iron headboard.

She remained wildly aware how close his cock was—to her mouth, her breasts—and she wished madly that he were naked. But she dared not say a word.

Backing off of her, he said, "Lift your ass," then harshly pulled down her panties. He tossed them aside as he rose from the bed and reached into his bag, extracting…something black, a large swath of leather, but she wasn't sure what it was until he said, "Lift," again, and this time slid it under her. He drew it around her waist and began to lace it by hand. It stretched from her rib cage to her hips and she realized it was a waist-cincher, an item that struck her as somewhat Victorian and completely wicked in terms of bondage—especially when he laced it tight, tight, *tight*, making her feel utterly imprisoned in the thing before finally finishing.

Next he withdrew a thick, black leather collar from the bag, which he fastened around her neck. Like the waist-cincher, it made her feel pleasantly trapped, forcing sensation on her with each and every move she made.

And then he left. Just left the room—picked up his bag and walked out!

Minutes began to pass and she wondered if he'd departed from the apartment completely and meant to leave her here like this, trussed naked except for a bit of black leather, until she called out for help and someone found her. God, talk about payback.

And on top of that, her pussy wept for him. She could feel the comforter dampening beneath her. She'd been a little frightened and totally unsure what would happen to them once this was over, but from the moment he'd shown up at her door, she'd been aroused and ready for whatever this evening held, for whatever he *wanted* it to hold. If he wanted to punish her, she figured she deserved it. She'd take whatever he dished out.

Just when she'd seriously begun to worry that maybe he'd left her like this, he tramped back into the room—no longer a lighthearted beach boy, but now clearly a god of all that was dark and dangerous.

She gasped at the sight of him, and her cunt spasmed. Across his chest he wore a black halter-like apparatus constructed of thin leather strips connected by silver rings. His eyes still shone through his sexy black mask, and now his neck was adorned with the same sort of collar she wore. Thick leather cuffs circled both wrists, and below, he'd donned black leather pants—with no crotch. His big cock stood at full attention between the leather leggings, completely exposed. She was stunned speechless. And so damn hungry for him. To think this man had wanted to be tied up—when he was clearly born to be a woman's master.

As he stood looking at her, tied to the bed in her scant leather regalia, she felt a whole new kind of beautiful, and she *relished* submitting to him. She still feared for tomorrow and the future of their relationship, but for tonight, she was going to soak up every bit of domination he wanted to heap on her.

"Are you ready to be my sex slave, Mia?" he asked sharply.

She nodded, answering with one quiet word. "Yes." *So very ready.*

He walked to the bed and straddled her again, but higher up this time, his thighs settling across her shoulders, the black leather of his pants rubbing warm on her skin. "Then suck my cock, slave," he demanded, rising on his knees and holding his shaft down to insert it in her mouth. She opened wide, accepting it with ease.

To have him between her lips, sinking deep, near her throat, without having any control over it, was breathtaking. She felt so owned, so wholly possessed—but in this moment she *wanted* to be owned by him, *wanted* to be whatever he wanted to make of her. Her pussy fluttered with delight as he slid his hard, lovely cock in and out of her mouth, slow at first, but then slightly harder, deeper, until he was groaning with each stroke between her lips. Her mouth felt so stretched, to a degree that—under normal circumstances—would have made her back off slightly, take a break. But like this, now, she couldn't *choose* to take a break—and it was arousing to have the option stolen from her, to be gently forced to suck his cock until he decided he'd had enough.

When finally he withdrew the massive shaft, her mouth felt instantly empty, abandoned—but joyfully well-used.

What now? she wondered, thinking, *More, I want more of this. I want to be his slave*, but not daring to speak.

That angry fire still lit his eyes as he shifted back, still straddling her—until his erection came to lay between her breasts. He reached down and pressed the soft mounds up into his hard cock, beginning to slide back and forth, fucking them. She moaned at the raw heated delight of having that ultra-hardness enclosed by her sensitive, tender flesh, glad she'd left him so wet that he could glide with slick ease between her breasts. Above, he groaned deeply, watching the connection of their bodies, and she was thrilled to see that even amid his anger, she could still bring him pleasure.

His thrusts turned rough, intense, making her feel it all the more, and love it all the better. *Yes, yes*, she thought, still not brave enough to utter a word. *Fuck my breasts, Ty. Fuck me every way possible.*

Finally, he released her breasts and moved still farther down her naked body, pushing her legs apart and kneeling in between. Her heart threatened to pound right through her chest as she lay bound and watching him study her pussy. Planting his palms on her thighs, he spread them farther, opened her wider. Oh God, she wanted him inside. *Please, Ty. Please.*

Without warning, he drove two fingers into her cunt, making her sob at the hot, pleasant intrusion. "Your pussy's wet, slave," he said, although his voice seemed slightly calmer now than before.

"Because I'm excited. I want you inside me," she said between heated breaths.

"You're supposed to be *scared*," he said, his tone taking on a rough edge again. "You're supposed to worry I might *hurt* you."

She only shook her head, moaning lightly as he continued thrusting his fingers into her hungry little passageway. "Whatever you do, I deserve. I shouldn't have lied to you. I never thought about...well, so many things. I never thought about how you'd feel if you found out. I was selfish. Whatever you want from me tonight is okay. I owe it to you. Do anything you want to me, Ty. *Anything*."

His face looked almost agonized with lust as he stared into her eyes, then dropped his gaze back to her cunt. She bit her lip, knowing it must be glistening for him, knowing his fingers must be drenched.

"God," he murmured finally, and in quick succession, he withdrew his fingers, lifted her thighs, and rammed his cock deep inside her.

She cried out at the blow—hard and filling and all-consuming, and somehow, even then, she wanted more of him. His shaft was enormous inside her, yet she still managed to yearn for more. She wanted to hurt for him, to somehow atone for what she'd done. She truly wanted to be his sex slave in every way.

"I'm gonna fuck you so hard, Mia," he bit off, his voice gritty, gone back to pure, unadulterated heat now, and she thought, *this is how it should be. This*—it turned out—was *her* perfect fantasy coming to life. Ty calling her by name, promising her an incredible fuck that would leave them both well-pleasured and spent.

He pummeled her with his huge cock, driving, driving, deep inside her, so that she felt his thrusts everywhere— pulsing through her arms and legs, her breasts, even her head. The leather at her waist and neck created a hot friction with each rough jolt of his pounding shaft, and his leggings rubbed at the backs of her thighs. They both cried out at each mind-numbing thrust.

Her breasts bounced and he closed his hands greedily around them, kneading, massaging. She pulled involuntarily at the leather binding her wrists, frustrated at not being able to touch him. He released her breasts, yet closed his forefingers and thumbs around her nipples, pinching them tight and pulling, drawing them upward—making her grit her teeth at more pleasure-pain—until he let them go and she released a screech.

She writhed in his grasp then, overcome with pleasure and pain and frustration and heat, taking each stroke of his cock deep within her being, feeling wild and crazed inside, his new grip on her breasts turning needy and rough. She suddenly knew that he wanted her to struggle, and so she did, thrashing about as he filled her, absorbing more kinds of friction and hot delight than she could easily comprehend, and she sensed it making them both even more reckless and untamed. His heated cries turned to harsh growls, hers to groans drawn up from deep in her gut. "Oh, fuck me," she begged through clenched teeth. "Fuck me. *Fuck me.*"

It was all so good. The binding, the battle, his hands, his cock. His face, above her. Even soaked in his anger, she loved it because…well, maybe she was angry, too! Angry that she'd wanted him for so long without having him until now. That's why she struggled at her bindings for him, even as she wrapped her legs around his back. There was anger and frustration and a deep, forbidden sort of passion all lurking inside her and needing to get out—now—in his arms.

"Come in me, Ty! Come in me. I want to make you come so bad, so hard," she sobbed.

But then, clenching his teeth and looking agonized to the depths of his soul, he pulled his cock out and dropped her ass to the bed.

She felt abandoned. "What are you doing?" she practically shrieked.

"You can't fucking tell me when to come!" he boomed. "You're not in charge this time, Mia! This time it's all about *me*, punishing *you*!"

She had a feeling they'd both forgotten that for a few intense minutes, but now they remembered. Her body heaved with frustration where she lay stretched out on the bed.

"And we're not done here," he added in a low voice, his eyes shining hotly on her. "We're not even *close* to being done."

"What now?" she asked, suddenly reminding herself of *him* when their positions had been reversed, always wondering what came next.

In response, he reached up over her, his slick erection dangling down to touch one breast as he untied her from the bed — but he didn't untie her hands from each other.

"Now, I'm going to spank you. Hard!"

She tensed in a combination of fear and anticipation as he maneuvered her body, face down, over his lap, on the edge of the bed, and leaned down near her ear. "Tell me you've been a bad little girl," he said, no hint of playfulness coloring his voice.

"I have. I've been a *very* bad girl." She meant it. She believed it.

"Beg me to punish you for it."

She drew in her breath. "Punish me. Yes. I deserve it. Spank me."

The first slap of his hand across her ass landed with a sting that echoed all through her. Mmm, *God* — still more of that strange pleasure-pain. She wanted it, and when the flat of his hand struck her again, she cried out — in joy, because it hurt. Because she felt it everywhere. *More*, she thought, not daring to speak now. *I want more.*

He spanked her in a smooth, hard, even rhythm, each strike flaring through her with power and heat. The spanking radiated through every limb, each slap of his palm coming before the vibrations from the last had faded. She cried out—all pleasure now, even as her ass stung and grew sore, so very sore. But it was a *good* kind of sore, the same lovely kind of sore she'd first experienced when he'd whipped her the other night. Only this was more intense than that. This was not a playful game—this was a strong, forceful man dominating her, and she was joyfully lost in the power of that domination.

And then...something new! What was he doing *now*? Even as he spanked her, even as she cried out, she swung to look over her shoulder and saw—oh God!—he was...he was putting something inside her ass—a string with little balls placed every couple of inches. Anal beads—she recalled seeing them at the sex shop when she'd bought her rope and riding crop. He was inserting them, one by one, sending tiny explosions of pleasure through her nether regions with each added ball. She gaped, trying to watch even as she drank in his blows, her ass red now from his perfect spanking.

By the time he was done with the beads, she could no longer discern what was happening to her body. She lay writhing, whimpering across him, lost in the tumult of sensation. It was almost more than she could take, pushing her to the edge of sanity.

And then he was bending over her, whispering, "Now fuck me, Mia. Fuck me. Ride me."

She gazed over her shoulder, up into his eyes this time.

He peered heatedly at her and said it again. "Ride me...lover." As she'd called him in her role as Mistress Mina.

Slowly, she rose to her knees next to him. He reached for her thigh, prodding her to straddle his hips. She glanced down between them at his tremendous, straining cock. She'd never wanted anything more than she wanted this man back inside her right now. She didn't know if he was still angry or not—she had no idea how he might feel about her now—she only knew she needed him inside her body. Because she loved him. She loved him deeply.

She sank slowly down on his erection, pleased at how enormous he felt filling her. "So big," she breathed, her eyes falling shut, head dropping back with the ecstasy of his size combined with the beads that seemed to ripple gloriously about inside her ass.

A soft kiss brushed her neck. "Do you like my cock, Mia?" he whispered.

She lowered her head and opened her eyes, meeting his gaze. "Oh, God, yes."

She saw his lips move more than she actually heard his nearly inaudible request. "Fuck me."

She leaned deeper into him, beginning to move in the most ancient rhythm, her instincts instantly taking over. They both moaned as she undulated against him. Her bound arms circled his neck, his hands splayed wide on her ass. She fucked him slowly, their foreheads touching. Her breasts raked against his chest, the leather that crisscrossed it abrading her nipples lightly.

But soon she was driven to move faster, to fuck deeper, her clit brushing against him, her pussy beginning to reach for release. The beads inside her anus jiggled and rubbed in response to her movements, heightening every sensation. He kissed her hard, deep, as they moved, and she pushed her tongue into his mouth, hungering for still more of him. His hands roamed her shoulders, her back, one sliding around to caress her breast, raking his thumb across the sensitive peak.

But then his hands both returned to her ass and she rode him in hot circles that brought her closer and closer to ecstasy, making the desire churn and rise. He lifted to suckle at her breast, and she sobbed lightly, murmuring, "Yes, suck me. So good, so good," as she held his head there, watched him tugging on her nipple with his eager mouth.

And then—ahhh!—he pulled the string and one of the beads left her in a hot little blip of pleasure that made her moan.

Her breath went ragged as she rode him harder, as he suckled her, and he drew another bead out, pushing her still closer to the edge.

He began pulling the beads faster, in a slow rhythm that matched the hot circles in which she writhed, and she was lost, so lost in him and in the pleasure, that there was no thought, only feeling, stretching through her like an electrical line giving off immeasurable heat and energy.

"So close," she whispered in his ear, still moving, grinding her body against his—and then he extracted the last bead and she fell off the edge, the climax pulling her deep within herself, burying her in hot pulses of delight that echoed through her, coming out in low groans wrenched deep from her gut. And also in words. "I love you. God, I love you," she murmured up into the air without thought.

"Damn, I'm coming, too," he breathed upon releasing her breast from his mouth and as before, when he came, he lifted her body from the bed with his orgasmic thrusts, making her feel exactly what she *wanted* to feel—overpowered by him, possessed by him.

They both fell back on the bed in a heap and lay that way, silent, for a long moment.

When Mia finally opened her eyes, he was looking at her. He shifted his gaze to her hands, and reached to undo the leather strip, setting her free. Her first move was to slip the sexy black mask from his head—completely understanding now his previous need to see her face. She wanted nothing more in this moment than to see his.

Although she didn't know what to say, what to expect from him now. She only knew she'd just had the most phenomenal sex of her life, and it had been reckless and scary and infinitely exciting, and it had been with Ty, the man she loved.

"I've been a fucking idiot," he said, gazing at her.

"Huh?"

He shook his head against the comforter, then ran one hand through his hair. "I don't know what I was so mad about."

"Because I lied to you," she reminded him, thinking it made perfect sense. "I tricked you."

"But you were right when you said I never would have given us a chance otherwise. I just...never thought of you this way."

"I know. And there were times when I tried to hint to you that maybe I wasn't the girl you thought I was..." She stopped, confused by her own words. "But the thing is, Ty, I *am* that girl you thought I was. I'm a nice person and a dependable, capable worker, and I'm Tim's little sister. And I'm *this* person, too." She looked away, toward the ceiling. It was stupid to bother being embarrassed *now*, but... "This person who loves to fuck and play sex games and sometimes be *really, really* dirty." She sighed. "Only..."

"Only what?"

She wasn't sure she wanted to tell him this, but at this point—what the hell. "Only I've never gotten nearly so dirty with anyone as I have with you."

She felt his eyes on her and dared to lower her gaze and meet them. "Because of what you said?" he asked. "When you were coming just now?"

She took a deep breath. "Yes."

"That was real? You love me?"

God, was he *still* trying to torture her? "Yes. Yes, it was real. I'm in love with you, okay?" She turned her head away instantly, unable to believe she'd just blurted that out.

"Like I said, I've been an idiot. Please look at me."

She didn't, couldn't. He reached over, pressing his warm palm to her cheek, turning her face toward his.

"I didn't think a girl could be as sweet and nice as you are and also be into hot sex."

She blinked. "Why?"

He shook his head. "I don't know. If you don't count Jack's wife, I've never met any hot, sexy girls who seemed all that nice. And vice versa. Just my dumb luck, I guess. And I just didn't think the two things could reside in the same woman."

"Surprise," she whispered.

"You can say that again."

They lay silent for a moment, until he leaned in and gave her a soft kiss on the lips. He didn't pull back afterward, so their faces lay only a couple of inches apart. His eyes looked enormous and deep and beautiful. "Did you know," he said softly, "that I fell in love with Mistress Mina?"

The words left her dumbfounded. "Uh, no."

"I did. And I couldn't understand it. Couldn't understand how I could fall for a stranger in a mask who I didn't even know, whose face I couldn't even see. But now, I get it. It makes sense. Because things were so...*right* with her. With *you*. Because you're you, and you and I have always just...clicked."

"Yeah," she agreed. "I guess we have." From the beginning. From those very first easy, playful flirtations nearly twenty years earlier.

"So it's not Mistress Mina I'm in love with anymore, Mia. It's you."

Mia sucked in her breath. "*God.*" She dropped her gaze away, then lifted it again, not quite able to believe. "Really?"

He nodded. "Deeply."

Her heart felt like it would burst up through her chest at any moment, like it was physically...growing.

"And I'm so fucking sorry about tonight—about how mad I got, about...well, if I forced you to do anything you didn't want to just now..."

She hated the remorse in his expression and shook her head vigorously. "No, baby, you didn't. I promise. Because there's nothing I wouldn't want to do with you. I *love* you."

Ty took her face between his hands and lowered a long, deep kiss to her waiting mouth. It swirled down through her, more powerful than any sex with any man she'd ever had. She could still scarcely believe it. *He loved her. He really loved her.* After so many years, it seemed too good to be true, but she could tell now, looking into his eyes, that it was real. She'd never seen this expression on his face before—but it was undeniably love that poured from his gaze.

"God, this is so good," she said as the elation traveled through her. She suddenly couldn't stop smiling. "So incredible."

He returned the smile she'd been pining for all these years, only now it unexpectedly felt as if his smile belonged to *her*. "Just one thing I gotta know," he said, his voice taking on a familiar teasing quality.

"What's that?"

"Do you really dig guys with tattoos?"

She shrugged, feeling slightly guilty, then gave him a sweet grin. "Afraid so, but don't worry, I'll keep you anyway."

He gave his head a playful tilt. "Who knows. Be a good girl and maybe you can talk me into getting one," he finished with a wink.

"Mmm," she said, liking the sound of that. "Just think of how excited you'd get me *then*."

"Mistress Mina rides again?" he asks, raising his eyebrows.

"Perhaps, if you'd like. *Ride* being the operative word, of course."

They shared a bit of laughter and an easy kiss, and he said, "So where did you come up with the name Mina anyway?"

She made a resistant face, but admitted the truth. "Okay, you may as well know. My real name is Wilhelmina."

"Really?" He grinned. "I'll have to call you that from now on."

"Don't you dare. I much prefer 'sweet thing'."

"But you're not exactly sweet anymore, are you?" He leaned closer to her and whispered, "Maybe I'll call you '*sexy* thing', or '*naughty* thing'."

She offered a light smile. "Those are kind of fun, but...well, the truth is—I've always cherished the way you call me 'sweet thing'. I wait for it every single morning. It always makes my pussy tingle."

She watched the heat re-invade his gaze. "Okay. Want to fuck me, *sweet thing*?"

Rolling into his arms, she pressed her breasts against his chest, pulling him into another deep, hot kiss. "I think that can be arranged. But..." On impulse, she slipped his black mask over her head, peering out at him through it. "For right now, you can call me Mistress Mina."

Also by Lacey Alexander

❧

Hot In the City: French Quarter
Hot In the City: Key West
Hot In the City: Sin City
Hot For Santa!
Seductress of Caralon

About the Author

❧

Lacey Alexander's books have been called deliciously decadent, unbelievably erotic, exceptionally arousing, blazingly sexual, and downright sinful. In each book, Lacey strives to take her readers on the ultimate erotic adventure and hopes her books will encourage women to embrace their sexual fantasies. Lacey resides in the Midwest with her husband, and when not penning romantic erotica, she enjoys history and traveling, often incorporating favorite travel destinations into her work.

Lacey welcomes comments from readers. You can find her website and email address on her author bio page at www.ellorascave.com.

Tell Us What You Think

We appreciate hearing reader opinions about our books. You can email us at Comments@EllorasCave.com.

HIDDEN DESIRES

Elizabeth Lapthorne

Trademarks Acknowledgement

∞

The author acknowledges the trademarked status and trademark owners of the following wordmarks mentioned in this work of fiction:

Ben and Jerry's Chunky Monkey and Phish Food: Ben & Jerry's Homemade Holdings, Inc.

M&M's (peanut and chocolate variety): Mars, Incorporated

Reese's Peanut Butter Cups: Hershey Chocolate & Confectionery Corp.

Chapter One

Ah yes. My favorite time of all the year. The Mardi Gras. Fat Tuesday. The carnival to end them all. What self-respecting mask doesn't just live to enjoy the biggest bash, the grandest carnival of them all?

I shudder to think just how many of these I have seen over the years. In fact, if I cast my mind back far enough, I can recall the very first one of all. All those delicious Femmes Françoise, the dapper young men so eager to eat, drink and be extremely merry. It is so much fun being able to see the true person underneath all the exterior maskings when I am worn — and even better is when I am worn by a truly intriguing woman and can set her up with her soul partner. Yes, those are definitely the best of times.

Yet this year I seem to be all dressed up with no one to take me! With only twenty-four hours to go until the Big Start, I might have to get out of this dive and entice some fair damsel into rescuing me.

Aha! Here we go. Tall, but not too tall, lovely legs and firm rounded breasts — exactly what I want in a woman upon whom I must be placed. Short blonde hair pulled casually back into a ponytail but wisps are falling out around her face. She must have had a tough day. She appears to have entered and not fully realized just what sort of shop this is. Brilliant. A definite dame, worthy of such a mask as I. That extra sparkle in her eyes really draws to my inner soul.

She's looking for something and I bet I'm it. Yep, here she comes. Her eyes are roving, searching. She's obviously no green young girl, despite her youthful appearance; she's going straight past the dross and to the gold — me that is! You little beauty. Yep, she's seen me and now all I need to make this a truly memorable carnival is for her to try me on.

Oh fantastic. She's got guts, this one; she's taking the plunge.

Ah! How I have missed the carnival season. If she's lucky I might even let her wear me after I've done my business and found her soul partner for her. It's felt so long since last year...

Here we go again!

* * * * *

Lily had no idea what made her enter the tiny, darkly lit secondhand store—obviously some imp of mischief. She had spent the entire day roaming the streets, looking for the perfect mask. She had left shop after shop, always disappointed. As the day had worn on and her spirits had flagged, the shops she graced became seedier and seedier. Her footsteps became heavier and her frustration grew.

Nothing seemed to please her! She began to wish she had created her own mask. Everything was the wrong color, too gaudy, not sparkly enough, too depressing, too short or too long. She felt like the biggest cretin on earth as dusk drew and she became truly desperate.

Finally, a block from her hotel, she saw a chink of light coming from a shop with a wooden doorframe and chipped painted sign claiming "Ye Olde Store". Heaving a sigh, she weighed in her mind the option of trudging through another store versus removing her shoes and massaging her aching feet.

Even though the temptation to ignore the small store was great, she mentally shrugged her shoulders and, thinking of the not particularly appetizing frozen sausage rolls waiting for her in her hotel mini-freezer, she trudged across the street, automatically dodging the early-evening traffic.

Pushing open the door while still managing to juggle the few shopping bags of junk she had managed to find, she heard a bell tinkle overhead. Pausing inside, looking around, squinting to try and see in the dim inner light, Lily felt almost disorientd for a moment.

"Look around, take your time, dear," a cheerful call came from the back. Mentally shrugging, Lily began to cruise along the aisles. Taking everything in at a glance, she realized it was a rather decrepit resale store. As she only had minutes to travel to the hotel, she figured, *why not look around?*

Her eye became caught as she saw a bunch of used paperbacks on a bookshelf. Smiling to herself, hoping maybe the day wouldn't be such a waste if she found a good old romance novel, Lily shuffled over to the bookshelf, trying not to knock anything over in the process.

Lily carefully placed her shopping bags between her feet, angling them so she could reach most of the bookshelves without having to move and possibly forget her bags. Casting her eye professionally over the authors' names, ignoring the covers and most of the titles as any experienced book scrounger would, she felt her breath catch as the reflected sparkle of a bead caught her eye.

There, wedged half behind a stack of old tattered romance novels, was a satiny, deep navy blue beaded three-quarter facemask.

Her heart pounding, half afraid she was dreaming or had hit her head and was fantasizing, Lily reached back to grasp the delicate fabric and remove the old mask.

Oh man, it's almost exactly what I've been searching for all day.

Taking deep breaths, hoping not to hyperventilate in her excitement, Lily turned the mask over, determined to find what was wrong with it.

The mask would cover the top of her head, down to just below her nose and above her mouth. The perfect dark navy blue, it would match her costume as exactly as she could have hoped. With wide eyeholes, so she wouldn't have to scrunch her face up to see, the sequins and beads sewn into the face would gaily reflect the lights and colors of the carnival. It was sophisticated and elegant, yet still bright and fun.

Absolutely perfect, she thought, amazed she could find something so perfect so close to her hotel. With growing excitement, Lily turned the mask over and brought it to her face.

Slipping it on, she could almost believe she felt the mask itself grow with excitement. The mask slid on perfectly, as if it had been made for her, and settled upon her face as if they were meant to be.

She closed her eyes in the blissful satisfaction a shopaholic such as herself always found with the perfect item.

As she closed her eyes to adjust to the lack of light, she relaxed and breathed a huge sigh of relief. The strangest vision entered her mind.

She saw herself, in her blue beaded Regency-style dress, masked, out in a garden somewhere. She was laughing and being chased by a black masked and caped man with a tricorn. She dodged between trees, laughing and calling out to the man. Suddenly, he pounced on her around the tree. Grabbed by her arm, she squealed half in fright, half in delight. When he pulled her down on top of him on the grass, her legs trapped between his, she felt her heartbeat accelerate. He held both her hands in his and rolled them both, so she lay beneath him. Without removing either of their masks he bent his head and kissed her.

Lily blinked in a dazed manner totally unlike her. She felt as if she were waking from a dream instead of merely opening her eyes. Surprised to still find herself in the shop, rather than in a garden somewhere underneath a masked man, she took a deep breath.

"Lovely old mask, isn't it dear?" came a friendly old voice from behind her.

"Uh…" stammered Lily, removing it hastily and trying to grope for her shopping bags with her other hand.

"A dear old friend of mine brought that in. Said she had no more use for it. Boasted all her grandkids were happily married and she herself had met the man of her dreams on a cruise just six months ago. Tempted me to try it myself, but my old Mortimer would never want to go on one of those fancy cruises. You been looking for a mask for the carnival tomorrow, dear?" Lily opened her mouth to say she had but the old lady continued on as if she had already agreed. "Of course you have. You look to have been doing it all day, too. You look plumb worn-out, dear. You visiting for the big bash?"

Lily merely nodded, not wanting to interrupt the flow of conversation.

"That's just fine. This old mask match your dress, does it? You're rather lucky to have found him. I was toying with the idea of keeping him myself, but got distracted by my book collection. Didn't realize I had left him there." Reaching her hand out, Lily gave the mask to the old lady, amused by her candid chatter, but still a little off balance by the vision she had seen. Did the mask give visions? Or aid clairvoyance or something? Maybe she was just exceedingly tired and had dozed off for the moment?

Tired and hungry as she was, all Lily wanted to do was head home and put the mask back on to test it out again.

"How much is it?"

Following the old woman as she shuffled to the ancient cash register on the crammed desk by the front door, Lily pulled her thin wallet from the back pocket of her jeans. Juggling her shopping bags, she managed to retain hold of everything.

"Hmm…well, as this was a gift from Mavis, I really shouldn't charge you too much at all. How's five dollars sound, dear?"

Lily smiled. Even with the glint in the old lady's eye, she knew the mask was a steal for such a small sum.

"Done," she laughed, handing over the bill and waiting for the decrepit register to spit out her receipt.

Lily waited patiently as the old lady carefully placed the gorgeous mask with her receipt in a white shopping bag and handed it over. Thanking the lady profusely, Lily headed out of the shop, smiling at the tinkling of the bell.

Elizabeth Lapthorne

Walking quickly back to the hotel, very excited to have finally found her mask, she kept her head bent low, not wanting anything to come between her and the privacy of her room where she could once more put the mask on.

Looking carefully for a break in the oncoming traffic, she jaywalked to reach a short side street she had discovered earlier in the morning. Cutting across a number of blocks to speed herself up, it only took her a few minutes to finally reach her destination.

Smiling politely and waving at the concierge, a thin red-haired young man named Lee, she hustled her tired body to the lifts. Tapping an impatient foot, she felt an overwhelming relief when a set of elevator doors opened immediately and proceeded to carry her up to her floor.

Grateful to have the elevator to herself, she rustled around in the bags, peering inside the one holding her mask. Interrupted by the *ding* of the doors opening, she sighed in resignation and almost sprinted in eagerness to her door.

Juggling for her keycard, grateful she had kept it in her back pocket and not in a bag somewhere, she entered her small room, finally able to lock the door and the rest of the world out behind her.

Lily dropped all her other bags carelessly on the floor, kicked off her sneakers and, carrying the beautifully beaded blue satin mask with her, sat comfortably on the couch.

Holding her breath, half afraid nothing would happen, Lily put the mask back on. The rest of the world receded as her eyes closed once again.

This time she was thrown back into the dream-vision picking it up almost to the second of where she had left it.

The man in the mask and tricorn held her underneath him and he kissed her fiercely. His mouth gently pressed down on hers and she felt herself arch up into it – trying to reach further into him. His weight crashed down on her and she burned for more. His free hand roamed over her navy dress, crushing the fabric and finally settling

268

over her now mostly exposed bosom. Dipping in, he palmed her nipple and she moaned with the pleasure his skillful, thick fingers gave.

Arching into his hot palm, Lily raised a hand to bring his dark head down to hers. Finding his lips with hers, she felt amazement as a wealth of knowledge started flowing into her mind. His lips were soft, soft and warm. He opened his mouth in invitation, just as his skilled fingers began to tweak at her nipple.

Lily moaned again and speared her tongue into his mouth. He tasted of heat, salty masculinity and very faintly of a fine wine, or maybe champagne. So many different textures of his tongue and mouth warred within her she could barely concentrate on the mixture of tastes.

All she knew was that she wanted this man, needed to feel his hot skin cover and touch her own, wanted to feel his immense shaft penetrating her and not just resting hotly against her leg. She wanted to tear her own carefully crafted dress from her body and strip him of his own pants and shirt and ride him until sweat covered both their bodies.

Panting, Lily pulled the mask off, stunned by the realistic vision. She could feel the heat of the man's hands on her breasts, feel the softness of his lips bearing down on hers, taste his spicy, masculine scent as his tongue delved into her.

Carefully placing the mask on the desk near her laptop, Lily paced in the small kitchen area, determined to have something solid to eat and brew up a fresh pot of coffee.

She didn't even know if she wanted to think further about this mask or whether she should just have something to eat and then have a decent twelve hours' sleep. Her mind was crammed with a million questions. Was it a vision or merely a dream, a fantasy? Was she finally cracking under the strain of working too many hours? She had specifically taken the two weeks off to come down and be here in New Orleans for the Mardi Gras, to have a bit of fun. Maybe she needed a little more time away?

Before you need the men in white coats, her mind said nastily. Lily pushed aside the thought, focusing instead on the dream-vision-whatever she had experienced.

Hearing the coffee pot finish dripping, Lily pushed all her thoughts to the back of her head. She was here in the heart of the French Quarter for two whole weeks. Tomorrow night was the biggest party New Orleans would ever see and she was a part of it.

She began to toast some bread and cheese; the frozen sausage rolls held no appeal anymore. Lily knew getting something to eat, and then a lot of sleep, would help her relax and enjoy the big bash tomorrow. She had plenty of time to sort out the mask later on, after the party her old high school friend, Susy, was holding.

Finally she sat down, wriggling her feet into the soft sofa cushions, overjoyed to finally have her usually comfortable sneakers off. Lily sipped her coffee and let the melted cheese fill her mouth, carrying away all her problems.

When her belly was warm, if not full, she stood up quickly and returned to her discarded shopping bags. Removing the fresh fruit and placing it in the mini-fridge, and tossing the silk scarves she had purchased into her opened suitcase, she squashed the bags for recycling.

Smiling happily, she carefully picked up the mask and placed it on the bedside table, letting the lights reflect prettily from the beads. With a secret smile of pride only a dedicated shopaholic could understand, Lily stripped and headed toward the shower to get ready for bed.

Under usual circumstances she would curl up under the covers and read one of her romance novels to wind down from her hectic day. Yet knowing tomorrow she likely wouldn't get to bed before five or even six in the morning, added on to the fact she could *never*, no matter how tired, sleep past nine in the morning had her knowing she needed as much sleep as possible.

Usually Lily cursed this inability to sleep in, yet tonight she didn't mind going to sleep early. Visions and half-formed fantasies of a highwayman complete with tricorn and a body-to-die-for danced in her head, hopefully to be carried through into some explicit and highly erotic dreams.

Added on to that, her main task for the day had been completed even better than she had hoped. She had found her mask and that was the most important goal she had set herself for the day.

Life was good.

Chapter Two

ಬ

Ah yes, I do so love to see inside people's minds and souls. Such a useful skill! And Lily is fiery plus some. Being ravished by a highwayman! My, my! Such fiery, feisty fantasies. Of course, she doesn't fully understand just yet but I shall hopefully be able to show her very soon. After all, there's no use in being able to read one's innermost thoughts and desires if one can't help to bring them about, now is there?

Thankfully I am able to read Lily's most hidden desires and I am well-versed enough with the masculine thought patterns that scouting out a suitable candidate shouldn't be too hard. It's part of my charm, after all.

Lucky for me, Lily seems to have taken us to a truly fantastic masked ball, held by an old friend of hers. Yes, indeed. Plenty of opportunity here for a matchmaking mask. Lily seems to have calmed down, mellowed a bit, and decided to let herself enjoy the atmosphere. Brilliant idea.

Hmm…what's this? She seems to have had her eye on that caped fellow for a bit over the last hour. Big black cape, black facemask and tricorn. Let me get a good look at him. Hmm. He's eyeing her while she's not watching, too. Good start.

Well, well, well. Maybe my part this go-around will be easy. Mr. Tricorn is heading our way. Heads up, Lily-girl, looks like someone is interested in making you "stand and deliver". Heh, heh, heh. Might have to keep an eye or two on this one. By the fierce, eager look in his eye, my Lily might be having an interesting night.

With or without much of my help.

* * * * *

Lily sipped her champagne while standing on the edge of the dance floor and mentally breathed a huge sigh of relief.

She had finally shaken off the jester who had been following her like an adoring puppy all night. She felt quite guilty palming him off to the young little gypsy girl who didn't look a day over sixteen but the sweet little thing had seemed so eager for the jester, Lily didn't have the heart not to set them up.

Tapping her foot in time to the sounds of the swinging band, she took another sip of the champagne and looked around for a spot to leave the glass. She didn't want to waste a moment of the rest of the night and who cared if she entered the dance floor alone? She certainly wouldn't be *leaving* it alone and the time left until midnight was too precious to waste.

Pouring the ruinously expensive champagne into a convenient potted plant and resting the glass on the edge of the huge pot, she shook out her dress and looked around, feeling guilty. It was a waste of champagne, but she wanted to dance far more and, if she simply left it sitting around, it would almost certainly be thrown out anyway.

Taking eager strides toward the dance floor, dodging the people hanging around chatting, she felt a huge grin cross her face, reminding her of the extraordinarily comfortable mask covering her features.

Free at last! She chanted to herself in glee. Less than four steps from the dance floor, she heard a husky, masculine sound voice her thought from a second ago.

"Free at last, I see. I sincerely hope you didn't kill that poor jester trying to woo you. May I have this dance? As you do seem so eager to hit the floor."

Confused for a moment, shocked that someone appeared to read her mind, she turned around. Unfortunately, she turned so quickly she almost lost her balance on the newly waxed dance floor and she skidded slightly on her stilettos.

"Whoops! Had a drink or two, my dear?"

The man caught her arm easily, and steadied her. As she laughed and stood fully upright again, she had the grace to blush as she realized that, while she hadn't made a fool of herself, if this man hadn't steadied her, she might have.

As she ran her eyes down him critically, she realized he truly seemed a steady man. Large, but by no means fat, he filled out his black pants and black shirt rather well. A knee-length cape covered much of his body from her view but the smiling dark brown eyes and shoulder-length brown hair softened the full black of his costume. Nothing, however, could hide his impressive width and height. This was a man one could romp with and not be afraid of. It wasn't until she saw the tricorn that she felt a twinge of doubt.

Had she met him before? Did she know him? Did he recognize her?

"I know I'm a highwayman but I promise not to ask you to stand and deliver your goods. I merely wanted to join you on the dance floor."

Lily laughed. "I'm sorry, I was just…surprised. Do I know you?"

This time it was the highwayman who laughed. "Now, what fun would a masked ball be if one gave out one's name?" Taking her hand he began to negotiate their way onto the huge dance area. Lily frowned, but had been much too eager to get onto the floor to bother complaining now.

"That doesn't really answer my question." She laughed, enjoying the quickness of his wit. Obviously the man wasn't a doofus, or extremely young, like the jester.

"I wasn't aware this was a game of twenty questions," he remarked. Lily laughed as he swung them into a leisurely waltz. The music was slow and so she couldn't complain about the way he held her closely. *As soon as the music picks up I'll free myself and begin to truly jive*, she promised herself.

"So, fair maiden," he continued, "what brings you here?"

Lily smiled, dazzled by his dancing skills. The man might be a highwayman and look similar to the man in her flash with the mask yesterday but, boy, could he lead a girl around the dance floor.

"I know Susy from way back. I contacted her when I decided I wanted a break from work and decided to take a vacation. I figured everyone should experience a real Mardi Gras down here in New Orleans and here I am. Besides, it seemed like Fate taking a hand when I called some of the local hotels and there had been a last minute cancellation the week before the Mardi Gras." Lily couldn't help but smile at Fate and Luck taking a hand in her impromptu holiday. She couldn't help her pride and satisfaction at how well and easily everything had turned out. "How about yourself?"

"I also decided I needed a break from work, but came here by pure luck. Thankfully, my luck seems to have held in finding you."

Lily laughed. "Oh, I don't know. There seems to be some sort of magic floating about during the Mardi Gras, don't you think? Something sparkling in the air, or so I could easily believe."

The man smiled down at her and she noticed a slight dimple in his cheek. It managed to make him look mischievous and sexy at the same time. Lily swallowed. The man could be dynamite if he chose to be.

"Yes," he huskily agreed with her. It took her a moment to remember what he agreed with. "I do think there might be some magic or witchery sparkling in the air. You seem to have cast a fair dose of it over me."

Lily merely smiled and tried not to let it widen into a face-splitting grin. No sense in letting the man know she felt weak in the knees just yet.

Just then the slow music came to an end and the band struck up a faster number. Regretfully, Lily pulled herself from his tight embrace and let the rhythm and beat sink into her soul. Raising her arms, she swung her hips and enjoyed the fast beat pounding through her body. Her dance companion stayed close, but thankfully wasn't macho enough to try and hold her again. He, too, swung his hips and began to dance to the energetic beat of the music.

In the bliss only brought by releasing one's tension and energy through music, Lily closed her eyes, let her head fall back and truly enjoyed the music and dance floor.

After a number of more upbeat tunes, a slower song struck up and Lily's highwayman stepped closer and took her into his arms again.

"You sure know how to dance, sweetheart. Lucky for me, I'm a guy with confidence or you might have made me feel self-conscious."

Lily looked up to his masked face, dark brown eyes gleaming with laughter, dimple showing underneath his simple black mask. When she felt her face blush slightly, she saw his grin widen and she laughed.

"I don't think anything could shake your confidence." Grinning back at him, she knew her mischievous and naughty thoughts would be shining in her own light brown eyes.

Her highwayman grinned back at her and pulled her closer. She could feel a massive erection straining against his pants. Lily drew in a quick breath, feeling her blush come back again. It had been so long since she had let herself indulge in some nooky. Yet now that the chance was before her, she hesitated.

Thankfully, her highwayman was in no way concerned, nor did he seem uncommonly eager to push her. Or so she thought.

"Shall we take a stroll around Susy's gardens? We can stay on the back patio if you like. Not even a desperate highwayman would ravish a young lady with a dozen or more people around him."

Lily smiled. Never having had exhibitionist fantasies, she wasn't keen to be seduced physically on the back patio, where much of the party had spilled out to, yet neither was she completely adverse to a bit of nooky with said highwayman.

"You said I had cast a spell over you. Well, you seem to have a good bit of that old magic yourself. Let's go."

Pulling herself from his embrace, even though he tried to tighten his arm around her, she took his hand and led him out toward the large French doors, open to the patio.

Passing one of the many waiters wandering around with trays of drinks, they both grabbed a flute of champagne on their way out. Lily mentally commended her highwayman on being able to negotiate the crowd with his arm still around her all the while holding his glass and not spilling a drop.

No two ways about it, the man had talent and style. Her very own James Bond, or a bad-boy James Bond-turned-highwayman. Seated by the edge of the garden, looking in at the massive party in full swing, Lily breathed in deeply, enjoying the scents of freshly mown grass and flowers in full bloom.

Much like any garden, private or public, in New Orleans during the Mardi Gras, it was well maintained with lush green grass, flowers spread everywhere and a number of trees. While it didn't exactly look like the scene she had experienced in her "vision", neither did it look dissimilar to it.

Lily smiled.

She would love to cast off her responsible side and run naked through the trees with her highwayman chasing her, only to let him catch and seduce her. But something inside her rebelled at acting purely out of a fantasy she had. Why not create her own memories, instead of enacting others?

"That's a mighty big grin you have there, my dear. Care to share the joke?"

Looking at him, *really* looking at him, Lily pondered her two choices. To seduce or not to seduce. Lily took in his eyes, the set of his body, the casual, yet slightly tense way he held himself. Lily easily came to her decision.

She didn't know him exactly but she could only see kindness in his eyes, could only see the tension in his body of a man waiting for a woman. The sort of tension that meant, with the woman's approval, he would pounce. Nodding to herself, she smiled and leaned closer, so no one else on the patio could overhear her naughty comment.

"I was just deciding to take you back to the hotel with me. I'm not really one for a quickie out in the backyard; I think we're both a little old for that. But I'm not adverse to a one night stand, back at my hotel."

The dimple came back as her highwayman smiled.

"A one night stand? Who says I won't rock your world and you'll want to marry me and chain me to your bed?"

Laughing, Lily placed her flute of champagne on the thick concrete rail that surrounded the patio. Noticing her highwayman also set aside his glass and turned to face her gave her courage.

He is definitely interested in me too, she silently acknowledged to herself.

Glasses dispensed of, she moved even closer into him as he slid his arm around her shoulders, creating a strange intimacy between them. Even among fully a dozen couples on a cramped back patio, there seemed to be only the two of them in their own little world.

"Well, having my own personal sex slave chained to my bed twenty-four seven *is* quite a dream come true. But I think we both have our own lives and I intend to go back to mine after my holiday here is over."

"Mmm," he muttered, leaning in so his lips rested just above hers.

She smiled as the thought, *Here comes the pounce,* rushed through her brain.

"Let's discuss tomorrow when tomorrow comes, hmm? I'd much rather enjoy you and this night right now."

He bent down and took her mouth in a fierce kiss. Barely giving her time to orient herself, he opened her mouth and his tongue gave her his taste. She sucked on his tongue, enjoying the jerk of surprise she felt go through his system.

In the background, she could hear the ballroom go quiet, as she heard Susy ordering the waiters to give everyone a glass of champagne for the countdown to the official beginning of the Carnival.

Lily wanted to pull away, wanted to watch the clock tick over, but her highwayman was invading her senses. She felt as if she drowned in his scent, in his heat, in the fierce possessiveness she could feel in his kiss.

In the back of her mind, Lily heard the waiter chuckle and pass them by.

"Don't look like you two need a glass of bubbly," he commented and continued to pass around the glasses of celebratory champagne.

Her highwayman grunted and nipped at her lips, demanding her attention. Lily wrapped her arms around his neck and lost herself in his heat and passion.

All too soon streamers were released and whistles blew. Lily relaxed into the kiss as midnight clocked over. Recalled to their surroundings, Lily unwound her arms and rested her hands against her partner's large chest. Leaning into him she began to nip at his lips, demanding to be released.

Finally, once he had taken his time, she felt his arms let go and he pulled back, sucking at the air.

"Now *that* was a Mardi Gras start-up to remember."

Grinning, Lily couldn't help but agree. She took a step, and then two backwards, and held out her hand to her highwayman in invitation.

"Care to be taken home by a strange Regency England woman?"

He grinned, his dimple showing, "Damn straight, if you can cope with being *taken* by a highwayman."

She smiled, enjoying the easy camaraderie between them. "Oh, I think I can handle being taken by a highwayman. I always enjoy a good ride."

Chuckling, she let herself be led away by her new partner.

Chapter Three

SO

Andrew had to keep himself from grinning manically as he led Lily out of the huge mansion still in the middle of its reveling. He *finally* had his Lily-girl just where he wanted her. For too many months he had been ogling her in his rare spare time at their workplace. As badly as he wanted to ask her out, the right time and place just never seemed to come up. Either he had been just returning or just heading out on the road, or she had been working on a major project and looking far too frazzled and stressed for him to want to try his luck.

He could still remember the instant lust and falling-out-of-the-sky feeling he had experienced the first time he had seen her, a number of months ago.

He had been headhunted from a rival company and basically dropped into a sea of internal company problems. Simply keeping his head above water, metaphorically speaking, had kept him busy for weeks. He only had seen tantalizing glimpses of Lily after that first casual, all-too-brief introduction and exchange of names by the CEO.

Lily had been in the middle of a crisis, and had barely paid attention to him at the time. Not that she had any reason to be more than superficially polite. She worked in a different division and so he had no reason for a follow-up coffee, or more personal contact. Yet just seeing her pass in the corridor sporadically had been enough to brighten his day.

He found it ironic the only reason he had taken on the position in the company had been to earn enough money to nest egg for a mortgage in the suburbs. He had decided it was time for him to settle down, maybe open his own much smaller consulting firm. It was well past time for him to settle down and start thinking of his own family, a wife and kids, maybe a dog and cat or two plus all the trimmings.

Yet the months had seemed to flit by and still he came no closer to introducing himself to Lily, or even setting up a few casual getting-to-know-you-better dinners. Time just seemed to slip away from him and every time he thought he solved one problem and could ask Lily out, another problem cropped up and he had to either leave to go fix it or, worse, bury himself in paperwork and solve the issues himself.

He smiled as he recalled his fierce determination two weeks ago. He had cleared his calendar, even been toying with the idea of taking annual leave so they could escape for a romantic week away and get to know each other properly. He had seen her talking to a workmate over the watercooler, gesticulating excitedly.

Feeling like a sneak, he had walked close enough to hear what she was talking about. Even coming in halfway through the conversation as he had, her excitement to her friend had bubbled over him and all his plans easily clicked together.

"…and don't you think everyone should experience at least *one* real Mardi Gras down in New Orleans? And what better way than to go to Susy's masquerade ball? All the excitement, romance and mystery, with none of the ramifications! I can go pick up a masked stud, have my wicked way with him and still have a week to recuperate! Trust me, Darla, annual leave was *invented* for weeks like these."

Andrew tightened his hold on Lily's hand as his memories came to a halt. Oh yeah, he had spent the last two weeks plotting and planning this night, and hopefully the following week of fantastic sex and intimate getting-to-know-you time. He shied away from the mental question of why he was going to so much trouble for one woman and one week of sex. He didn't want to think about the long-term. He felt far too eager to enjoy the next week.

"Your hotel room, my dear, or mine?" *That's it,* he patted himself mentally on the back, *keep it in the present. No knowing how long this will last.*

He paused just outside Susy's huge plantation-style home, letting Lily make the decision with no pressure. It honestly didn't make any difference to him whether they used his room or hers; all he felt interested in was stripping them both bare and plunging balls-deep inside her. He had been wearing his hard-on since the moment they had been introduced. The following months of trying to set something up between them had been a slow burning foreplay session peppered by casual smiles and intense fantasies.

He was more than eager now to start the *real* seduction and see where they ended up.

Lily looked at him a moment, then surprised him.

"What's your name? Much as I enjoy calling you my highwayman, I think I'd prefer a name for a man I'm about to 'sleep' with." Andrew could only smile at the emphasis on the word *sleep*. Both of them knew damn well not much sleeping would occur.

The highwayman, who until he had discovered this costume he had no realization resided inside himself, grinned charmingly. "I'm Andrew," he said.

Lily smiled back. "I'm Lily."

They solemnly shook hands and then both laughed simultaneously. "It does seem slightly bizarre to introduce yourself to the woman you're about to have mind-blowing sex with, doesn't it?"

"Yes," Lily agreed, shivering slightly at his not-so-subtle hint at the heat and intensity of the sex to come. "I was just thinking the same thing myself." Andrew smiled as she looked up and down the crowded street, filled with revelers enjoying the carnival atmosphere. "Where are you staying?" she continued.

Andrew pointed in the direction he knew was close to Lily's own hotel, and named a well-known hotel branch. He had purposely chosen a hotel close to Lily's, but not close enough to arouse her suspicions. Lily appeared to think a moment, then nod her head with the decision she had made.

"Let's use your hotel then."

Andrew held out his arm in an old, courtly gesture, totally at odds with his highwayman costume and his raging desires. They turned to begin the short walk back to his room.

As they chatted, Andrew carefully watched Lily. He wanted as much warning as possible if she felt any tension about taking a "stranger" to her bed. Her posture seemed calm enough and her voice didn't shake but he could see a little bit of tension in her arms.

Looking carefully into her eyes, even masked as she was, he could see the deep hunger buried in their brown depths. They glittered in the street light, reflecting the dozens of colors shining from the beads, stars and moon from the gaily lit city.

Oh yeah, the heat from that gaze could burn a lesser man than I, he admitted. She felt the same attraction he had been slowly burning from for months now. She might not consciously know who he was but, deep inside herself, she must know she either knew him, or recognized him from somewhere.

He breathed in deeply, wishing he could already smell the tang of her desire. He knew he would have to wait until they reached the hotel room for that. But aching as he was, he could hardly wait.

Instead, they chatted about social niceties, the weather, how long they were staying in the city. As they strolled casually, in absolutely no hurry, they then moved on to restaurants, shops and arcades they had each visited and could recommend.

Andrew, desperately trying to ignore the double entendres Lily teased him with, enjoyed the fresh night air, the definite sense of "party" on the streets as houses were thrown open, loud music playing everywhere and parties spilling onto the streets. While nowhere near as crowded as when the main parade came through, the streets were still full of partiers even now, after midnight.

He slowly wound them along to his hotel, tipping the doorman, who had a profusion of beads, stars and streamers covering his uniform as he held the door open for them both. The doorman, Tom, grinned at them, tipping his hat and rattling his beads.

"You two have a great night, eh?"

Andrew laughed and handed Lily into the foyer of the hotel.

"I intend to, Tom. I certainly intend to."

Lily glared at him but Tom laughed jovially at them both. Andrew smiled and retook her hand, placing a soft kiss on her chin, the only area of skin, other than her mouth, exposed by her mask.

"Tom is a nice guy. He didn't mean anything by his comment."

Lily's face split into a grin. "I know; I was just teasing."

They both nodded to the concierge, also covered in beads and streamers. Balloons floated everywhere in the foyer. An extremely loud party could be seen and heard from the conference room. Shouts and music and whistles being blown all leaked out into the main hotel space.

Hurrying them over to the elevators, Andrew pressed the call button and felt relief when a door opened immediately. Under normal circumstances, he wouldn't have minded taking Lily and joining the main party for another hour or so but he was hard as a rock and far too eager to begin their *own* little party to want to postpone it even a minute longer.

As the doors closed behind them, Andrew turned them both gently so they looked into the reflective surface of the back of the elevator. Lily looked excited and flushed behind her beautiful mask. Her eyes glittered, a strange light brown color that could be amber, or maybe it was simply the light in the elevator. Behind the satin blue mask it seemed hard to tell.

Enjoying their first moments alone together, Andrew placed his hands gently on her shoulders, holding her against his hard body. He saw a slight flush creep up her neck and, looking into the mirror, began his seduction.

Chapter Four

දැ

Lily looked at her reflection in the elevator and found she had trouble breathing correctly. This man, Andrew, her highwayman, seemed familiar somehow. She couldn't pin it down—a part of her didn't even want to pin down how she seemed to know him. She felt caught up in the fantasy, lost in the colors and dazzle of the carnival atmosphere.

Thankfully, they were alone in the elevator and, as she watched the reflection of Andrew's hand caress down her shoulder and around to her partially exposed breast, she felt her heart beat faster. She could feel his breath, warm across her ear, as he inhaled the mingled scent of her shampoo and perfume. He seemed to breathe it deeply inside him as his hand flicked over where her erect nipple stood just under her thin layer of silk.

He caressed the hard point, once, then twice. Lily leaned back into his body, warm and solid behind her. She reached back, her eyes closed to the bliss his hand created, and pulled his ass closer, so they ground together. Her hand squeezed, testing the strength of his ass cheek, strong and solid like the rest of him.

He groaned into her ear, a hoarse, almost desperate sound.

"Andrew," she panted, needing more of him, "I hope you plan to do more than just feel the silk of my dress."

As if her taunting him gave him permission, he groaned again, blindly reached out across the small elevator and pressed the red "stop" button. The elevator jerked to a stop and, obviously knowing they only had a few minutes at best, dipped his hand beneath the bodice of her dress to touch the creamy swell of her breast.

While not overly large, her breasts were a handful and Andrew didn't seem to have any complaints about them. Lily arched up, never having even considered something as naughty as making out in a stopped elevator before. It had a ring of wicked to it, knowing sooner or later security would ring them and ask if everything was okay.

When he flicked her nipple, making her gasp with the sensation, she lost her train of thought. Arching into his hand, Lily felt the dampness between her legs and she ground back onto his erection, straining the black pants he wore. The seconds ticked by and Lily could feel herself heating up more.

Just as Lily turned into him, deciding to raise the stakes of the game by touching some of *his* hot spots, Andrew reached out once more and pressed the stop button, letting the elevator continue its rise to their floor.

In a few seconds the elevator dinged and the doors slowly opened.

Blinking, feeling as if she were waking from a dream, Lily smiled as Andrew hastily removed his hand and smoothed down the front of her dress. Looking left and right, he took her hand again and led her away from the elevator.

The muted sound of music came from a few of the rooms but, by and large, the corridor was silent. Lily listened carefully, only hearing the odd muted sound, almost completely suppressed. If she hadn't been listening so carefully she would have missed it altogether. *Lovely to know most sounds are dulled in these rooms. They're obviously well insulated,* she thought.

Standing outside room 403, Andrew dug into his pocket and produced a key card. Opening the door, he stood back and waved her in. Lily could see a chink of light where Andrew had obviously left one of the lamps on to have some light in the room.

"After my lady," he grinned.

Tilting her chin, Lily regally swept into the room. Continuing over to the window, she looked down upon the still avidly partying streets of New Orleans, and dimly registered the thud of the door shutting behind them.

She heard Andrew cross the room after her. There was a slight clink as he dropped keys and the keycard onto the side table. Lily heard his footsteps cross the carpet and then he pressed himself against her, much as they had been in the elevator.

He reached inside her bodice once more, taking the same breast in his hand, and toyed with the nipple again.

"Would you like a drink of something?" he huskily murmured in her ear, absently caressing her breast and nipple.

Lily saw their reflection in the window, not as clearly as the mirror in the elevator, but still there against the black of the night and the small amount of light given off by the lamp. The erotic possibilities for the night ahead danced in her head, a feast before the starving.

She swallowed, arching into his touch as the sensations overwhelmed her. The night held endless possibilities.

Chapter Five

ഇ

Andrew tried to swallow a moan, to clear his throat, anything to clear his head as passion overtook him. Lily's breasts were perfect. An easy handful, firm and round with delicious nipples one could suck forever. He felt his mouth water at the thought of playing with these beauties for a whole week.

Over the last few months, dreaming and fantasizing about *how* he would get Lily into his bed, not in his wildest fantasies had he pictured a hotel room in the middle of the Mardi Gras and a large window looking out into the world.

He smiled, amused at the twists of Fate.

Bending over her, nibbling her shoulder as he began to unbutton her blue silk dress, he decided to tease her, as she had unwittingly teased and tempted him for so many weeks back at work.

"No drink..." she panted as he eased the silk from her shoulders.

He paused for a moment, remembering he had offered her a drink in the attempt to forget his aching cock.

He smiled against her soft skin, letting his curved lips show her without words his amusement. He continued removing the delicate silk of her dress. When he eased the bodice down her chest, it sat, pooled at her waist, and he returned his hands to cup her breasts, as they had itched to do forever.

"Place your hands upon the glass, Lily."

Hands cupping her breasts, watching over her shoulder, he blindly looked out the window. Watching their reflection, he tried to memorize the details. His much larger body standing behind Lily's half-naked perfection. High up as they were, as well as still masked, he felt it highly unlikely anyone would recognize them, let alone be able to watch them.

He felt a thrill when Lily obeyed his command. He smiled. While never having entertained dominant fantasies, he certainly wouldn't mind being master of Lily every now and then. Maybe he could test the waters.

"You ever have submissive fantasies, Lily?"

Lily swallowed and for a split second her mind flashed back to the fantasy she had seen when she first put the mask on. A highwayman holding her hands above her head and taking her, the feeling of his body pressing into hers, the tender yet rough way he thrust inside her. She had been more than willing but he took her nevertheless.

While she wouldn't consider it a "submissive" fantasy as such, the new thought of being taken by this man, of having his much larger body over and under her, had definite appeal. Even so, the desire was new enough she didn't feel comfortable admitting to it just yet.

She looked into the window to stare at Andrew's reflection.

"Not really," Lily answered his curious question. He had watched her as she had stared into the distance, a slight flush creeping over her flesh. He had a feeling her mind had been cast back to something he had said and, from the dilation in her pupils and the quickening in her breathing, it had been something erotically stimulating she had been thinking of.

Before he could probe deeper into the issue, she had continued. "I'm not into pain or anything but a strong man, an alpha man, is almost always a turn-on, no matter what a woman says."

Andrew smiled. He could tell now she was telling the truth, but not the whole truth. That suited him just fine. He wasn't into bondage—he wasn't even sure he would know how to perform it safely if she had asked—but being dominating in an alpha manner, he was more than used to.

Deciding to seduce her first, he began to play with her nipples once more. He used his mask as a tool, letting his close-shaven cheek and soft lips caress her shoulder, her neck, her exposed skin and the slightly rougher edge of the mask to counteract that softness of his flesh. The play between soft lips and cheek and the harder edge of the mask seemed to work as her breath came harder and faster in pants.

"Look out into the world, Lily. Everyone is partying, having a grand old time. Lovers old and new are meeting, getting acquainted, playing that strange game of two animals coming to mate."

He continued to caress her skin; he could hardly believe how satin soft it felt. In the last hour or so, he had become a dedicated breast man. Lily's breasts seemed to be so much more responsive than any other set he could remember.

The nipples were a pale pink color, long and so easily peaked. He couldn't help but tweak them, watching her back arch in pleasure and her mouth open on a long moan. He loved to play with her breasts and nipples, letting the weight of the globes sit in his hands, thumbs caressing the erect nipples.

As he spoke softly, continued to explain the different sights they could see outside the window, he played with her lovingly, kneading and using a gentle force to spike her desire higher.

He wanted her hot and ready, prepared for his penetration but, more than that he wanted her to be anticipating their joining, to realize how important it was in the big picture, how inevitable it had become in their life.

Andrew knew he had been fantasizing about Lily for weeks, months now. The fact he needed to seduce her, prepare her for him, excited him. She knew him in passing but they had never had the chance to get to know each other. They worked in different divisions and he was in the management team, while Lily was still working her way up the corporate ladder.

Everything, the carnival, the lights, the party atmosphere, as well as the culmination of his fantasies, turned him on more than he could ever imagine.

As he described the scenes in the streets below them, his aching need to possess her increased. He felt her nipples harden to tight buds and heard her panting breaths.

"I want you." He couldn't help the growl in his voice. He had trouble containing himself. "I want nothing more than to press you up against this glass, tear the rest of this beautiful dress of yours off and plunge myself inside you. I want you to feel the force of my need, understand just how much I want this night from you."

He could hear her panting cries, the wail that seemed stuck in the back of her throat. Even though he couldn't see them, he could just imagine how dilated her pupils would be, slightly glazed with the passion of their position as well as his words.

He leaned closer, so he could whisper in her ear. Even though they were alone, as if they were the only two lovers in the entire Mardi Gras, let alone the world, he wanted his next naughty words to be just between them, a secret they could share and hold forever.

"I want to fuck you," he started, surprised at himself. He had never uttered words quite this raw to anyone before. "I want to press you tight against this window, and be so deep inside you for the rest of our lives you won't be able to feel complete without me thrusting inside you. I want to pump so hard inside you no one else will ever be able to satisfy you. I want to fill you full of my seed, so full it runs down the side of your thigh in excess. And when we're both spent, collapsed on the floor, I want to lie still inside you, and start this thing all over again."

"Oh, yes," she murmured softly and Andrew knew without a shadow of a doubt if he touched her lower curls she would be flowing with her heated dampness. Never had he wanted a woman as desperately as he wanted to be inside Lily right now.

She ground back against him, urging him to move faster, and he couldn't deny her. While working her up into a pitch of erotic fever, he had only been adding fuel to his own fire. Even so, he desperately tried to draw this out, to make as many memories as humanly possible for them both.

"Patience, my dear, we have all night. Why rush things now?"

"Because I feel as if I'm about to explode," she moaned.

"Well, darling, if you must come, you must. Feel free to start ahead of me."

Andrew could feel her shuddering, feel the fine tremors running along her arms, knew they would also be in her legs, hidden beneath all the silk of her skirt. For a moment, he wondered if the tremors were Lily holding on to her climax, or her about to start it.

He continued to play with her breasts, to kiss and nibble her neck, her cheek, up to her earlobe. Tasting her with his tongue, he relished the salty taste of her skin. Even on the knife-edge of desire, standing on the brink of exploding, she still tasted of feminine heat, of salty sweetness.

His masculine ego now demanded for him to bring her to climax without actually stripping her bare. He grazed his teeth along the sensitive run of her neck, nibbling at the pulse points he could tell were strewn along there from her shivers and moans.

Tweaking her nipples simultaneously, he could *feel* her climax build inside her, knew without a doubt she had nearly thrown herself over the edge of her desire.

A minute later, she pushed back onto his hard body, arching her back and throwing her head onto the curve of his shoulder, crying out in her completion.

Andrew watched her reflection in the window. When she relaxed and leaned back passively in his embrace, he looked down at her softened features.

Even though his fingers itched to touch her curls, to thrust inside her damp heat, to bring her to another climax, hard on the heels of her last one, he let his girl rest, get her breath back.

Plenty of time later to bring her to peak over and over until she can't remember anything, except the pleasure you bring her, he assured himself.

Andrew waited patiently until her breathing returned to normal and she was back to squirming in his embrace.

Then he began the procedure all over again.

He kissed and nibbled his way around her neck and cheek, touched and played with her breasts. This time, however, Lily was far more actively involved.

He felt a purely masculine smile cross his face as she removed her palms from the window, leaving clear palm-prints from where she had them pressed against the window all through their previous play. He smiled, thinking of what the cleaning crew would think about such delicate marks so clearly imprinted on the window.

She reached both her hands back to grab his ass, pulling him closer, so even through the thin material of his pants his hot, incredibly aroused hard-on laid against the silk of her dress. Andrew lowered his hands to her waist. Slowly, careful to not rip or tear the delicate silk, he pushed the dress from her hips and it pooled in a mess down by her ankles.

Andrew looked down her entire length in the window. The light from inside made the large window act like a two-way mirror. The outside world could be clearly viewed, yet so could the sexy reflections of him and Lily. It had become a very useful tool for them both.

Lily stood before him, perfect pale beauty, rounded in all the right places men never complained about, long legs that he ached to have wrapped around his own hips in indescribable passion. His hands tightened for a moment, until he realized it might be painful for Lily. The pleasure he could bring her, the shared sexual joy they brought each other, had him erect like never before. He felt his jaw muscles tighten in pure, unadulterated lust for this woman.

A tiny wisp of silk she probably thought passed for a thong teased his eyes, running slimly along the vee between her legs.

Lily hesitated a moment, then obviously caught his ravenous gaze in the reflection of the window. She smiled teasingly at him and stood up, braced her legs apart, replaced her palms on the window and arched her deliciously naked body into the chill glass.

He couldn't help but notice as her breasts pressed oh-so-lightly against the glass her nipples hardened even more.

With her back arched, her delicious ass sticking out and wearing only her mask, heels and thong, she looked like a centerfold spread from his horniest teenage fantasies.

"Well, Andrew," she pouted, "I seem to only have my thong and mask on and here you are, fully dressed and masked. That seems a little unfair from here."

He grinned, his dimple flashing beneath his mask.

"Oh, I don't know," he drawled. "From where I'm looking, it seems absolutely perfect."

She flushed and he felt his heart turn over. They might be playing right now but he fully intended to brand her, to make her totally his and then confess all in the morning.

He wanted her to know how long he had been fantasizing about her, how many lunch breaks he had sat a few tables over in the staff room cafeteria and watched her wildly gesticulating a particular point in a funny story she told her coworkers.

He wanted her in his life and in his home. Yet first, he wanted her, most importantly, in his bed. Idly stroking her round and firm ass, he indulged in a moment of pure fantasy. Naked on his large bed at home, her on all fours and him on his knees behind her. He loved taking a woman from behind, because he could plunge inside her to the balls, yet at the same time caress her breasts and play with her nipples.

Next time, he promised himself. *When we both return home, I'll have ample time to indulge in our every fantasy and desire. And my bed is big enough for anything.*

Pulling himself from his ever-growing fantasies and desires, he remembered his need to possess Lily in the here-and-now. Shedding his cape, leaving it crumpled in a ball on the floor, he unbuttoned the first few buttons on his formal black shirt. Falling down onto his knees, he smiled inwardly at the small gasp of surprise that escaped Lily's lush lips. Turning her around with gentle hands on her hips, he angled her toward him, so he was perfectly level with her pelvis.

Spreading her legs wider so he had the perfect view of her pussy, he bent forward and licked a slow, long stroke, taking her juices inside him. Closing his eyes, enjoying her sweet, hot taste, he hurriedly went back for more. She tasted divine, hot and sweet and spicy and so delicious he doubted he could ever get enough.

Lapping at her like a cat with his bowl of cream, he quickly finished all her juices. By pushing aside the scrap of lace, he was able to spear his tongue fully into her. She cried out, arching back, pressing herself against his face. He tried to hide his smile, but couldn't.

Thrusting his tongue into her, again and again, he moved his hand around so he still held her in the perfect position, but could also rub her clit. Her sensitive bit of flesh felt fully engorged, hard and swollen between her folds. Fiercely

Elizabeth Lapthorne

thrusting his tongue into her, rubbing her clit, he could feel the excitement and sexual energy build in his Lily.

She began to buck, to thrust herself upon him in time to his tongue's thrusts, to moan as his thumb circled around and around.

"Faster," she panted, an aching need evident in her tone. "Please, Andrew, just a little faster and I can come again."

Smiling, muttering, "As you wish," against her heated, swollen flesh, he speared her pussy faster with his tongue and frantically rubbed her clit.

In seconds, he could feel the contractions begin in her womb, could taste the extra flow of her juice and felt the gathering inside her body, held so closely to his own.

She arched, screamed her release as her body contracted over and over again. He lapped the extra juice, startled by how sweet it was, how delicious it tasted to him.

Finally, she collapsed against the chill glass, replete and satisfied.

He let her stand there for a moment, drinking in the sated, tousled look she had about her whole body. Her face was flushed beneath the silk mask. The blush managed to run all the way down to her chest, a delicate tinge of red across her skin.

Lily stood there before him, almost naked with only her mask, heels and a slightly torn scrap of lace between her folds. Her legs were still splayed widely, her pussy a warm, fleshy red from his rough tongue and her own fierce arousal.

He stood, the image of her splayed against the window, satisfied from his lovemaking, burned forever on his brain. Without even a single coherent thought, he shed his shirt and unbuttoned his pants.

Reaching one arm under her legs and the other around her back, he easily picked her up. Her eyes remained closed, her smile on her face.

"I'm too heavy," she murmured, not particularly caring.

He smiled.

"You're perfect. And I am a highwayman, after all. We highwaymen have to take what we want. And be sure, I definitely want you."

She smiled and opened her eyes.

"I seem to be pretty sated right now. I think it's my turn to drive you wild."

He laughed.

"Not a chance, dearest. I'm not even close to being done with you."

Lily merely smiled. Her eyes glittered sexily from behind her mask and Andrew felt himself falling deeper and deeper into their game. *Best to stay in control*, he reminded himself. Confessions of eternal and undying love had no place here in their magical night. Best keep it to sex and games. There would be plenty of time for confessions later and the love could grow between them after that.

Stepping through the bedroom door, he crossed over to the bed and tossed her down onto its softness.

Lily laughed, and bounced once, instantly climbing onto her knees. Slipping her stilettos off and wriggling her torn thong down her legs, she dropped them on the floor, totally uncaring where they ended up. Returning to her kneeling position, she came right up close to where Andrew stood, watching her in awe, and placed her hands on the hips of his pants.

"Come on, Mr. Highwayman, surely you're not shy?"

He grinned. Let her see him in his aching arousal; it would certainly prove he wasn't *shy*.

Slowly, teasingly, he let his hands drop to the zipper on his pants.

Chapter Six

* හ*

Lily found herself holding her breath, waiting for Andrew to remove his pants and show himself to her. Even if he was only a few inches long, he had more than proved he could satisfy her without the usual slam-bam-thank-you-ma'am methods.

She still had that niggling sensation of knowing him but the night was too perfect, too wonderful, for worrying about such things. She wanted to bask in her sexuality, enjoy every decadent moment. There would be plenty of time for recriminations and what-ifs tomorrow or even next week, once her fantastic holiday was over.

Lily banished the thought with a shudder. She had come here to rest and relax. Fantastic, multi-orgasmic sex was an added bonus.

She had no idea when he had lost his shoes and socks. She couldn't remember seeing him take them off but she had been so lost in her own passions, he could have started contacting people on the moon. As long as he had kept on tasting her and touching her, she doubted she would have noticed.

Shaking her head slightly, she reached once again for his pants. As she gently unzipped them, being careful not to catch anything delicate in its metal teeth, she smiled up at her lover. She loved his dark eyes, his dark hair and wicked smile. The dimple peeking in and out of his cheek drove her wild. She found herself surprised that, instead of being shy or worried about her instant attraction to this man, she felt energized by it. He lent her a feeling of safety, of protection, and in this magical atmosphere she embraced the incredible magic of their time together.

As she helped him shuck his pants over his hips and skim his black briefs along with them, his erection sprang free and she caught her breath at its magnificence. While not the biggest cock she had ever seen, it was a more than healthy length and beautifully thick. More than enough to fill her and satisfy the heat he had built up in her.

As he came over her, leaning his weight on his arms as his body caged hers deliciously, she reached one hand up to touch the edges of his mask. She thought it funny how she had totally forgotten her own mask, comfortable and silky as it was.

"Should we...?" she trailed off, not knowing if he preferred the masks on or if he was just being polite in not removing hers first.

He smiled, his dimple playing in his cheek again. She found his smile so warm and sexy she couldn't help but smile back at him.

"Nah. Let's leave the masks on for tonight. Tomorrow we can take them off. I think the masks add to the magic of the night, don't you?"

She nodded. The masks did add to the mystique of the evening. Also, since that niggling doubt that she knew him wouldn't go away, she didn't want to spoil the evening by looking disappointed if he removed the mask and she realized she *didn't* know him. Her look of disappointment could easily be misconstrued as disappointment in *him*.

As he bent down to kiss her, he whispered, "Besides, there will be plenty of time for us to make love without the masks, after tonight."

She raised an eyebrow. "Sure of yourself, aren't you?"

Instead of replying, he kissed her, which felt more than fine to her. The feeling of his lips against hers, of his tongue darting and playing with her, sent fire racing over her skin.

Never had she been the type of woman to blush at anything, yet his every touch seemed to make her skin burn and her body ache.

As he lay over her, his naked body sent darts of fire along her skin. He seemed to create a fire inside her; the skin-on-skin contact seemed to create a delicious friction within and she couldn't help herself. She could feel her pussy creaming again, could feel the aching tension inside herself. Despite having two fantastic orgasms, she was climbing, aching for more.

She touched his skin, ran her hands gently over his chest and shoulders, drawing him closer, eager to explore his body. She arched into him as he also explored her. His mouth plundered hers, yet his hands rubbed over her skin, sensitizing her for him.

Eagerly, she spread her legs, enjoying the solid, warm feeling of him lying cradled between her thighs. Blindly, without thinking or caring about the consequences, she arched herself up into him, trying to get his heated tip to enter her and begin their night of fun.

"Hang on, darling," he panted, pulling his mouth away from hers. He shuffled over to the side table, pulling open the nightstand drawer and removing several foil packages.

With more haste than grace, he sheathed himself in the latex.

"Damn, a few kisses and your divine skin under my hands and I'm worse than a fifteen-year-old virgin. I doubt you'd appreciate the lack of protection."

Lily smiled, glad one of them had some brains left. "I wasn't thinking about it, myself. But yeah, I'm glad you're gentleman enough to think of it."

"Gentleman? Woman, I'm supposed to be a highwayman. Now, you need to stand and deliver, so I can keep my head high with pride."

Lily laughed and pulled him back into her embrace, eager for him to keep going. "I am very keen for your head to stay high. I don't think I can stand but I can certainly deliver."

Kissing her highwayman again, Lily moaned as his tip entered her pussy. Even through the latex she could feel the heat of his cock, could feel the power resonating from him. He paused, just barely inside her, pulsing and throbbing with his own need and heat. She could feel her own moistness easing his thick passage inside her.

"Please don't tease," she panted, canting her hips, trying to draw him deeper inside her.

"How much do you want me?" he teased. If not for the breathlessness of his own question, Lily might have been worried.

Instead of responding, she reached one arm up to drag his face down to her; the other reached around to grasp his exceedingly firm ass and, crossing her legs behind his hips, she pulled him deeply inside her.

With a groan of approval, Andrew plunged, filling her so full, so deeply, she wondered if she might split. "I can't wait, oh shit, I'm sorry, love."

Andrew started withdrawing and plunging, faster and faster. Lily felt the friction inside her and closed her eyes against tears of ecstasy. As hot and tight as she felt, she couldn't believe how magnificent the feel of Andrew moving inside her was. Over and over he thrust into her, seemingly reaching deeper and deeper each time.

Lily felt her orgasm gather inside her. It was as if a storm was about to break. Every nerve ending tightened, Lily threw her head back in complete abandon. She panted for breath and as the wave crashed over her she couldn't even scream, so intense was her pleasure.

Her mouth open in a silent scream, something she had only previously read about, never experienced. She could feel

Andrew tighten, as if his cock were gathering itself for something. And then he *exploded* inside her.

He shouted out, a hoarse, indescribable sound of a male releasing himself inside a woman. Even though she couldn't feel his seed inside her, she could feel his contractions inside the latex, as her own pussy contracted around him, milking him for all his juice.

As the wave subsided, Lily fell back onto the bed, replete and totally spent. Panting for breath, she barely noticed Andrew fall down to her side, half on top of her, half off.

She panted and caught her breath as the minutes ticked easily by. As her brain stopped whirling and everything seemed to right itself, she curved semi-consciously into Andrew's warm body.

Happy to spend more time collecting herself, she felt her skin begin to cool slightly. After a short period of time had passed, she shivered. Partly, she knew, the shiver was her body's reaction to the incredible sex. As her hearing returned from the white noise of her orgasms, she recognized an air conditioner as the muted, almost silent hum in the room. The shiver was because the air-conditioned room had a faint chill against her naked skin.

As she shifted to crawl under the covers, Andrew stood for a moment and headed for the bathroom, pulling the condom from his flaccid cock. Lily had barely managed to crawl beneath when he had returned and joined her.

Without a word, they snuggled up with each other, enjoying their shared heat. Andrew had an arm around her. Enjoying the comfort of the intimate moment, Lily gently stroked his chest. Neither said anything but nothing needed to be said. They were feeling the uncanny emotion and intimacy of newly made lovers.

"You still have your mask on," Andrew purred, nuzzling her chin. Lily smiled and arched back to give him better access down her neck and toward her now ultrasensitive breasts.

"I think I've decided to become a mysterious woman of the night." When Andrew snickered, but continued to nuzzle his way down her throat toward her erect nipples, she took a deep breath to still the incipient laughter and continued.

"You can snicker but I think it's a fantastic idea. I can seduce hordes of young men into eager and willing slaves and no one would ever know of my secret identity. I would be 'that mystery woman' young men across the globe would sigh and moon over. They would wonder where I come from and when I'll return."

At this, Andrew couldn't muffle his laughter. He pulled his head away from her, righted his mask, which seemed to bounce with his cheekbones moving so much, and laughed his head off.

"And what about your faithful sidekick?" he asked, still chuckling. "The mysterious masked highwayman to whom you always return?" Lily joined in his laughter, enjoying their sparring.

"Oh," she said airily, waving a hand as if he hadn't crossed her mind. "He's around somewhere...or maybe he's the man who started the whole thing, the man who started me on this path, the one all the young studs have to thank for *creating* the mysterious masked woman."

Smiling proudly at her logic, a logic which didn't necessarily leave room for him in her future, Lily lay back against the pillows and pulled the comforter up around her shoulders.

Immediately, Andrew lay down next to her, snuggled under the comforter with her and wrapped her in his tight embrace.

"Okay, my mystery woman, let's nap for a bit. You can practice your seduction skills on me later, when we've both rested up a bit, hmm?"

Lily smiled. "I think that's a great idea. We mystery women of the night need our practice."

Lily snuggled back into his warm chest, her ass resting easily in the curve of his pelvis and stomach. She could feel his warm cock stir at her small movements, seeking a comfortable sleeping spot.

Smiling, she closed her eyes and evened her breathing. It had been a truly magical evening, one she would never forget. She smiled as she knew she would be able to return to this moment of sexual satisfaction, and relive both it and the memories of the incredible sex she had shared with him when she returned home. This definitely was a night to fantasize about over and over through the long winter nights.

She smiled even wider. She knew everyone should experience at least *one* real Mardi Gras. This was obviously hers.

Chapter Seven

෩

Lily wondered why she had gone to bed with a hot water bottle. Was it cold outside? Turning slightly to ease the ache of sleeping on her numb arm, Lily realized it wasn't a hot water bottle sharing the bed with her; it was a very hot man. *Man!*

Susy's masquerade party came back to her, along with Andrew, her highwayman.

She smiled in satisfaction. As her eyes adjusted to the early morning dawn, she stretched and turned over onto her stomach to look down at her lover.

His simple black mask had fallen down around his neck during the night. Lily frowned and looked closer at the man who shared her bed.

She knew him. She felt certain she knew this man. But where? As the fog of sleep cleared from her mind, she tried to jog her memory. Andrew, Andrew, Andrew.

With the blinding flash only brilliance seems to bring, Lily recognized her bed partner. It was Andrew Morrisey, a manager. If work gossip held any truth, a genius when it came to troubleshooting problems, from one of the higher divisions from work.

Oh shit. What on earth was he thinking? Could this be some stupid male prank, or dare? Panicking, Lily jumped out of bed and began to hunt around for her clothes and underwear. Shivering in the chilly pre-dawn air, she tried to make sense of the last twelve hours.

She had become more and more aware of Andrew over the last few weeks. He always seemed to be nearby, either hanging around the cafeteria, or personally passing memos around to her bosses. She herself was busy trying to claw her way up the corporate ladder and, while consensual after-hours contact wasn't forbidden, neither was it actively encouraged, sexual harassment lawsuits being what they were.

Lily frowned and halted in the act of searching under the bed for her thong. While it wouldn't be overly healthy for her career, neither would the knowledge that she had been sleeping with Andrew on her week off be detrimental to her career. And she certainly could not really see her highwayman blackmailing her with their fling.

The scrap of lace came within view and Lily pulled it out, sighing as she realized the expensive item was not re-wearable.

Lily pulled her mask off her face and sat down in one of the comfy chairs. The air conditioner was off and so sitting naked in the chair was not overly uncomfortable.

She needed to think this through.

What if Andrew had overheard her plans to come out here, and decided to use the opportunity to start an affair? It made a strange, male sort of logical sense.

Besides, if he did try to do something stupid, she could simply lodge a complaint with her bosses and find another position. It might put her career behind by a few months, even a year, but it wouldn't signify the end of her life.

Lily felt an evil smile cross her face.

Maybe she should turn the tables on her lover.

Renewed with energy, Lily hunted around the hotel room. Armed with two silk ties and a sleeping facemask the hotel had obviously provided, she returned to the king-sized bed.

So Andrew thought he could play with her, did he? Let's see how he enjoyed *her* playing with *him*.

Chapter Eight

ॐ

Andrew awoke to the most delicious sensations. Warm hands traced his chest, playing with his nipples and tugging gently, erotically, on his chest hair. Warm breath caressed his iron-hard cock, ruffling his pubic hair and making him ache to feel the wet heat of a woman's mouth close around his aching shaft.

Smiling lazily, he opened his eyes, only to feel his lashes rub against the rough yet silky feel of a sleeping mask. Frowning, he tried to sit up, only to feel thin, silken bonds restraining his wrists.

"What the hell—"

A feminine snicker caught his attention and he recalled the previous night's intense lovemaking.

"Lily," he groaned, "what the hell are you doing?"

"Well, Andrew, in case it's not blindingly obvious," she snickered again at her pun, "I thought it time to take control of our sex games."

Leaning over him, she took one of his nipples in her mouth. Rising up, he arched his back, completely stunned by the electric feelings coursing through his body.

"Shit, woman! Don't do that!"

"But why not?" she murmured against his chest, laving his nipple with her tongue. The air conditioner had obviously turned itself back on first thing in the morning, making the air chilly. Lily took advantage of the cool air to help make his nipple stand erectly to attention, her warm breath teasing him with how achingly hot her mouth could be. Andrew tugged at his restraints, unable to believe how erotic her ministrations felt.

"Because..." he mumbled, trying to order his scattered wits, "because...I don't know, shouldn't it be me teasing you in the restraints? I never realized you had dominatrix fantasies."

"Ahh," his vixen purred, "I thought you happened to meet me at Susy's party. I thought we happened to meet by chance. I didn't realize you were Andrew from work, the company's genius and secret weapon, the manager who happened to be in the cafeteria most times I took my lunch break."

Andrew felt his body temperature rise. He couldn't see shit and, with his sight gone, all his senses were heightened. Every breath she puffed over his body sent his blood pumping; every touch of her hair draped over his skin, every caress from her hands, her arms, her legs, every skin-on-skin contact drove him madder. Was it possible to expire from overstimulation?

Desperately, he urged his brain to come up with some plausible explanation. With Lily touching his skin, setting his senses on fire and teasing him as he lay helpless, he didn't have a hope in hell.

"I overheard you talking to Darla about Susy's masquerade party and taking this time off. I've been meaning for months to approach you but either you were snowed under with work or I was heading out of state on business."

Panting, Andrew tried to understand what the hell was going on. Lily was fondling his balls, weighing them in her hands and gently manipulating them, toying with them and driving him insane.

"Lily! Let me free. I can pleasure you and we can talk about this. How can you be mad after the ecstasy we shared?"

"Oh, I'm not mad, Andrew, just...curious."

"About what?" he panted, hoping like hell something would turn in his favor.

"I'm curious what *this* will do to your body."

Andrew arched up, crying out in pleasure, a guttural, incoherent sound of pleasure as she took his red-hot tip into her mouth, sucking hard on him.

With a wet *pop* sound, she pulled her mouth away, ignoring his moan of disapproval. "Or maybe curiosity about how men react to this..."

Lily tasted and teased, touched and probed him. Andrew began to burn with desire and the ache to possess her. She touched him intimately, taught herself his every crease and hidden spot. She found his sensitive flesh between his balls and anus, found his ticklish spots on his side, just underneath his ribs. Her warm fingers explored him all over. She murmured to him, talking about how interesting she found his body, how his reactions to her explorations turned her on and how excited and damp she became as he reacted to her.

She drove him mad with desire.

Andrew promised himself as soon as he were free he would bind and gag her, so her soft, femininely husky voice couldn't drive him mad any longer. So her sweet words wouldn't drive his lust even hotter.

He would bind her to his bed and keep her there a year or so until he had sated himself.

"And now," she purred, unknowing of his raging lust and simmering frustrations, "I think I'm ready for a ride."

Earlier, when he still had been sleeping peacefully, she had sheathed him in a condom. She had enjoyed rolling it over his thick length with her mouth, encasing him in the latex but, more importantly, her heated, damp mouth. When he had realized he was wearing a rubber, he had thought she would put him out of his misery quickly and sate both their rising lusts. But she had proved him wrong, teasing him and taunting him verbally and with her delicate hands.

He cried out as he felt her straddle his waist, felt her damp slit press into his stomach. Her hands had begun to toy with his nipples again. Never had he realized just *how* sensitive a man's nipples could prove to be. Who would have guessed? He bit his lip, tasted the blood that flowed from the tiny cut. He had spent ages begging her, now he refused to beg any more. He would rather go insane with the unrequited lust.

He did, however, groan as she lowered herself along his thick, incredibly engorged shaft. He held on to his control by the thinnest of threads. He was so hot, so primed to explode, he knew the merest friction would send him spilling himself like a seventeen-year-old youth, a horny teenager with the least amount of experience. Andrew refused to disgrace himself, even if he had been provoked so badly.

Yet as Lily raised and lowered herself, he felt his control unravel.

"Faster," he panted, canting his hips and bucking her. "Move faster, Lily, or this will be over before you've even begun."

"My," she panted, her voice betraying her own excitement, "impatient, aren't we?"

"Not impatient, love," he bit out, desperately holding onto his control, forcing himself not to come this instant, "practical. There's only so far you can push a man before he explodes and I'm mighty close to the point."

"Well then, we best see what we can do to help you."

With that, Lily began thrusting herself upon him in fierce, forceful strokes. The delicious sensations had them both moaning, both enjoying the sensitive friction between their flesh.

With a cry, he felt Lily begin to milk him, her contractions allowing him to finally release himself. He desperately wished he could hold her hips still while he thrust himself up into her, faster and more forcefully. Instead, he had to hold on to the headboard, digging his fingers into the wrought iron lacework, until he felt sure either it or he would break. Yet he didn't care; the pain helped him to concentrate, to focus. Lily held onto his shoulders, bracing herself as he thrust himself deep inside her pussy. He shouted out, finally letting himself convulse and heave, pressing his cock as deeply inside her as he could possibly fit.

Andrew panted, tried to catch his breath as Lily fell down on his warm chest.

"That was certainly interesting. Are you going to release me now or am I playing captive slave a while longer?"

Chapter Nine

∽

Lily blinked and nuzzled her head into the warmth of Andrew's chest. Had she really tied this man to his own bed and had her wicked way with him? Such stuff usually only resided in her fantasies, not her reality.

Wearily lifting her head, she visually confirmed that yes, she did have a stud from work tied with his own silk ties to the hotel bed. He had a mask covering his eyes and beads of sweat running down the side of his face. His arm muscles seemed to twitch with the force of his earlier release.

Mmm…this hunk was definitely a superior specimen of masculinity, certain to make her drool.

The question was, should she release him?

Why not? one side of her debated. *You took charge of him once. You can do it again.*

Sure, except for the fact he was asleep and tied up when we took charge of him, the other side of her mind insisted.

"Well?" Andrew drawled, seemingly in no hurry either way.

Hesitantly, Lily sat up and leaned over him. She fumbled a bit with the knots; they had been pulled exceedingly tight during the course of their passion. Finally, one broken nail later, she managed to release both his wrists.

Sitting back, poised to flee, she watched him lift his own hands, shake some feeling into them and remove his mask.

Dark brown eyes clashed with her own lighter brown ones.

"Do you think we'll know how to do it without one of us masked?"

Lily smiled, relieved he was taking this so well. Her body relaxed. So it took her completely by surprise when he pounced across the bed and pinned her down, spread-eagle, on the enormous mattress.

"What the…? You sneak!"

Andrew laughed, feeding her fury. "Look on the bright side, darling, I have no intention of tying you down or blindfolding you, much as I fantasized about it while you had *me* trussed up like a turkey."

Lily pouted. "I just felt a need for some revenge. I felt deceived when I realized you had known who I was all along and I had no idea who you were."

"Don't worry, honey, as of now the slate is blank. You've had your revenge and I had my seduction. We're starting out even now."

Lily laughed huskily, "Oh, a clean slate. Well, that sounds incredibly interesting. So you won't retaliate if I touch you *here*." Lily lowered her hand and gently scraped one nail along his hairy sac. Andrew uttered a sound somewhere between a groan and a girlish shriek.

"Uh…"

Lily chortled, and continued to massage the sensitive flesh underneath his hugely upstanding erection through the ultra-thin latex. Touching him as much as possible, she removed the condom, sliding across the bed to wrap it in some tissues and pass him a few to clean himself up.

Dropping the used condom in the wastebasket, she came back next to him on the bed feeling much better and in control of herself and her emotions.

"So you won't retaliate if I lean over and do *this*," she murmured as she placed herself over his hips and lowered her head to lave and nibble the skin under his scrotum.

Between one breath and the next, Lily found herself roughly turned over onto her back and pinned by two large, powerful, hairy arms.

"No, darling," he purred, "I won't retaliate. I'll simply reciprocate the torture."

So saying, he lowered his head, his heated breath causing her nipples to come to painful arousal and he teased, nibbled and taunted her hot flesh with his teeth and tongue. Lily found herself moaning, twisting in his embrace and enjoying their erotic play.

Refusing to simply lie back and let him do all the work, she found a few of his sensitive spots and they both enjoyed teasing and taunting each other.

Dawn crept over the horizon, beautiful in its brilliant colors, welcoming the new day to one and all. But Lily and Andrew were far too occupied to even notice the brilliance of the new day.

Chapter Ten

ട

Ah yes. A new day, a new set of perfect lovers. Nothing like setting up a matched pair and these two certainly know how to set the sheets alight! It does my old soul proud to see such – Hang on a minute! Why is Mr. Highwayman, our resident Romeo, crawling out of bed? Pacing up and down like a nervous mother hen?

Hmm…seems our dear boy has a few qualms. I do wonder what is going on in that oddly masculine head of his. I do understand how some of the less magnificent examples of the masculine breed can second-guess themselves into a pit but I had hoped Our Esteemed Highwayman wasn't one of these.

Oh well, let's hope I can get his attention and help out our dear old Lily with whatever maggot has entered his mind…

* * * * *

When Andrew woke up for the second time that morning, he could feel the mandatory post-sexual-romp aches and pains in his body. They were a delicious ache and a good long soak in the tub would certainly ease them. He tightened his hold on Lily, still sleeping soundly next to him. Everything had just seemed to click into place, fall into his open palm like a perfect ripe plum.

Andrew frowned.

He didn't want to borrow trouble but surely everything had clicked into place a little too easily.

Being extra careful not to wake up Lily, he crawled out of bed. How was it Lily didn't get upset when she realized his identity? Why didn't she enact the usual female scene of tears and recriminations? He certainly felt grateful none of those had occurred but why did everything seem to move so smoothly?

Pacing up and down the room, feeling rather stupid, Andrew headed toward the bathroom. A shower would clear his head and everything would be fine. He could wait for the luxurious bath until after Lily had woken up, and maybe even until after breakfast or lunch, seeing as the morning was now mostly over.

As he headed toward the bathroom, Andrew noticed a glint of blue light. The morning sun reflected from one of the beads on Lily's beautiful, satin mask. It lay on the floor, probably where she had dropped it when she had awakened so early in the morning.

It was a gorgeous old thing. He bent down to pick it up, not wanting to step on it later by accident and ruin the silky satin and exquisite beadwork.

As his hand closed over it, Andrew thought he felt a jolt of electricity flow through him. Blinking, he wondered at his imagination. He mustn't have had as much sleep as he thought. Looking at the old mask, he smiled at the fool notion that popped into his head.

Why not try it on? his brain urged. Mentally shrugging, he brought the delicate mask up to his face, and placed it firmly over his own features.

The faint electric pulse he had felt when picking it up returned again. Instead of seeing the rest of the hotel room, as he had anticipated, Andrew saw flashes of the night before.

Lily underneath him, open to him, stretching upwards, embracing him, taking all of him inside her wet warmth. Andrew felt his breath hitch as the scene melded and became later on, as she had straddled him. She looked glorious, riding him hard, panting and taking all of him as he lay beneath her, bound and blindfolded.

Andrew felt his blood pressure rise as scene after erotic scene flashed before him. He couldn't understand exactly how it worked, but he seemed to not only view the incredibly erotic scenes, but he felt his own reactions simultaneously feeling what Lily felt.

On and on the erotic snapshots flashed before his eyes, showing him and Lily locked in almost every erotic embrace imaginable. Strangely enough, he saw both erotic acts they had performed and also acts they had not performed. Each picture, however, melded into a mural of mouthwateringly erotic acts.

Side by side, one on top of the other, backwards, standing, over and over the scenes of him and Lily so intimately entwined flashed before him. The visuals were so erotic, so decadent, they made him bone-hard with the need to create these scenes in the flesh instead of just in his imagination.

Just as he was about to remove the mask, he heard Lily sitting up in the big bed.

"Why are you wearing my mask, Andrew?"

He whipped the mask off, stunned by the visions of the last few minutes.

"Uh, just looking."

Lily frowned. Andrew felt surprised to see her pull the comforter up over herself, covering herself from the neck down.

For a moment, they just looked at each other, each one thinking their own thoughts.

Lily broke the heavy silence first. "Where do we go from here?" she asked him softly.

Andrew smiled. He knew how women liked to hear positives and affirmations the morning after fantastic sex. Even better, he knew he could truthfully give them to her. He wanted Lily to be a part of his life; he just wanted to start with small steps. No need to rush into anything.

"Well, I was thinking about taking a bath together, resting up all those aching muscles. And then we can order in some breakfast and spend the day indoors. You have a week, right?" He smiled at her confirming nod, continuing jovially. "Well, I have the next two days off before I have to return to work, so I thought we could make the best of them."

Lily's frown deepened and Andrew felt himself sweat a bit. What else could she possibly be asking?

"I meant, after we leave New Orleans. When we return back home."

"Oh." He breathed a sigh of relief. If that was all she fretted over then maybe there wasn't anything to worry about. "I assumed we'd continue our affair. See each other outside of work, on weekends maybe…" he trailed off when his words sounded lame, even to his own ears.

Lily nodded. "Baby steps, huh? We share fantastic sex and I get to mold myself into your life. You keep your cushy job, while I get to hang around and wait until you return from another trip and we can fuck again."

Andrew opened his mouth as she climbed out of the bed and began to hunt around for her clothes.

"Lily, it's not like that and you know it. I want you to be part of my life but I don't see why we should make such a big deal out of something that's only just beginning. What's the problem with taking small steps at the start?"

Andrew watched as Lily pulled her gown down over her head. Even crinkled and squashed from a night on the floor, she still looked amazing.

Lily sighed. "You're right. I know you are. I just think I need to go back to my hotel, soak alone in my bath and change into some jeans. What say we meet up for lunch before you head back to work tomorrow?"

Andrew ran an agitated hand through his hair. He felt frustrated at the feeling of losing control of the situation. He hadn't been planning on leaving until late tomorrow evening but maybe a bit of breathing space would do them both good. Once they brought their affair back into the real world, instead of the glitzy, glamorous world of the Mardi Gras, everything would hopefully settle back down.

Taking her arm and leading her to the door, he kissed her. Running his tongue across her plump lower lip, he enjoyed her taste, the taste of himself on her.

Finally pulling back, forcing himself to open the door and let go of her arm, he named a well-known café halfway between their hotels. "Let's meet up for a late lunch in, say, two hours. That should give us both plenty of time to cool down and see where we want to go. I seriously doubt there will be many people around anyway—the Mardi Gras went well into the late hours of the morning. We shouldn't have any trouble getting a table."

Lily smiled and ran a hand down his chest, arrowing toward his cock.

"Yeah. Maybe a bit of air will clear everything up."

Winking and swishing her hips as she walked down the corridor, Andrew watched his woman leave and questioned his sanity. No one else had ever had him standing naked watching a gorgeous woman leave his hotel room, uncaring if the entire world would come and watch his stupidity. Thankfully the corridor was deserted after such a long night.

He probably should have seduced her, forced her to listen to him while they both lay sated in his big bed. Yet he didn't want to push his skittish woman; more than likely it would only serve to make her dig in her heels even more.

Sighing, he closed the door and sank against it. He desperately needed that shower. Not only to wash the sweat and smell of sex from his body, but also to relieve some of the tenseness from the muscles in his arms and legs that seemed determined to cramp.

He had two hours to lay out his plan of attack and, at the moment, he didn't have a clue as to what to do to convince Lily to commit to him.

Chapter Eleven

ഔ

Lily sat in the corner booth of the old style café and fiddled with her double chocolate mocha latte. Wrinkling her nose, she tried to sort out her thoughts again. Sure, Andrew was a splendidly built man, bulky and muscular in all the right places, lean and lithe in all the other right places. Yet she wasn't sure she felt ready to commit to one man just yet. The magic and fantasy of the Mardi Gras had seemed to penetrate her brain and make her crazy.

Stupidly, she had hoped by pushing him to commit she would scare him off. How could she have known it wouldn't have worked? It certainly was enough for any other man of her experience! Try to get a commitment out of any other breathing male and they ran a mile. Yet Andrew was happy to commit, only he wanted to move slowly. For a moment she had wondered if she was still dreaming or if she had suddenly become the commitment-shy male and he the commitment-hungry female.

She didn't know too much about Andrew back in their normal lives. She didn't know where he lived, whether he rented or owned, or even if he wanted to own his own house. She didn't know anything about his family, how close he was to his siblings or parents, or even how he felt about children! Their masquerade ball had circumnavigated all the usual dating issues and they had landed squarely in bed in the one night stand basket.

As Lily had fallen asleep after their mini-romp in the bondage arena, she had planned on waking up after a brief nap, dressing herself and sneaking out of the hotel room. It would have been easy to avoid any of Andrew's attempts to regain contact and then pretend nothing had happened.

But no. He had to wake up first. Not even asking the classically annoying, taboo-morning-after-questions had dampened his enthusiasm. And now she had no idea how she felt. She didn't know if she wanted to turn their fantasy into a reality. Most women would rush to grasp this opportunity with both hands, yet Lily found herself hesitating.

She knew herself well enough to know that, after the incredible sex the previous night, there was no way could she move back to the platonic "getting-to-know-you" stage that began many relationships. Yet neither could she jump from one night of fantasy and incredible sex into a serious, committed relationship.

The problem she faced seemed to be how to work a relationship where one had begun in the middle? They had skipped past the usual icebreaking questions of how many siblings and what sort of relationship with their family one had, and dived directly into the screaming, make-your-panties-wet orgasmic sex side of a relationship.

Stewing in her own questions and doubts for the past two hours hadn't really helped Lily either.

She had changed into one of her oldest pair of well-worn jeans. The soft denim molded her ass and had long ago become frayed at the cuffs. The denim was almost bare at the knees and ass. Only a whim of thinking she needed something comfortable to travel in had made her pack them. Lily wasn't a happy flyer. She wasn't scared but neither did she enjoy traveling by means other than car. They were the perfect comfort-and-thinking pair of jeans. While not indecent, she made sure to be careful how she bent over.

Lily hadn't cared about decency this morning; she simply wanted to be as comfortable as possible. With her already donned favorite pair of jeans, she pulled on her oldest and most stretched Winnie-the-Pooh navy blue T-shirt and a ratty woolen sweater.

Taking a spoonful of the frothy milk from the top of her latte, Lily pondered whether she would be able to bear drinking it if she added any more sugar.

More sugar at this point would possibly make her think better but the alternate reaction her body might give would have her bouncing off the walls, or even going into cardiac arrest from sugar overload.

Before she could make up her mind, she could feel her highwayman enter the café.

Andrew. She reminded herself. He wasn't her highwayman any longer; he was simply a man who worked in the same company as she. Andrew.

Lily looked up from her latte and felt her breath catch. *Not your highwayman, hmm?* Her brain mocked her earlier determination.

Andrew passed the other customers, not even glancing at them. He seemed purely focused on her. He wore fresh black jeans, with no stains, no apparent wearing and a designer label she would bet large amounts of money would be sewn in on the back pocket. A dark navy blue shirt gave some light to his dark hair, still wet from his recent shower. Squirming, Lily felt slightly underdressed.

Immediately, she straightened in her seat, proud in her appearance. She might not be as spick-and-span as the man looming over her table but she looked mostly neat and presentable with the ratty sweater, which she had removed after her walk, resting on her lap. As long as she didn't split her jeans open later in the day, she might be able to pass off merely being hung over and looking for comfort, instead of heartsick and on a binge.

"Hey there, Andrew," she greeted the man, idly waving one hand toward the empty seat opposite her in the booth. "I've just got my chocolate mocha— Oh, here she is," she mumbled as the waitress fairly knocked the other patrons down in her eagerness to come and serve the new studly customer.

Spooning some more of the frothy milk into her mouth and sucking on the spoon, Lily watched, amused, as the young girl stammered and drooled all over Andrew. *Seems like some people didn't get lucky last night at the carnival*, she snickered to herself.

The busty waitress did everything to make Andrew pay attention to her exceptionally large cleavage except actually pull her shirt off for the poor man. Lily felt relieved when Andrew smiled and replied to her enquiries politely, and then ordered a short black. Realizing her time here was over, the waitress huskily informed Andrew, "If there's *anything* else you'd like to order…?"

Andrew smiled politely, much to Lily's amusement, and said they'd like to wait to order their lunch until after their drinks. The waitress slinked away, making sure to add an extra swing in her hips as she negotiated the tables.

Lily laughed. "'If there's *anything* else you want…'" she teased softly, running her finger along the rim of her cup suggestively.

Andrew leaned in, crowding Lily and giving her a whiff of his spicy cologne.

"From you, my dear, I might just take you up on that offer, so be careful what you say."

Lily sat back in the booth. "Well, at least you have a sense of humor."

"Afraid I wouldn't?"

Lily frowned and considered the question seriously. "I was just thinking before you came in. We seemed to have missed the 'getting-to-know-you' stage most relationships have. We seemed to have jumped into the middle without actually realizing what sort of relationship we have."

Andrew leaned back into the booth and stretched his legs out beneath the table. Lily felt his jeans-clad leg brush past hers. Shocked at the current that ran from him to her, she lifted one leg and crossed it underneath her.

"Well," he said, eyes twinkling merrily, "that's an awful lot of big words for so early in the day."

Lily snorted. "It's early afternoon."

Andrew smiled as the busty waitress placed his coffee in front of him, making sure to shove her breasts as close to his face as she dared.

"Yes, but as you know, darling, neither of us slept much last night."

Lily felt a blush creep across her face as the waitress shot her an envious glance. Lily kept her mouth closed until the poor girl had sashayed over to a group of four snappishly grumpy men in one corner, obviously still hung over from their party last night.

"Okay, okay," she sighed. "You're a stud-muffin. I certainly know it, the poor waitress knows it, every woman with blood and breath in her body would know it. My point is, where do we go from here?"

"I tried to answer that last question and it had you freaking out on me. How about this time you offer a solution?"

Lily sipped her drink, enjoying the mingled tastes of coffee and chocolate. She needed to be careful here. She wanted to entice Andrew into continuing their sexual affair, but give herself time and room to breathe.

"How about we continue the affair, but try to keep it quiet? If we can keep the sexual side away from work, we can probably start to date during our lunch breaks without raising much suspicion or angst from work. That way, we can get to know one another, but also continue the incredible sexual side of what we have. What do you think?"

Lily found herself holding her breath as Andrew looked at her. After a moment, when she felt sure he was going to tear her plan to shreds, he smiled, picked up his tiny cup and took a sip of his coffee.

"That sounds perfect."

Feeling a huge grin spread across her face, Lily felt her spirits lighten like never before. "Fantastic. Let's get your little waitress over again. Suddenly I am *ravenous*. Man, I could eat a whole cow right now."

Laughing, they picked up their menus and started chatting. Lily had never laughed as much as she did with Andrew. He had a wicked sense of humor and she found a surprisingly large number of points they agreed on.

The extra large chicken and pineapple pizza with barbeque sauce, which they bought to share, quickly disappeared as they laughed and talked and shared their opinions and details. Lily enjoyed the surprisingly mature and romantic outlook on life Andrew seemed to have. The time and pizza easily slipped away and, before she knew it, she was beating him by mere seconds to the last slice of pizza, literally snatching it just out of his grasp.

She laughed as she took a giant-sized bite out of it and offered him a bite.

"I need to keep my energy up," he complained good-naturedly. "How am I supposed to keep up with you if you steal the last slice?"

Lily smiled around the slice, taking her time. Enjoying the dilating of his pupils, she slowly, slowly opened her lips, slid her mouth along the slice, then bit down gently into the soft dough. Moving her lips away, she began to chew, daintily flicking her tongue out to pick up any of the sauce that might have escaped.

Lily enjoyed watching Andrew squirm and groan at her naughty play. Biting into the crust, she rubbed her sneaker-clad foot against his strong leg.

"We need to go for a walk," he insisted, bringing out his wallet and leaving a number of bills on their table. Lily happily popped the last of the slice into her mouth and wiped her hands on a napkin.

He easily caught her hand and helped her out of the booth, half-dragging her out of the small café.

Laughing, she let him lead her wherever he wanted—for now.

Chapter Twelve

ॐ

Andrew looked out onto the half-dead street. Everywhere there were signs of the Carnival last night. Streamers, beads and stars were scattered everywhere. Strange how he hadn't noticed them earlier, when he walked from his hotel room to the café to meet Lily.

Lily.

She had taken over his mind, taken over his heart and soul sometime over the last few days or months when he hadn't been looking. She had just been teasing him with the pizza, yet he now had the intense desire to take her, brand her, make her his in every way.

There were a few people roaming the street, one or two couples who seemed to be only now heading home from a full night and day of partying.

Andrew smiled, he could well understand the feeling. If he hadn't been so desperate for Lily, both then and now, he, too, might have spent over twenty-four hours at a party.

Turning away from the direction of both their hotels, Andrew led Lily across the street and down the block. He knew from his research there should be a secluded park a few blocks away. He had intended to take one of the recommended nature trails if things hadn't worked out.

Now, he could think of a few perfectly *natural* things to show and do with Lily. Even though it was the middle of the day, the city seemed quite deserted, licking its wounds and recovering from the incredible party last night, and the one to surely follow later tonight after the sun set.

Andrew grinned and bent down to retrieve one of the many strings of beads.

Looping it over Lily's head, he smiled as she grinned back at him.

"Where are we going, hot stuff?" she easily inquired.

"Why, the park, sexy," he just as easily replied.

For a moment, Lily's eyes widened and he wondered what it was he had said to cause that reaction. A smile quickly replaced the flare of surprise and…desire? Anticipation? He couldn't really put his finger on it.

"Sounds good," she laughingly said, causing his stomach to flip.

Andrew shook his head and held her hand. If they only had the rest of the day and night, he wanted to use as much of it as possible to convince her they belonged together, forever.

* * * * *

Lily didn't know what it was exactly about the park, or more accurately, nature paths that reminded her of…something…but they did seem vaguely familiar. Obviously the Council had wanted to bring in some of the native plants and agriculture into the middle of the city and a winding, bending group of walks had been the result. They were green and lush, yet compact enough to only take up a half block of room or so.

They were beautiful, yet Lily knew she had never been here.

Shaking her head, she smiled, knowing she probably just felt the excitement and magic of the moment and being with Andrew.

They chose a path at random, and meandered their way along the soft trail, stopping every now and then to pause and read the description of a certain flower or tree. When they were well out of sight of a casual passerby, Andrew let go of her hand.

Turning in surprise, Lily opened her mouth to ask what he was doing. Before she could ask, however, he bent forward and kissed her.

"Run, Lily," he whispered to her.

"Huh?" Blinking, trying to focus her cloudy, lust-riddled thoughts, she couldn't understand what he meant.

"I want to chase you. You do know how to play Chase, right? You run, I run after you and when I catch you I can do what I want to you."

Lily smiled. "Confident you'll catch me, huh?"

The smile that Andrew gave her was in itself answer enough. Lily arched an eyebrow, amused at how confident he felt.

"I'll always catch you, Lily-girl, remember that—*always*."

Her eyebrow raised even further at such male arrogance, Lily made a face at him, then turned and ran off into the trees. Dodging and weaving, she felt laughter bubble up in her throat.

Stopping behind a tree, Lily turned and peered around the thick trunk. She could hear Andrew nearby, his feet crunching between the twigs and dried leaves. Deciding to tease him a little, she called out to her lover.

"If I can hide from you, does this mean I can tie you up again and make you my sex slave?"

Knowing her taunting would give him an indication of where she hid, she carefully moved to a different tree, watching her feet, trying not to give away her movements.

There was a pause for a moment, then two. Lily looked around. Not seeing Andrew boosted her confidence, until he replied to her earlier jeer.

"Does that mean when I catch you, you will be *my* sexual slave for the night?"

The absolute conviction and masculine assurance in the words halted Lily. How the hell does a modern, confident woman respond to such a challenge?

Thinking hard, Lily turned around to flee once again, only to slam into a very solid, very masculine chest.

When she felt Andrew wrap his arms around her waist, Lily's breath escaped her lungs.

"Ah ha," he proclaimed, completely satisfied, "my slave for the evening."

Lily raised herself onto her tiptoes and kissed his mouth.

Feeling his hands loosen their hold, she wrenched herself away and quickly ran through the trees, running as far and as fast as she could. Teasing about binding Andrew up was one thing; allowing him to bind her up without any sort of fight was completely another.

From the heavy footfalls sounding behind her, Lily knew he was in hot pursuit. The chase spurred her on more. Running, panting for her breath, Lily dodged and weaved between the trees, hoping to lose Andrew. If she could just get her sense of direction back for a moment, she could point herself toward the hotel and meet Andrew back at his room.

Feeling a stitch form in her side, Lily looked around. Not seeing Andrew pounding behind her, she stopped to get her bearings.

Turning around, she realized, even though she couldn't be that far away from the street, she had no idea which direction to turn. Panting hard, catching her breath, she turned around a few times in a circle. Everything looked the same.

The snap of a twig directly behind her had her gasping and turning, only to see Andrew come out behind a tree.

"*That*," he chastised, waggling his index finger at her, "was a low-down, mean and dirty trick. Baffling me with the lust of your kisses and then running off on me was sneaky, underhanded and has made me harder than a pole."

Smiling, Lily shrugged. "Can't blame a girl for trying."

Andrew took one last step between them, closing the distance.

"You're not really scared of me tying you up, are you? You know I'd never do anything you didn't like."

Lily smiled, wrapping her arms around his waist.

"I know, but I couldn't just tamely submit to you either. Without a bit of a challenge, you'd never really enjoy your reward, would you?"

"Mmm," he murmured, "speaking of rewards —"

Lily felt Andrew press his lips against hers. Almost chastely, he let the gentle press of his lips bear down on hers. When she felt his tongue dart out between his lips, seeking entrance, she held no reservations in opening her lips to meet his.

The sun beat down on them. In the distance she could hear the odd car driving down the street, yet it almost seemed as if they were in their own little world, separate and apart from everyone and everything.

When Lily felt Andrew's hands slide under her sweater and T-shirt, she shuddered with the pleasure he could bring her. Her nipples pebbled and she arched into his touch.

When he pulled his hand away, firmly replacing her sweater, she pulled away from the kiss, clearly at a loss.

"Not here. Let's go back to my room. I think I want you properly tied up so I can take my time with you," he smiled, showing only eager anticipation at the thought of having her to himself.

Smiling, Lily let him take her hand and lead her out of the park.

Chapter Thirteen

ဢ

Lily pulled to test one arm on the same crumpled silk tie. Her circulation was in no way impeded and the tie did not chafe on her skin, yet she could barely move her arms an inch to either side.

"You haven't done this before by any chance, have you?" she asked more from nerves than any real desire to learn his sexual history.

The masculine, feral grin he gave her had her pause a moment.

"Tell me you're not some deviant sexual dominant, eager to devour young maidens and corrupt a woman into your bondage sexual slave for life?"

Lily felt her heart accelerate at the only half-jesting manner she asked the question.

When Andrew threw his head back and laughed his familiar laugh, genuinely finding humor in her query, she felt herself relax a bit.

"Lily-girl, I've never tied a woman up, either for her pleasure or my own. You're the first, I promise. It just doesn't take a rocket scientist to work out the balance between tight enough to keep you in place, but loose enough not to cause you harm. Relax, I have a feeling we're *both* going to enjoy this."

Her doubt fully assuaged, Lily leaned back into the mountain of pillows Andrew had put at her back for her comfort, and spread her legs invitingly.

"Well then," she purred, "aren't you a little overdressed for this party? I seem to be fully naked and bound, as ordered, yet you seem to still have pants on."

Lily felt her body dip slightly as Andrew climbed onto the bed with her. Earlier, he had removed his boots and socks, his shirt and the belt buckling his jeans. When he had moved to begin to strip her, she had shuddered at his sensitive touch, his gentle caresses. For a minute or two, she had truly thought they wouldn't reach the binding stage.

Yet he had exhibited far more restraint than she could lay claim to. When she had been gutturally begging him to take her, to thrust inside her, he had pulled away from her burning body. He had removed her panties, swiped one teasing lick of her creaming cunt and stood up to stare at her spread body. After looking his fill, he had positioned her hands as he wished them, and bound her with his crumpled silk ties.

Even now, he simply kneeled on the bed, staring at her as if she were some pagan goddess spread before him for his enjoyment alone. Feeling herself creaming, eager to begin their play, Lily spread her legs wider, invitingly, eager to rekindle the heat he had created when stripping her.

When he bent over her body and dipped to kiss her neck, Lily felt her heartbeat accelerate again. He seemed so gentle, so self-possessed, she felt it hard to believe he was as turned on as she.

Lily had never thought she had bondage fantasies but she was desperate to feel his penetration, felt as if a fire burned beneath her skin. The simple act of restricting the movements of her hands turned her on incredibly. The feeling of giving over control, of being able to lose herself in her passions and desires, was an incredibly erotic feeling she had never been able to indulge in with any of her other lovers.

She wasn't convinced she would ever let Andrew, or any other lover, do this to her again. She wasn't even certain she would enjoy sex being bound but the foreplay, the mental images crossing her mind, heating her blood, was more than enough for her to be a willing participant at the moment.

Andrew gently bit down at the juncture between her neck and shoulder and an electric feeling arched from his heated mouth through to her erect nipples and all the way down into her creaming pussy.

"Oh!" she cried out, unable to articulate anything else. She felt Andrew smile against her skin.

"Felt that all the way down into your cunt, didn't you, love? This is one of your erogenous zones—one of the most common zones in the female body, even though every woman is different. You must tell me how this feels."

When his warm hands began to caress her chest and the globes of her breasts as well as her bare and twisting torso, Lily knew she was in for a long night of intensive lovemaking.

Having her hands bound almost seemed to heighten her senses. As she couldn't move her hands, couldn't be thinking about how to please *him*, it made her concentrate more fully on how *he* pleasured *her*. It didn't fully make sense but, in the red-hot haze of passion, desire and lust that fully overtook her, Lily understood what was happening.

For what seemed like hours, Andrew carefully built the fire raging in her. He touched her gently, he ran his hands, his tongue, his lips and all the soft parts of his body over her. He traced and tasted every inch of her body, inside and out. He ate her to a raging, screaming orgasm that rocked her world and blew her away. Then calmly, as if he were completely unaware of the earth-shatteringly intense pleasure he had given her, went back to nibbling on her skin and setting the fire to burn again.

Lily thought she would go mad from the love and lust he incited in her.

As the afternoon waned into the evening, Andrew didn't even pause for breath. She could feel his cock, iron-hard and obviously in desperate need of release, cased inside his pants.

Yet even when she begged him to enter her, he would tease her, licking her with his tongue, or teasing her with his fingers. He had lovely fingers, long and thick, but, even as he entered two or three into her, they were insufficient to slake her burning desire for his shaft. Nothing else would be able to ease the desperate ache inside her.

And still he teased her.

She cried for him. She begged him. She pleaded with him to complete her.

And still he teased her.

It was agony. It was ecstasy. It was better than any fantasy she had ever dreamed, yet it was still not enough and she didn't understand why. She had her stud, satisfying her every craving, bar one, and still she begged, *pleaded* for the one thing he hadn't given her.

As she screamed out her third orgasm, feeling the aching, pleasurable, but still somehow painful peak rip through her body, tears entered her eyes. Somehow she didn't feel complete without him inside her and that knowledge, more than anything else, worried her.

Chapter Fourteen

ಞ

As Andrew watched Lily's body convulse and clamp around his drenched fingers in her third orgasm, he felt himself begin to sweat.

He had always dreamed of having a luscious woman, bound and naked for him to perform all kinds of erotic acts upon. And he indeed loved having his Lily-girl spread before him for his pleasure. Yet he ached to be inside her, ached to possess her. Feeling her body spread even wider after she came down from her climax, he could no longer deny himself or her. She had been pleading from her second climax for him to possess her, yet he had wanted to make sure she was ready, had completely forgotten her act of trust in letting him bind her.

He hadn't exactly been selfish, yet a part of him relished the knowledge that she trusted him so deeply.

With far more haste than grace, he shed his pants, smiling sourly at how eagerly his cock leapt from his pants.

He was more than ready.

He bent down, inhaling the salty, tangy, feminine scent of Lily once more.

"No!" she cried out, surprising him, "don't you dare eat me again, Andrew! Fuck me *right now* or I swear I will never smile at you again."

He smiled, amused at her threat. Strangely enough, it held enough threat to make him pay attention.

"My lady is eager," he teased.

"Your lady is about to jump you, bound or not."

Andrew held her hips, cupped her as delicately as if she were made of thin china. She was so precious to him, he feared to hurt her with his aching desire.

"*Right now*, Andrew, or I swear you'll regret it."

Laughing aloud, never having had so much fun and enjoyment with any other woman in his life, Andrew pulled himself back. Taking a deep breath, knowing their marathon bout of incredible sex was about to come to an end, he plunged himself balls-deep with one fierce, firm stroke.

Amazingly, almost instantly, Lily began to convulse around him. She screamed a high, almost unheard, scream of completion. He felt her womb contract around him, her walls milking him, her grasping him as if he were the last thing in the world.

He groaned, determined to last more than one stroke. Drawing back, he felt amazed as Lily wound her legs around him, pulling him closer into her. Not even a few inches removed from her, he thrust himself back in her and, amazingly, began to spurt his seed. His shaft ached, burned inside her as his seed poured forth inside her womb.

He felt as if a bomb had detonated in his balls. His shaft was like a burning beacon, pouring his essence, his very soul, deep into Lily. He came over and over, hoarsely crying out his ecstasy.

When he finally finished convulsing, he fell to his side, still entwined with Lily, unwilling or unable to let her go. He gasped his breath back into his lungs, unsure when he had stopped breathing.

Lying there tangled with her, feeling her warm and pliant, probably half unconscious in his arms, he felt a peace settle over him. As if with that one remarkable act of trust and faith, they had sealed their relationship.

Andrew listened to his heart rate settle, felt his body relax and return to normal. Sitting up with a jerk, he leaned over Lily to unbind her.

"Sorry, sweetie, I didn't forget exactly...but I didn't precisely plan it either. The blood is only just now returning to important organs like my brain."

The sweet, sensitive smile she directed sleepily at him melted his heart. Getting up, he retrieved the comforter from where he had earlier moved it and snuggled next to her in the giant bed, covering them both.

"I'm clean and I know you wouldn't have done it if you weren't clean either. I trust you, hon. We can order dinner and pack later, and then exchange boring things like tests and all when we get back. What say we just lie here and pretend we're not sleeping for now?"

"Sounds good to me..." she huskily murmured and Andrew knew she was asleep before she had even finished the thought.

Chapter Fifteen
One month later

ஐ

Andrew checked himself once more in his own private bathroom. Grateful to not have any one of the other men peering over his shoulder at his sweating palms and constant stupid fiddling with his hair, he cursed at his own nerves.

It was quite late, after seven on a Friday evening, and so he found himself hedging his bets that there wouldn't be anyone else around the offices. He *sincerely* hoped there wouldn't be anyone else around at this hour. Tucking one last stray lock of hair away from his face, he took a deep breath.

Stop procrastinating, you jerk, and get on with it.

Looking back down into his gym bag, which now held the crumpled remnants of his business suit, he bent down and picked out the last item. He had already donned his highwayman pants, his black shirt and the cape. Only the facemask remained.

Holding the black mask in his hands, he wondered again at the lengths Lily had pushed him to.

One whole month of mind-blowing sex had passed. Each encounter miraculously seemed better than the last. It was the frustrating lunch dates she continued to insist they have each week that drove him insane.

If he happened to try and play footsie with her, she smote him with a glance. If he made even the mildest of risqué comments to her, she kicked him in the shins. If he *dared* look at her funny in front of her colleagues she gave him the longest lecture over the phone that evening.

Enough was enough. He had tried jumping through her hoops and all he had to show for it was a boner that never went away, and an astronomical dentist's bill for all the grinding of his teeth.

He had tried and tried to talk Lily into moving in with him or getting engaged to him. Nothing seemed to work. She insisted she wanted to "take her time". She said he couldn't possibly have fallen in love with her so quickly and he couldn't seem to convince her he was serious, that he wanted marriage, babies and the white picket fence.

He had had enough with the waiting and procrastinating. It was well past time she jumped through some of *his* fricking hoops and she could start with the three-day weekend he had planned for them both. No clothes allowed!

Zipping up his gym bag, he stashed it in the back of his office, hoping his suit and shirt wouldn't crease too badly with his gym gear. Anyone desperate enough to steal the crumpled suit was welcome to it. The two silk ties, however, he had stashed in his pants pockets. Those would undoubtedly come in handy later on in the evening.

Taking one last glance in the mirror, Andrew assured himself he looked as close to the same as he had that fateful Mardi Gras evening as possible. His mask in place, the cape flapping in the breeze, he smiled to his reflection and mentally wished himself the best of luck.

Let's hope I don't make a complete ass of myself.

Striding confidently out of the men's bathroom, Andrew headed down the corridor to the elevators. Even though the offices were deserted, he kept his head high, his posture firm and his strides confident. If he happened to pass someone, he had far more chance of brazening it out if he looked as if he lived here, rather than sneaking about stealthily.

Also, the security cameras were monitored and sneaking about seemed far more likely to gather their attention than striding purposefully about.

The elevator *pinged* and Andrew stepped in and pressed the floor number Lily should be working late on.

He couldn't believe how relieved he had felt when she cancelled their date tonight, insisting she had to work late on the finishing touches to her project. He knew she already had it perfect; she simply felt the need to nitpick at it.

Besides, he had briefly spoken to her boss when he had arranged for their annual leave. Her boss was more than satisfied with her work, had even hinted that the upcoming promotion was in the bag for her, yet still Lily fretted and worried.

He smiled. While Andrew-the-average-businessman might not have dared encroach on her work time, Andrew-the-highwayman felt no remorse at all about his upcoming plans.

The elevator *pinged* again and the doors slid open with barely a whisper of sound.

Andrew raised his head, cocked it at the arrogant angle he could easily picture any highwayman worth his salt holding it at. Striding forward again, he headed in the well-known direction of Lily's office. Though many of the lights still shone in the corridors and offices, thankfully each office he passed was empty.

He heard Lily before he could see her.

"So you see my problem, Darla?"

"Mmm," came the muffled response. Andrew paused, wondering what the hell she and Darla were doing. Lily's voice sounded thick. Not husky, but as if she were doing something with her mouth.

For the briefest of seconds, Andrew had a mental flash of Lily going down on Darla and then he shook his head.

No way. If Lily had planned anything like that and not invited him, he would kill her with his bare hands.

Reality intruded and he realized Lily didn't feel so inclined *that* way.

"Very tricky," came the muffled response from Darla. The clink of silverware on silver could be heard from Lily's small office. Andrew felt his breathing return to normal.

No lesbian voyeuristic fantasies would be played out tonight. He must be hornier than he realized.

Andrew tried to stifle his laughter, and continued into Lily's office anyway. The sight that greeted his eyes amazed him.

Feminine decadence abounded.

One crushed, empty pint of Ben and Jerry's Chunky Monkey lay on the floor near the wastepaper basket. One almost empty pint of Phish Food lay on the desk, mostly-melted chocolate ice cream stickily seeping out the bottom.

An extra-large indulgence packet of Reese's Peanut Butter Cups spilled out over the paperwork spread helter-skelter across the desk. M&M's—both the chocolate variety as well as the peanut variety he noted, completely amused—and strawberries and cream also fought for space among the cluttered desktop.

Both girls had changed from their suits and jackets into baggy sweat suit pants and torn T-shirts.

Andrew raised an eyebrow as they scrambled to pick up the scattered suckers and clean up the mess from the ice cream with a man-sized box of tissues they had obviously brought for such a purpose.

"Andrew!" Lily cried out. "I thought you were going bowling with the guys."

"And I thought you were working late, my dear," he purred, not wanting to ruin the moment. He had never felt so amused, seeing Lily and her friend scramble to right the small office.

"This isn't what it seems," she panted as she finally collected the last of the chocolates from the desk.

"This isn't really a girls' night, as such," Darla confirmed, mopping up the dripping ice cream, "despite how it looks— Why the hell are you wearing that outfit?"

Andrew leered at Darla and chuckled as she cringed back in confusion. Her comment about the mask had Lily stopping her collection of the candies and turning fully to face him.

"Oh my goodness. Andrew! You're not—"

Deciding his little pre-prepared speech was not meant for Darla's ears—why not let Lily embellish it herself after their weekend away?—he strode forward and scooped Lily up into his arms.

She shrieked, but didn't fight him and so, with a wink for Darla, he carried his woman back down the corridor and to the elevators.

* * * * *

"So, the highwayman of my dreams returns?" Lily cooed in his ear as the elevator descended.

She smiled as her masked man turned to look down upon her. She was in her oldest, dowdiest "got-my-period-with-cramps-to-die-over-leave-me-the-hell-alone" clothes and his eyes still glittered as they had that first night when she had been dressed to kill.

"The nice, polite, patient Andrew didn't seem to be getting anywhere. We decided it was time for the highwayman to return. Highwaymen don't wait patiently and get their shins kicked for risqué comments. Highwaymen take what they want and damn the consequences."

Lily wriggled until he set her down on the floor. Keeping her arms wrapped around his neck, she pulled him down for a deep, drugging kiss. Neither one moved an inch as the elevator jolted to a halt and the doors opened softly.

"Freeze! Cops are on their way!"

Both Lily and Andrew broke apart, startled by the one well-known, supremely overweight security guard, shaking as he held his gun on them both.

"Uh, Niles, it's Andrew from…"

Elizabeth Lapthorne

"Don't you talk to me, buddy. I've radioed the cops and the city's finest will be here in a moment for you. Let go of Miss Lily now."

Sighing, wondering why the hell old Niles wasn't snoozing or munching his nachos like normal, Andrew stuck his hands in the air. He felt it far safer for his piece of mind to keep his hands where Niles could see them. He would hate for the old man to have to give himself a heart attack by pulling the trigger of his gun.

"Darling, can you talk to him?"

Lily stepped out of his embrace and threw him a saucy glance.

"What happened to 'stand and deliver?'" she teased.

He glared at her.

Laughing, she exited the elevator and held Niles' hand, lowering his gun carefully.

"Niles, sweetie, you're the very best of security guards but this is Andrew Morrisey, from the Troubleshooting Division. Let him get his ID out, okay?"

Andrew dug into his pocket carefully and *very* slowly withdrew his swipe card. The photo was appalling but, as he removed his mask and handed over the card, the flush creeping up old Niles' face was enough to convince Andrew they were in the clear.

"Oh sir! I am so sorry, sir!"

"No problems, Niles. It's encouraging to know the women are safe at night. Though maybe you should call the cops. Lily and I are on our way out and, while I trust you implicitly, I wouldn't like our chances if the cops thought we were making a dash for it."

Fumbling, still apologizing for his actions, Niles hastily radioed the cops to explain the mess-up.

Lily stepped back toward him, wrapped her arms around his neck again. Replacing his mask, he bent down to kiss her fully.

A full minute later they broke apart, panting, as Niles got off his radio.

"Everything is clear now, sir. And again—"

"No problems, my man. Like I said, it makes me feel much better allowing Lily to work late to know you're on the job. Darla is still up there, though I doubt for much longer, so keep an eye out for her, okay?"

Niles nodded and opened the front door for them. Holding her hand tightly, Andrew hailed a cab, thanking Niles as the man shut the door behind them.

"To the airport," he instructed the driver.

"Airport? Andrew, what have you planned?"

Leaning back in the cab, Andrew pulled his woman toward him.

"Andrew-the-businessman has been jumping through your hoops for over a month now. Andrew-the-highwayman has taken over, I told you. Highwaymen do not wait for what they want. I cleared the next three days off with your boss. We're making a trip back to New Orleans. I have the paperwork all done and an appointment later this evening at the courthouse near our suite. I figure the highwayman can bind you to him this weekend and we can enjoy those three days of nonstop screaming sex you promised me and then we can return back here and work the rest out later."

Lily laughed.

"You have to be kidding. I am not getting married in my oldest pair of sweatpants and a torn shirt. I don't have anything with me, not even my purse."

"Mm..." he murmured, kissing her again. "Wasn't there that resale shop near the hotel where you found that mask? I bet we can find something there for you to wear."

She hit his chest, with no real force, but with enough to make him draw back and laugh.

"Okay, okay, I packed a suitcase for you, and for me as well, as I don't like my chances of getting through security dressed like this. It should be waiting in the locker the courier mailed me the key to. Your blue Regency dress is freshly pressed and all those naughty camisoles and garter belts you've been holding out on me are packed in a bag. Other than that, you can be naked all weekend for all I care."

When the cabbie cleared his throat, face flaming red, they both laughed and sank back into the cab to wait until they reached the airport. Lily kept fingering his mask.

"I do love the highwayman. I think I love the businessman more but the highwayman certainly has his uses."

"This highwayman is glad and he just can't wait to order you to 'stand and deliver' tonight. As his wife, you won't be allowed to turn him down."

Lily laughed huskily and caressed his jaw.

There is definitely a lot of good to be said for going to a "real" Mardi Gras.

Also by Elizabeth Lapthorne

ಌ

Desperate and Dateless

Ellora's Cavemen: Legendary Tails I *(Anthology)*

Lion In Love

Merc and Her Men

Payback

Rutledge Werewolves 1: Scent of Passion

Rutledge Werewolves 2: Hide and Seek

Rutledge Werewolves 3: The Mating Game

Rutledge Werewolves 4: My Heart's Passion

Rutledge Werewolves 5: Chasing Love

About the Author

ഇ

Elizabeth Lapthorne is the eldest of four children. She grew up with lots of noise, fights and tale-telling. Her mother, a reporter and book reviewer, instilled in her a great appreciation of reading with the intrigues of a good plot.

Elizabeth studied Science at school, and whilst between jobs complained bitterly to a good friend about the lack of current literature to pass away the hours. While they both were looking up websites for new publishers, she stumbled onto Ellora's Cave. Jumping head-first into this doubly new site (both the first e-book site she had ever visited, as well as her first taste of Romantica) they both devoured over half of EC's titles in less than a month. While waiting for more titles to be printed (as well as that ever-elusive science job) Elizabeth started dabbling again in her writing.

Elizabeth has always loved to read, it will always be her favourite pass-time, (she is constantly buying new books and bookshelves to fill), but she also loves going to the beach, sitting in the sun, having coffee (or better yet, CHOCOLATE and coffee) with her friends and generally enjoying life. She is extremely curious, which is why she studied science, and often tells "interesting" stories, loving a good laugh. She is a self-confessed email junkie, loving to read what other people on the EC board think and have to say, she laughs often at their tales and ideas. She recently has developed a taste for the gym. She's sure she read somewhere it was good for her, but she is reserving judgment to see how long it lasts.

Elizabeth welcomes comments from readers. You can find her website and email address on her author bio page at www.ellorascave.com.

Tell Us What You Think
We appreciate hearing reader opinions about our books. You can email us at Comments@EllorasCave.com.

Why an electronic book?

We live in the Information Age—an exciting time in the history of human civilization, in which technology rules supreme and continues to progress in leaps and bounds every minute of every day. For a multitude of reasons, more and more avid literary fans are opting to purchase e-books instead of paper books. The question from those not yet initiated into the world of electronic reading is simply: *Why?*

1. ***Price.*** An electronic title at Ellora's Cave Publishing and Cerridwen Press runs anywhere from 40% to 75% less than the cover price of the exact same title in paperback format. Why? Basic mathematics and cost. It is less expensive to publish an e-book (no paper and printing, no warehousing and shipping) than it is to publish a paperback, so the savings are passed along to the consumer.

2. ***Space.*** Running out of room in your house for your books? That is one worry you will never have with electronic books. For a low one-time cost, you can purchase a handheld device specifically designed for e-reading. Many e-readers have large, convenient screens for viewing. Better yet, hundreds of titles can be stored within your new library—on a single microchip. There are a variety of e-readers from different manufacturers. You can also read e-books on your PC or laptop computer. (Please note that Ellora's Cave does not endorse any specific brands.

You can check our websites at www.ellorascave.com or www.cerridwenpress.com for information we make available to new consumers.)

3. *Mobility.* Because your new e-library consists of only a microchip within a small, easily transportable e-reader, your entire cache of books can be taken with you wherever you go.

4. *Personal Viewing Preferences.* Are the words you are currently reading too small? Too large? Too... ANNOYING? Paperback books cannot be modified according to personal preferences, but e-books can.

5. *Instant Gratification.* Is it the middle of the night and all the bookstores near you are closed? Are you tired of waiting days, sometimes weeks, for bookstores to ship the novels you bought? Ellora's Cave Publishing sells instantaneous downloads twenty-four hours a day, seven days a week, every day of the year. Our webstore is never closed. Our e-book delivery system is 100% automated, meaning your order is filled as soon as you pay for it.

Those are a few of the top reasons why electronic books are replacing paperbacks for many avid readers.

As always, Ellora's Cave and Cerridwen Press welcome your questions and comments. We invite you to email us at Comments@ellorascave.com or write to us directly at Ellora's Cave Publishing Inc., 1056 Home Avenue, Akron, OH 44310-3502.

erridwen, the Celtic Goddess of wisdom, was the muse who brought inspiration to story-tellers and those in the creative arts. Cerridwen Press encompasses the best and most innovative stories in all genres of today's fiction. Visit our site and discover the newest titles by talented authors who still get inspired - much like the ancient storytellers did, once upon a time.

25317903R00207

Made in the USA
Lexington, KY
19 August 2013